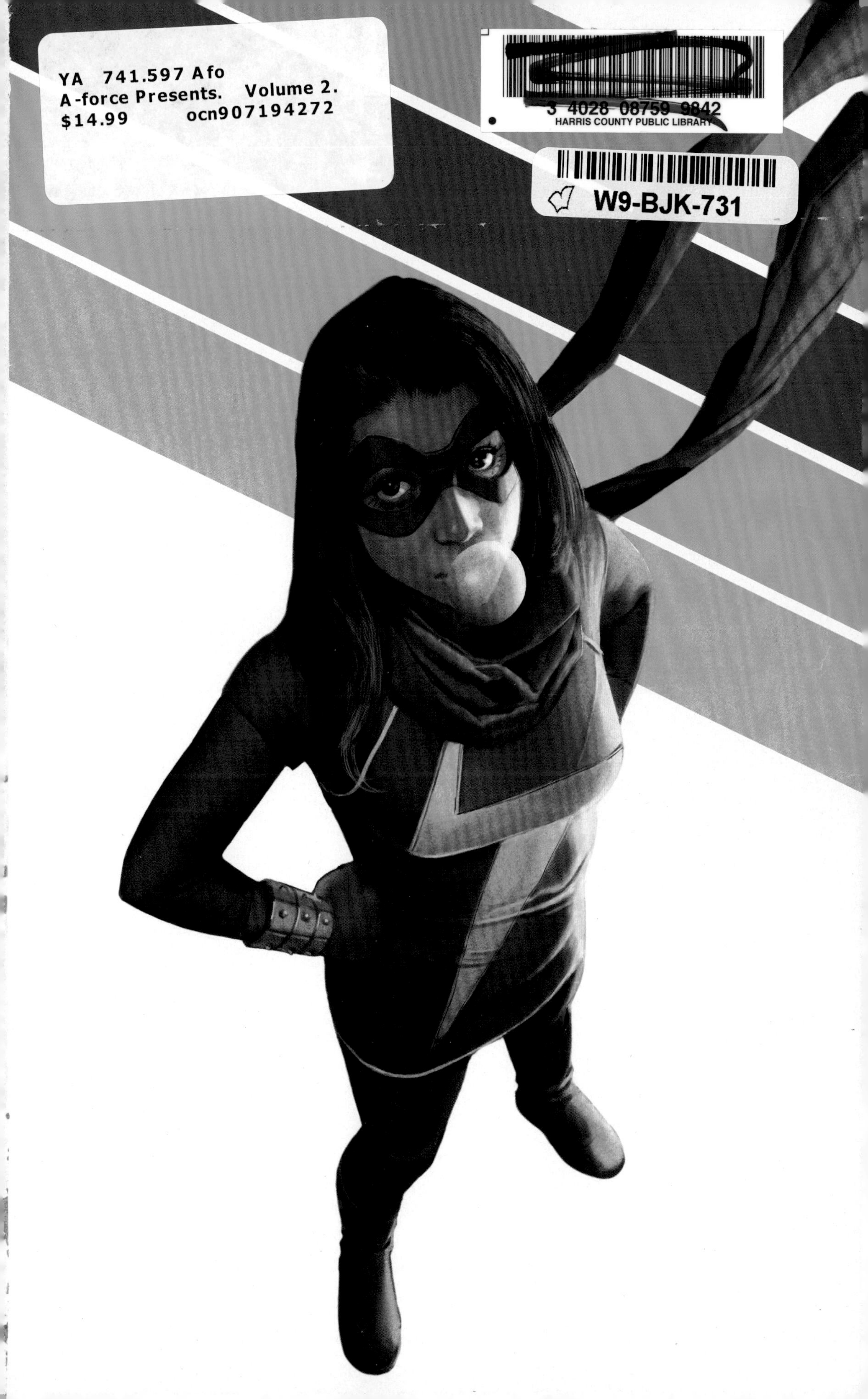

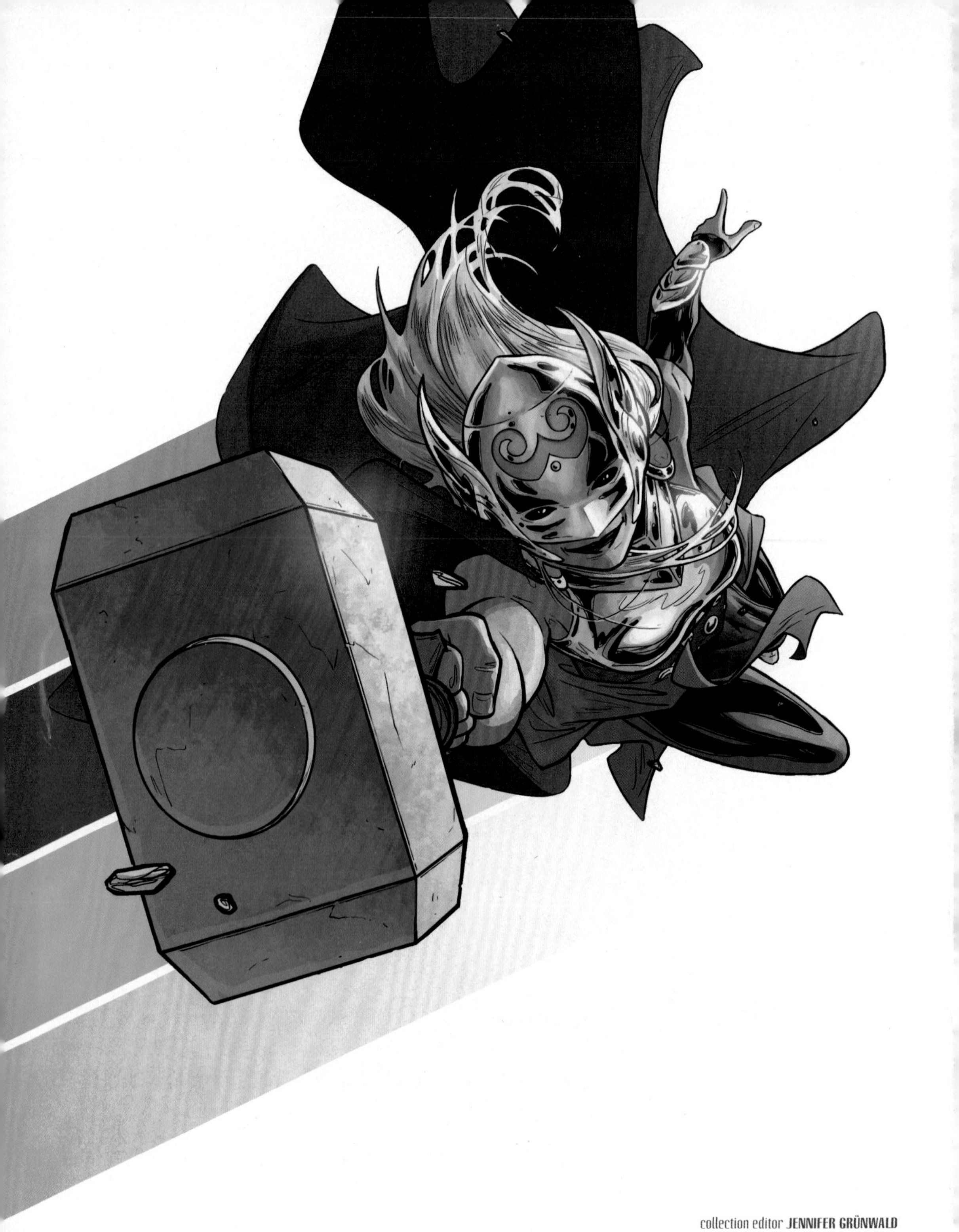

editor in chief **AXEL ALONSO**
chief creative officer **JOE QUESADA**
publisher **DAN BUCKLEY**
executive producer **ALAN FINE**

collection editor **JENNIFER GRÜNWALD**
assistant editor **SARAH BRUNSTAD**
associate managing editor **ALEX STARBUCK**
editor, special projects **MARK D. BEAZLEY**
senior editor, special projects **JEFF YOUNGQUIST**
svp print, sales & marketing **DAVID GABRIEL**
book designer **ADAM DEL RE**

A-FORCE PRESENTS VOL. 2. Contains material originally published in magazine form as BLACK WIDOW #2, CAPTAIN MARVEL #2, MS. MARVEL #2, SHE-HULK #2, THOR #2 and THE UNBEATABLE SQUIRREL GIRL #2. First printing 2015. ISBN# 978-0-7851-9899-4. Published by MARVEL WORLDWIDE, INC., a subsidiary of MARVEL ENTERTAINMENT, LLC. OFFICE OF PUBLICATION: 135 West 50th Street, New York, NY 10020. **Printed in Canada.** ALAN FINE, President, Marvel Entertainment; DAN BUCKLEY, President, TV, Publishing and Brand Management; JOE QUESADA, Chief Creative Officer; TOM BREVOORT, SVP of Publishing; DAVID BOGART, SVP of Operations & Procurement, Publishing; C.B. CEBULSKI, VP of International Development & Brand Management; DAVID GABRIEL, SVP Print, Sales & Marketing; JIM O'KEEFE, VP of Operations & Logistics; DAN CARR, Executive Director of Publishing Technology; SUSAN CRESPI, Editorial Operations Manager; ALEX MORALES, Publishing Operations Manager; STAN LEE, Chairman Emeritus. For information regarding advertising in Marvel Comics or on Marvel.com, please contact Jonathan Rheingold, VP of Custom Solutions & Ad Sales, at jrheingold@marvel.com. For Marvel subscription inquiries, please call 800-217-9158. **Manufactured between 9/18/2015 and 10/26/2015 by SOLISCO PRINTERS, SCOTT, QC, CANADA.**

10 9 8 7 6 5 4 3 2 1

A-FORCE PRESENTS

BLACK WIDOW (2014) #2
writer NATHAN EDMONDSON
artist PHIL NOTO
letterer VC's CLAYTON COWLES
cover art PHIL NOTO
editor ELLIE PYLE

SHE-HULK (2014) #2
writer CHARLES SOULE
artist JAVIER PULIDO
color artist MUNTSA VICENTE
letterer VC's CLAYTON COWLES
cover art KEVIN WADA
assistant editor FRANKIE JOHNSON
editors JEANINE SCHAEFER &
TOM BRENNAN

CAPTAIN MARVEL (2014) #2
writer KELLY SUE DeCONNICK
artist DAVID LOPEZ
color artist LEE LOUGHRIDGE
letterer VC's JOE CARAMAGNA
cover art DAVID LOPEZ
assistant editor DEVIN LEWIS
editor SANA AMANAT
senior editors STEPHEN WACKER &
NICK LOWE

MS. MARVEL (2014) #2
writer G. WILLOW WILSON
artist ADRIAN ALPHONA
color artist IAN HERRING
letterer VC's JOE CARAMAGNA
cover art JAMIE McKELVIE &
MATTHEW WILSON
assistant editor DEVIN LEWIS
editor SANA AMANAT
senior editor STEPHEN WACKER

THOR (2014) #2
writer JASON AARON
artist RUSSELL DAUTERMAN
color artist MATTHEW WILSON
letterer VC's JOE SABINO
cover art RUSSELL DAUTERMAN &
MATTHEW WILSON
assistant editor JON MOISAN
editor WIL MOSS

THE UNBEATABLE SQUIRREL GIRL (2015) #2
writer RYAN NORTH
artist ERICA HENDERSON
color artist RICO RENZI
letterer VC's CLAYTON COWLES
cover art ERICA HENDERSON
assistant editor JON MOISAN
editor WIL MOSS
executive editor TOM BREVOORT

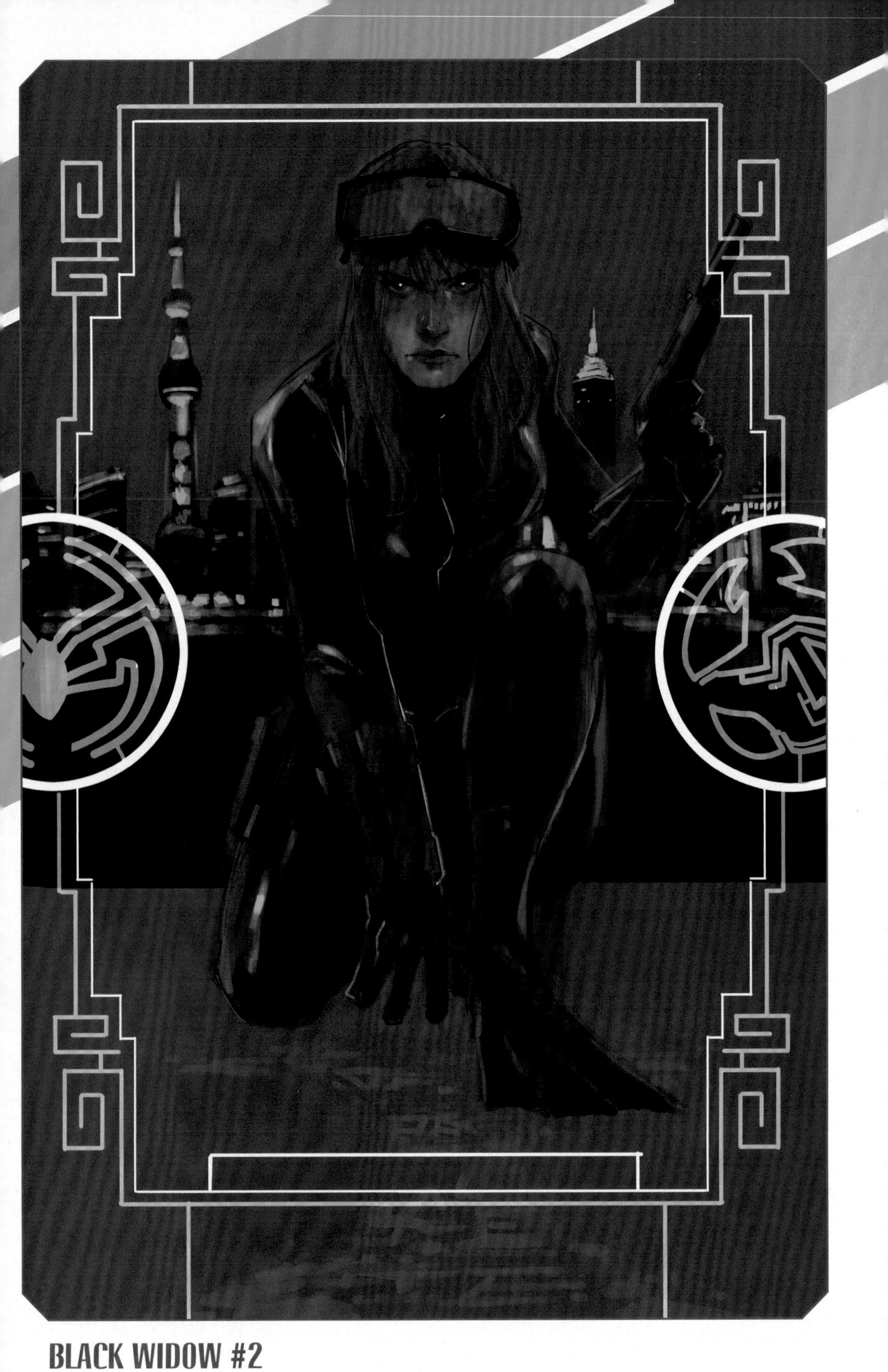

BLACK WIDOW #2

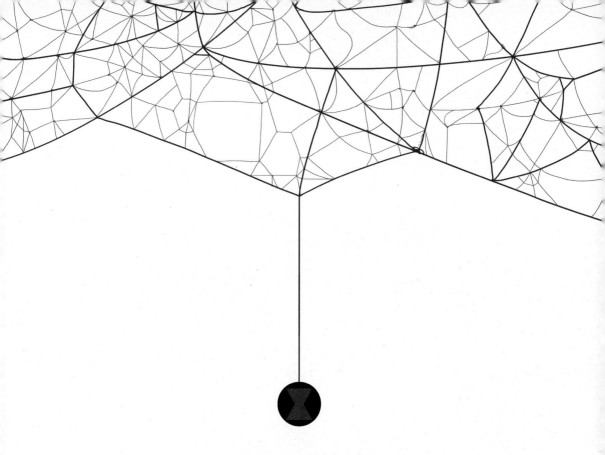

NATASHA ROMANOV IS AN AVENGER, AN AGENT OF S.H.I.E.L.D. AND AN EX-KGB ASSASSIN, BUT ON HER OWN TIME, SHE USES HER UNIQUE SKILL SET TO ATONE FOR HER PAST. SHE IS:

BLACK WIDOW

NATHAN EDMONDSON
WRITER

PHIL NOTO
ARTIST

VC's CLAYTON COWLES
LETTERER & PRODUCTION

ELLIE PYLE
EDITOR

**FRANK CHO
& JUSTIN PONSOR**
VARIANT COVER ARTISTS

**AXEL
ALONSO**
EDITOR IN CHIEF

**JOE
QUESADA**
CHIEF CREATIVE OFFICER

**DAN
BUCKLEY**
PUBLISHER

**ALAN
FINE**
EXEC. PRODUCER

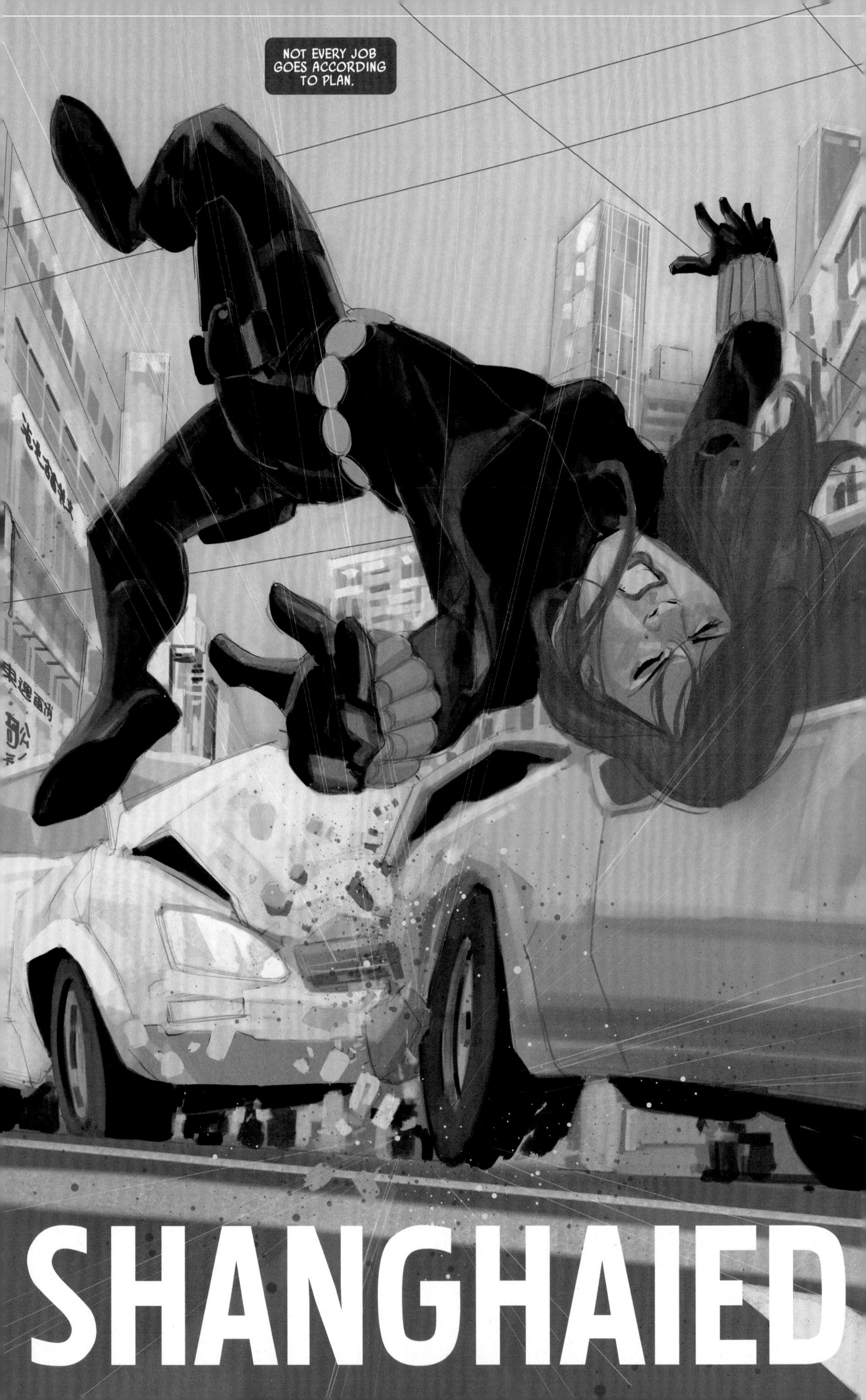
NOT EVERY JOB GOES ACCORDING TO PLAN.
SHANGHAIED

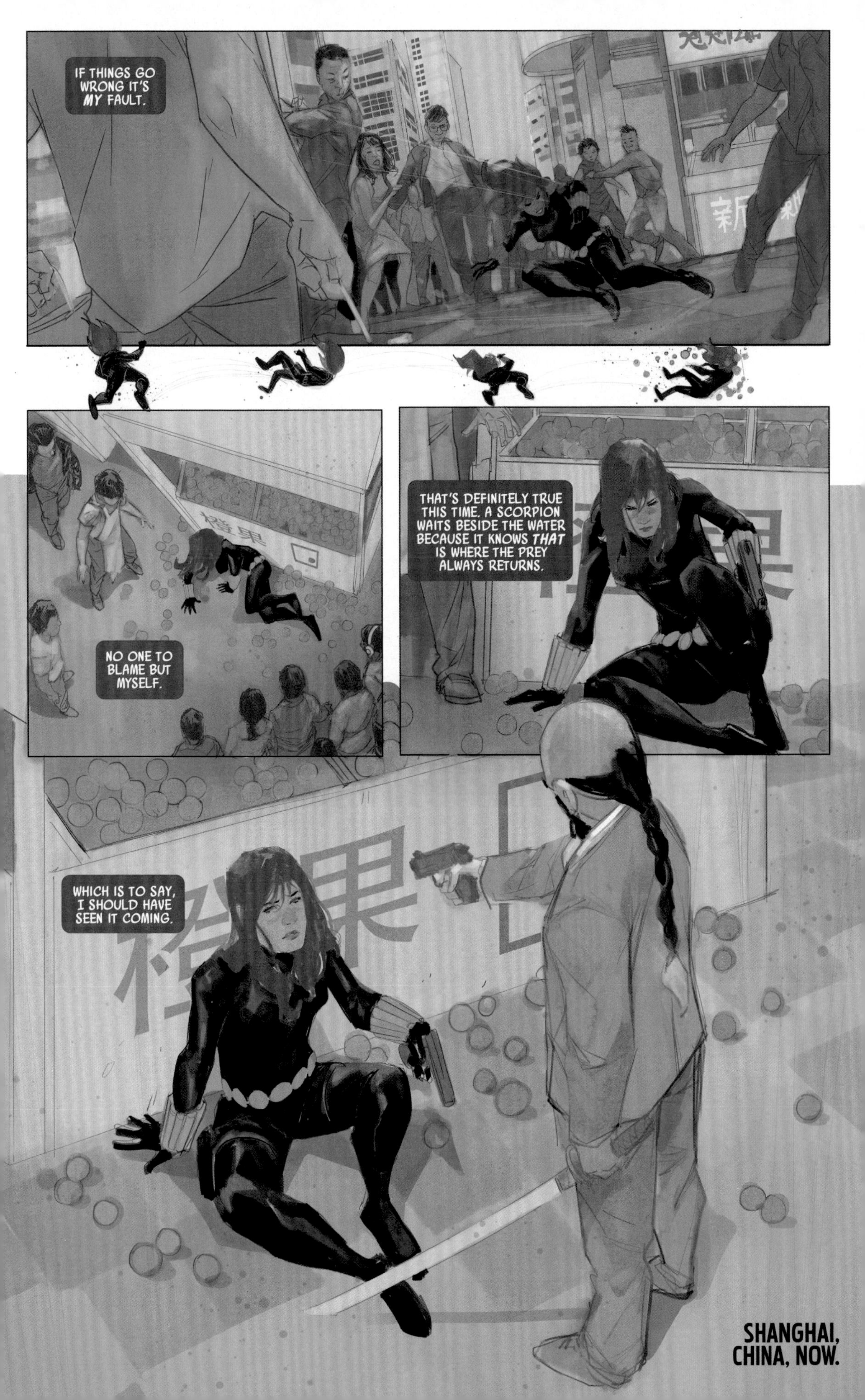
IF THINGS GO WRONG IT'S *MY* FAULT.
NO ONE TO BLAME BUT MYSELF.
THAT'S DEFINITELY TRUE THIS TIME. A SCORPION WAITS BESIDE THE WATER BECAUSE IT KNOWS *THAT* IS WHERE THE PREY ALWAYS RETURNS.
WHICH IS TO SAY, I SHOULD HAVE SEEN IT COMING.
SHANGHAI, CHINA, NOW.

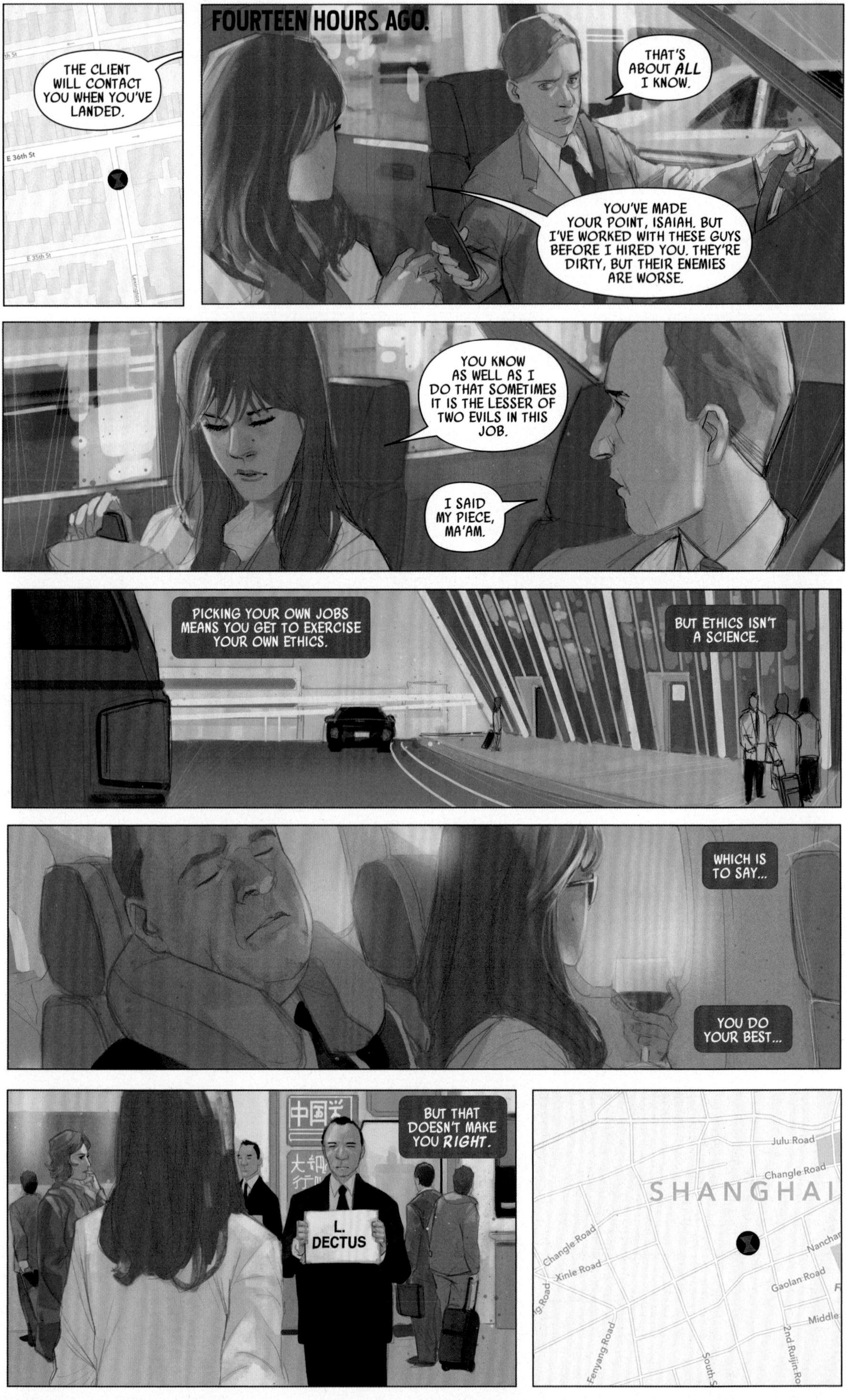
E 36th St
E 35th St
Lexington
THE CLIENT WILL CONTACT YOU WHEN YOU'VE LANDED.
FOURTEEN HOURS AGO.
THAT'S ABOUT ALL I KNOW.
YOU'VE MADE YOUR POINT, ISAIAH. BUT I'VE WORKED WITH THESE GUYS BEFORE I HIRED YOU. THEY'RE DIRTY, BUT THEIR ENEMIES ARE WORSE.
YOU KNOW AS WELL AS I DO THAT SOMETIMES IT IS THE LESSER OF TWO EVILS IN THIS JOB.
I SAID MY PIECE, MA'AM.
PICKING YOUR OWN JOBS MEANS YOU GET TO EXERCISE YOUR OWN ETHICS.
BUT ETHICS ISN'T A SCIENCE.
WHICH IS TO SAY...
YOU DO YOUR BEST...
L. DECTUS
BUT THAT DOESN'T MAKE YOU RIGHT.
Julu Road
Changle Road
SHANGHAI
Changle Road
Xinle Road
Gaolan Road
Fenyang Road

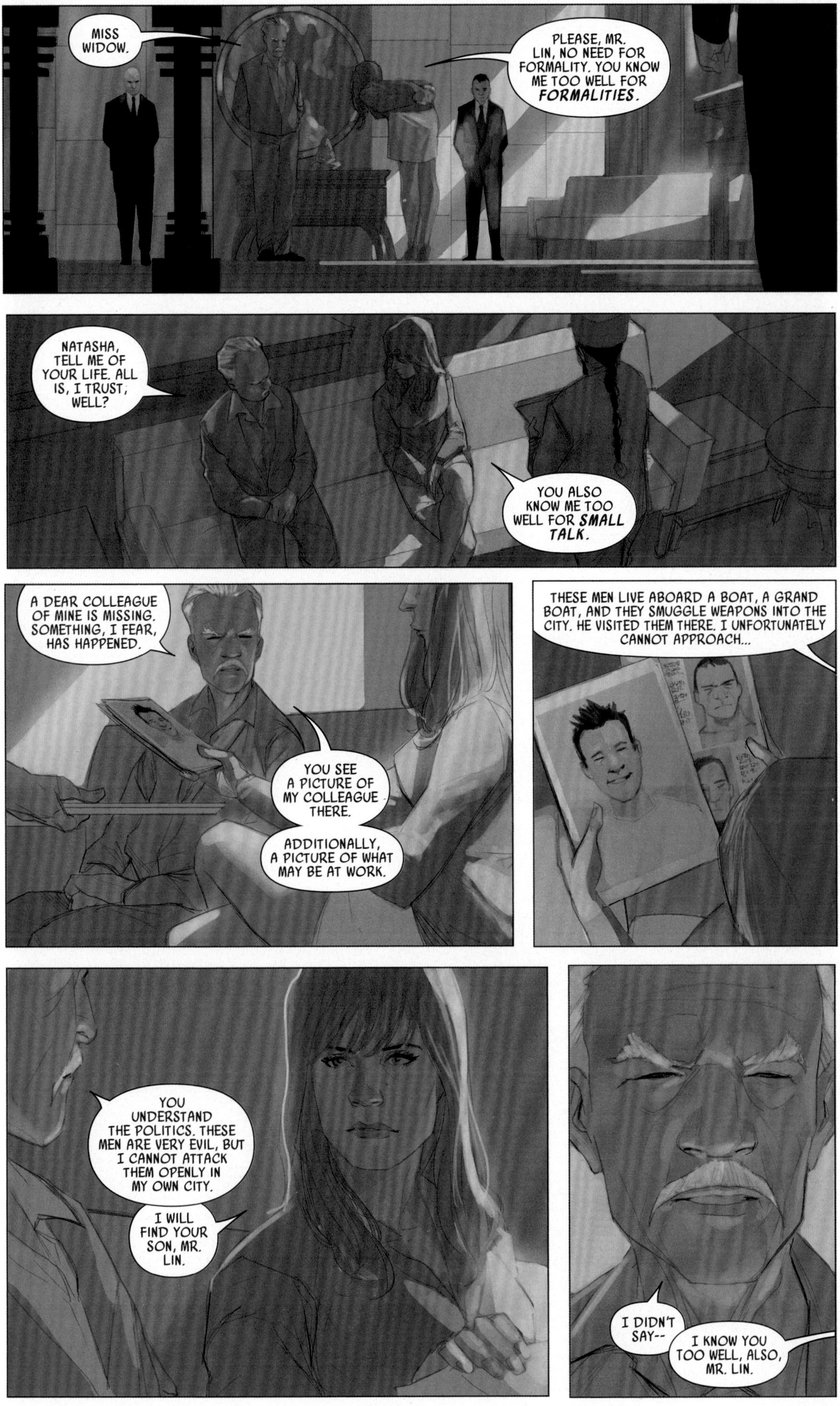
MISS WIDOW.
PLEASE, MR. LIN, NO NEED FOR FORMALITY. YOU KNOW ME TOO WELL FOR FORMALITIES.
NATASHA, TELL ME OF YOUR LIFE. ALL IS, I TRUST, WELL?
YOU ALSO KNOW ME TOO WELL FOR SMALL TALK.
A DEAR COLLEAGUE OF MINE IS MISSING. SOMETHING, I FEAR, HAS HAPPENED.
YOU SEE A PICTURE OF MY COLLEAGUE THERE.
ADDITIONALLY, A PICTURE OF WHAT MAY BE AT WORK.
THESE MEN LIVE ABOARD A BOAT, A GRAND BOAT, AND THEY SMUGGLE WEAPONS INTO THE CITY. HE VISITED THEM THERE. I UNFORTUNATELY CANNOT APPROACH...
YOU UNDERSTAND THE POLITICS. THESE MEN ARE VERY EVIL, BUT I CANNOT ATTACK THEM OPENLY IN MY OWN CITY.
I WILL FIND YOUR SON, MR. LIN.
I DIDN'T SAY--
I KNOW YOU TOO WELL, ALSO, MR. LIN.

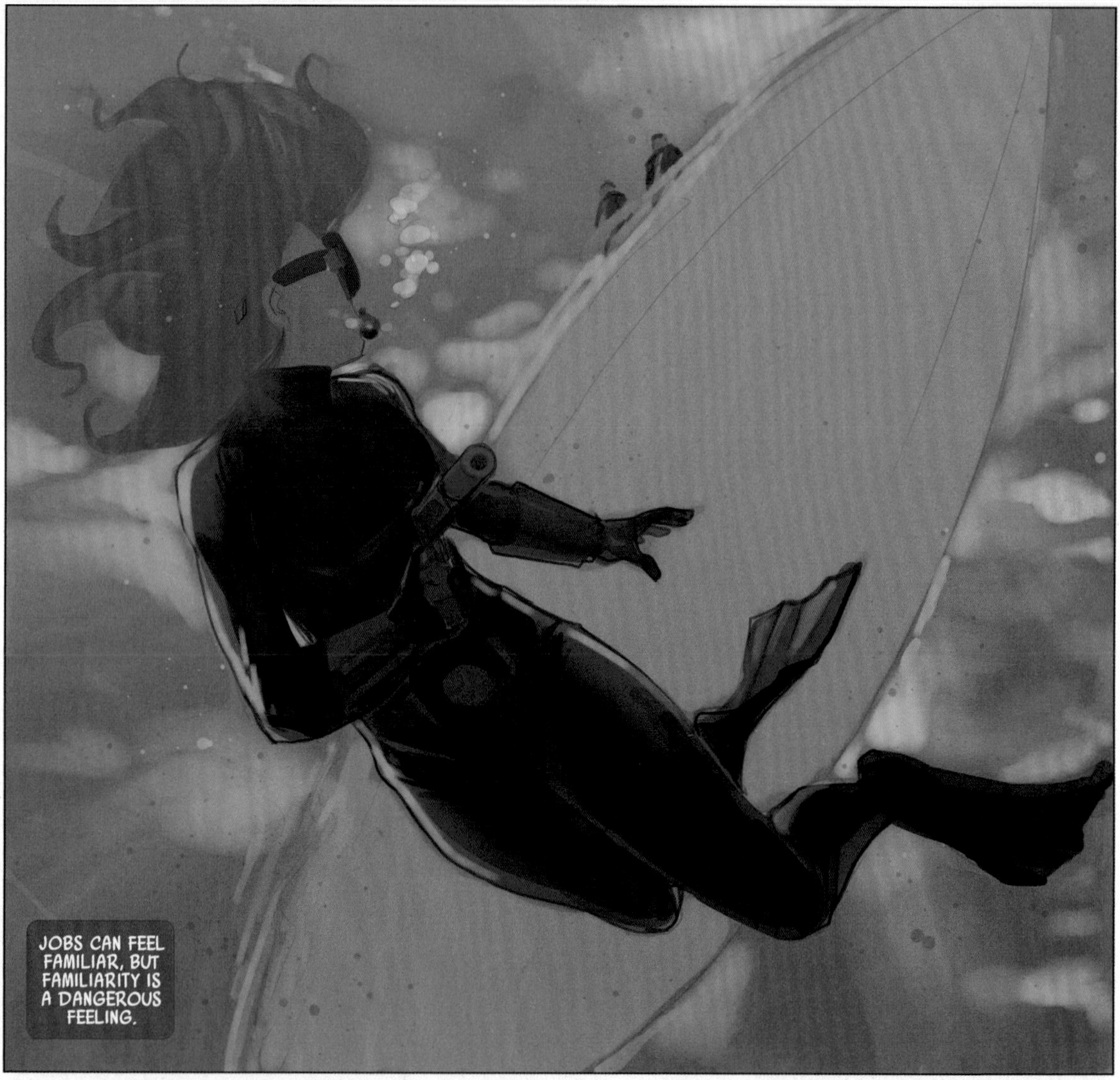
JOBS CAN FEEL FAMILIAR, BUT FAMILIARITY IS A DANGEROUS FEELING.

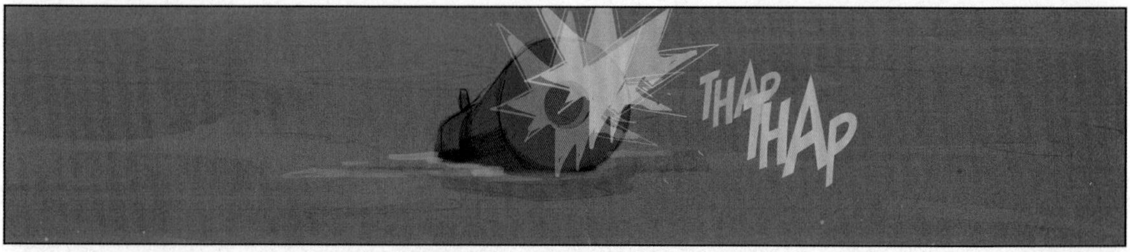
THAP THAP

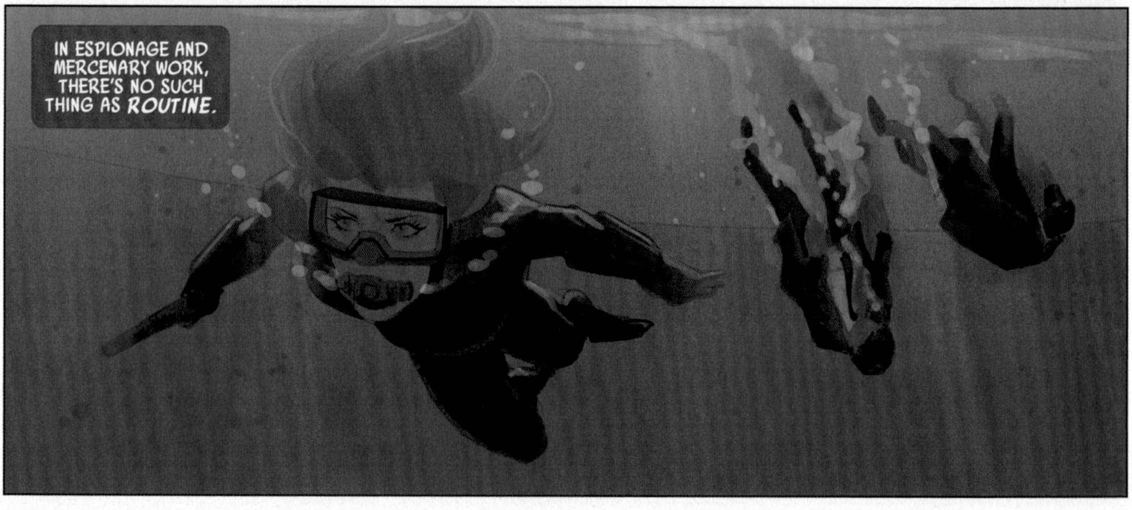
IN ESPIONAGE AND MERCENARY WORK, THERE'S NO SUCH THING AS *ROUTINE*.

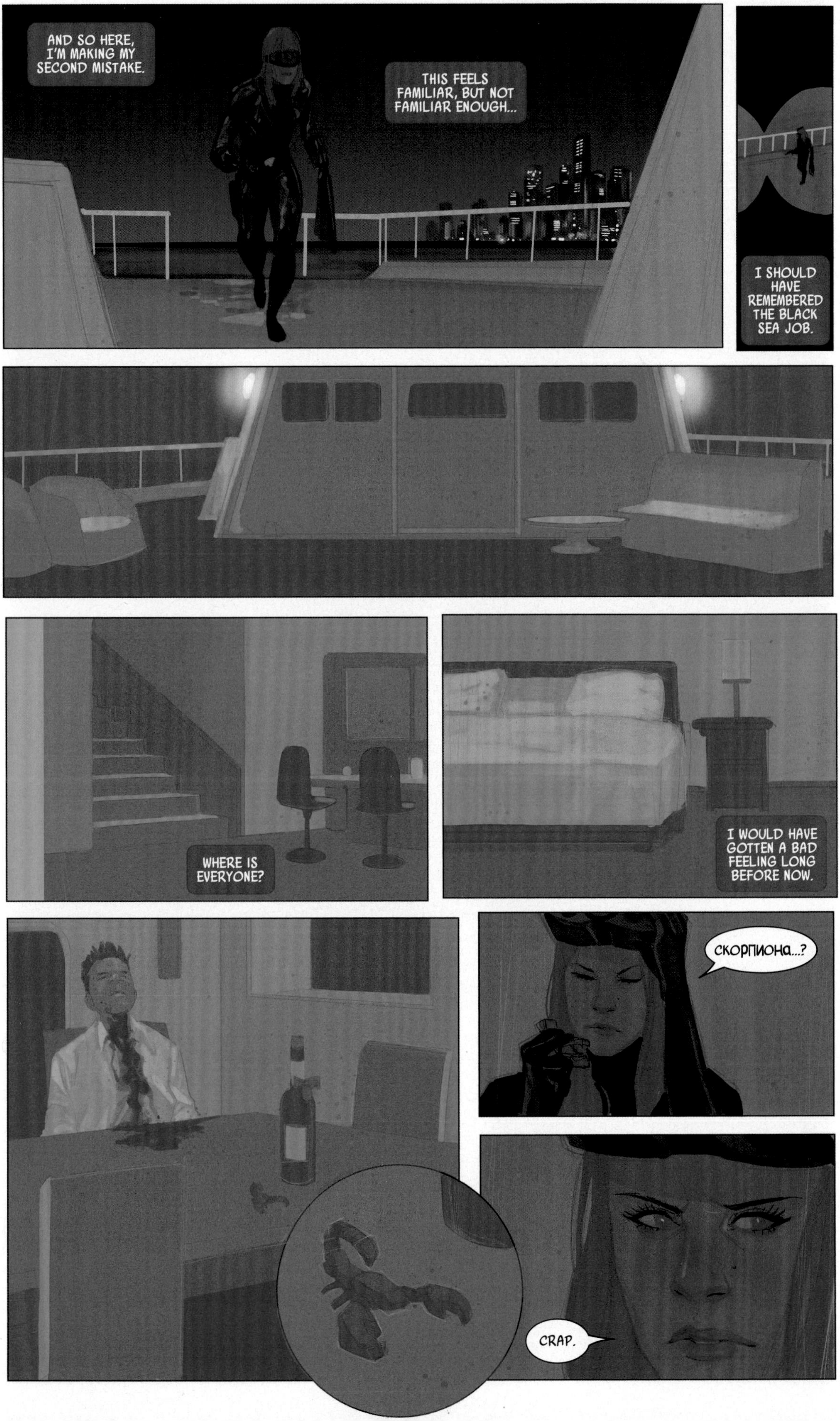
AND SO HERE, I'M MAKING MY SECOND MISTAKE.
THIS FEELS FAMILIAR, BUT NOT FAMILIAR ENOUGH...
I SHOULD HAVE REMEMBERED THE BLACK SEA JOB.
WHERE IS EVERYONE?
I WOULD HAVE GOTTEN A BAD FEELING LONG BEFORE NOW.
СКОРПИОНА...?
CRAP.

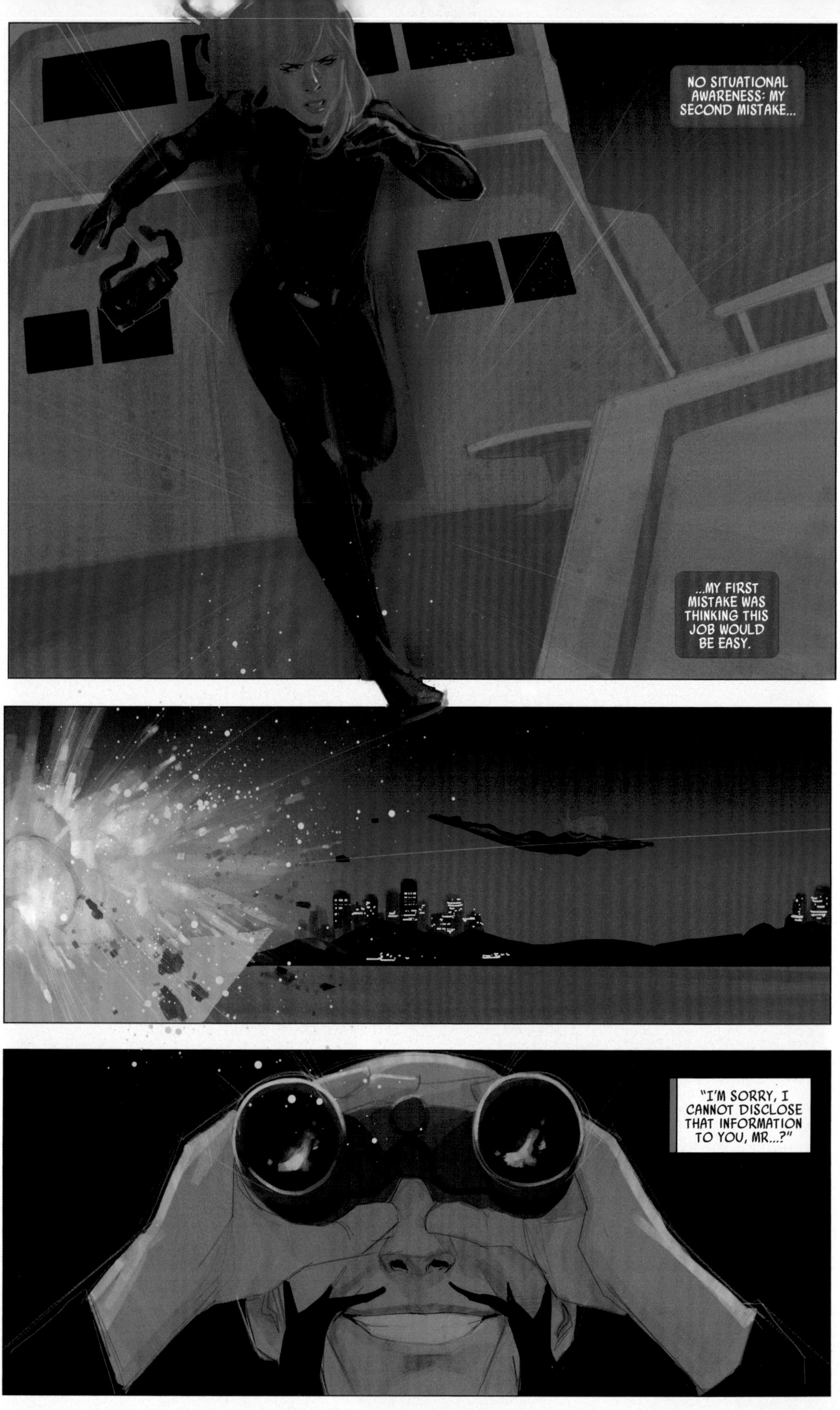
NO SITUATIONAL AWARENESS: MY SECOND MISTAKE...
...MY FIRST MISTAKE WAS THINKING THIS JOB WOULD BE EASY.
"I'M SORRY, I CANNOT DISCLOSE THAT INFORMATION TO YOU, MR...?"

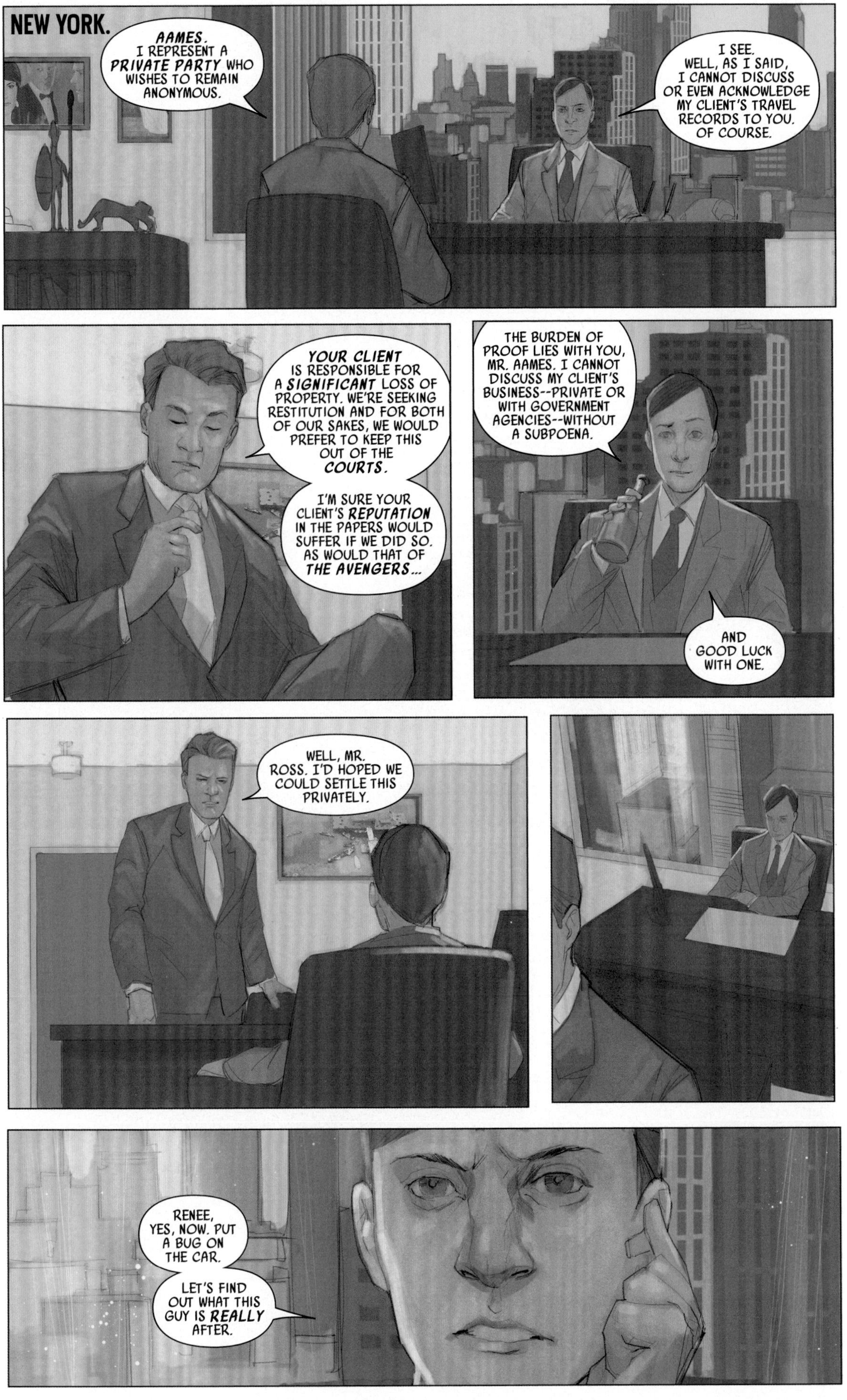
NEW YORK.
AAMES. I REPRESENT A PRIVATE PARTY WHO WISHES TO REMAIN ANONYMOUS.
I SEE. WELL, AS I SAID, I CANNOT DISCUSS OR EVEN ACKNOWLEDGE MY CLIENT'S TRAVEL RECORDS TO YOU. OF COURSE.
YOUR CLIENT IS RESPONSIBLE FOR A SIGNIFICANT LOSS OF PROPERTY. WE'RE SEEKING RESTITUTION AND FOR BOTH OF OUR SAKES, WE WOULD PREFER TO KEEP THIS OUT OF THE COURTS.
I'M SURE YOUR CLIENT'S REPUTATION IN THE PAPERS WOULD SUFFER IF WE DID SO. AS WOULD THAT OF THE AVENGERS...
THE BURDEN OF PROOF LIES WITH YOU, MR. AAMES. I CANNOT DISCUSS MY CLIENT'S BUSINESS--PRIVATE OR WITH GOVERNMENT AGENCIES--WITHOUT A SUBPOENA.
AND GOOD LUCK WITH ONE.
WELL, MR. ROSS. I'D HOPED WE COULD SETTLE THIS PRIVATELY.
RENEE, YES, NOW. PUT A BUG ON THE CAR.
LET'S FIND OUT WHAT THIS GUY IS REALLY AFTER.

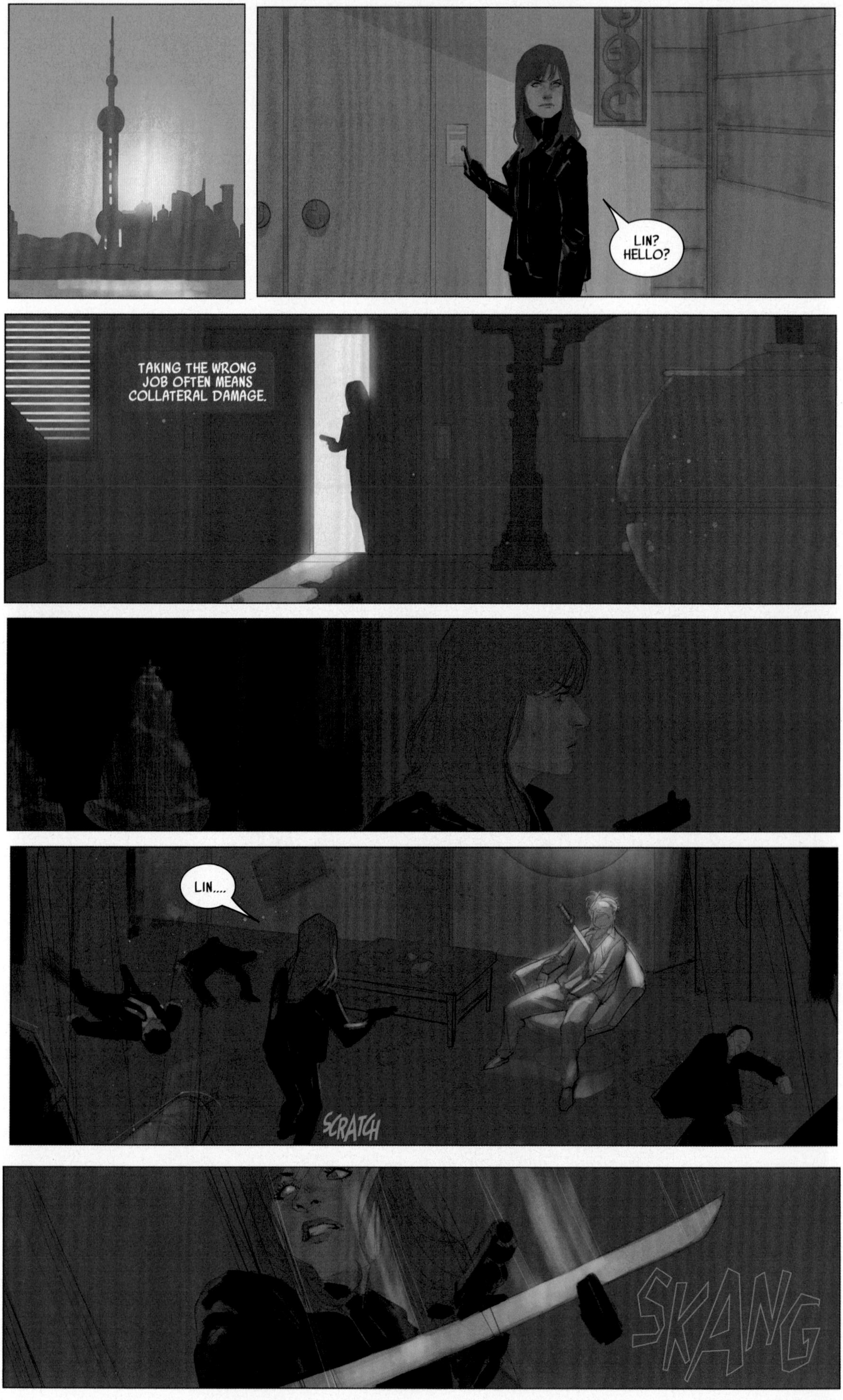
LIN?
HELLO?
TAKING THE WRONG JOB OFTEN MEANS COLLATERAL DAMAGE.
LIN....
SCRATCH
SKANG

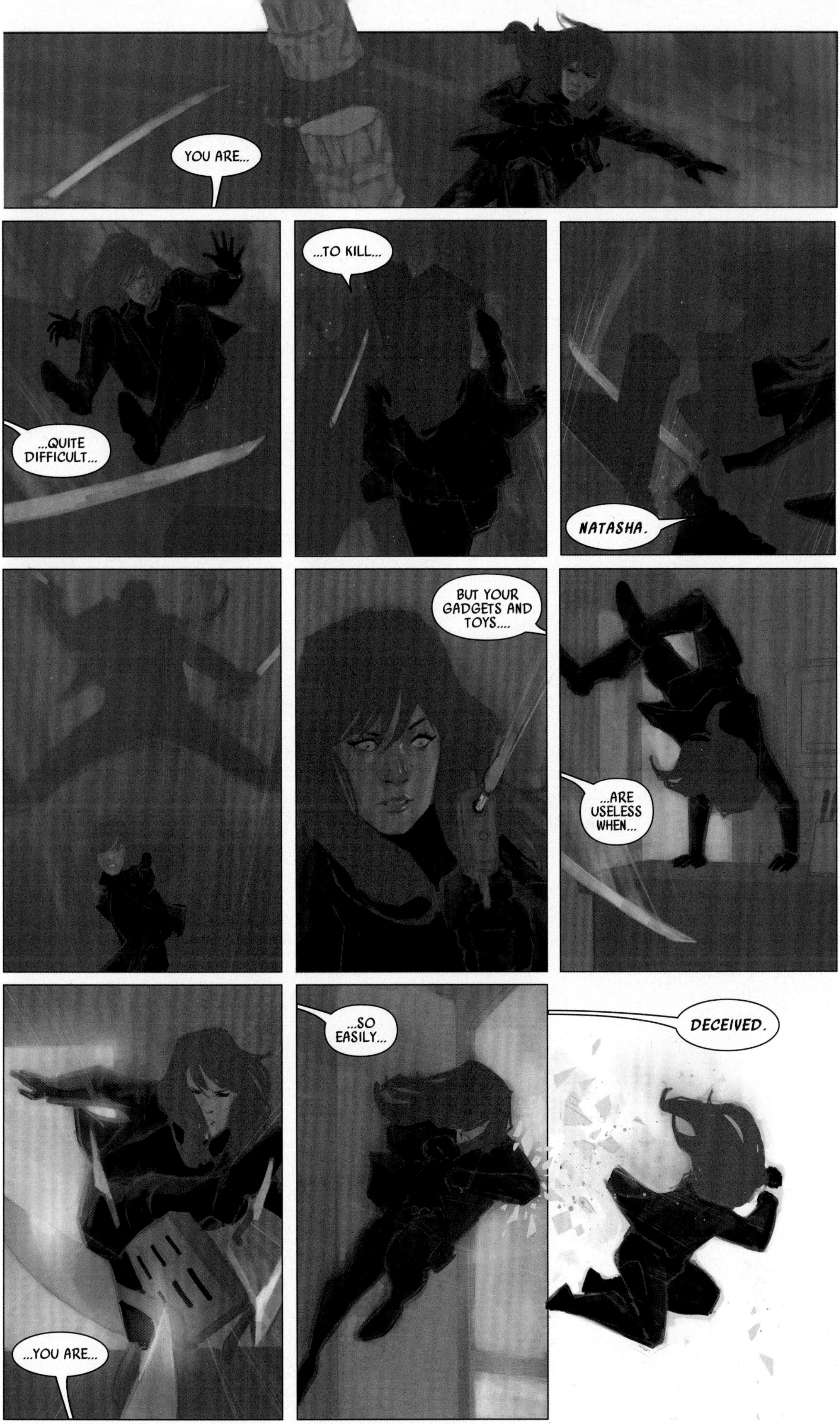
YOU ARE...
...QUITE DIFFICULT...
...TO KILL...
NATASHA.
BUT YOUR GADGETS AND TOYS....
...ARE USELESS WHEN...
...YOU ARE...
...SO EASILY...
DECEIVED.

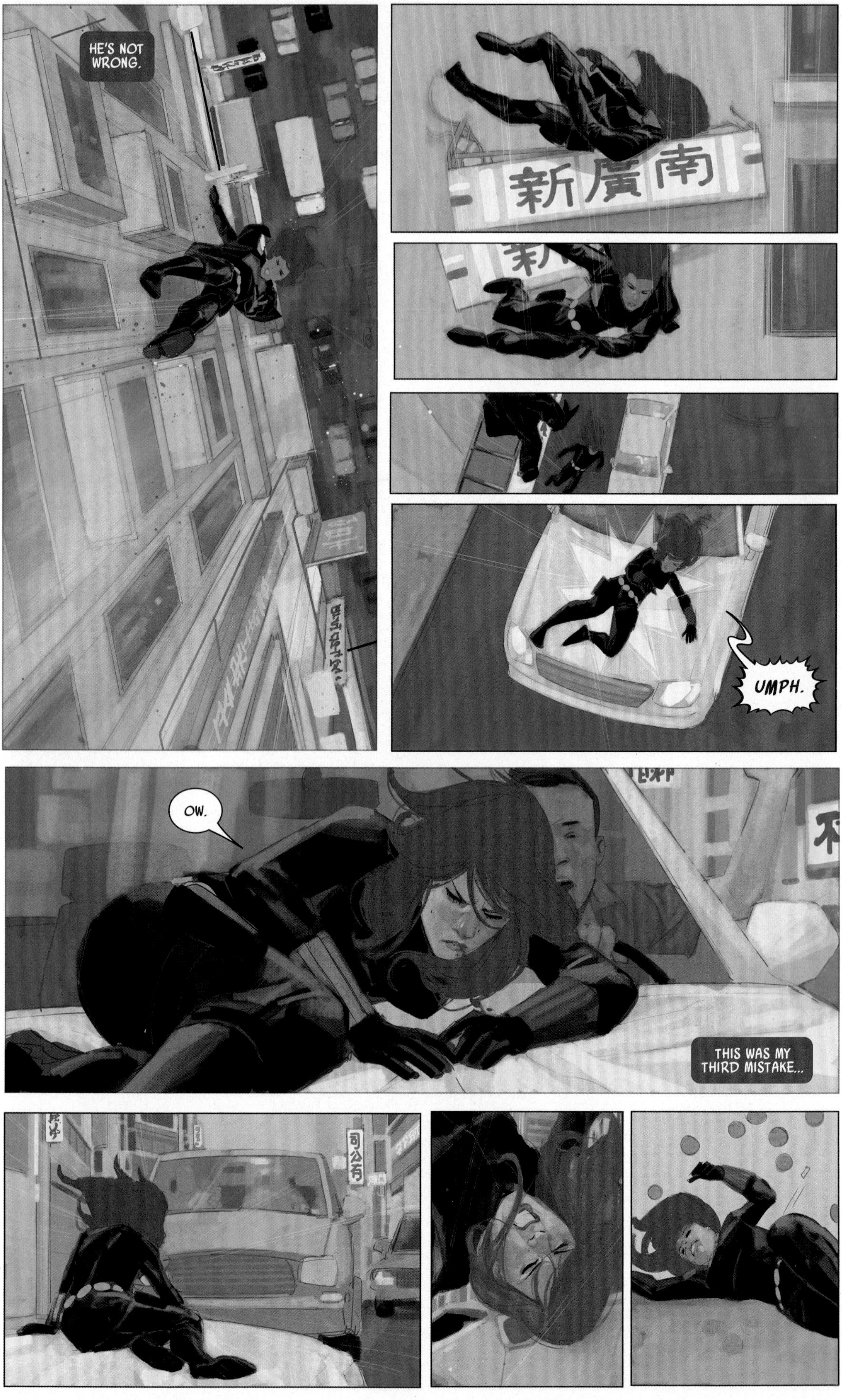
HE'S NOT WRONG.
新廣南
UMPH.
OW.
THIS WAS MY THIRD MISTAKE...
司公有

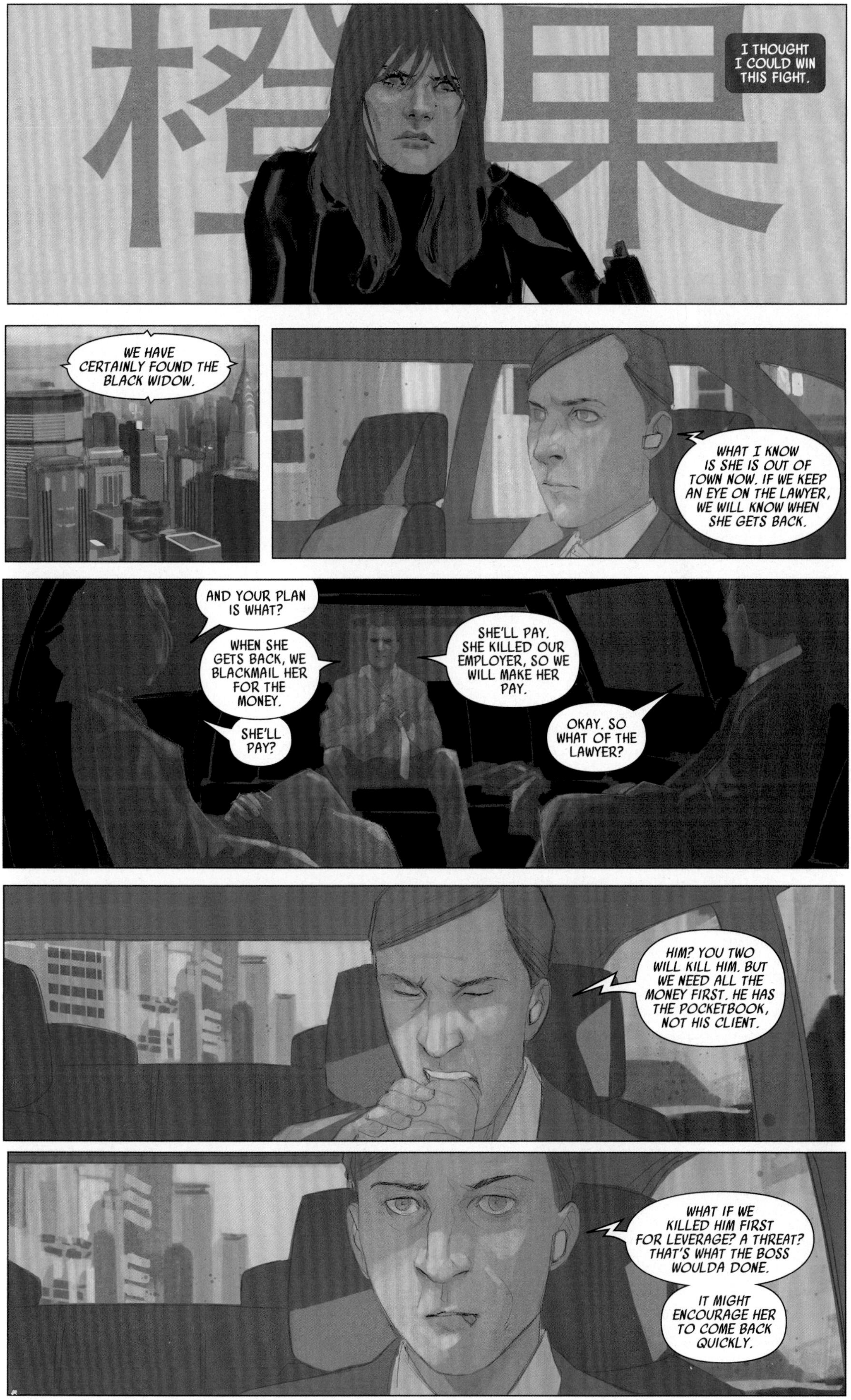
I THOUGHT I COULD WIN THIS FIGHT.
WE HAVE CERTAINLY FOUND THE BLACK WIDOW.
WHAT I KNOW IS SHE IS OUT OF TOWN NOW. IF WE KEEP AN EYE ON THE LAWYER, WE WILL KNOW WHEN SHE GETS BACK.
AND YOUR PLAN IS WHAT?
WHEN SHE GETS BACK, WE BLACKMAIL HER FOR THE MONEY.
SHE'LL PAY?
SHE'LL PAY. SHE KILLED OUR EMPLOYER, SO WE WILL MAKE HER PAY.
OKAY. SO WHAT OF THE LAWYER?
HIM? YOU TWO WILL KILL HIM. BUT WE NEED ALL THE MONEY FIRST. HE HAS THE POCKETBOOK, NOT HIS CLIENT.
WHAT IF WE KILLED HIM FIRST FOR LEVERAGE? A THREAT? THAT'S WHAT THE BOSS WOULDA DONE.
IT MIGHT ENCOURAGE HER TO COME BACK QUICKLY.

THE WIDOW. THE RUSSIAN AVENGER. THE SLAVIC SHADOW. THE RED DEATH.

THEY HAVE SO MANY NAMES FOR YOU.

YOU ARE HIS SERVANT...

"A DISGUISE, WIDOW."

YOU CAN CALL ME IRON SCORPION.

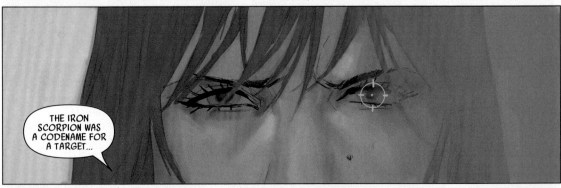

THE IRON SCORPION WAS A CODENAME FOR A TARGET...

"SIX YEARS AGO, ON THE BLACK SEA..."

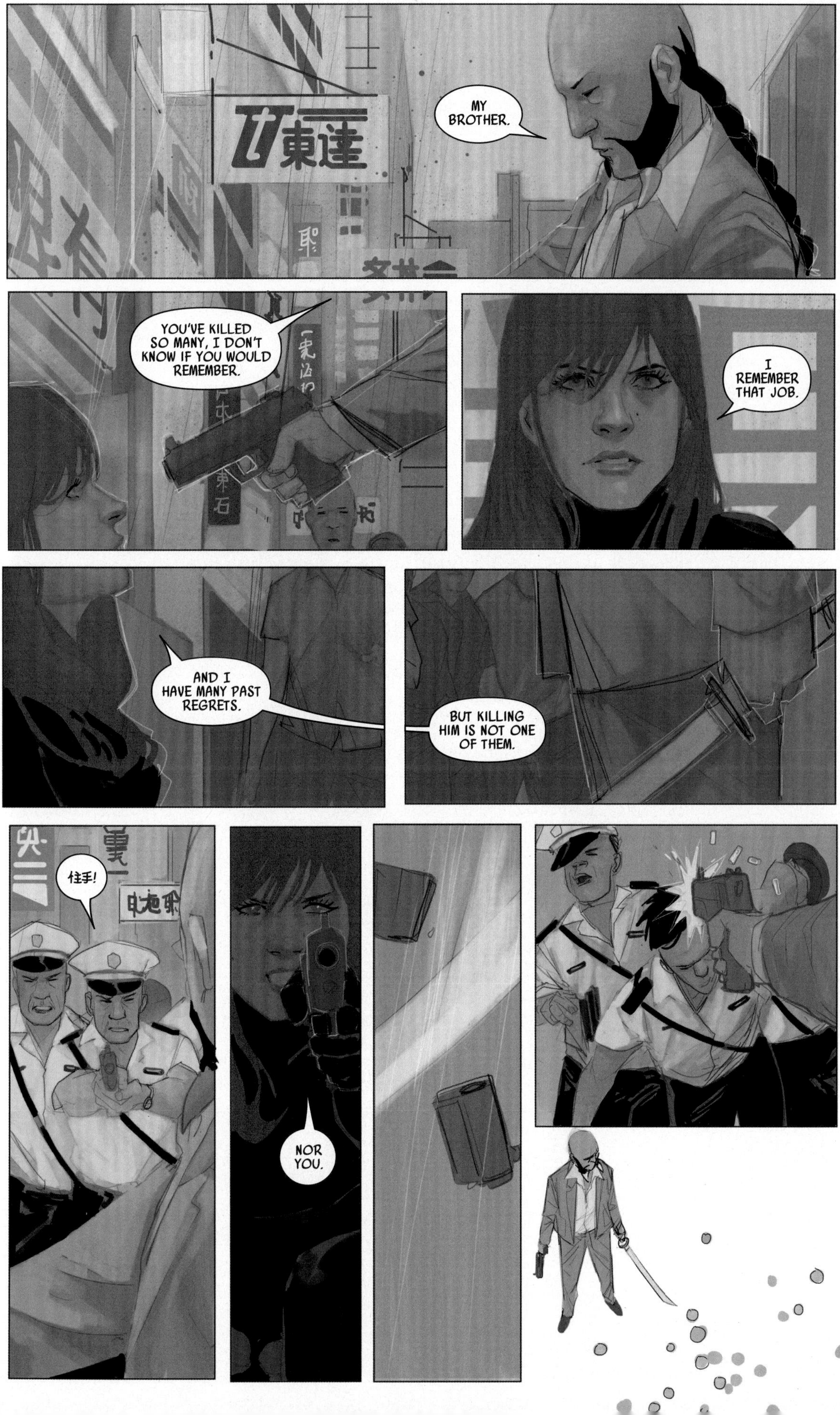

MY BROTHER.
YOU'VE KILLED SO MANY, I DON'T KNOW IF YOU WOULD REMEMBER.
I REMEMBER THAT JOB.
AND I HAVE MANY PAST REGRETS.
BUT KILLING HIM IS NOT ONE OF THEM.
住手!
NOR YOU.

WHERE HAVE YOU GONE, LITTLE SPIDER...

...YOU HAVE NO WEAPON, NO FRIENDS...

HERE.

I DO HAVE...

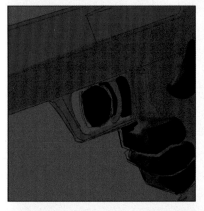

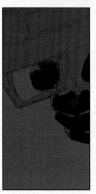

ONE REGRET:

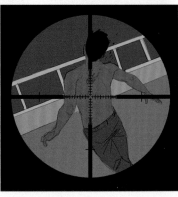

I HESITATED.

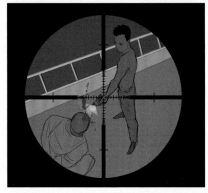

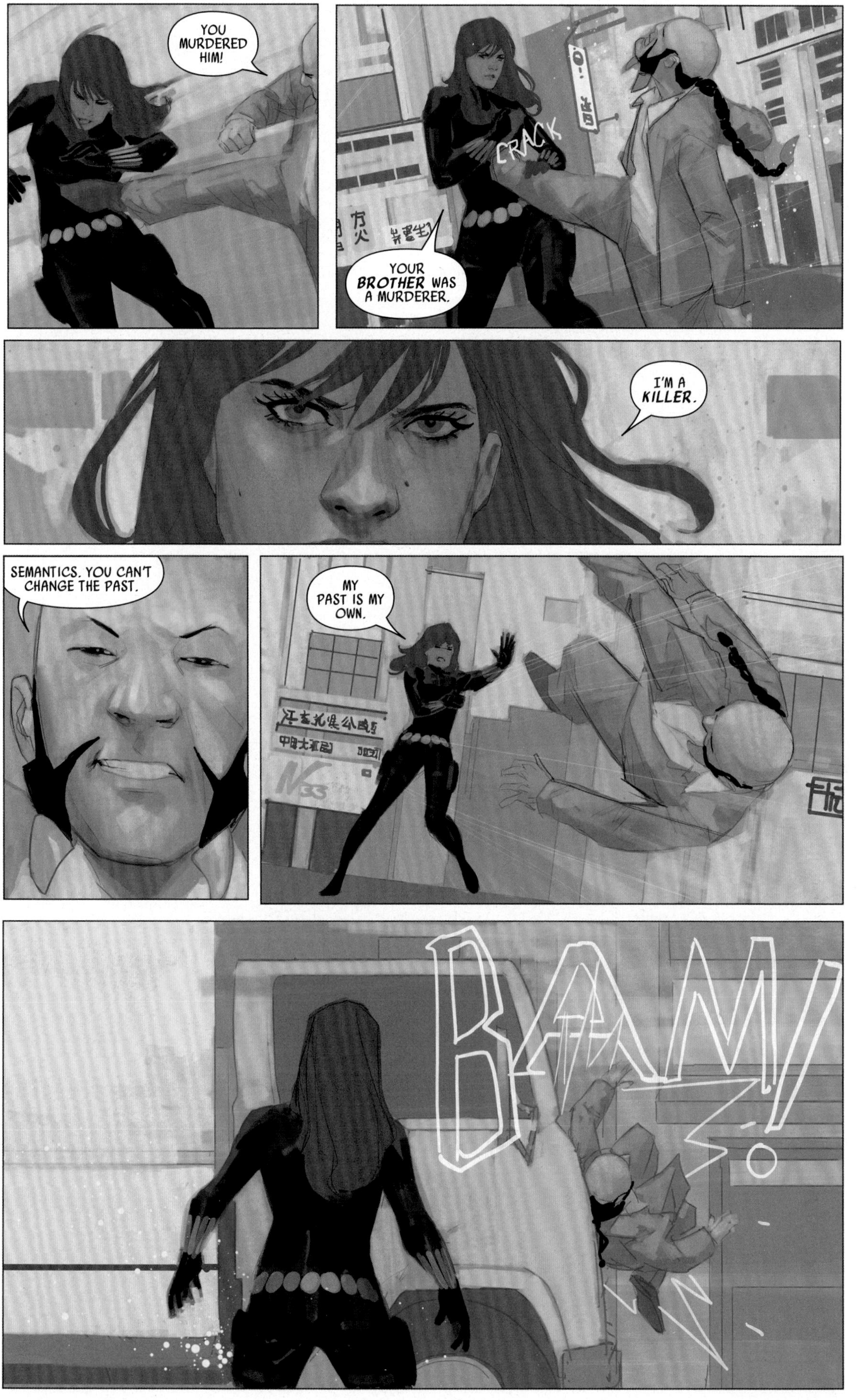
YOU MURDERED HIM!
CRACK
YOUR BROTHER WAS A MURDERER.
I'M A KILLER.
SEMANTICS. YOU CAN'T CHANGE THE PAST.
MY PAST IS MY OWN.
BAM!

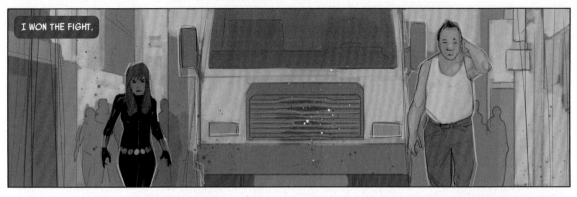

I WON THE FIGHT.

BUT THE IRON SCORPION IS STILL OUT THERE.

HE'LL FIND ME AGAIN. I CAN COUNT ON THAT.

THAT'S MY FOURTH MISTAKE...

...BUT I'M DONE COUNTING FOR TODAY.

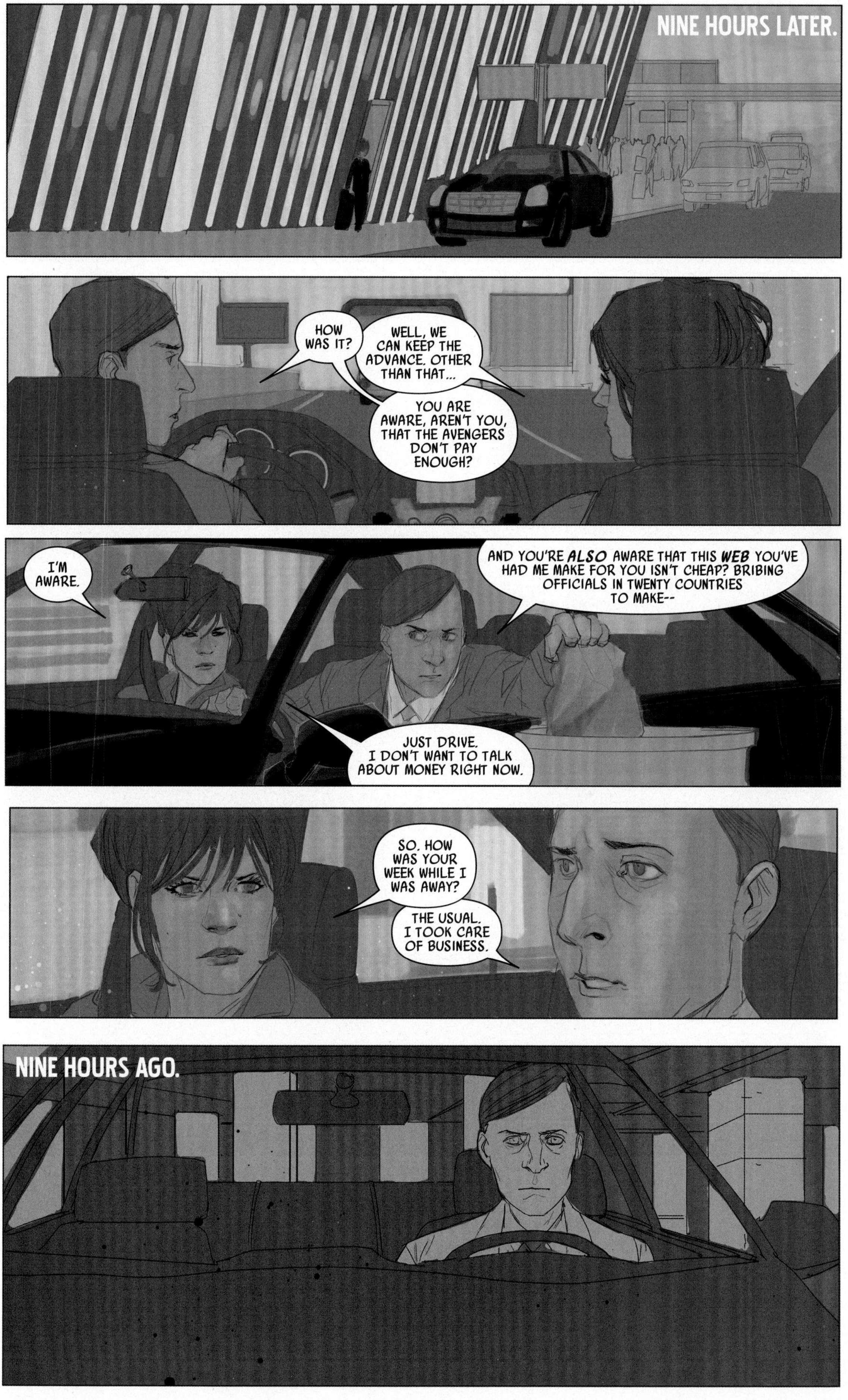
NINE HOURS LATER.
HOW WAS IT?
WELL, WE CAN KEEP THE ADVANCE. OTHER THAN THAT...
YOU ARE AWARE, AREN'T YOU, THAT THE AVENGERS DON'T PAY ENOUGH?
I'M AWARE.
AND YOU'RE ALSO AWARE THAT THIS WEB YOU'VE HAD ME MAKE FOR YOU ISN'T CHEAP? BRIBING OFFICIALS IN TWENTY COUNTRIES TO MAKE--
JUST DRIVE. I DON'T WANT TO TALK ABOUT MONEY RIGHT NOW.
SO. HOW WAS YOUR WEEK WHILE I WAS AWAY?
THE USUAL. I TOOK CARE OF BUSINESS.
NINE HOURS AGO.

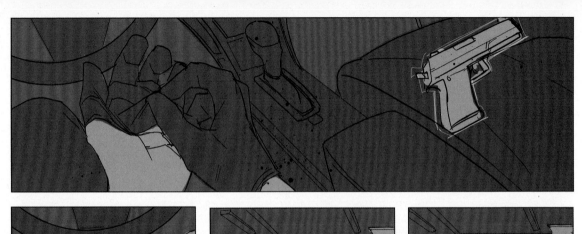

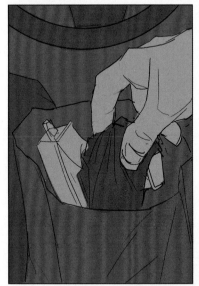

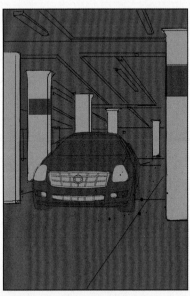

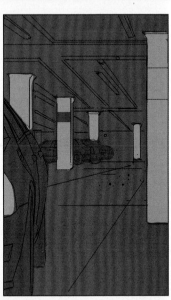

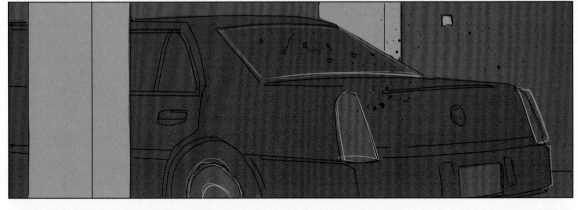

"SO, LIHO..."

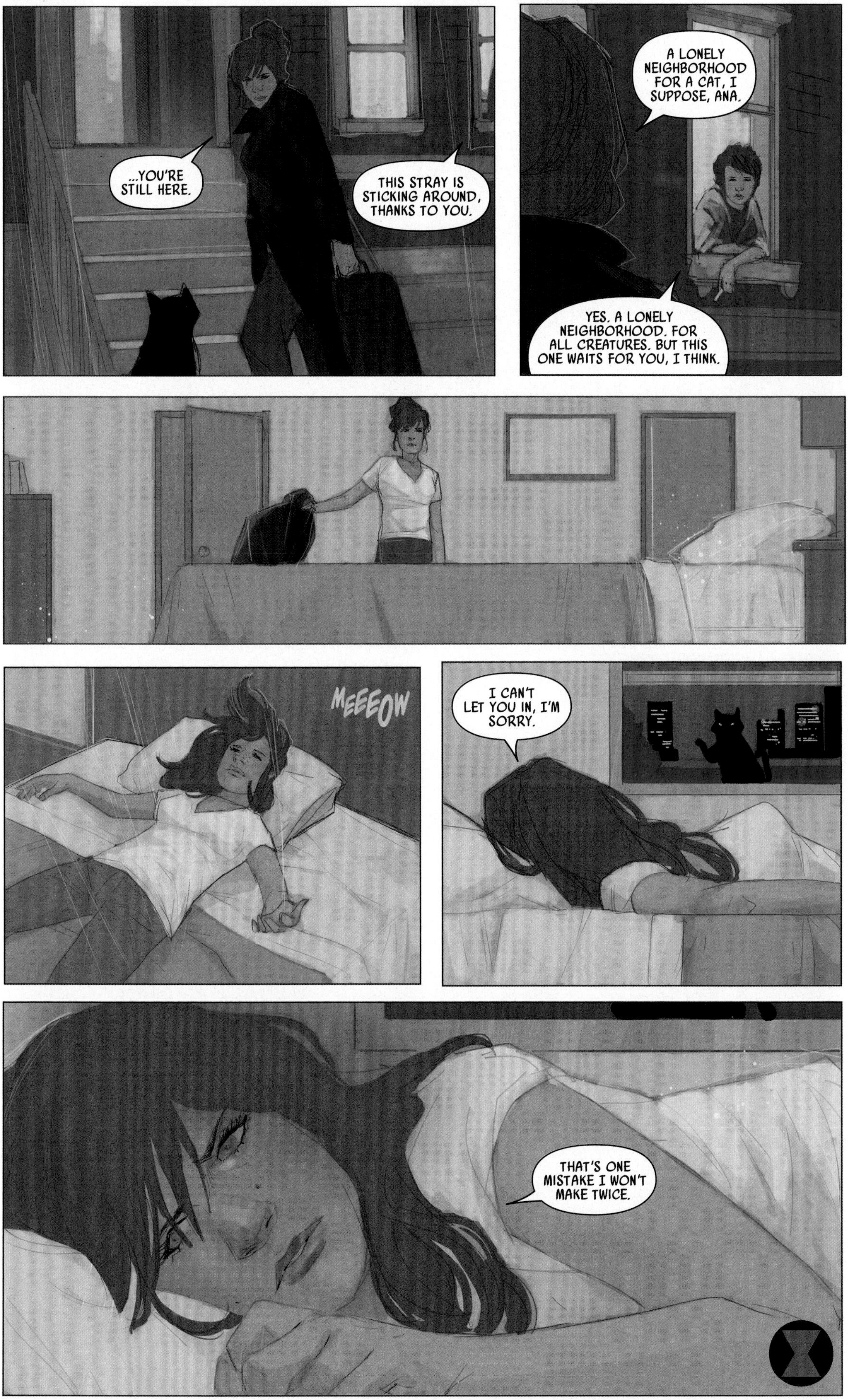
...YOU'RE STILL HERE.
THIS STRAY IS STICKING AROUND, THANKS TO YOU.
A LONELY NEIGHBORHOOD FOR A CAT, I SUPPOSE, ANA.
YES. A LONELY NEIGHBORHOOD. FOR ALL CREATURES. BUT THIS ONE WAITS FOR YOU, I THINK.
MEEEOW
I CAN'T LET YOU IN, I'M SORRY.
THAT'S ONE MISTAKE I WON'T MAKE TWICE.

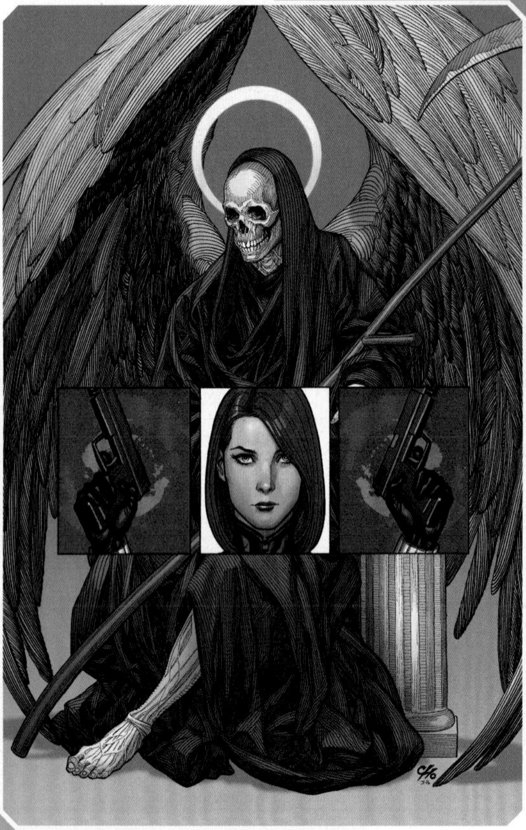

BLACK WIDOW #2
Variant by Frank Cho & Justin Ponsor

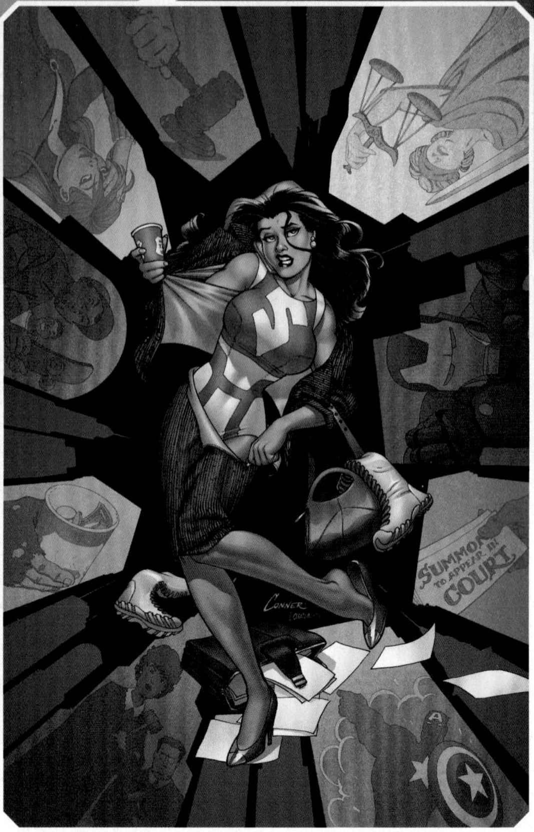
TO APPEAR IN
COURT
CONNER

SHE-HULK #2
Variant by Amanda Conner & Laura Martin

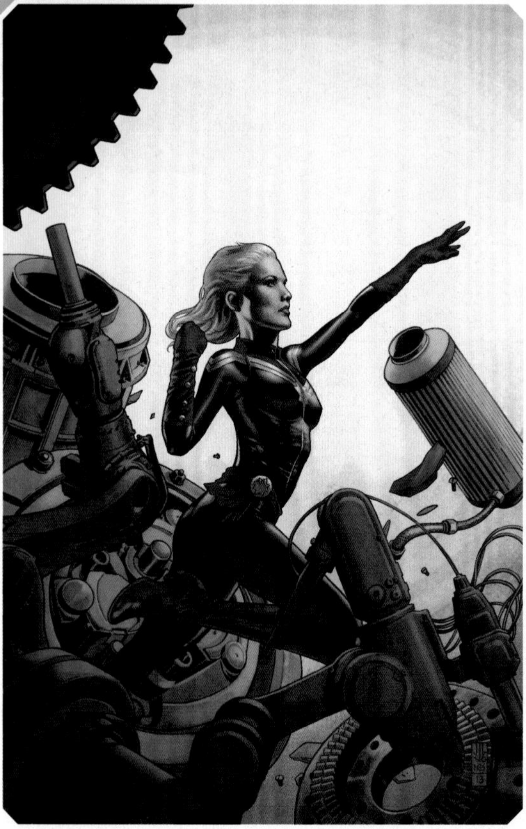

CAPTAIN MARVEL #2
Variant by J.G. Jones & Laura Martin

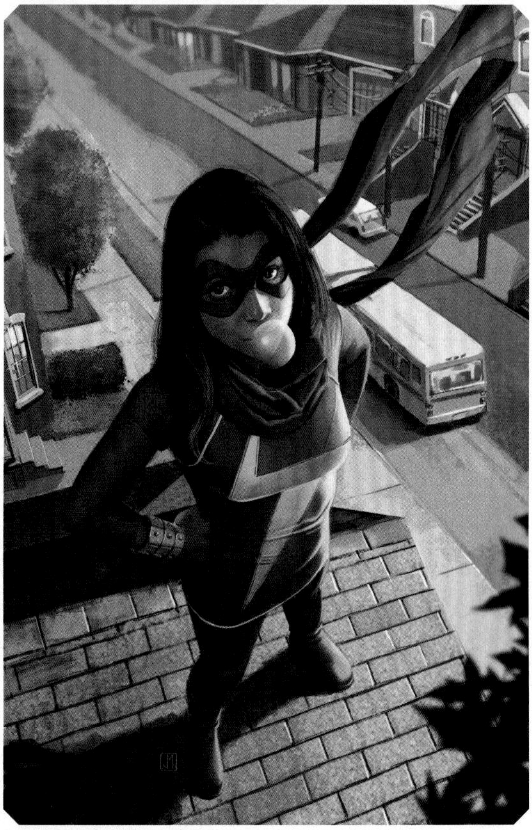

MS. MARVEL #2
Variant by Jorge Molina

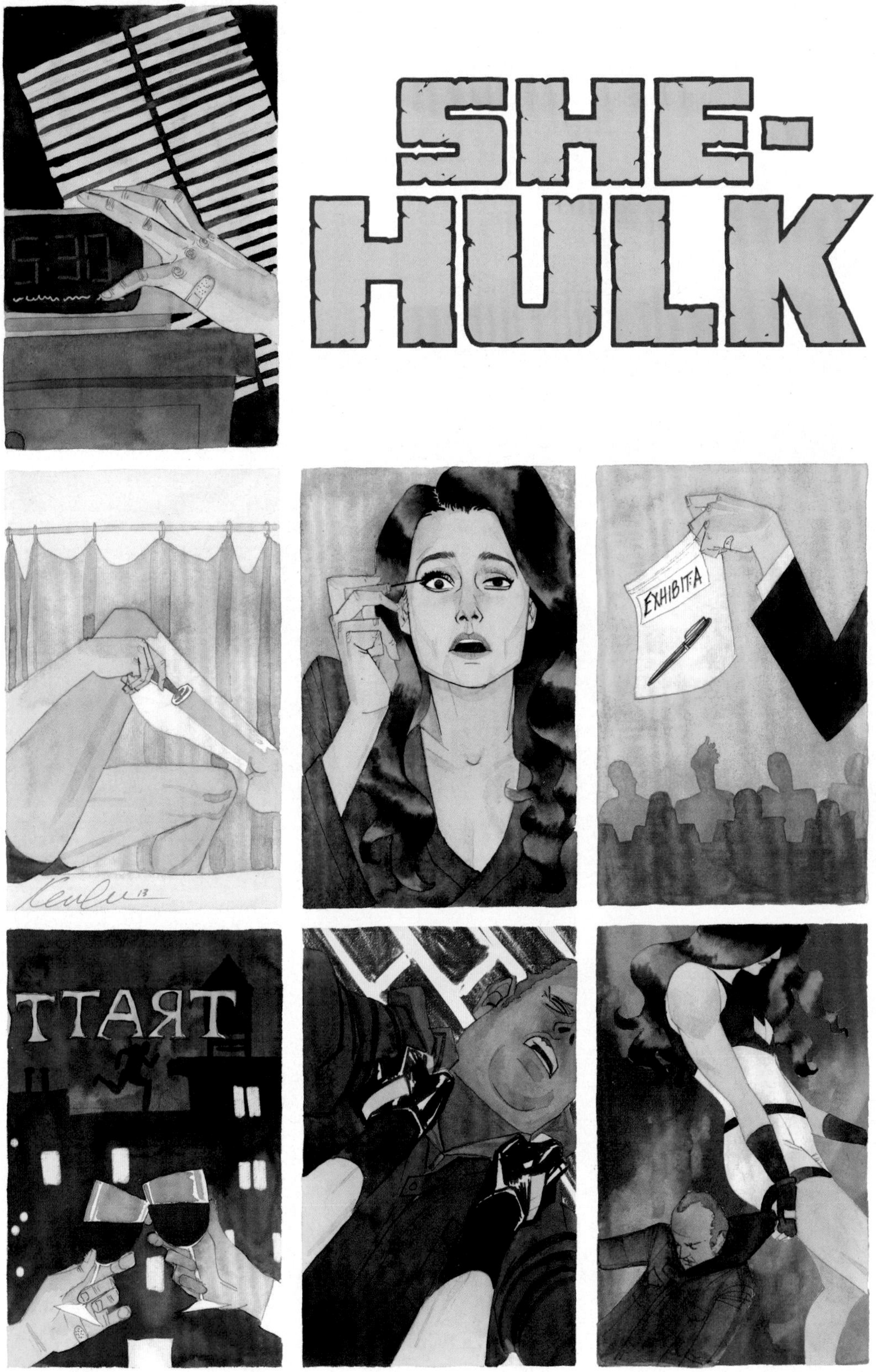
SHE-HULK
EXHIBIT A

SHE-HULK #2

Jennifer Walters was a shy attorney, good at her job and quiet in her life, when she found herself gunned down by criminals. A gamma irradiated blood transfusion from her cousin, Dr. Bruce Banner, aka the Incredible Hulk, didn't just give her a second chance at life, it gave her super strength and bulletproof green skin. Wherever justice is threatened, you'll find the Sensational…

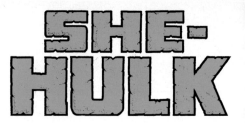

SHE-HULK

PREVIOUSLY...

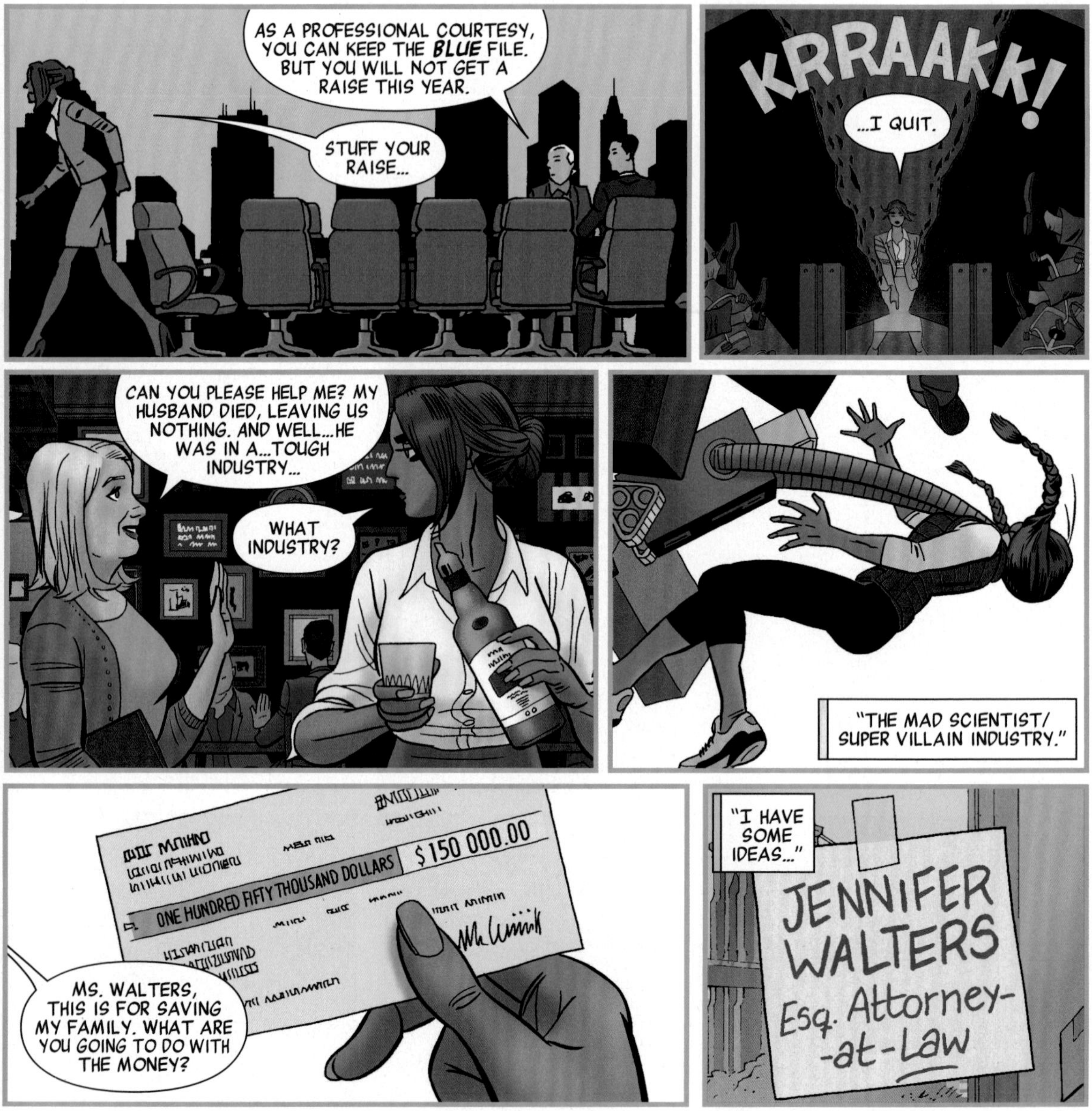
AS A PROFESSIONAL COURTESY, YOU CAN KEEP THE *BLUE* FILE. BUT YOU WILL NOT GET A RAISE THIS YEAR.
STUFF YOUR RAISE...
KRRAAKK!
...I QUIT.
CAN YOU PLEASE HELP ME? MY HUSBAND DIED, LEAVING US NOTHING. AND WELL...HE WAS IN A...TOUGH INDUSTRY...
WHAT INDUSTRY?
"THE MAD SCIENTIST/ SUPER VILLAIN INDUSTRY."
$150 000.00
ONE HUNDRED FIFTY THOUSAND DOLLARS
MS. WALTERS, THIS IS FOR SAVING MY FAMILY. WHAT ARE YOU GOING TO DO WITH THE MONEY?
"I HAVE SOME IDEAS..."
JENNIFER WALTERS Esq. Attorney-at-Law

CHARLES SOULE
writer

JAVIER PULIDO
artist

MUNTSA VICENTE
color artist

VC's CLAYTON COWLES
letterer

KEVIN WADA
cover artist

CONNER & MARTIN
variant cover artists

FRANKIE JOHNSON
assistant editor

JEANINE SCHAEFER & TOM BRENNAN
editors

AXEL ALONSO
editor in chief

JOE QUESADA
chief creative officer

DAN BUCKLEY
publisher

ALAN FINE
exec. producer

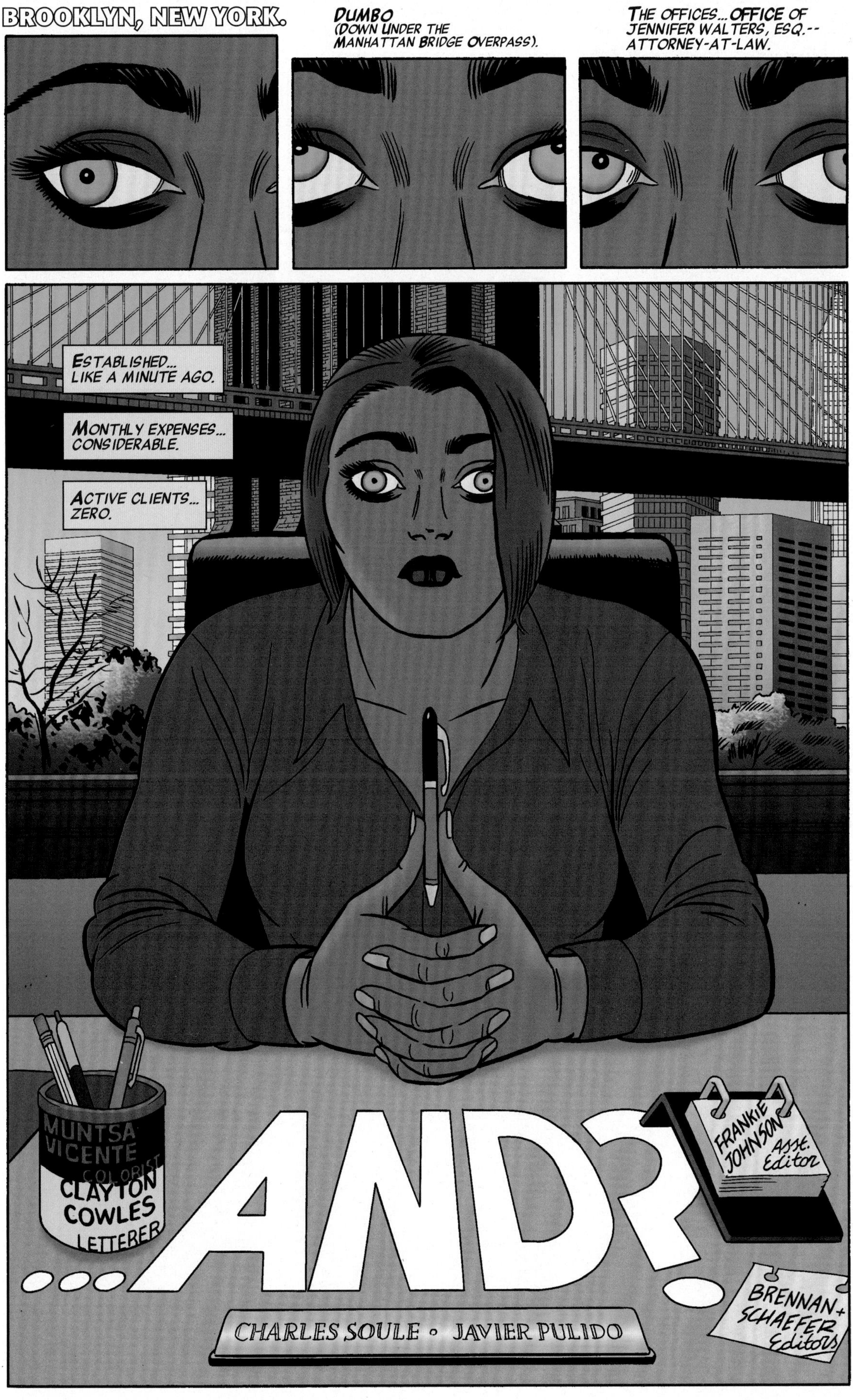

BROOKLYN, NEW YORK.
DUMBO (DOWN UNDER THE MANHATTAN BRIDGE OVERPASS).
THE OFFICES... OFFICE OF JENNIFER WALTERS, ESQ.-- ATTORNEY-AT-LAW.
ESTABLISHED... LIKE A MINUTE AGO.
MONTHLY EXPENSES... CONSIDERABLE.
ACTIVE CLIENTS... ZERO.
MUNTSA VICENTE COLORIST
CLAYTON COWLES LETTERER
FRANKIE JOHNSON Asst. Editor
...AND?
CHARLES SOULE • JAVIER PULIDO
BRENNAN + SCHAEFER Editors

ACTIVE CASES...

...ONE.

=SIGH.=

UNFORTUNATELY.

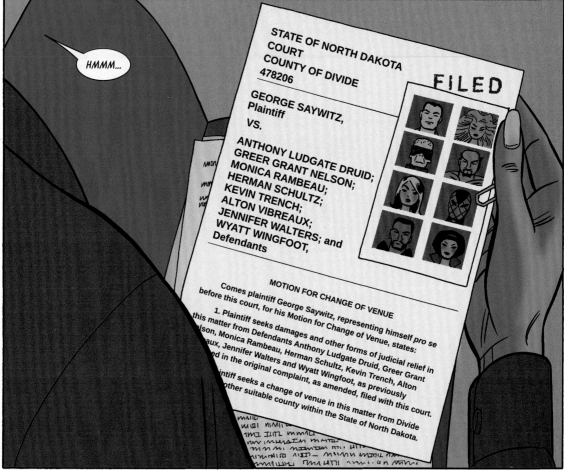

HMMM...

STATE OF NORTH DAKOTA COURT
COUNTY OF DIVIDE
478206

FILED

GEORGE SAYWITZ,
Plaintiff

VS.

ANTHONY LUDGATE DRUID;
GREER GRANT NELSON;
MONICA RAMBEAU;
HERMAN SCHULTZ;
KEVIN TRENCH;
ALTON VIBREAUX;
JENNIFER WALTERS; and
WYATT WINGFOOT,
Defendants

MOTION FOR CHANGE OF VENUE

Comes plaintiff George Saywitz, representing himself pro se before this court, for his Motion for Change of Venue, states:

1. Plaintiff seeks damages and other forms of judicial relief in this matter from Defendants Anthony Ludgate Druid, Greer Grant Nelson, Monica Rambeau, Herman Schultz, Kevin Trench, Alton Vibreaux, Jennifer Walters and Wyatt Wingfoot, as previously filed in the original complaint, as amended, filed with this court.

2. Plaintiff seeks a change of venue in this matter from Divide another suitable county within the State of North Dakota.

ARE YOU JENNIFER?

THAT'S ME. CAN I HELP YOU?

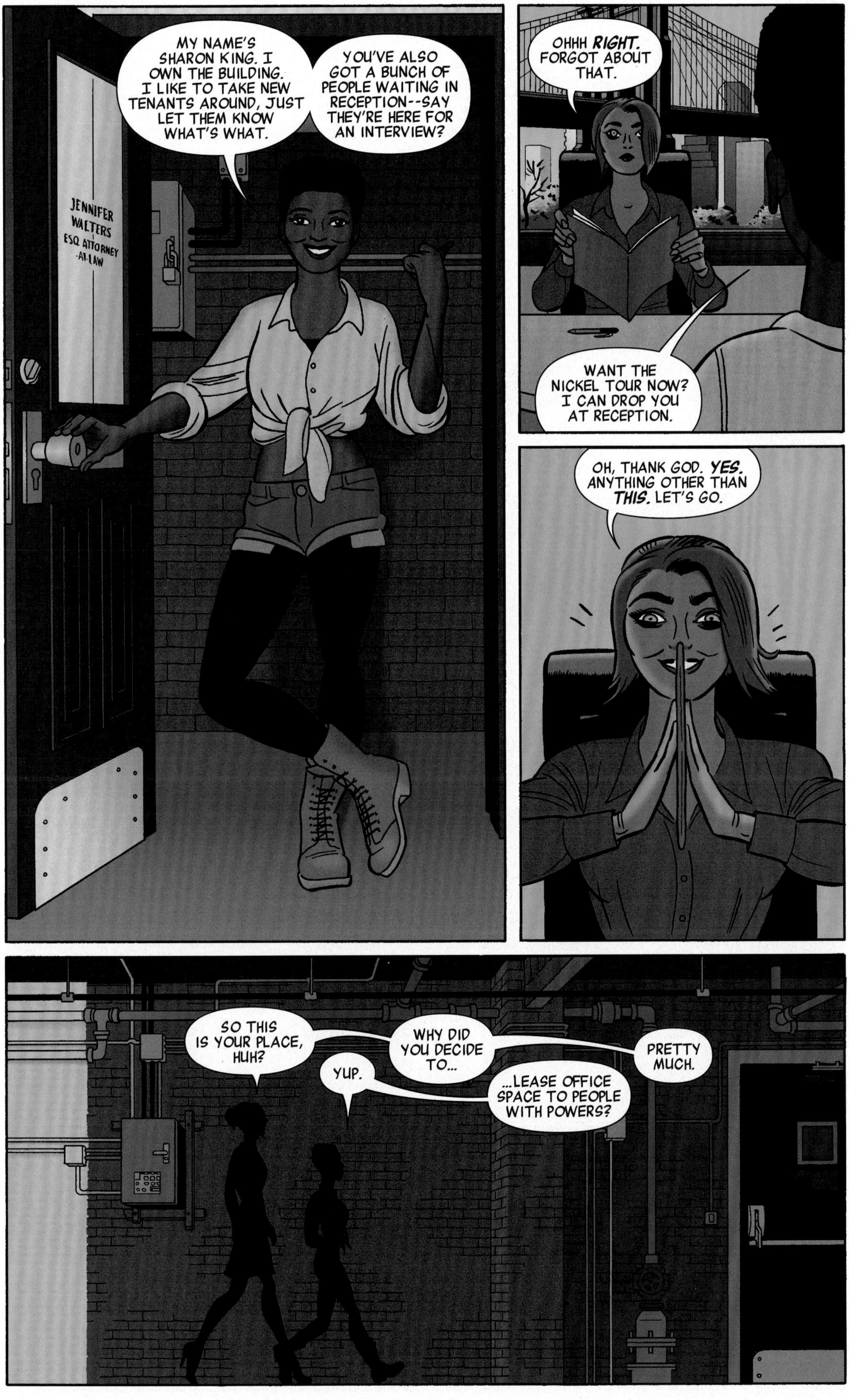
MY NAME'S SHARON KING. I OWN THE BUILDING. I LIKE TO TAKE NEW TENANTS AROUND, JUST LET THEM KNOW WHAT'S WHAT.
YOU'VE ALSO GOT A BUNCH OF PEOPLE WAITING IN RECEPTION--SAY THEY'RE HERE FOR AN INTERVIEW?
JENNIFER WALTERS ESQ. ATTORNEY -AT-LAW
OHHH *RIGHT.* FORGOT ABOUT THAT.
WANT THE NICKEL TOUR NOW? I CAN DROP YOU AT RECEPTION.
OH, THANK GOD. *YES.* ANYTHING OTHER THAN *THIS.* LET'S GO.
SO THIS IS YOUR PLACE, HUH?
YUP.
WHY DID YOU DECIDE TO...
...LEASE OFFICE SPACE TO PEOPLE WITH POWERS?
PRETTY MUCH.

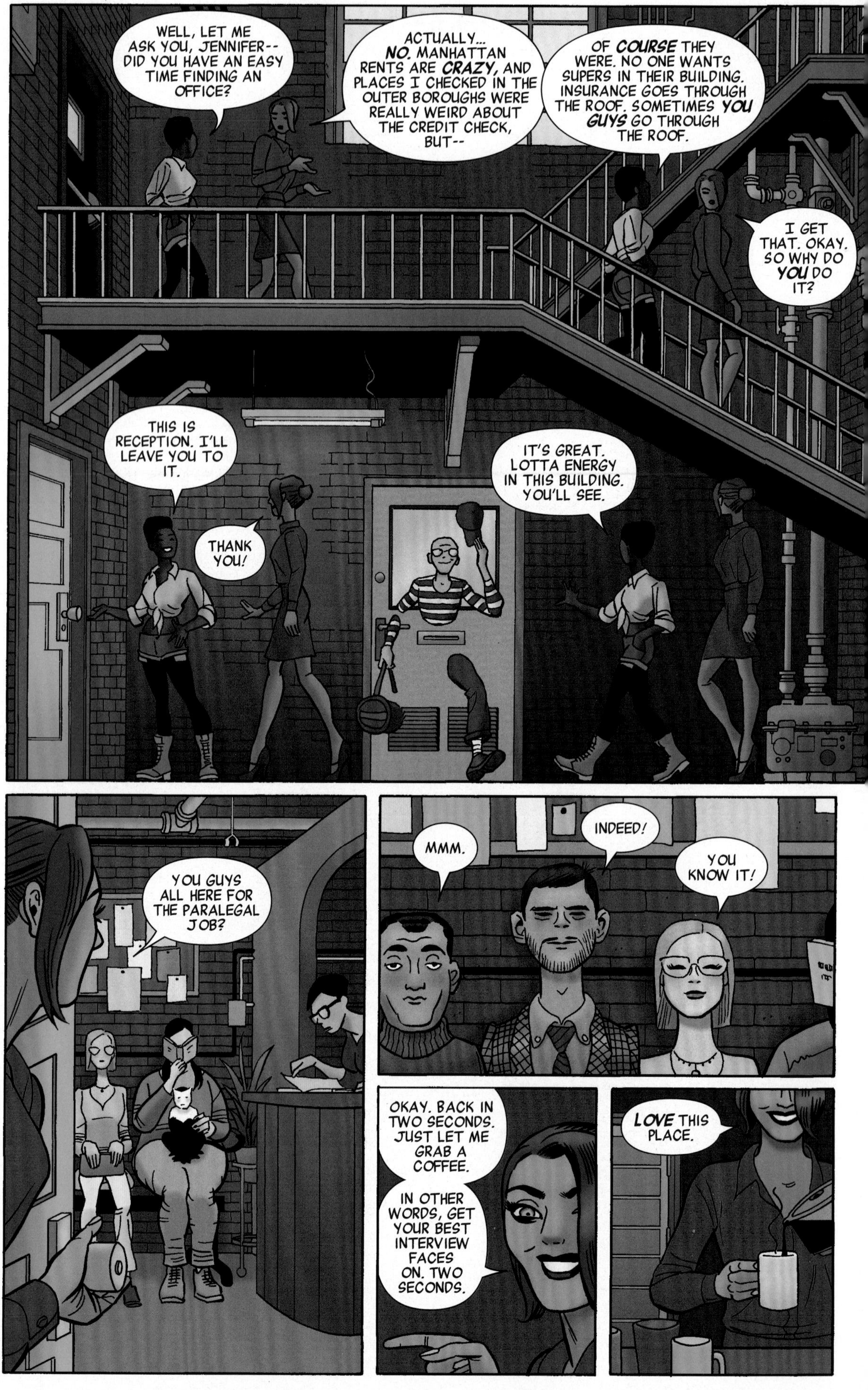

WELL, LET ME ASK YOU, JENNIFER-- DID YOU HAVE AN EASY TIME FINDING AN OFFICE?
ACTUALLY... NO. MANHATTAN RENTS ARE CRAZY, AND PLACES I CHECKED IN THE OUTER BOROUGHS WERE REALLY WEIRD ABOUT THE CREDIT CHECK, BUT--
OF COURSE THEY WERE. NO ONE WANTS SUPERS IN THEIR BUILDING. INSURANCE GOES THROUGH THE ROOF. SOMETIMES YOU GUYS GO THROUGH THE ROOF.
I GET THAT. OKAY. SO WHY DO YOU DO IT?
IT'S GREAT. LOTTA ENERGY IN THIS BUILDING. YOU'LL SEE.
THIS IS RECEPTION. I'LL LEAVE YOU TO IT.
THANK YOU!
YOU GUYS ALL HERE FOR THE PARALEGAL JOB?
MMM.
INDEED!
YOU KNOW IT!
OKAY. BACK IN TWO SECONDS. JUST LET ME GRAB A COFFEE.
IN OTHER WORDS, GET YOUR BEST INTERVIEW FACES ON. TWO SECONDS.
LOVE THIS PLACE.

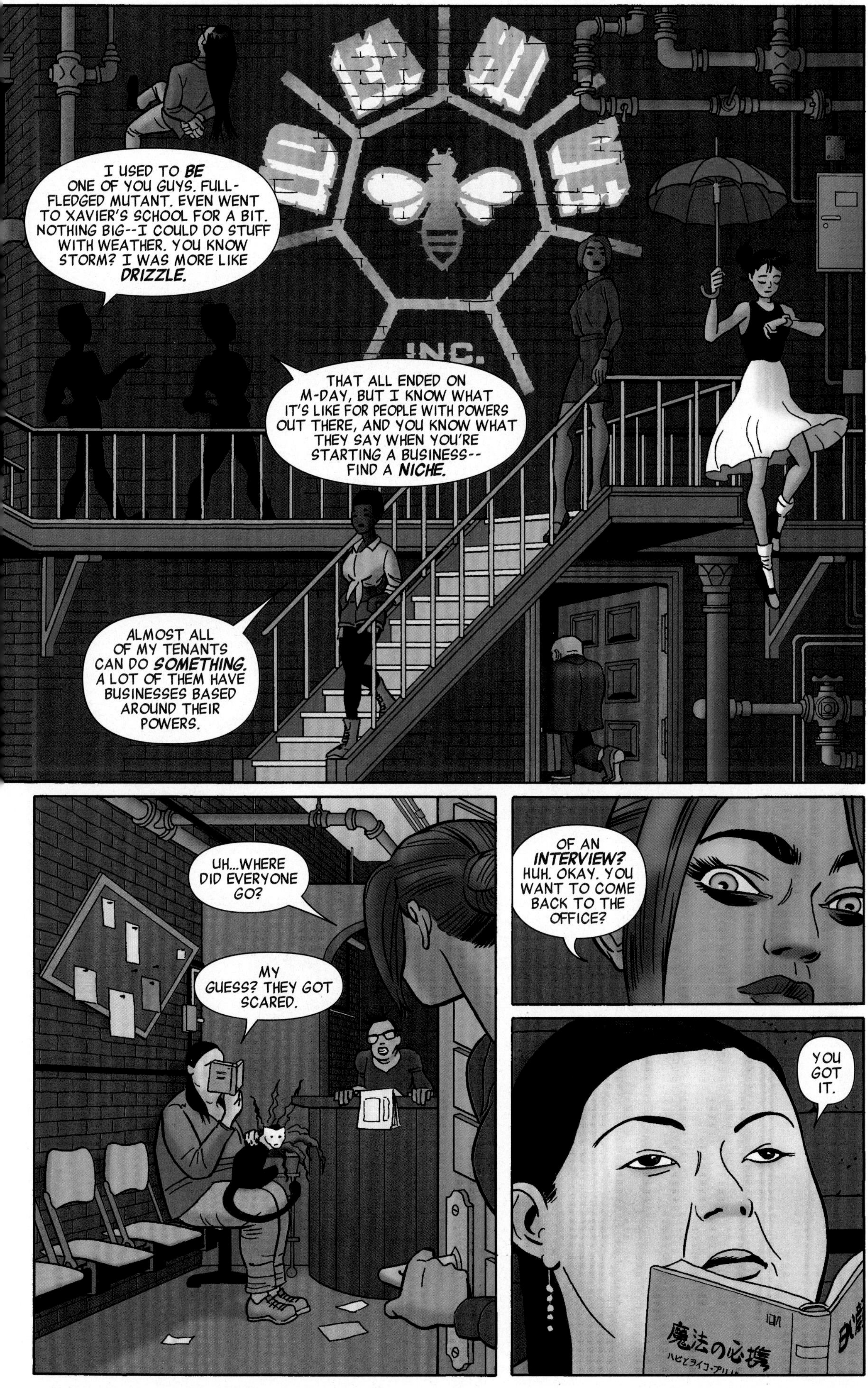
I USED TO *BE* ONE OF YOU GUYS. FULL-FLEDGED MUTANT. EVEN WENT TO XAVIER'S SCHOOL FOR A BIT. NOTHING BIG--I COULD DO STUFF WITH WEATHER. YOU KNOW STORM? I WAS MORE LIKE *DRIZZLE.*
INC.
THAT ALL ENDED ON M-DAY, BUT I KNOW WHAT IT'S LIKE FOR PEOPLE WITH POWERS OUT THERE, AND YOU KNOW WHAT THEY SAY WHEN YOU'RE STARTING A BUSINESS-- FIND A *NICHE.*
ALMOST ALL OF MY TENANTS CAN DO *SOMETHING.* A LOT OF THEM HAVE BUSINESSES BASED AROUND THEIR POWERS.
UH...WHERE DID EVERYONE GO?
MY GUESS? THEY GOT SCARED.
OF AN *INTERVIEW?* HUH. OKAY. YOU WANT TO COME BACK TO THE OFFICE?
YOU GOT IT.
魔法の必携

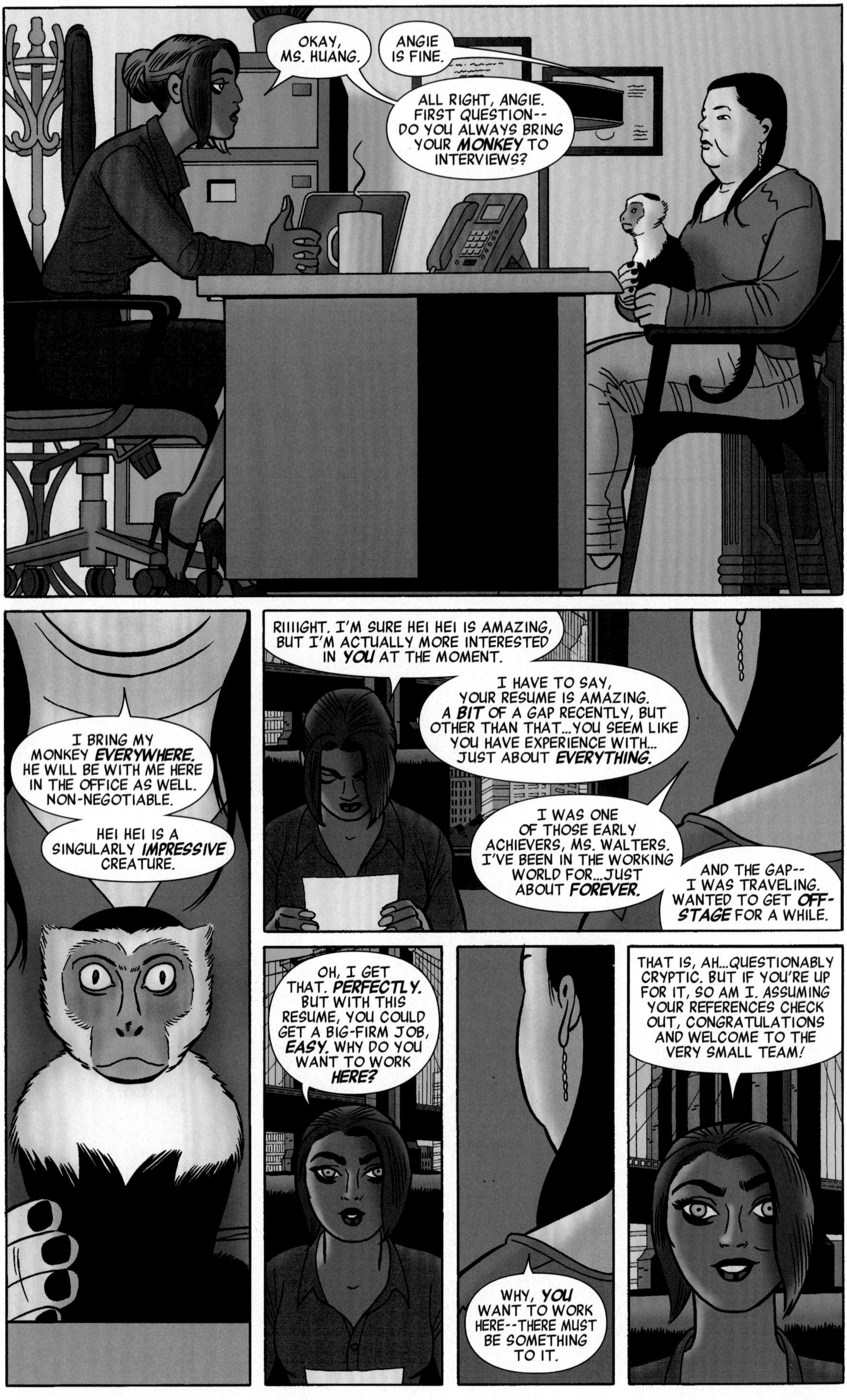
OKAY, MS. HUANG.
ANGIE IS FINE.
ALL RIGHT, ANGIE. FIRST QUESTION-- DO YOU ALWAYS BRING YOUR MONKEY TO INTERVIEWS?
I BRING MY MONKEY EVERYWHERE. HE WILL BE WITH ME HERE IN THE OFFICE AS WELL. NON-NEGOTIABLE.
HEI HEI IS A SINGULARLY IMPRESSIVE CREATURE.
RIIIIGHT. I'M SURE HEI HEI IS AMAZING, BUT I'M ACTUALLY MORE INTERESTED IN YOU AT THE MOMENT.
I HAVE TO SAY, YOUR RESUME IS AMAZING. A BIT OF A GAP RECENTLY, BUT OTHER THAN THAT...YOU SEEM LIKE YOU HAVE EXPERIENCE WITH... JUST ABOUT EVERYTHING.
I WAS ONE OF THOSE EARLY ACHIEVERS, MS. WALTERS. I'VE BEEN IN THE WORKING WORLD FOR...JUST ABOUT FOREVER.
AND THE GAP-- I WAS TRAVELING. WANTED TO GET OFF-STAGE FOR A WHILE.
OH, I GET THAT. PERFECTLY. BUT WITH THIS RESUME, YOU COULD GET A BIG-FIRM JOB, EASY. WHY DO YOU WANT TO WORK HERE?
...
WHY, YOU WANT TO WORK HERE--THERE MUST BE SOMETHING TO IT.
THAT IS, AH...QUESTIONABLY CRYPTIC. BUT IF YOU'RE UP FOR IT, SO AM I. ASSUMING YOUR REFERENCES CHECK OUT, CONGRATULATIONS AND WELCOME TO THE VERY SMALL TEAM!

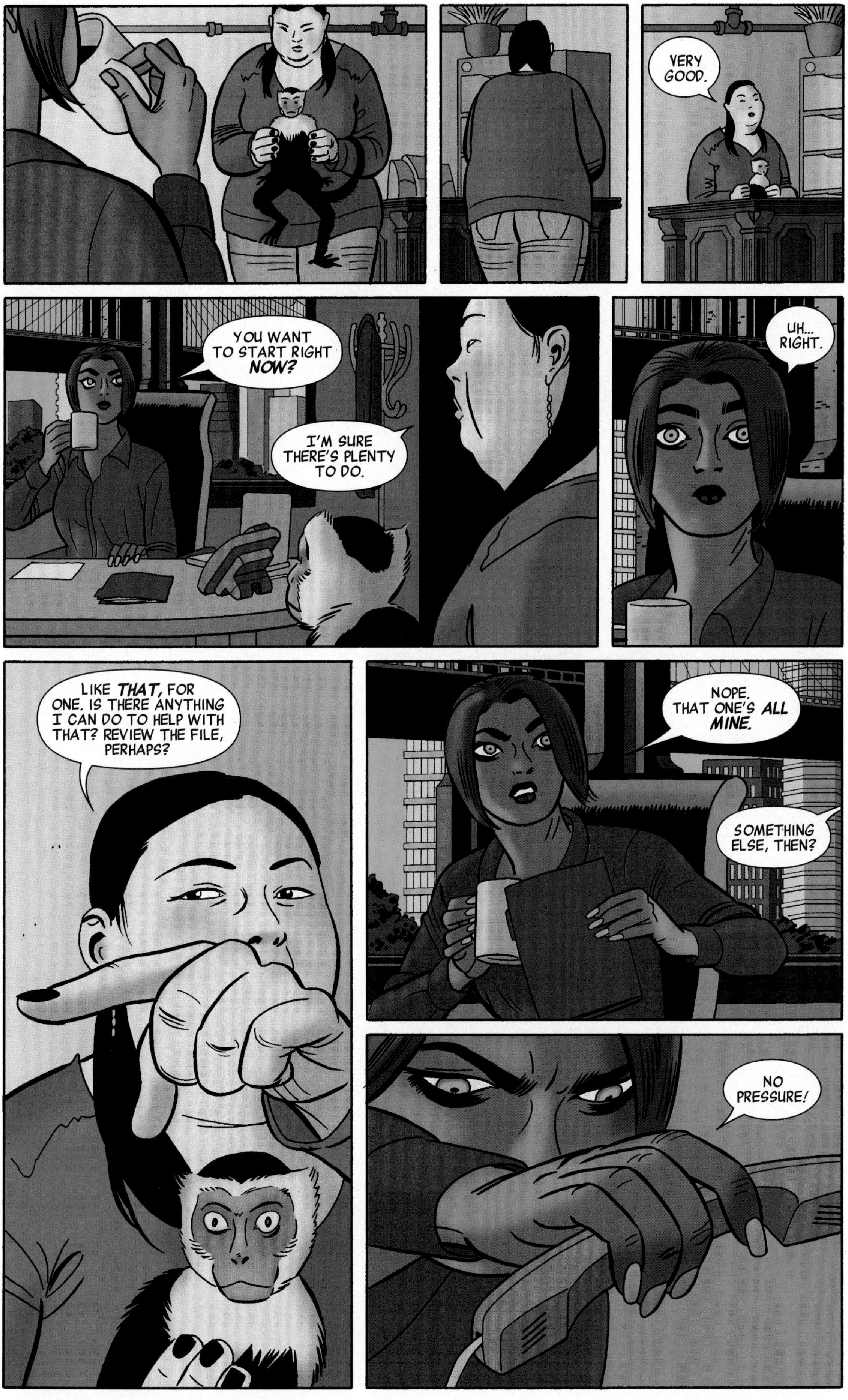
VERY GOOD.
YOU WANT TO START RIGHT NOW?
I'M SURE THERE'S PLENTY TO DO.
UH... RIGHT.
LIKE THAT, FOR ONE. IS THERE ANYTHING I CAN DO TO HELP WITH THAT? REVIEW THE FILE, PERHAPS?
NOPE. THAT ONE'S ALL MINE.
SOMETHING ELSE, THEN?
NO PRESSURE!

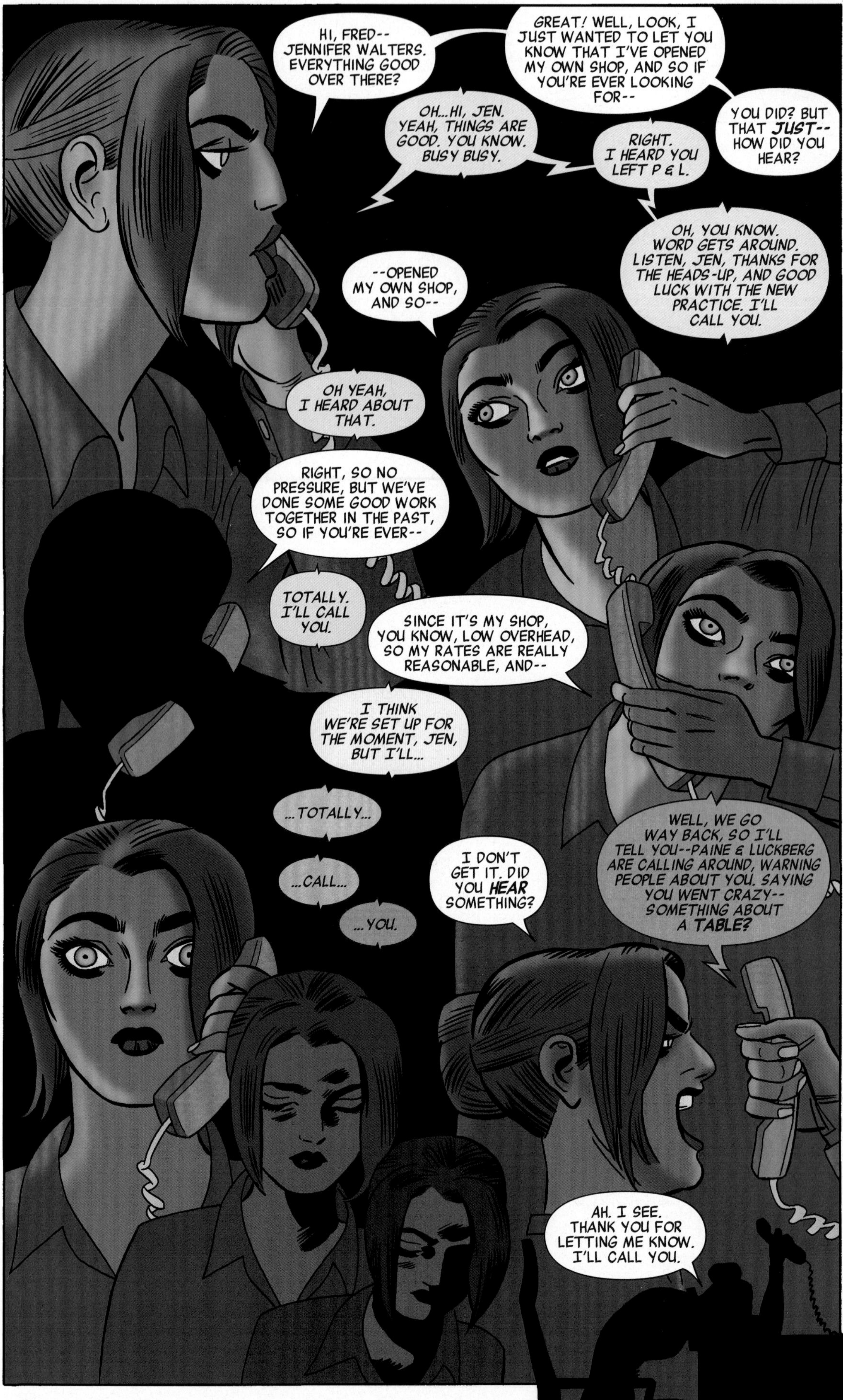
HI, FRED-- JENNIFER WALTERS. EVERYTHING GOOD OVER THERE?
OH...HI, JEN. YEAH, THINGS ARE GOOD. YOU KNOW. BUSY BUSY.
GREAT! WELL, LOOK, I JUST WANTED TO LET YOU KNOW THAT I'VE OPENED MY OWN SHOP, AND SO IF YOU'RE EVER LOOKING FOR--
RIGHT. I HEARD YOU LEFT P & L.
YOU DID? BUT THAT JUST-- HOW DID YOU HEAR?
OH, YOU KNOW. WORD GETS AROUND. LISTEN, JEN, THANKS FOR THE HEADS-UP, AND GOOD LUCK WITH THE NEW PRACTICE. I'LL CALL YOU.
--OPENED MY OWN SHOP, AND SO--
OH YEAH, I HEARD ABOUT THAT.
RIGHT, SO NO PRESSURE, BUT WE'VE DONE SOME GOOD WORK TOGETHER IN THE PAST, SO IF YOU'RE EVER--
TOTALLY. I'LL CALL YOU.
SINCE IT'S MY SHOP, YOU KNOW, LOW OVERHEAD, SO MY RATES ARE REALLY REASONABLE, AND--
I THINK WE'RE SET UP FOR THE MOMENT, JEN, BUT I'LL...
...TOTALLY...
...CALL...
...YOU.
I DON'T GET IT. DID YOU HEAR SOMETHING?
WELL, WE GO WAY BACK, SO I'LL TELL YOU--PAINE & LUCKBERG ARE CALLING AROUND, WARNING PEOPLE ABOUT YOU. SAYING YOU WENT CRAZY-- SOMETHING ABOUT A TABLE?
AH. I SEE. THANK YOU FOR LETTING ME KNOW. I'LL CALL YOU.

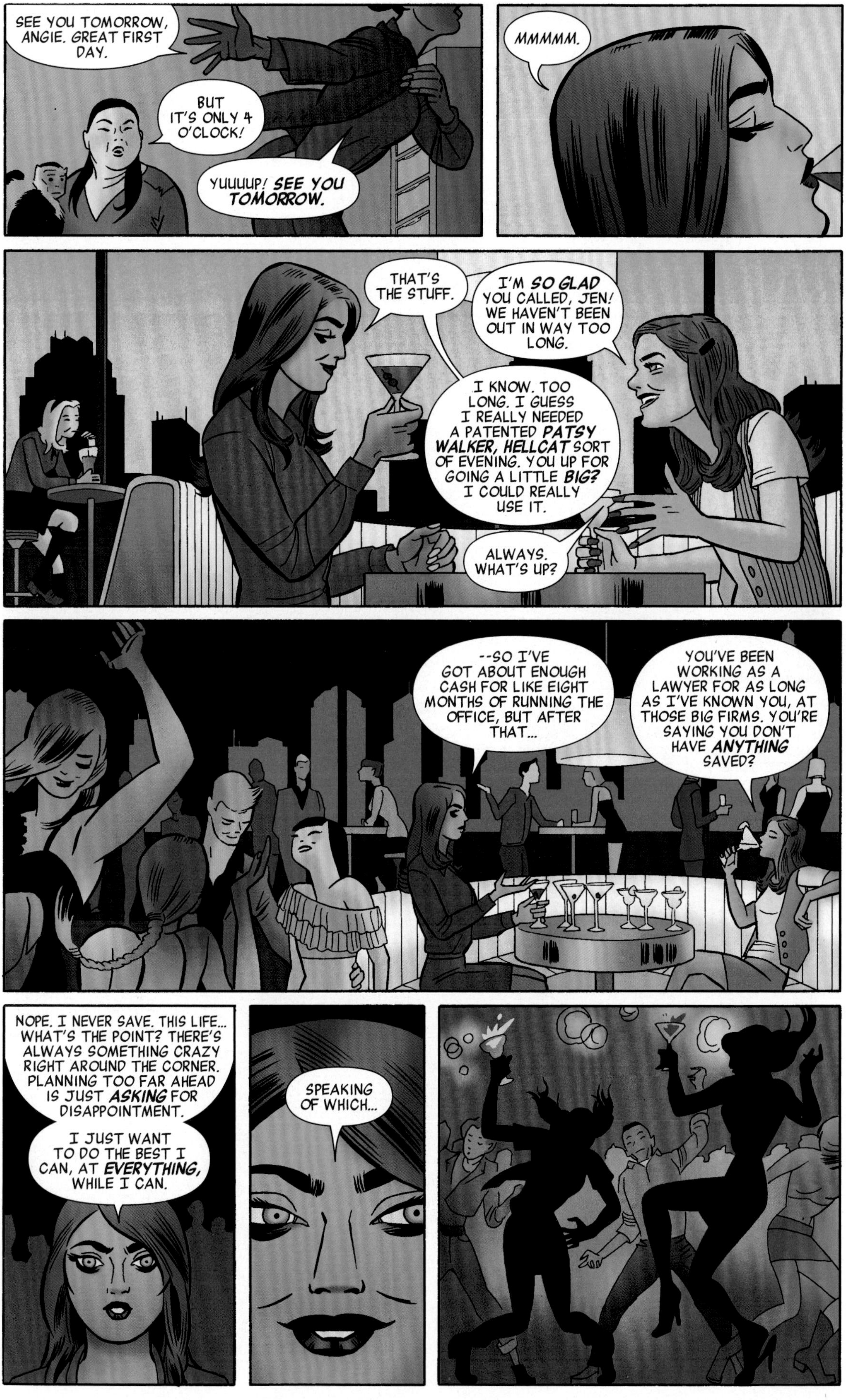
SEE YOU TOMORROW, ANGIE. GREAT FIRST DAY.
BUT IT'S ONLY 4 O'CLOCK!
YUUUUP! SEE YOU TOMORROW.
MMMMM.
THAT'S THE STUFF.
I'M SO GLAD YOU CALLED, JEN! WE HAVEN'T BEEN OUT IN WAY TOO LONG.
I KNOW. TOO LONG. I GUESS I REALLY NEEDED A PATENTED PATSY WALKER, HELLCAT SORT OF EVENING. YOU UP FOR GOING A LITTLE BIG? I COULD REALLY USE IT.
ALWAYS. WHAT'S UP?
--SO I'VE GOT ABOUT ENOUGH CASH FOR LIKE EIGHT MONTHS OF RUNNING THE OFFICE, BUT AFTER THAT...
YOU'VE BEEN WORKING AS A LAWYER FOR AS LONG AS I'VE KNOWN YOU, AT THOSE BIG FIRMS. YOU'RE SAYING YOU DON'T HAVE ANYTHING SAVED?
NOPE. I NEVER SAVE. THIS LIFE... WHAT'S THE POINT? THERE'S ALWAYS SOMETHING CRAZY RIGHT AROUND THE CORNER. PLANNING TOO FAR AHEAD IS JUST ASKING FOR DISAPPOINTMENT.
I JUST WANT TO DO THE BEST I CAN, AT EVERYTHING, WHILE I CAN.
SPEAKING OF WHICH...

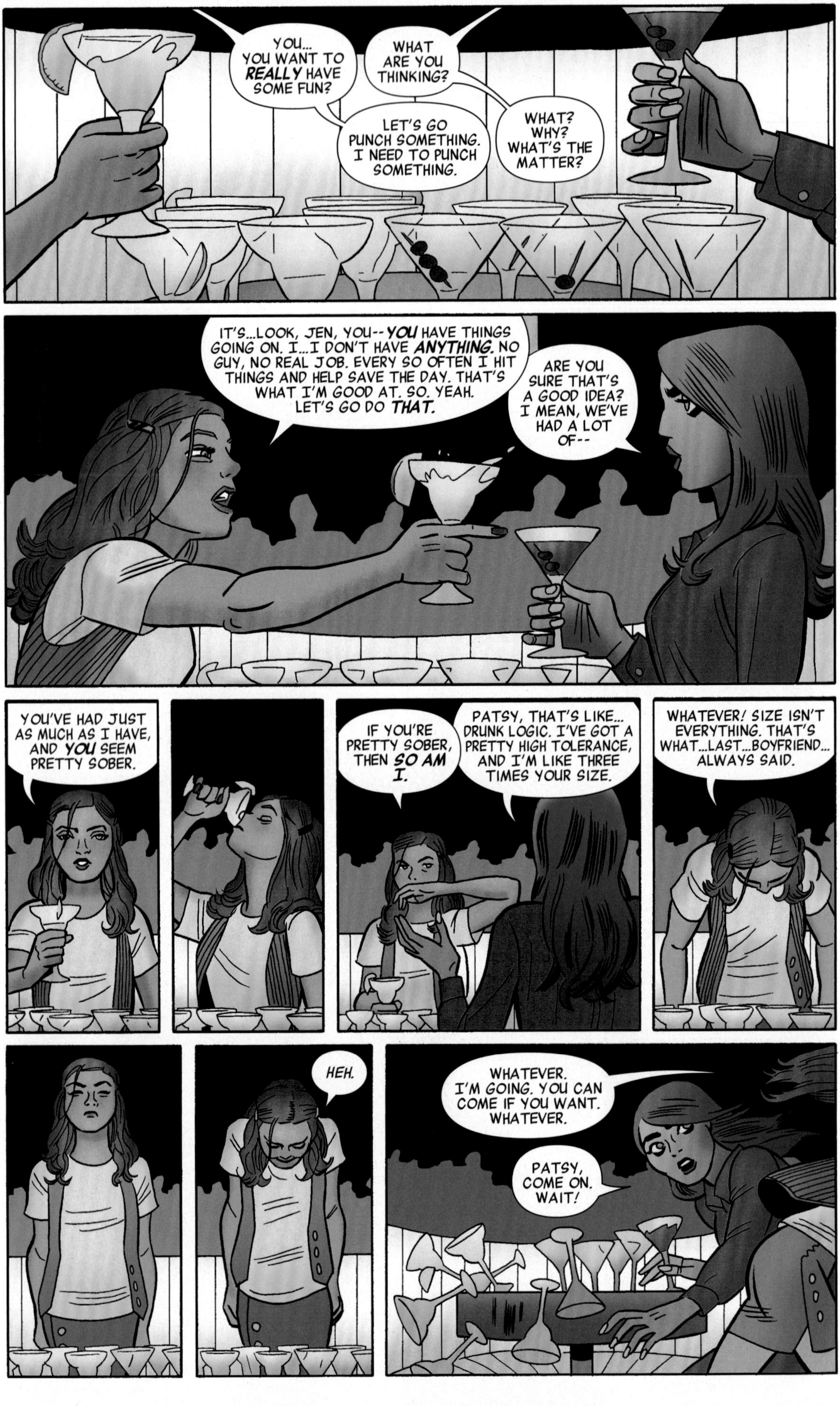
YOU... YOU WANT TO REALLY HAVE SOME FUN?
WHAT ARE YOU THINKING?
LET'S GO PUNCH SOMETHING. I NEED TO PUNCH SOMETHING.
WHAT? WHY? WHAT'S THE MATTER?
IT'S...LOOK, JEN, YOU--YOU HAVE THINGS GOING ON. I...I DON'T HAVE ANYTHING. NO GUY, NO REAL JOB. EVERY SO OFTEN I HIT THINGS AND HELP SAVE THE DAY. THAT'S WHAT I'M GOOD AT. SO. YEAH. LET'S GO DO THAT.
ARE YOU SURE THAT'S A GOOD IDEA? I MEAN, WE'VE HAD A LOT OF--
YOU'VE HAD JUST AS MUCH AS I HAVE, AND YOU SEEM PRETTY SOBER.
IF YOU'RE PRETTY SOBER, THEN SO AM I.
PATSY, THAT'S LIKE... DRUNK LOGIC. I'VE GOT A PRETTY HIGH TOLERANCE, AND I'M LIKE THREE TIMES YOUR SIZE.
WHATEVER! SIZE ISN'T EVERYTHING. THAT'S WHAT...LAST...BOYFRIEND... ALWAYS SAID.
HEH.
WHATEVER. I'M GOING. YOU CAN COME IF YOU WANT. WHATEVER.
PATSY, COME ON. WAIT!

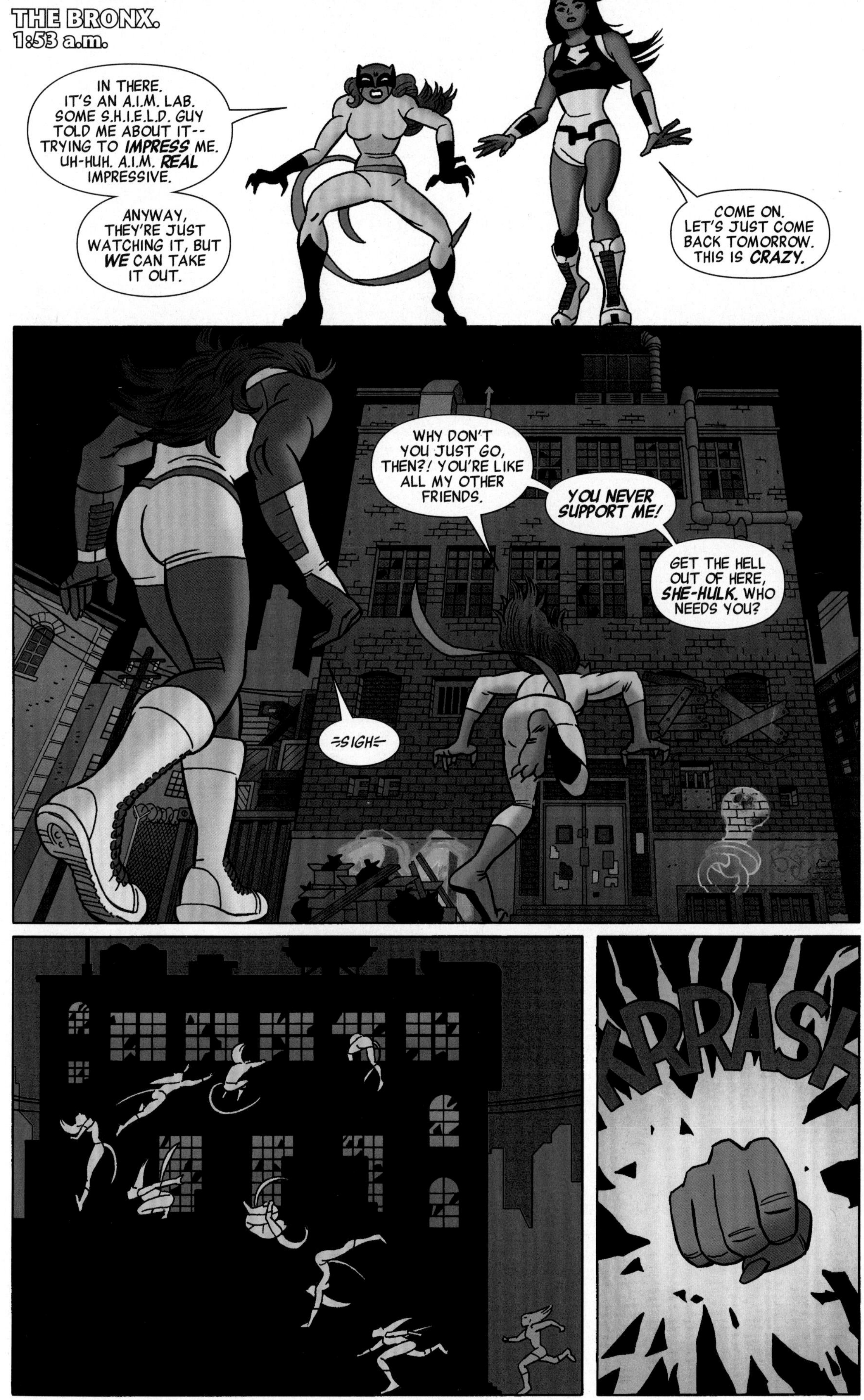
THE BRONX.
1:53 a.m.
IN THERE. IT'S AN A.I.M. LAB. SOME S.H.I.E.L.D. GUY TOLD ME ABOUT IT-- TRYING TO IMPRESS ME. UH-HUH. A.I.M. REAL IMPRESSIVE.
ANYWAY, THEY'RE JUST WATCHING IT, BUT WE CAN TAKE IT OUT.
COME ON. LET'S JUST COME BACK TOMORROW. THIS IS CRAZY.
WHY DON'T YOU JUST GO, THEN?! YOU'RE LIKE ALL MY OTHER FRIENDS.
YOU NEVER SUPPORT ME!
GET THE HELL OUT OF HERE, SHE-HULK. WHO NEEDS YOU?
=SIGH=
KRRASK

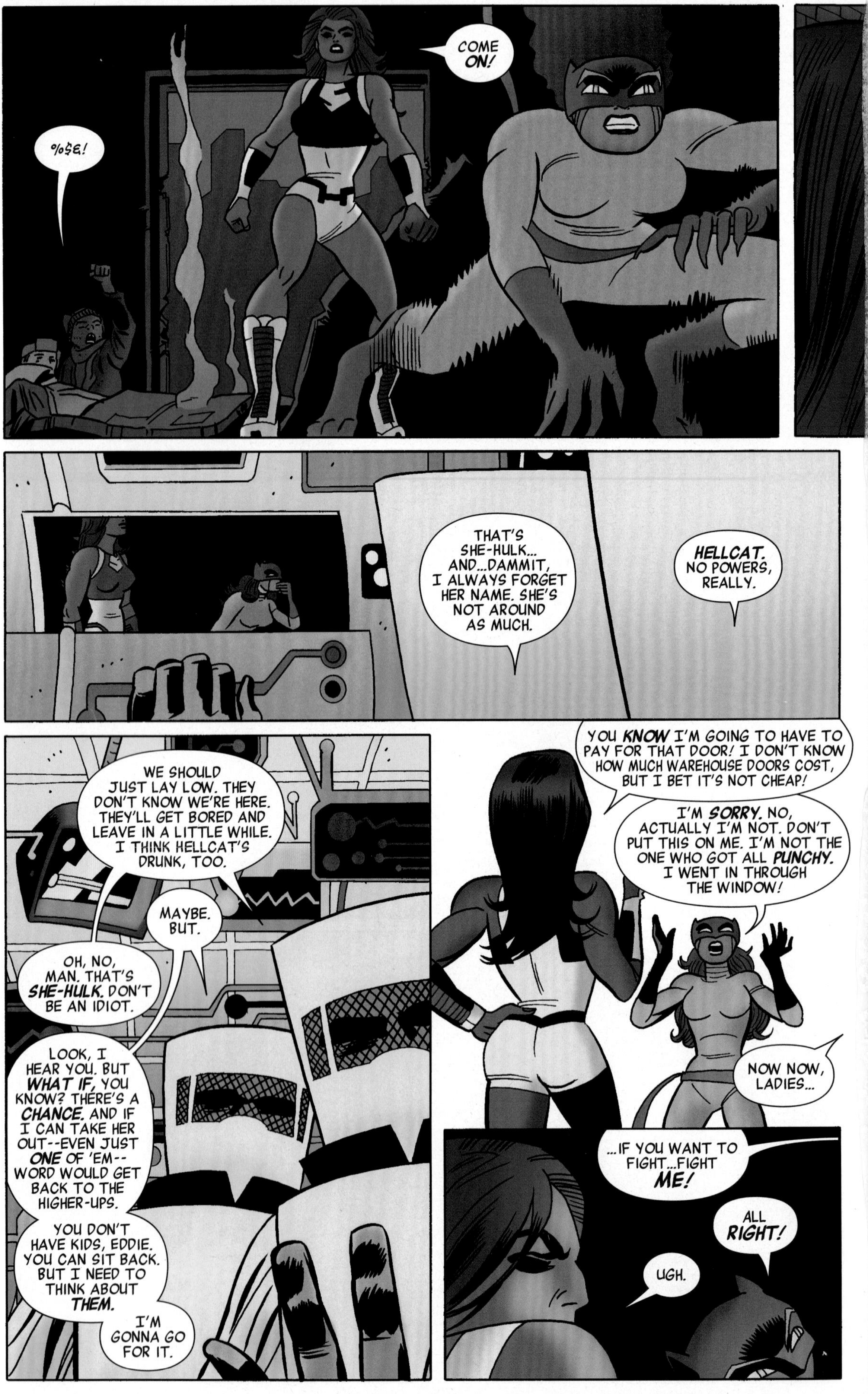

COME ON!
%$&!
THAT'S SHE-HULK... AND...DAMMIT, I ALWAYS FORGET HER NAME. SHE'S NOT AROUND AS MUCH.
HELLCAT. NO POWERS, REALLY.
WE SHOULD JUST LAY LOW. THEY DON'T KNOW WE'RE HERE. THEY'LL GET BORED AND LEAVE IN A LITTLE WHILE. I THINK HELLCAT'S DRUNK, TOO.
MAYBE. BUT.
OH, NO, MAN. THAT'S SHE-HULK. DON'T BE AN IDIOT.
LOOK, I HEAR YOU. BUT WHAT IF, YOU KNOW? THERE'S A CHANCE. AND IF I CAN TAKE HER OUT--EVEN JUST ONE OF 'EM--WORD WOULD GET BACK TO THE HIGHER-UPS.
YOU DON'T HAVE KIDS, EDDIE. YOU CAN SIT BACK. BUT I NEED TO THINK ABOUT THEM.
I'M GONNA GO FOR IT.
YOU KNOW I'M GOING TO HAVE TO PAY FOR THAT DOOR! I DON'T KNOW HOW MUCH WAREHOUSE DOORS COST, BUT I BET IT'S NOT CHEAP!
I'M SORRY. NO, ACTUALLY I'M NOT. DON'T PUT THIS ON ME. I'M NOT THE ONE WHO GOT ALL PUNCHY. I WENT IN THROUGH THE WINDOW!
NOW NOW, LADIES...
...IF YOU WANT TO FIGHT...FIGHT ME!
ALL RIGHT!
UGH.

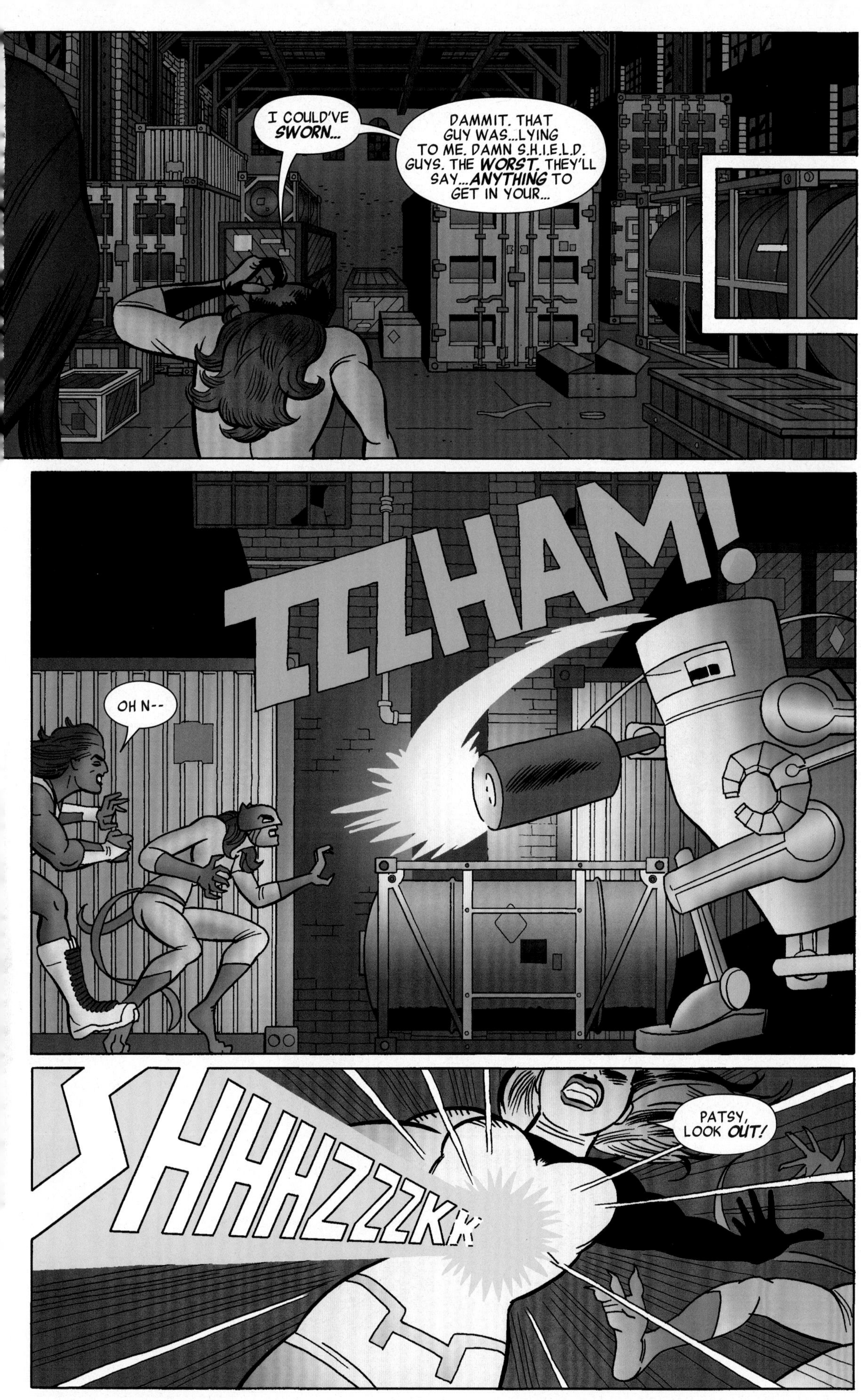
I COULD'VE **SWORN...**
DAMMIT. THAT GUY WAS...LYING TO ME. DAMN S.H.I.E.L.D. GUYS. THE **WORST.** THEY'LL SAY...**ANYTHING** TO GET IN YOUR...
ZZZHAM!
OH N--
SHHHZZZKK
PATSY, LOOK **OUT!**

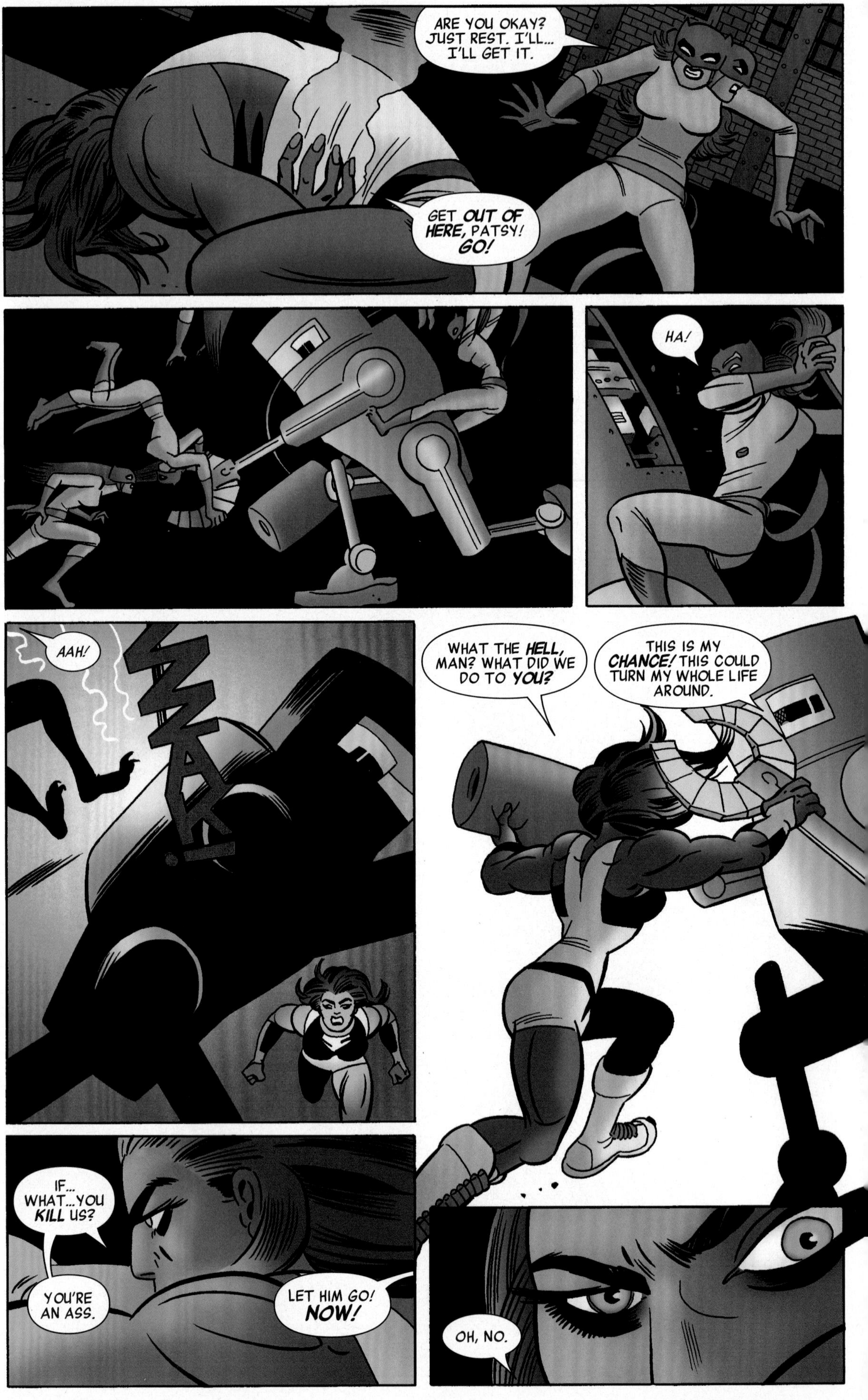

ARE YOU OKAY? JUST REST. I'LL... I'LL GET IT.
GET **OUT OF HERE,** PATSY! ***GO!***
HA!
AAH!
WAAK!
WHAT THE **HELL,** MAN? WHAT DID WE DO TO **YOU?**
THIS IS MY ***CHANCE!*** THIS COULD TURN MY WHOLE LIFE AROUND.
IF... WHAT...YOU **KILL** US?
YOU'RE AN ASS.
LET HIM GO! ***NOW!***
OH, NO.

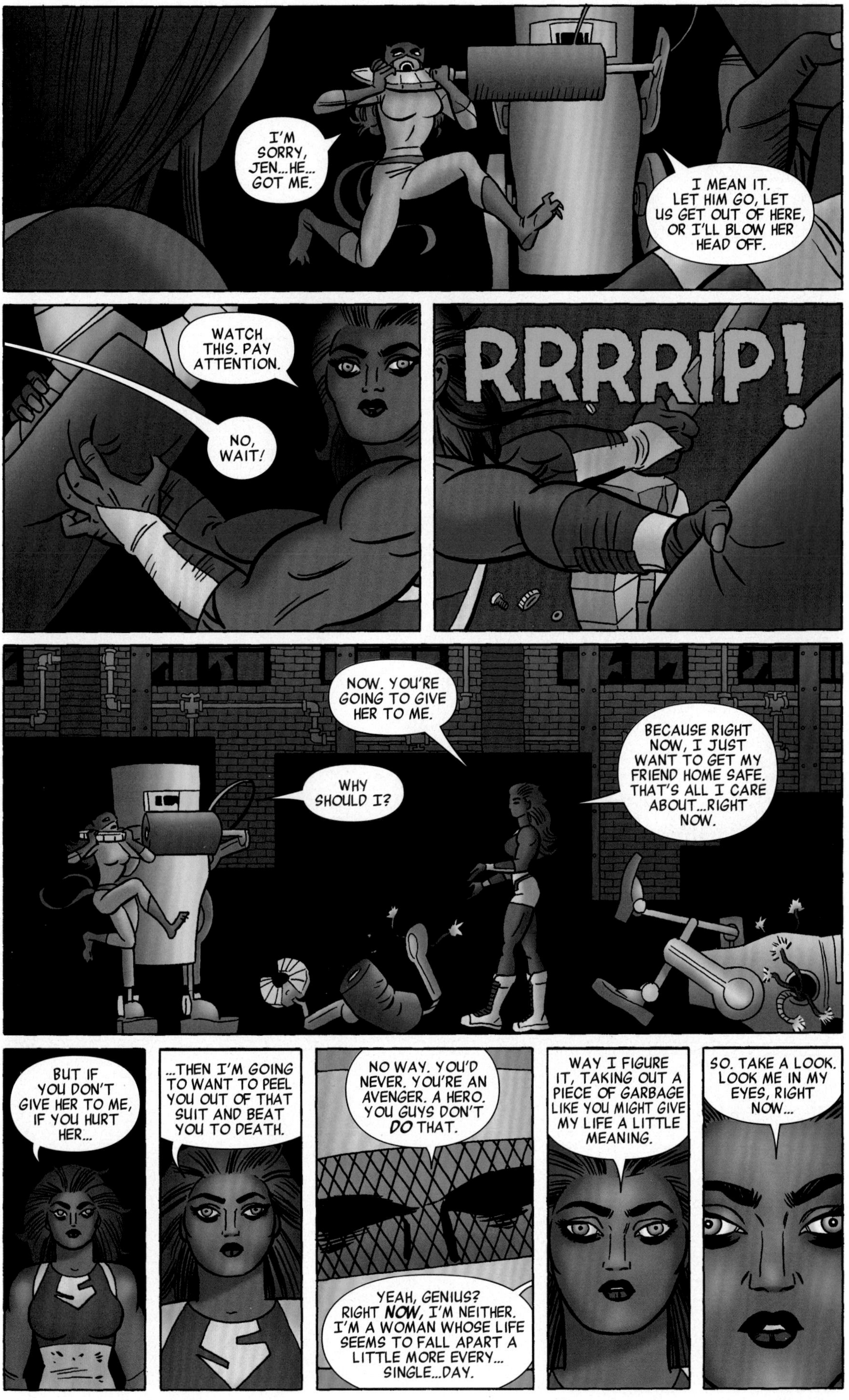
I'M SORRY, JEN...HE... GOT ME.
I MEAN IT. LET HIM GO, LET US GET OUT OF HERE, OR I'LL BLOW HER HEAD OFF.
WATCH THIS. PAY ATTENTION.
NO, WAIT!
RRRRIP!
NOW. YOU'RE GOING TO GIVE HER TO ME.
WHY SHOULD I?
BECAUSE RIGHT NOW, I JUST WANT TO GET MY FRIEND HOME SAFE. THAT'S ALL I CARE ABOUT...RIGHT NOW.
BUT IF YOU DON'T GIVE HER TO ME, IF YOU HURT HER...
...THEN I'M GOING TO WANT TO PEEL YOU OUT OF THAT SUIT AND BEAT YOU TO DEATH.
NO WAY. YOU'D NEVER. YOU'RE AN AVENGER. A HERO. YOU GUYS DON'T *DO* THAT.
YEAH, GENIUS? RIGHT **NOW**, I'M NEITHER. I'M A WOMAN WHOSE LIFE SEEMS TO FALL APART A LITTLE MORE EVERY... SINGLE...DAY.
WAY I FIGURE IT, TAKING OUT A PIECE OF GARBAGE LIKE YOU MIGHT GIVE MY LIFE A LITTLE MEANING.
SO. TAKE A LOOK. LOOK ME IN MY EYES, RIGHT NOW...

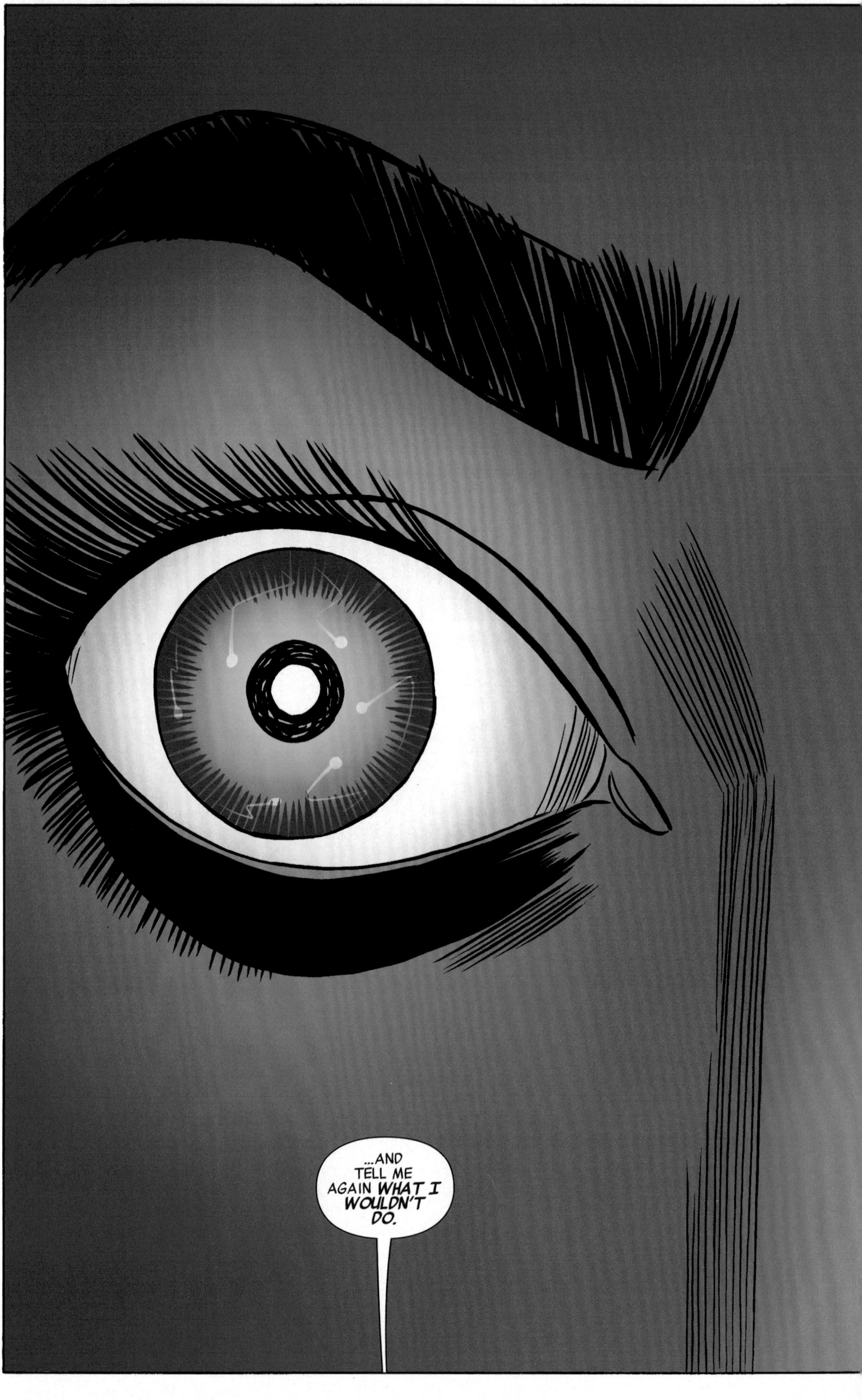
...AND TELL ME AGAIN WHAT I WOULDN'T DO.

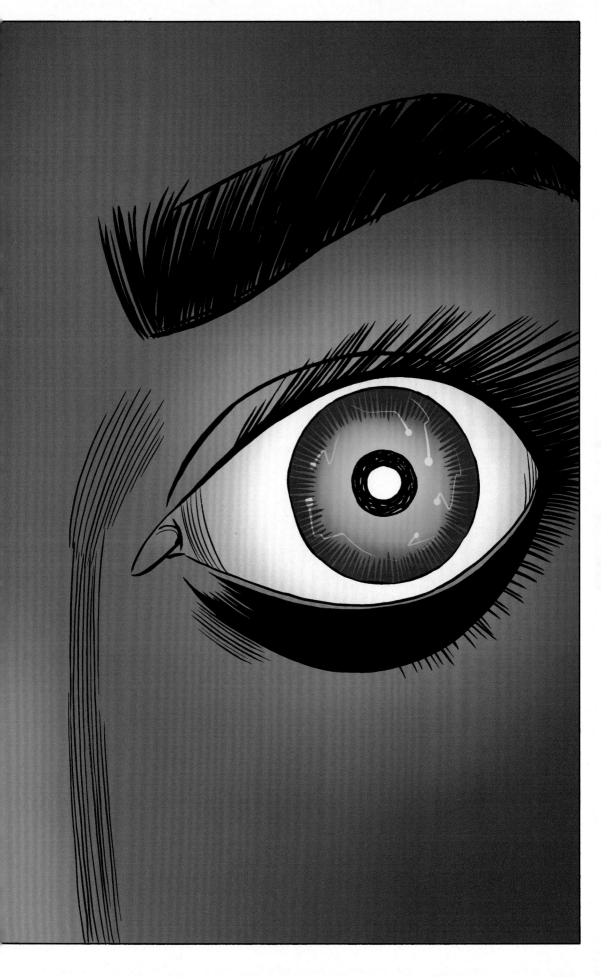

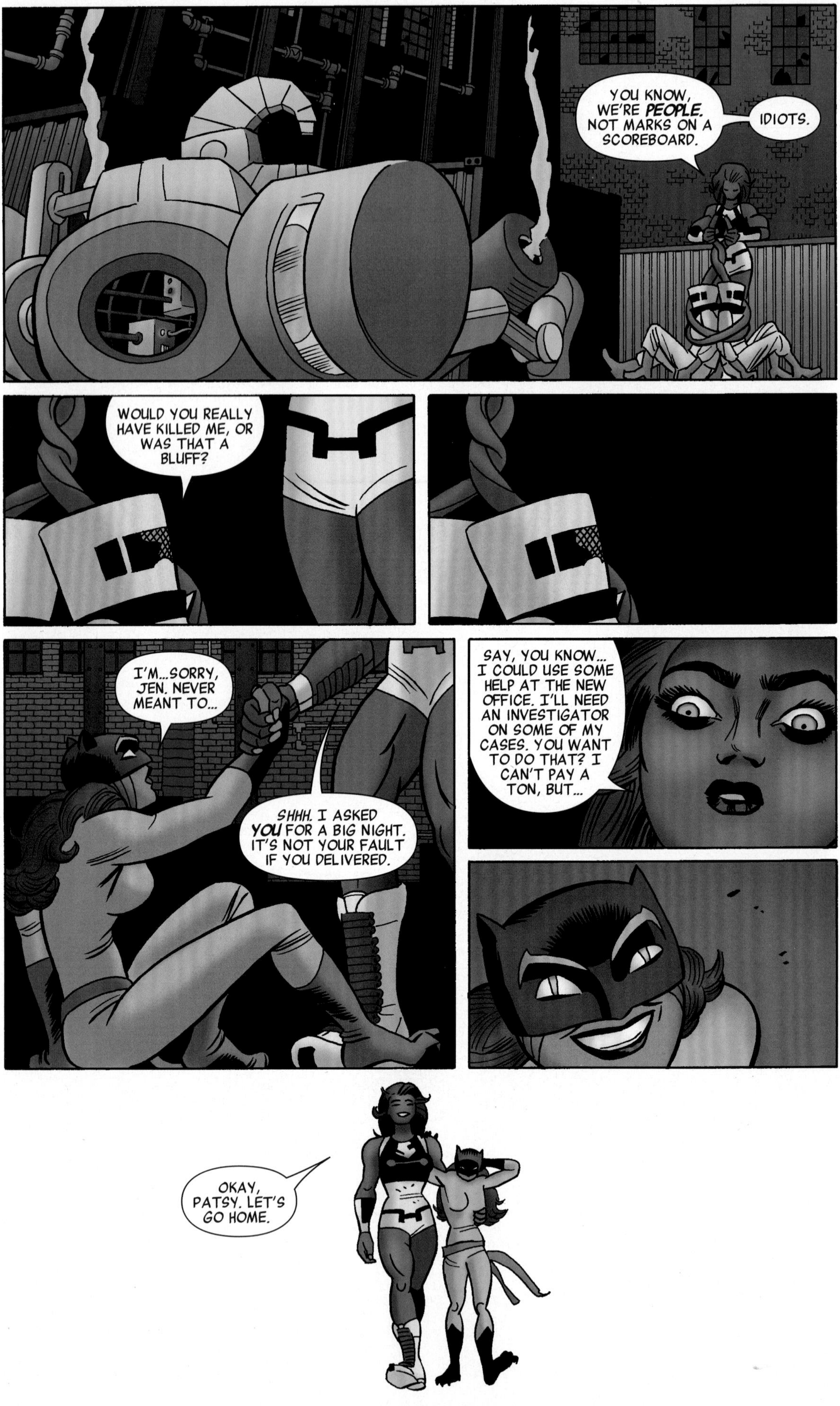
YOU KNOW, WE'RE PEOPLE. NOT MARKS ON A SCOREBOARD.
IDIOTS.
WOULD YOU REALLY HAVE KILLED ME, OR WAS THAT A BLUFF?
I'M...SORRY, JEN. NEVER MEANT TO...
SHHH. I ASKED YOU FOR A BIG NIGHT. IT'S NOT YOUR FAULT IF YOU DELIVERED.
SAY, YOU KNOW... I COULD USE SOME HELP AT THE NEW OFFICE. I'LL NEED AN INVESTIGATOR ON SOME OF MY CASES. YOU WANT TO DO THAT? I CAN'T PAY A TON, BUT...
OKAY, PATSY. LET'S GO HOME.

UUUUGH.

BEEP BEEP BEEP BEEP BEEP!

TAP!

MS. WALTERS! IT'S NEARLY 11 A.M.!

SO? IT'S NOT LIKE WE HAVE ANY CLIENTS. AND ANYWAY, I'M THE BOSS. I GET TO COME IN WHENEVER I WANT. ESPECIALLY WHEN THERE'S NOTHING TO DO.

YOU ARE MISTAKEN.

UH...I DON'T THINK SO. PRETTY SURE THAT'S MY NAME ON THE DOOR.

NOT ABOUT *THAT*, MS. WALTERS. THE *OTHER* PART. IN YOUR OFFICE. RIGHT NOW. HE'S BEEN WAITING FOR AN HOUR!

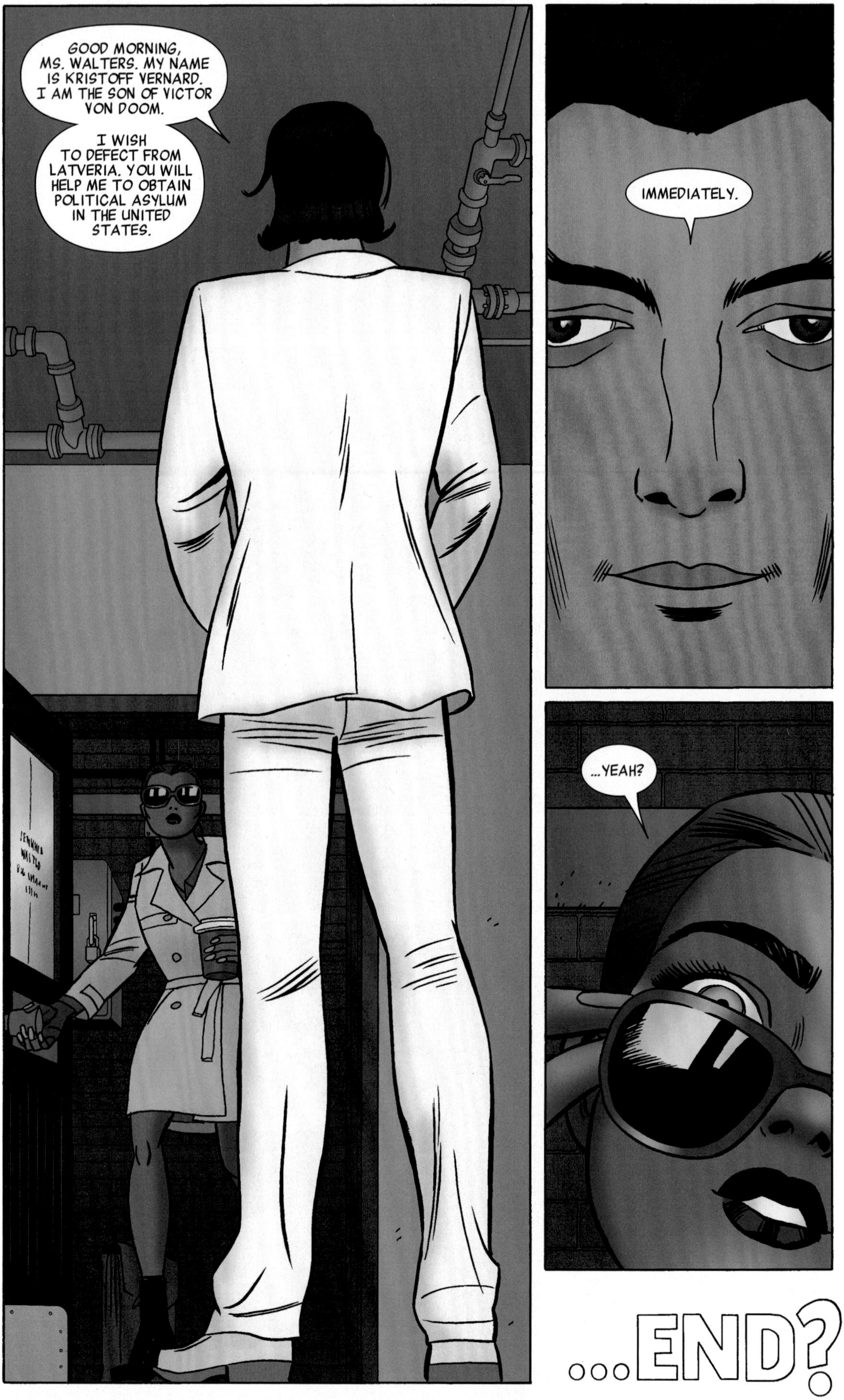
GOOD MORNING, MS. WALTERS. MY NAME IS KRISTOFF VERNARD. I AM THE SON OF VICTOR VON DOOM.
I WISH TO DEFECT FROM LATVERIA. YOU WILL HELP ME TO OBTAIN POLITICAL ASYLUM IN THE UNITED STATES.
IMMEDIATELY.
...YEAH?
...END?

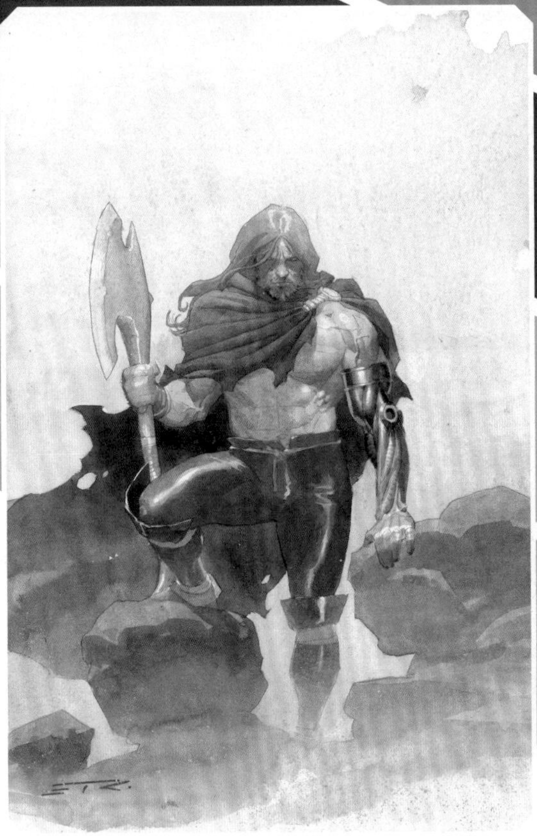

THOR #2
Variant by Esad Ribic

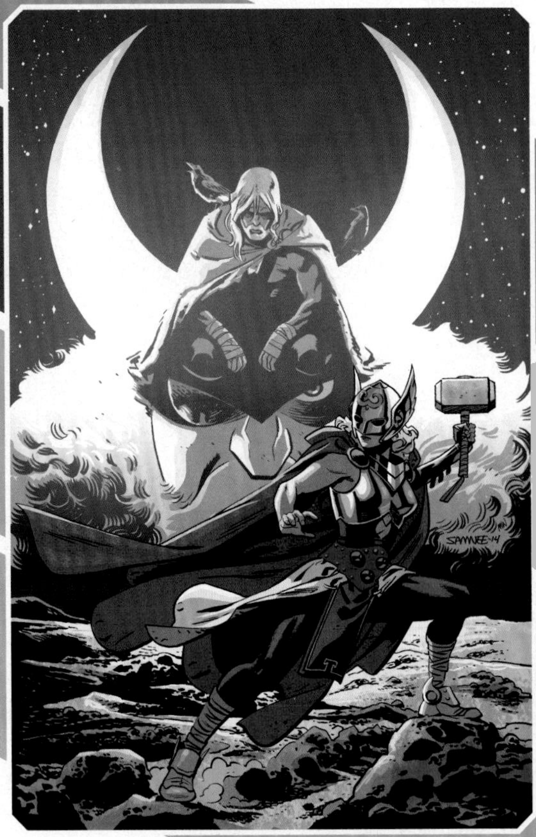

THOR #2
Variant by Chris Samnee & Matthew Wilson

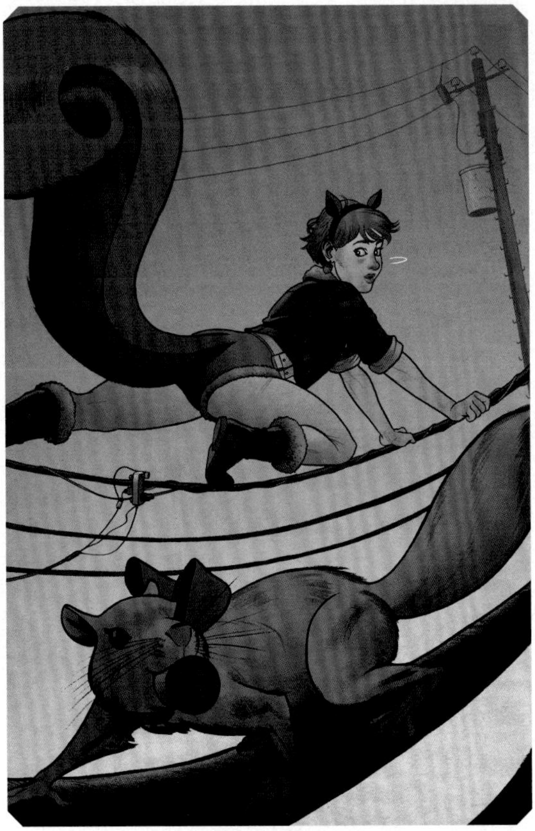

THE UNBEATABLE SQUIRREL GIRL #2
Variant by Joe Quinones

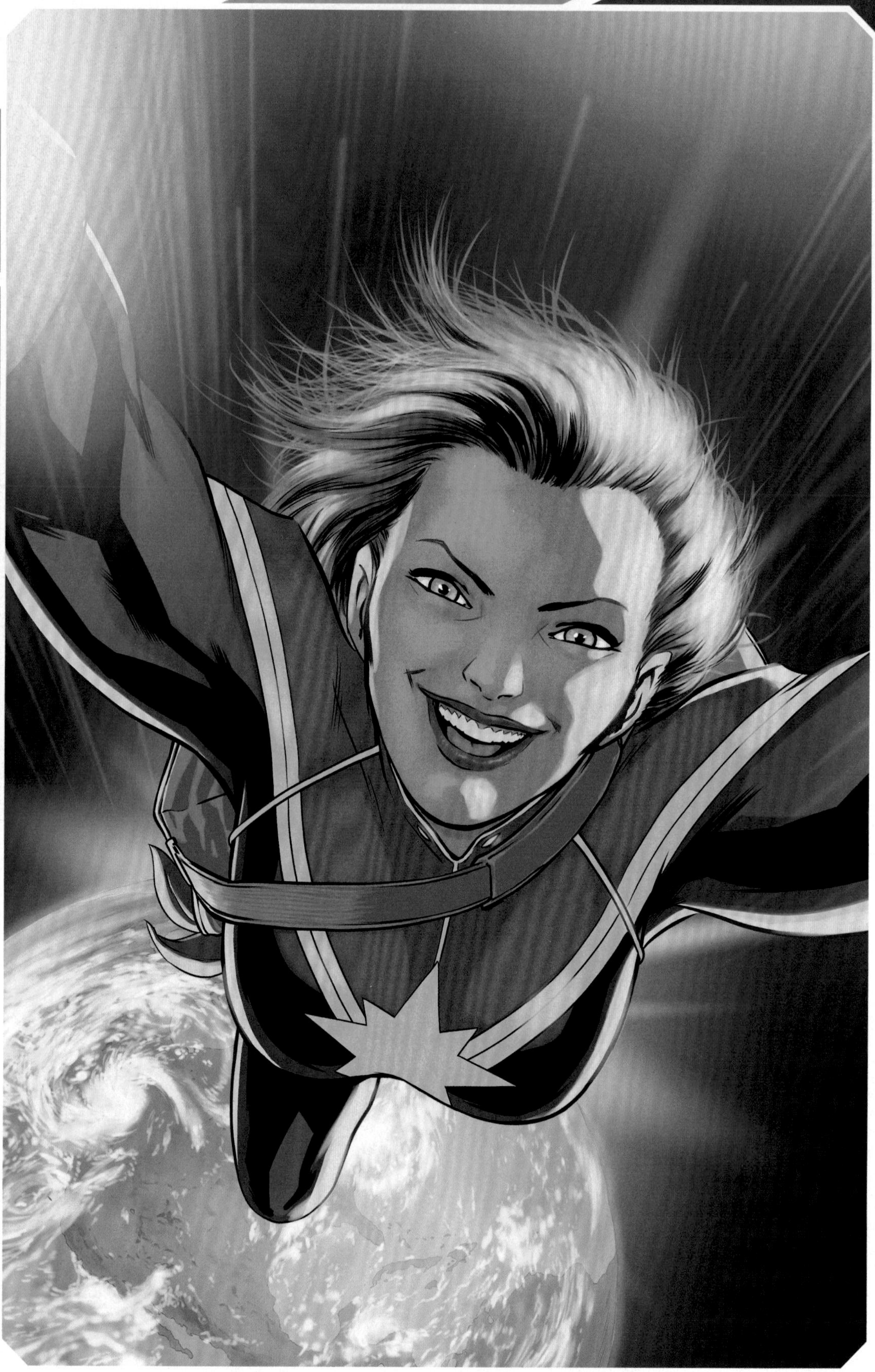

CAPTAIN MARVEL #2

When former U.S. Air Force pilot, Carol Danvers was caught in the explosion of an alien device called the Psyche-Magnitron, she was transformed into one of the world's most powerful super beings. She now uses her abilities to protect her planet and fight for justice as an Avenger. She is Earth's Mightiest Hero...she is...

CAPTAIN MARVEL

PREVIOUSLY
Captain Marvel became an Avenger in space.

HIGHER, FURTHER, FASTER, MORE. PART TWO

KELLY SUE DeCONNICK
WRITER

DAVID LOPEZ
ART

LEE LOUGHRIDGE
COLOR ART

VC'S JOE CARAMAGNA
LETTERER

DAVID LOPEZ
COVER ARTIST

J.G. JONES & LAURA MARTIN
VARIANT COVER ARTISTS

DEVIN LEWIS
ASSISTANT EDITOR

SANA AMANAT
EDITOR

STEPHEN WACKER & NICK LOWE
SENIOR EDITORS

AXEL ALONSO
EDITOR IN CHIEF

JOE QUESADA
CHIEF CREATIVE OFFICER

DAN BUCKLEY
PUBLISHER

ALAN FINE
EXEC. PRODUCER

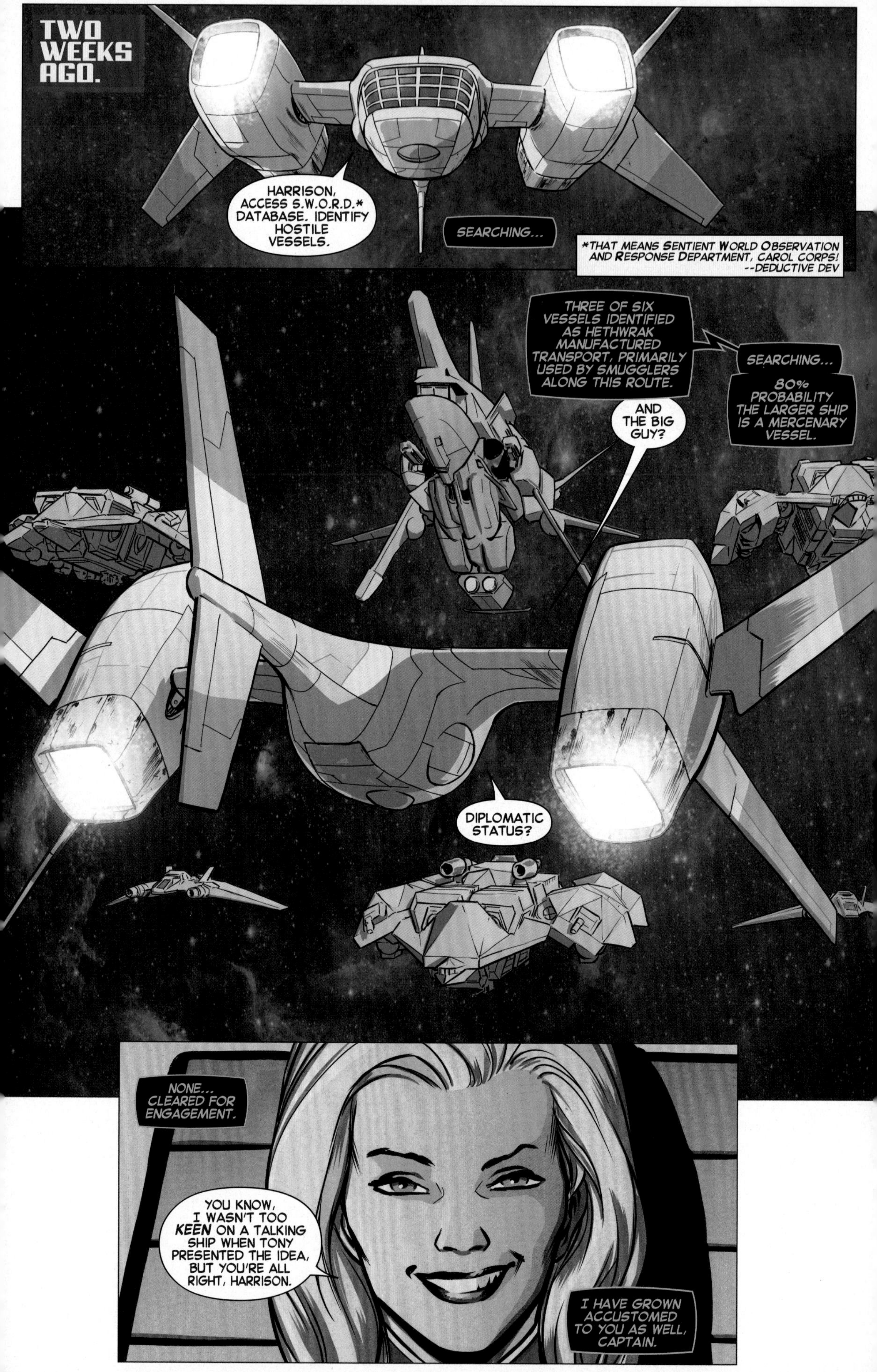
TWO WEEKS AGO.
HARRISON, ACCESS S.W.O.R.D.* DATABASE. IDENTIFY HOSTILE VESSELS.
SEARCHING...
*THAT MEANS SENTIENT WORLD OBSERVATION AND RESPONSE DEPARTMENT, CAROL CORPS! --DEDUCTIVE DEV
THREE OF SIX VESSELS IDENTIFIED AS HETHWRAK MANUFACTURED TRANSPORT, PRIMARILY USED BY SMUGGLERS ALONG THIS ROUTE.
AND THE BIG GUY?
SEARCHING...
80% PROBABILITY THE LARGER SHIP IS A MERCENARY VESSEL.
DIPLOMATIC STATUS?
NONE... CLEARED FOR ENGAGEMENT.
YOU KNOW, I WASN'T TOO KEEN ON A TALKING SHIP WHEN TONY PRESENTED THE IDEA, BUT YOU'RE ALL RIGHT, HARRISON.
I HAVE GROWN ACCUSTOMED TO YOU AS WELL, CAPTAIN.

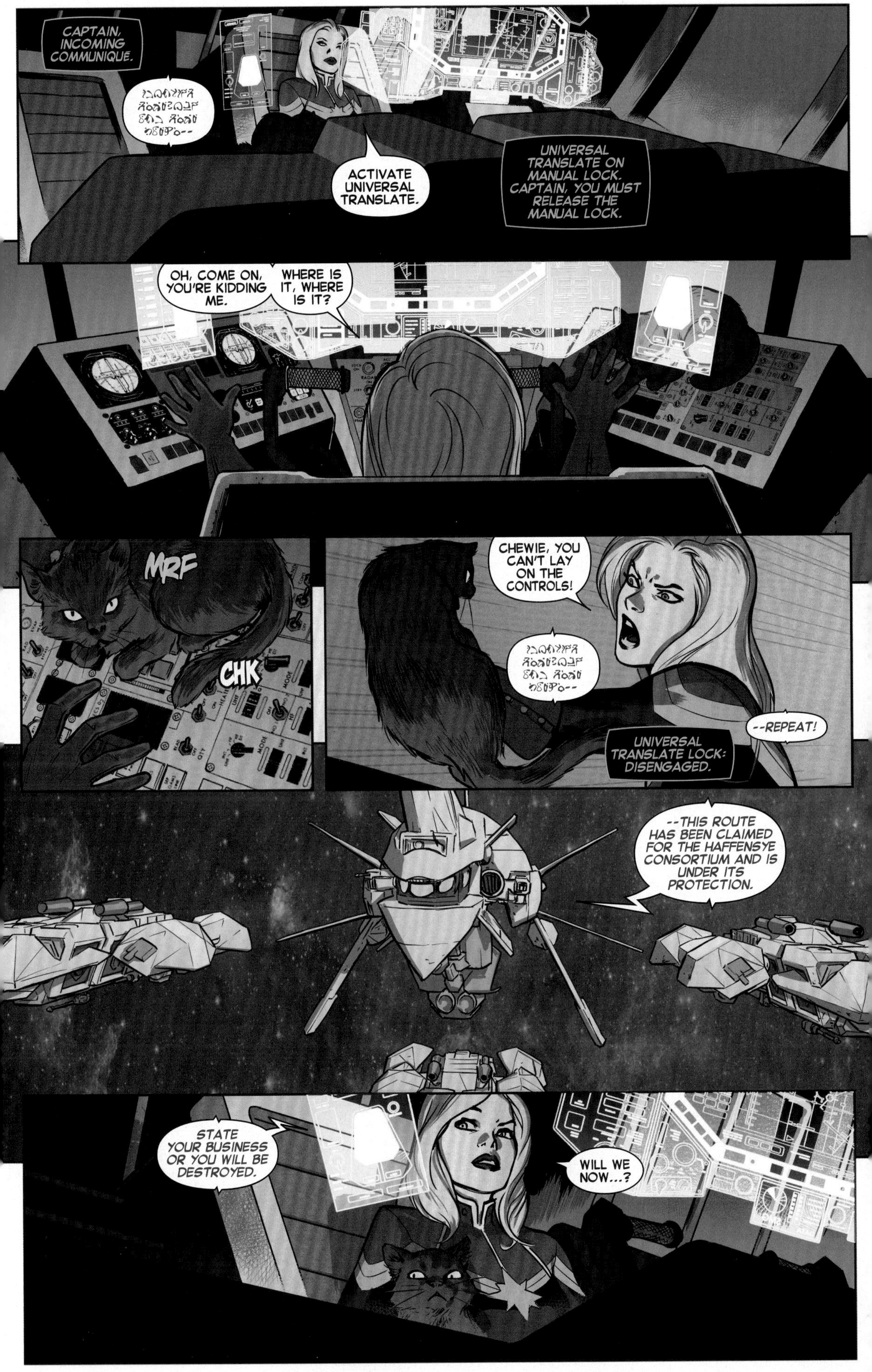

CAPTAIN, INCOMING COMMUNIQUE.
ACTIVATE UNIVERSAL TRANSLATE.
UNIVERSAL TRANSLATE ON MANUAL LOCK. CAPTAIN, YOU MUST RELEASE THE MANUAL LOCK.
OH, COME ON, YOU'RE KIDDING ME.
WHERE IS IT, WHERE IS IT?
MRF
CHK
CHEWIE, YOU CAN'T LAY ON THE CONTROLS!
UNIVERSAL TRANSLATE LOCK: DISENGAGED.
--REPEAT!
--THIS ROUTE HAS BEEN CLAIMED FOR THE HAFFENSYE CONSORTIUM AND IS UNDER ITS PROTECTION.
STATE YOUR BUSINESS OR YOU WILL BE DESTROYED.
WILL WE NOW...?

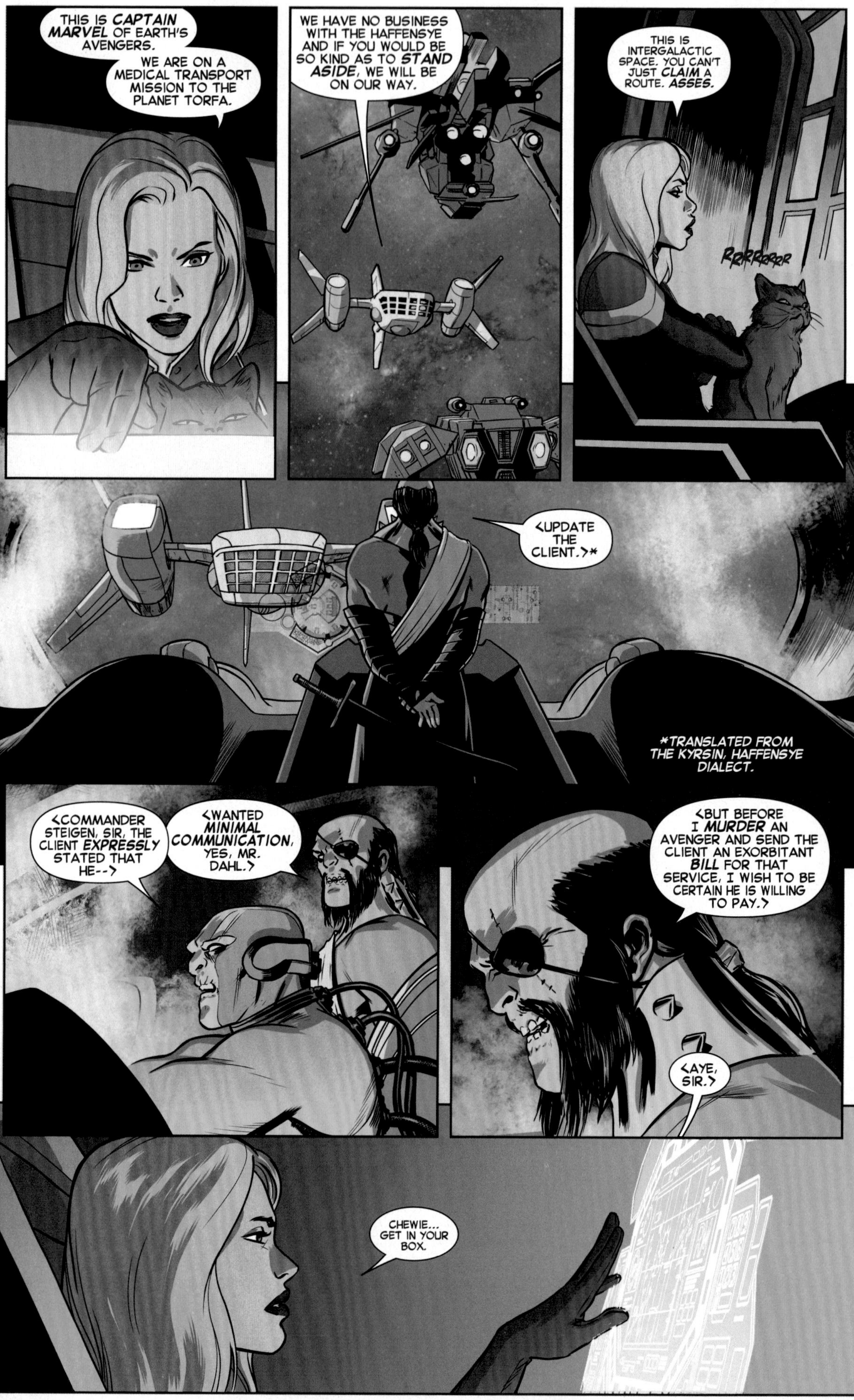
THIS IS CAPTAIN MARVEL OF EARTH'S AVENGERS.
WE ARE ON A MEDICAL TRANSPORT MISSION TO THE PLANET TORFA.
WE HAVE NO BUSINESS WITH THE HAFFENSYE AND IF YOU WOULD BE SO KIND AS TO STAND ASIDE, WE WILL BE ON OUR WAY.
THIS IS INTERGALACTIC SPACE. YOU CAN'T JUST CLAIM A ROUTE. ASSES.
RRRRRRRR
<UPDATE THE CLIENT.>*
*TRANSLATED FROM THE KYRSIN, HAFFENSYE DIALECT.
<COMMANDER STEIGEN, SIR, THE CLIENT EXPRESSLY STATED THAT HE-->
<WANTED MINIMAL COMMUNICATION, YES, MR. DAHL.>
<BUT BEFORE I MURDER AN AVENGER AND SEND THE CLIENT AN EXORBITANT BILL FOR THAT SERVICE, I WISH TO BE CERTAIN HE IS WILLING TO PAY.>
<AYE, SIR.>
CHEWIE... GET IN YOUR BOX.

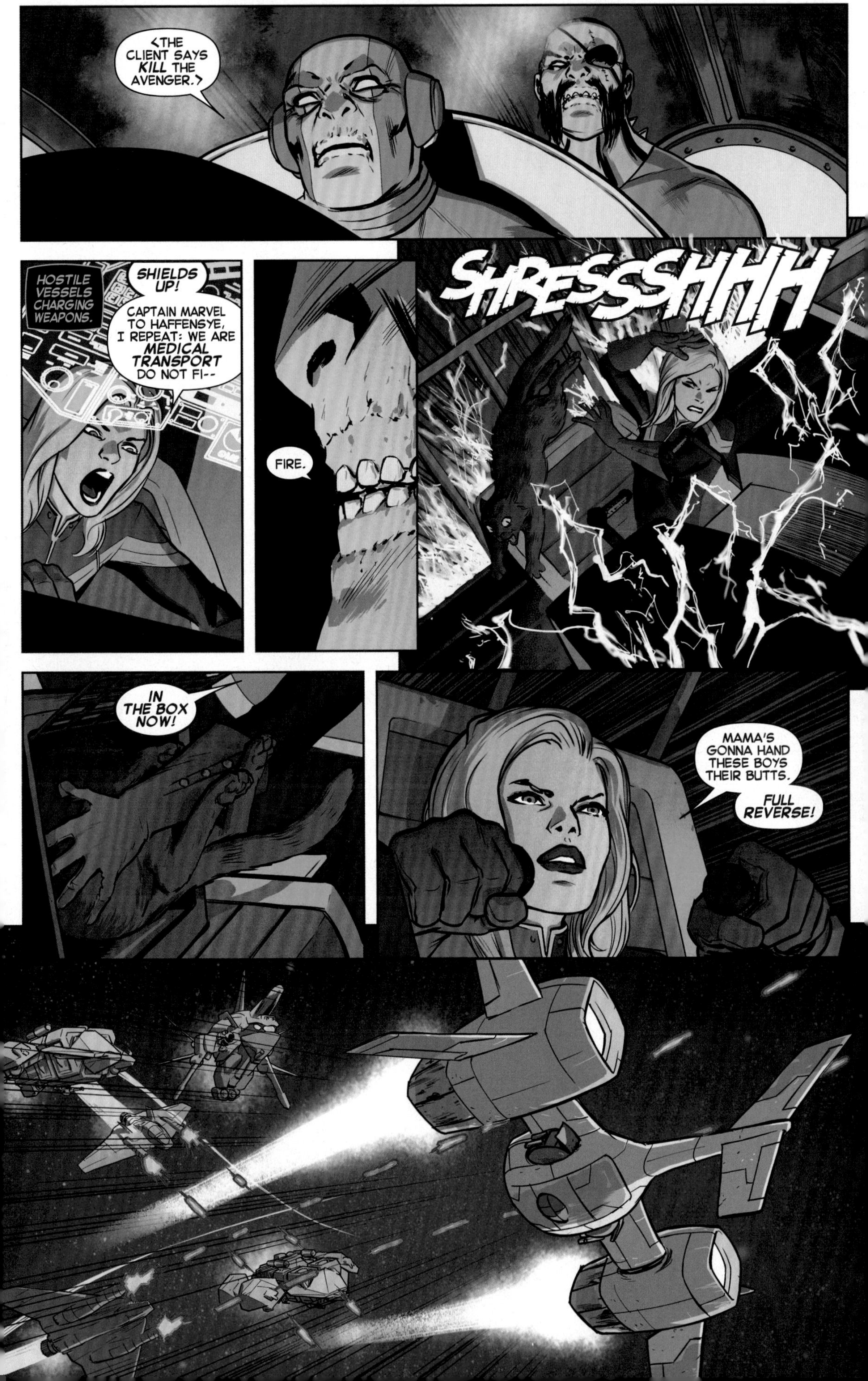
<THE CLIENT SAYS KILL THE AVENGER.>
HOSTILE VESSELS CHARGING WEAPONS.
SHIELDS UP!
CAPTAIN MARVEL TO HAFFENSYE, I REPEAT: WE ARE MEDICAL TRANSPORT DO NOT FI--
FIRE.
SHRESSSHHH
IN THE BOX NOW!
MAMA'S GONNA HAND THESE BOYS THEIR BUTTS.
FULL REVERSE!

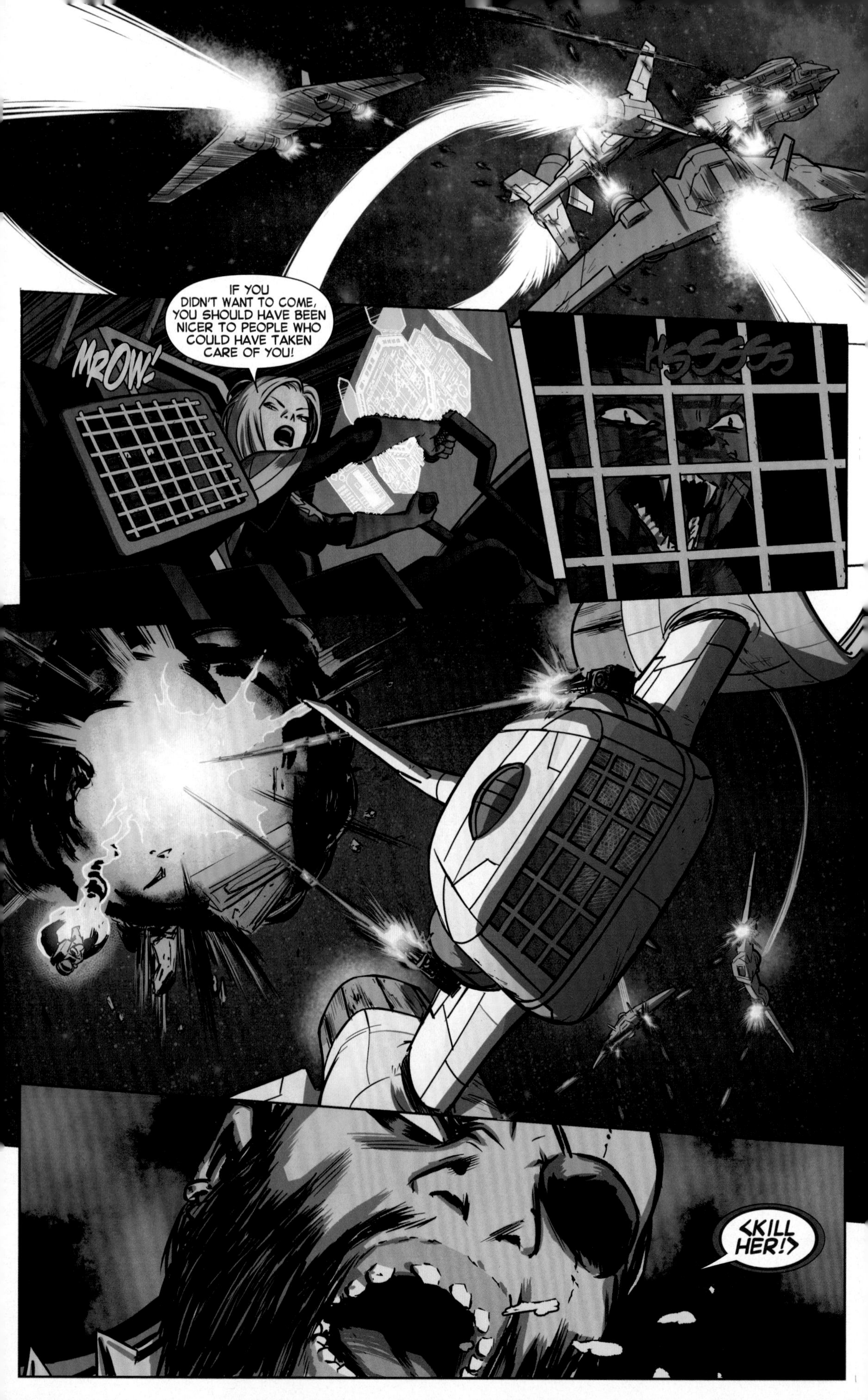
IF YOU DIDN'T WANT TO COME, YOU SHOULD HAVE BEEN NICER TO PEOPLE WHO COULD HAVE TAKEN CARE OF YOU!
MROW!
HSSSSS
<KILL HER!>

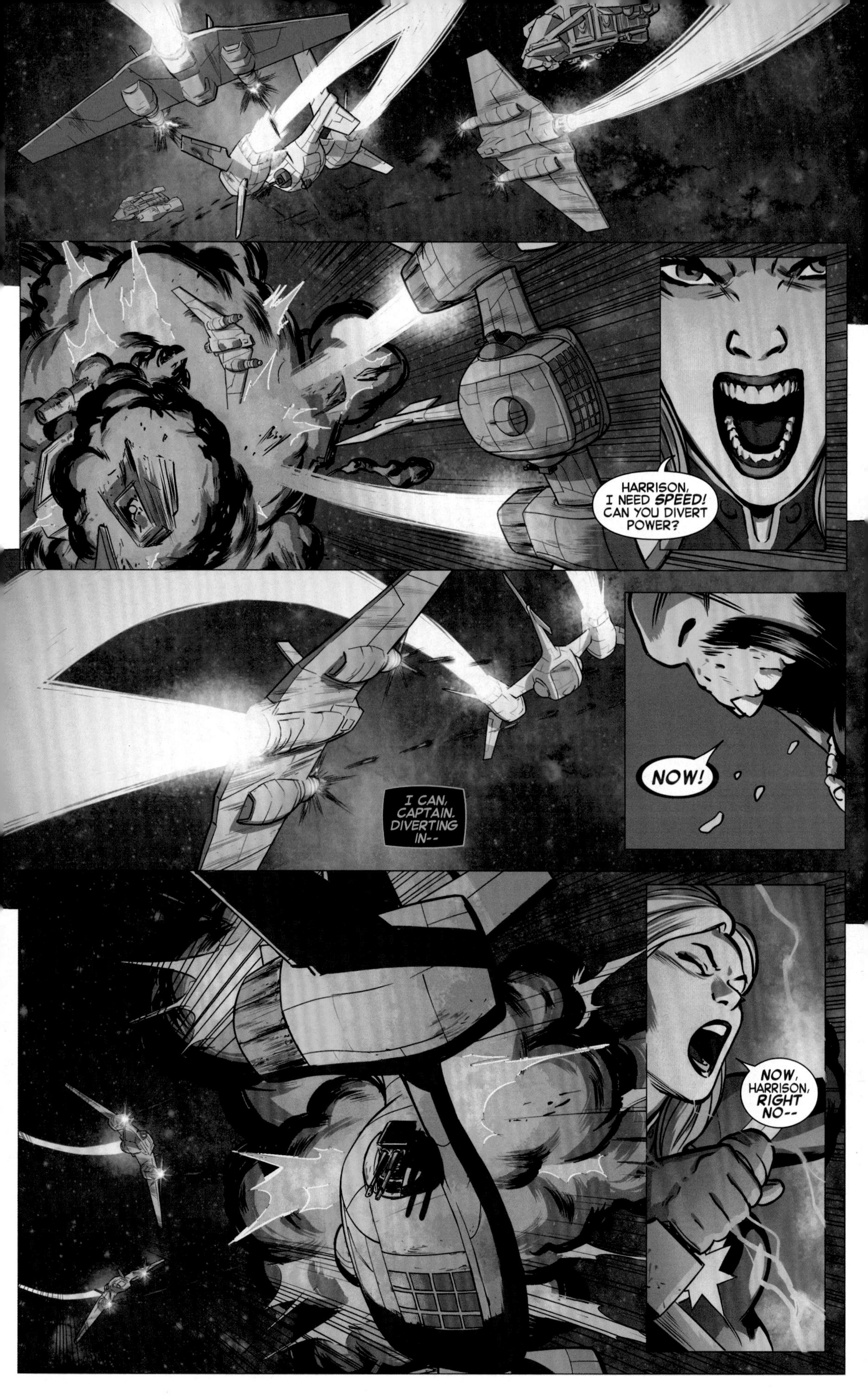
HARRISON, I NEED SPEED! CAN YOU DIVERT POWER?
NOW!
I CAN, CAPTAIN. DIVERTING IN--
NOW, HARRISON, RIGHT NO--

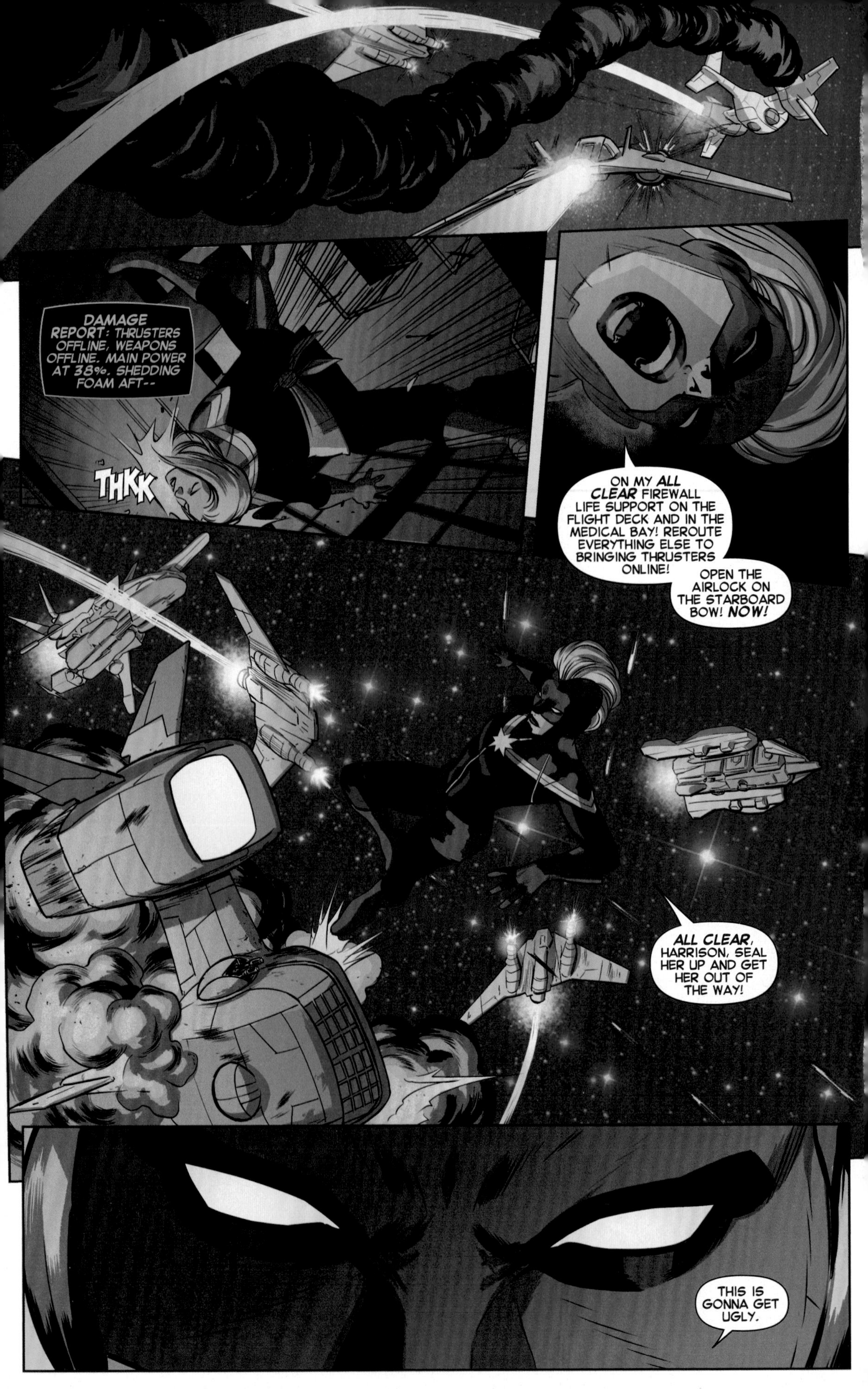

DAMAGE REPORT: THRUSTERS OFFLINE, WEAPONS OFFLINE. MAIN POWER AT 38%. SHEDDING FOAM AFT--
THKK
ON MY ALL CLEAR FIREWALL LIFE SUPPORT ON THE FLIGHT DECK AND IN THE MEDICAL BAY! REROUTE EVERYTHING ELSE TO BRINGING THRUSTERS ONLINE!
OPEN THE AIRLOCK ON THE STARBOARD BOW! NOW!
ALL CLEAR, HARRISON, SEAL HER UP AND GET HER OUT OF THE WAY!
THIS IS GONNA GET UGLY.

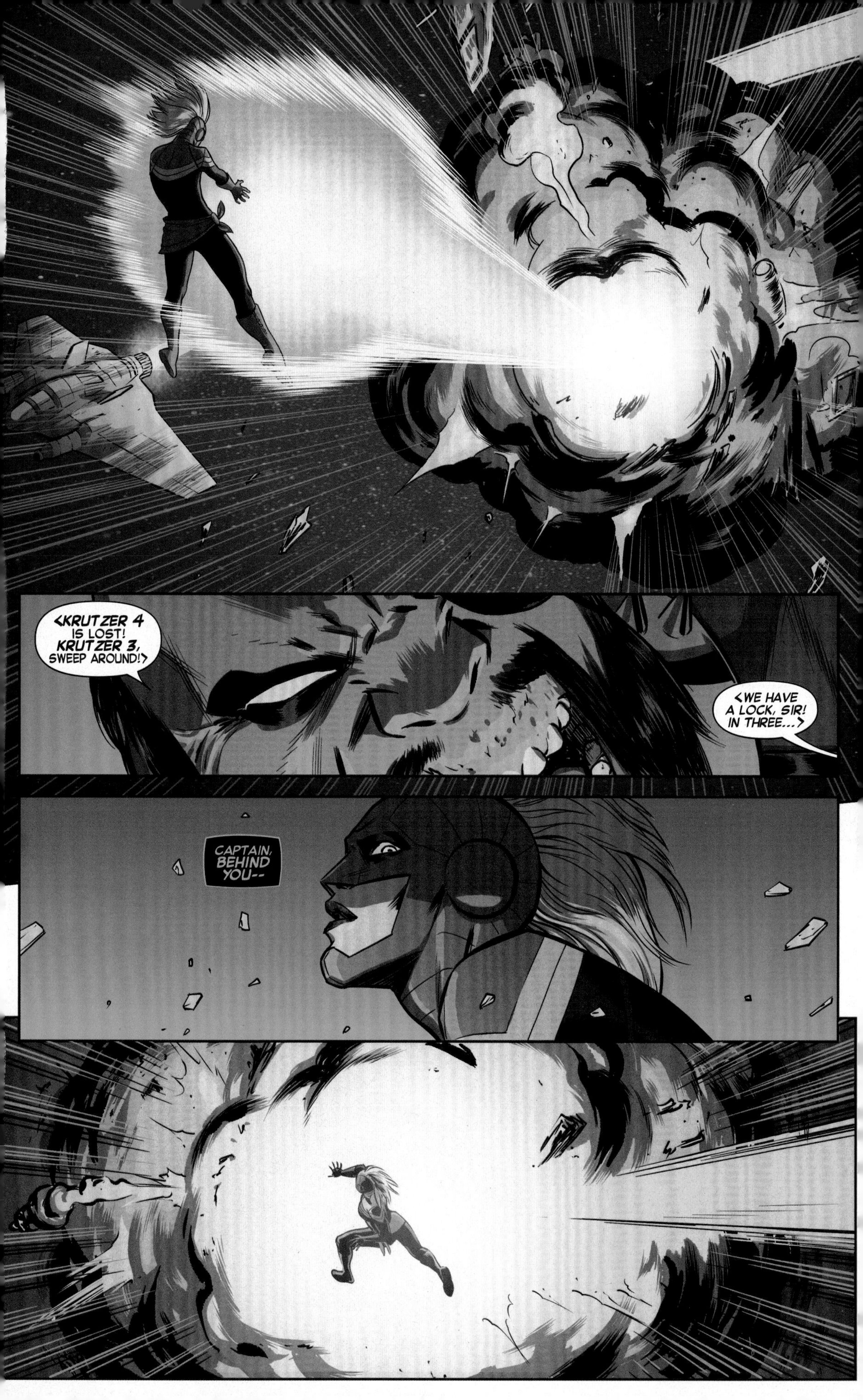
<KRUTZER 4 IS LOST! KRUTZER 3, SWEEP AROUND!>
<WE HAVE A LOCK, SIR! IN THREE...>
CAPTAIN, BEHIND YOU--

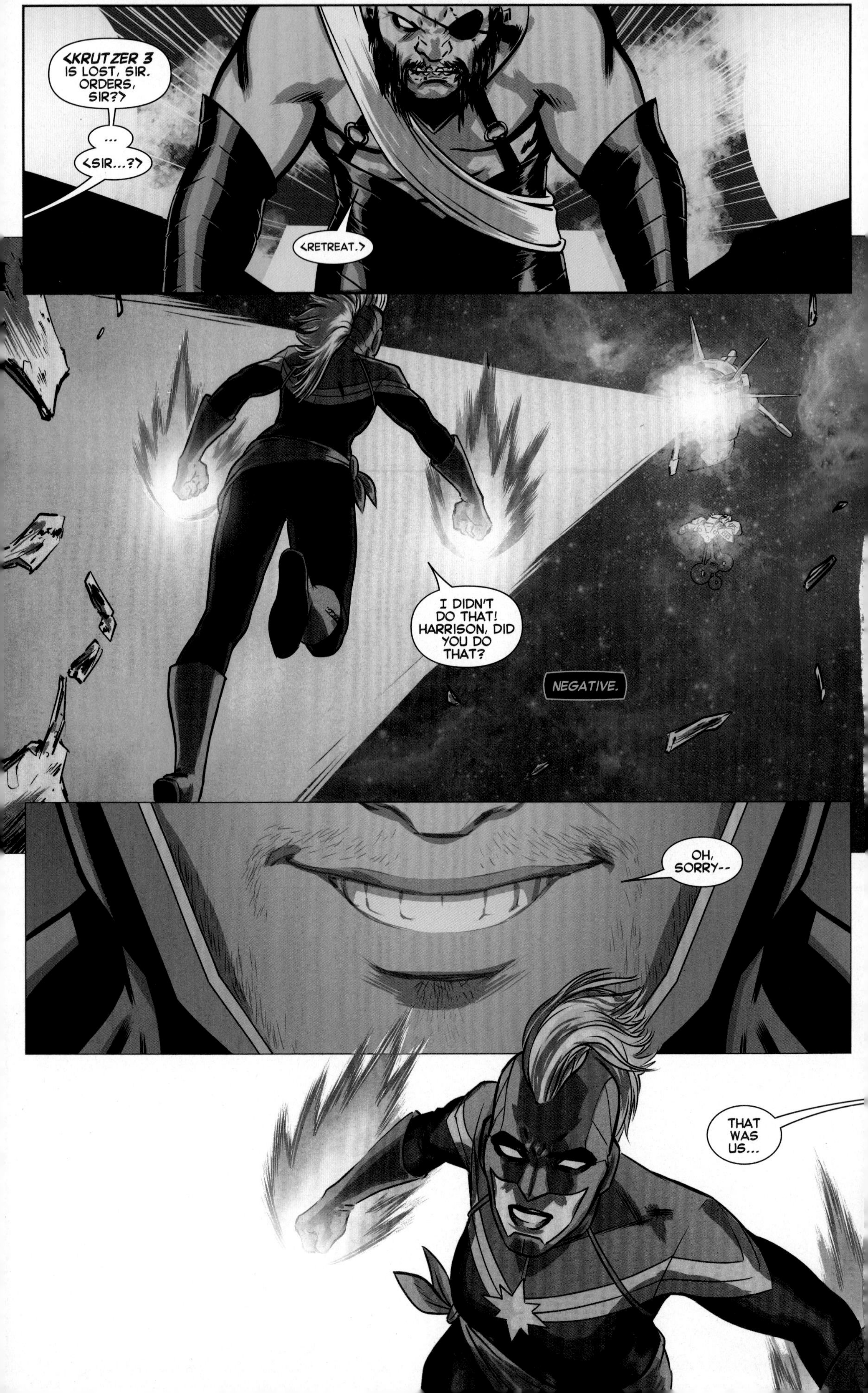
<KRUTZER 3 IS LOST, SIR. ORDERS, SIR?>
...
<SIR...?>
<RETREAT.>
I DIDN'T DO THAT! HARRISON, DID YOU DO THAT?
NEGATIVE.
OH, SORRY--
THAT WAS US...

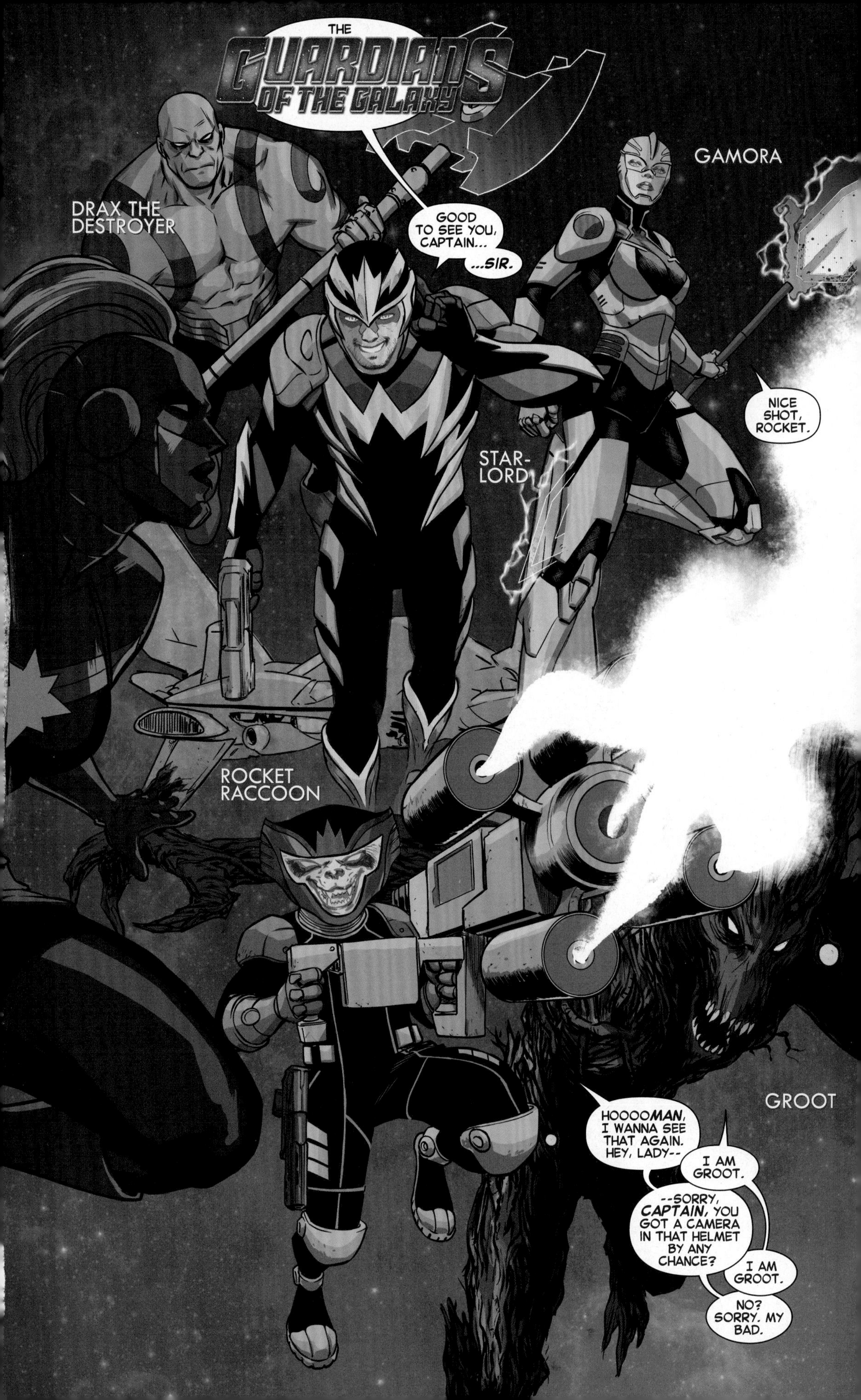
THE GUARDIANS OF THE GALAXY
DRAX THE DESTROYER
GOOD TO SEE YOU, CAPTAIN... ...SIR.
GAMORA
NICE SHOT, ROCKET.
STAR-LORD
ROCKET RACCOON
GROOT
HOOOOMAN, I WANNA SEE THAT AGAIN. HEY, LADY--
I AM GROOT.
--SORRY, CAPTAIN, YOU GOT A CAMERA IN THAT HELMET BY ANY CHANCE?
I AM GROOT.
NO? SORRY. MY BAD.

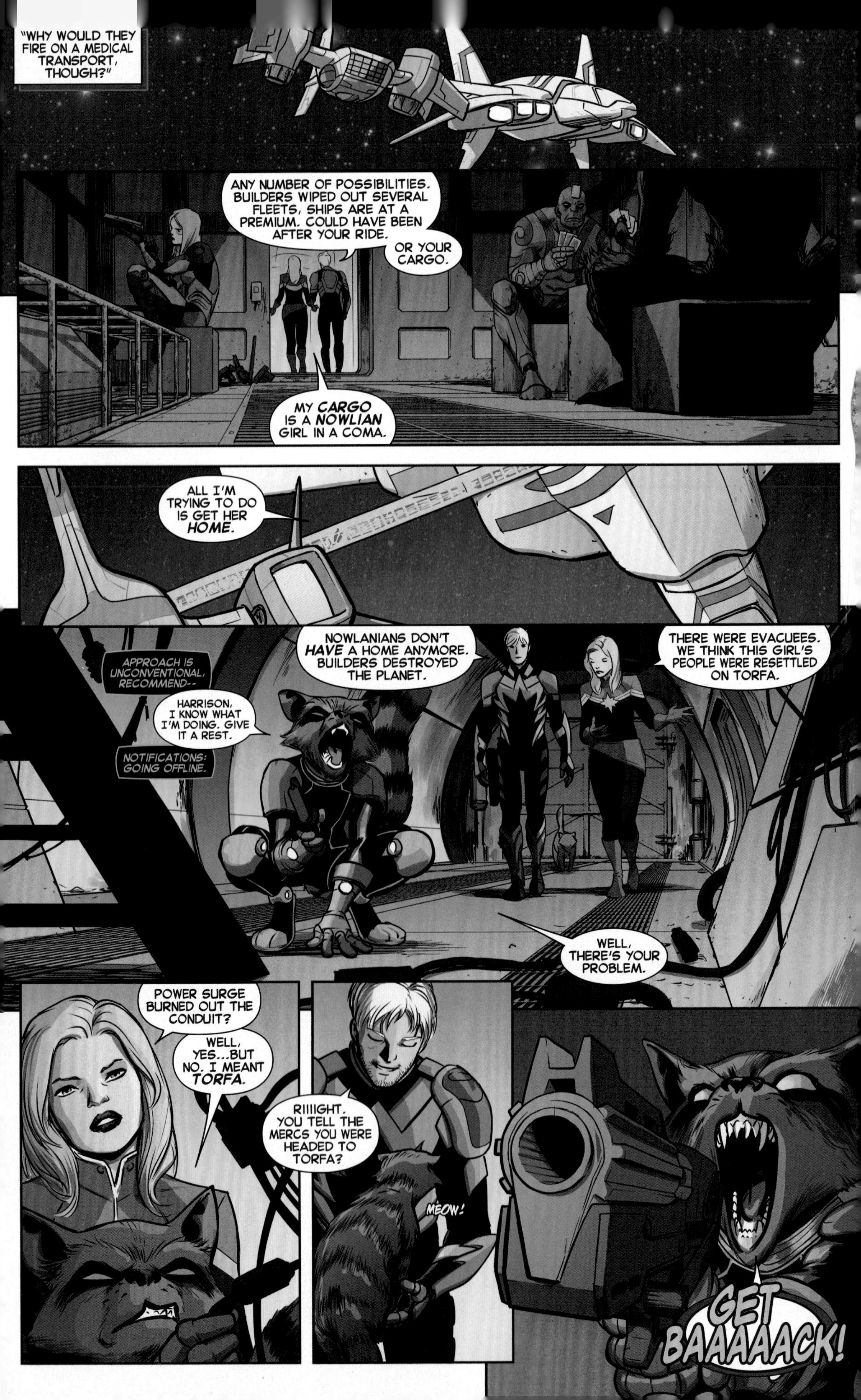

"WHY WOULD THEY FIRE ON A MEDICAL TRANSPORT, THOUGH?"
ANY NUMBER OF POSSIBILITIES. BUILDERS WIPED OUT SEVERAL FLEETS, SHIPS ARE AT A PREMIUM. COULD HAVE BEEN AFTER YOUR RIDE.
OR YOUR CARGO.
MY CARGO IS A NOWLIAN GIRL IN A COMA.
ALL I'M TRYING TO DO IS GET HER HOME.
APPROACH IS UNCONVENTIONAL, RECOMMEND--
HARRISON, I KNOW WHAT I'M DOING. GIVE IT A REST.
NOTIFICATIONS: GOING OFFLINE.
NOWLANIANS DON'T HAVE A HOME ANYMORE. BUILDERS DESTROYED THE PLANET.
THERE WERE EVACUEES. WE THINK THIS GIRL'S PEOPLE WERE RESETTLED ON TORFA.
WELL, THERE'S YOUR PROBLEM.
POWER SURGE BURNED OUT THE CONDUIT?
WELL, YES...BUT NO. I MEANT TORFA.
RIIIIGHT. YOU TELL THE MERCS YOU WERE HEADED TO TORFA?
MEOW!
GET BAAAAACK!

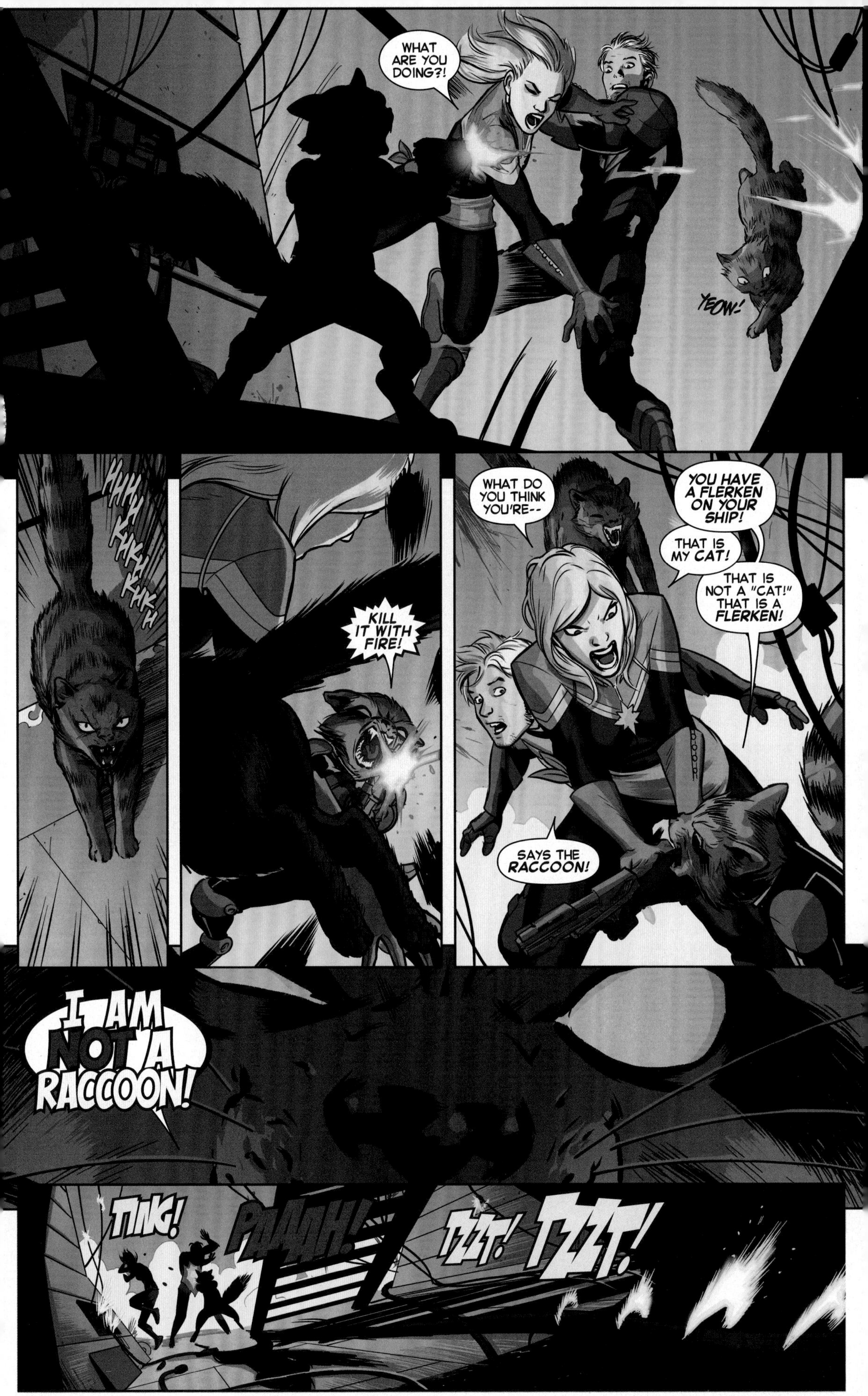
WHAT ARE YOU DOING?!
YEOW!
HHHHKHKHKHKHKHH
KILL IT WITH FIRE!
WHAT DO YOU THINK YOU'RE--
YOU HAVE A FLERKEN ON YOUR SHIP!
THAT IS MY CAT!
THAT IS NOT A "CAT!" THAT IS A FLERKEN!
SAYS THE RACCOON!
I AM NOT A RACCOON!
TING!
PHAAH!
TZZT! TZZT!

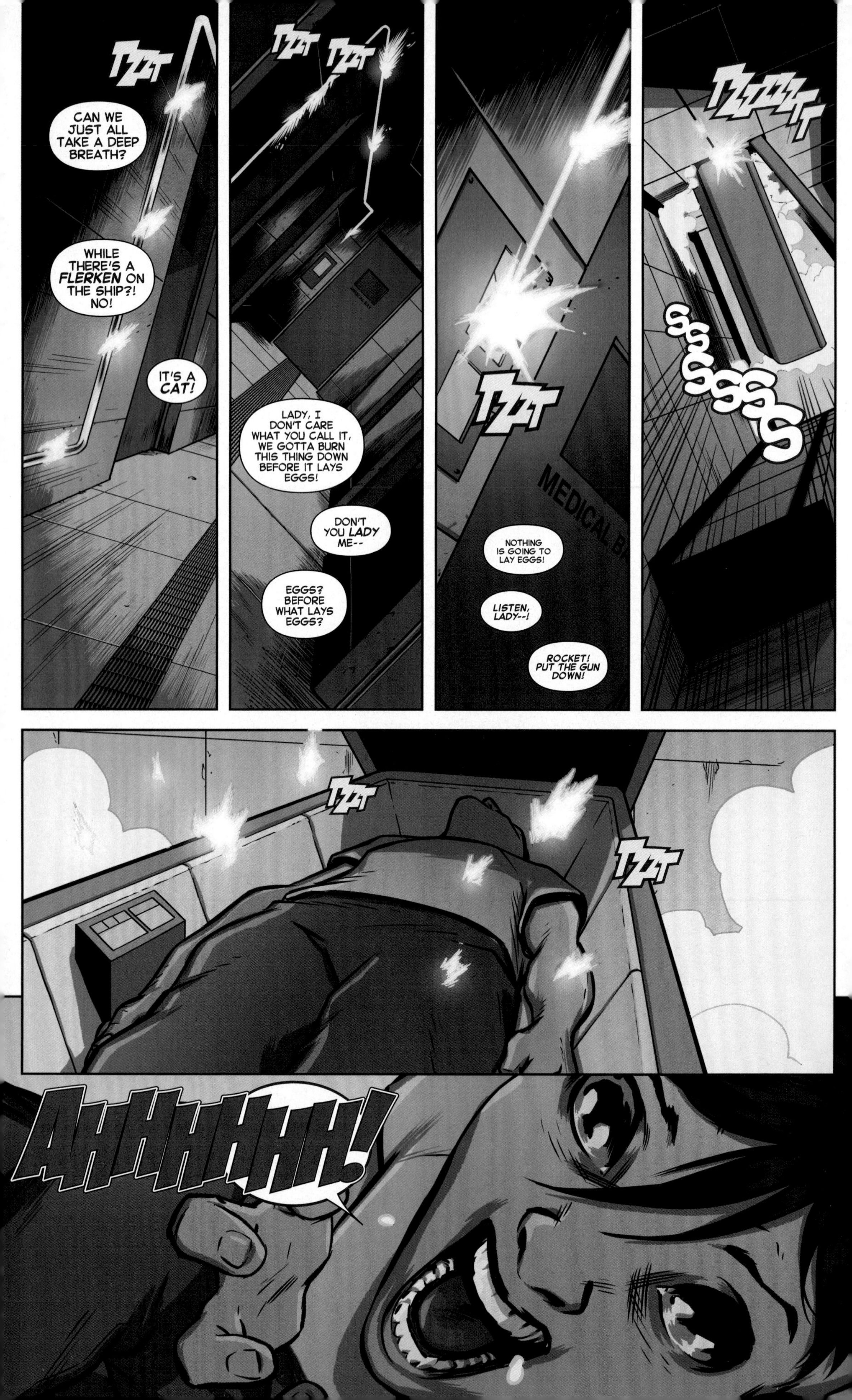
TZZT
CAN WE JUST ALL TAKE A DEEP BREATH?
WHILE THERE'S A FLERKEN ON THE SHIP?! NO!
IT'S A CAT!
TZZT TZZT
LADY, I DON'T CARE WHAT YOU CALL IT, WE GOTTA BURN THIS THING DOWN BEFORE IT LAYS EGGS!
DON'T YOU LADY ME--
EGGS? BEFORE WHAT LAYS EGGS?
TZZT
MEDICAL BA
NOTHING IS GOING TO LAY EGGS!
LISTEN, LADY--!
ROCKET! PUT THE GUN DOWN!
TZZZZZZT
SSSSSSS
TZZT
TZZT
AHHHHHH!

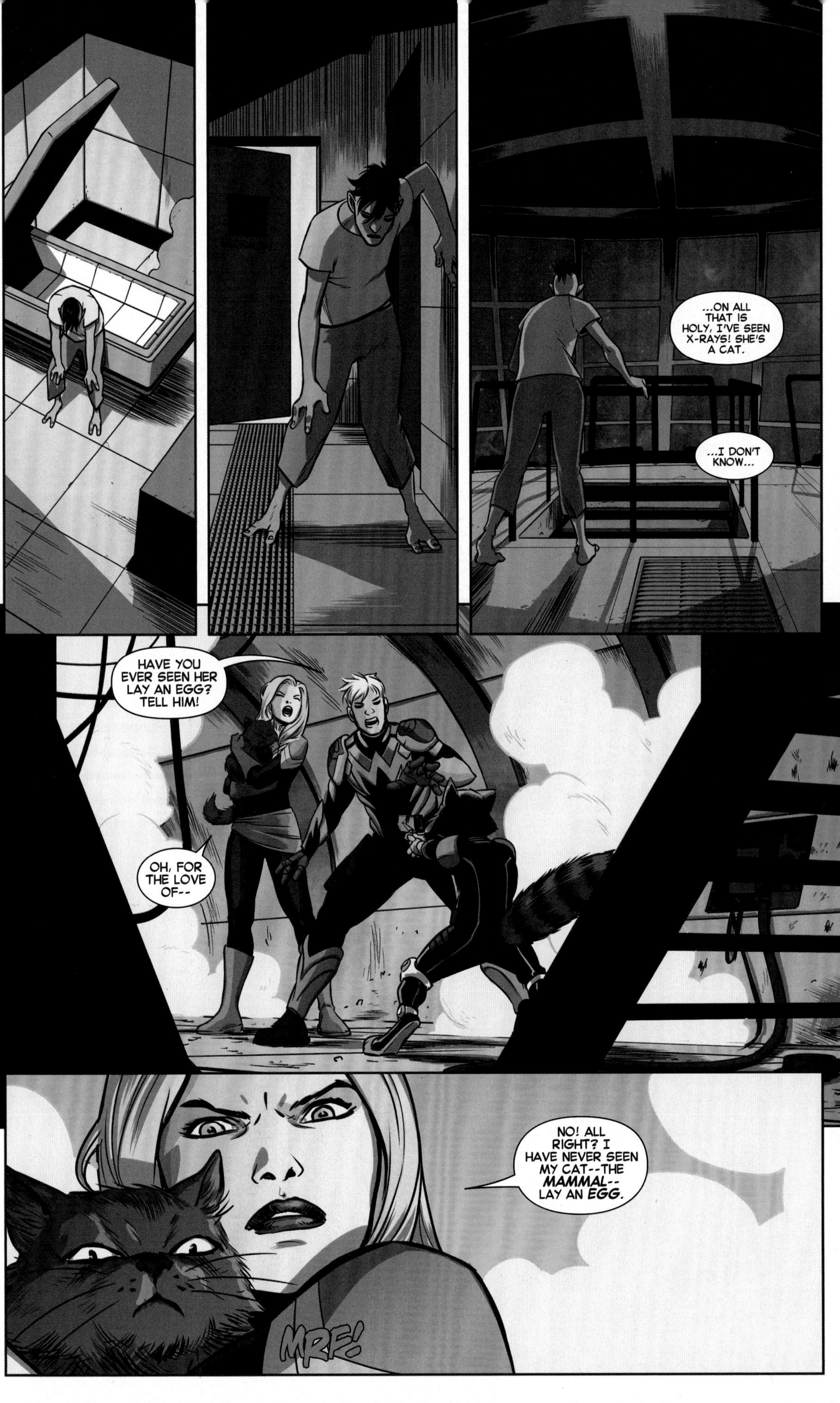
...ON ALL THAT IS HOLY, I'VE SEEN X-RAYS! SHE'S A CAT.
...I DON'T KNOW...
HAVE YOU EVER SEEN HER LAY AN EGG? TELL HIM!
OH, FOR THE LOVE OF--
NO! ALL RIGHT? I HAVE NEVER SEEN MY CAT--THE MAMMAL--LAY AN EGG.
MRF!

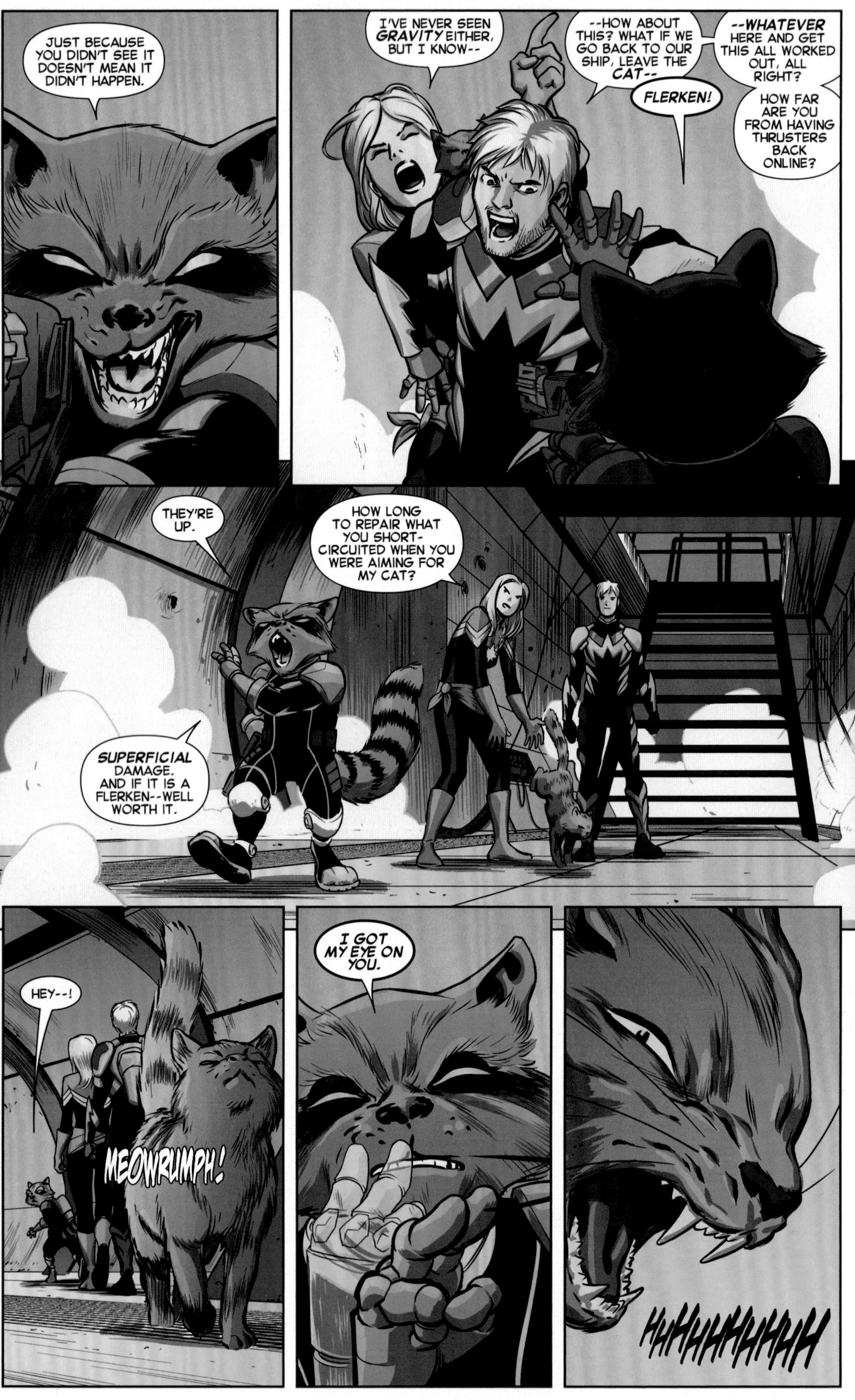
JUST BECAUSE YOU DIDN'T SEE IT DOESN'T MEAN IT DIDN'T HAPPEN.
I'VE NEVER SEEN GRAVITY EITHER, BUT I KNOW--
--HOW ABOUT THIS? WHAT IF WE GO BACK TO OUR SHIP, LEAVE THE CAT--
FLERKEN!
--WHATEVER HERE AND GET THIS ALL WORKED OUT, ALL RIGHT?
HOW FAR ARE YOU FROM HAVING THRUSTERS BACK ONLINE?
THEY'RE UP.
HOW LONG TO REPAIR WHAT YOU SHORT-CIRCUITED WHEN YOU WERE AIMING FOR MY CAT?
SUPERFICIAL DAMAGE. AND IF IT IS A FLERKEN--WELL WORTH IT.
HEY--!
MEOWRUMPH!
I GOT MY EYE ON YOU.
HHHHHHHHHH

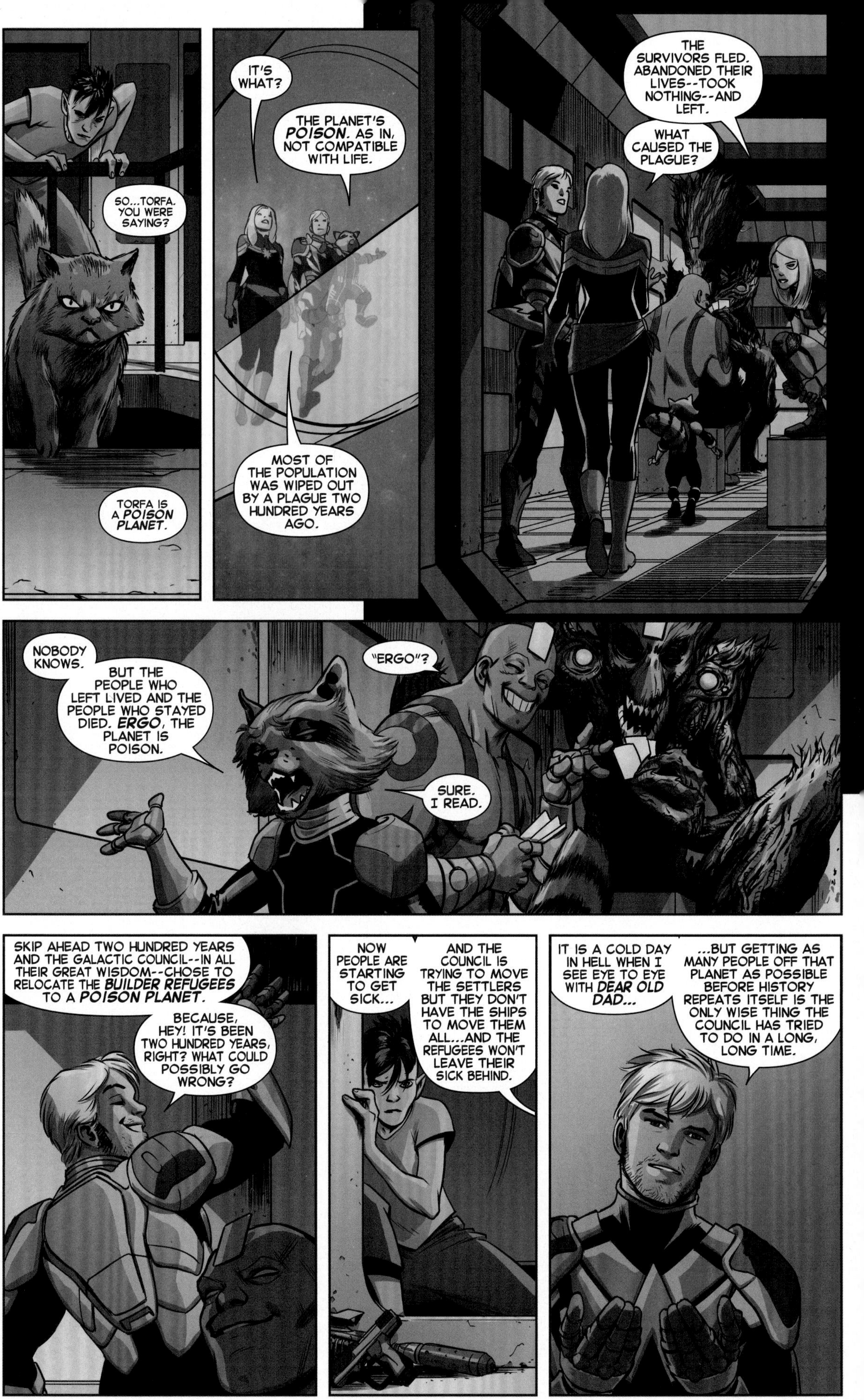
SO...TORFA. YOU WERE SAYING?
TORFA IS A POISON PLANET.
IT'S WHAT?
THE PLANET'S POISON. AS IN, NOT COMPATIBLE WITH LIFE.
MOST OF THE POPULATION WAS WIPED OUT BY A PLAGUE TWO HUNDRED YEARS AGO.
THE SURVIVORS FLED. ABANDONED THEIR LIVES--TOOK NOTHING--AND LEFT.
WHAT CAUSED THE PLAGUE?
NOBODY KNOWS.
BUT THE PEOPLE WHO LEFT LIVED AND THE PEOPLE WHO STAYED DIED. ERGO, THE PLANET IS POISON.
"ERGO"?
SURE. I READ.
SKIP AHEAD TWO HUNDRED YEARS AND THE GALACTIC COUNCIL--IN ALL THEIR GREAT WISDOM--CHOSE TO RELOCATE THE BUILDER REFUGEES TO A POISON PLANET.
BECAUSE, HEY! IT'S BEEN TWO HUNDRED YEARS, RIGHT? WHAT COULD POSSIBLY GO WRONG?
NOW PEOPLE ARE STARTING TO GET SICK...
AND THE COUNCIL IS TRYING TO MOVE THE SETTLERS BUT THEY DON'T HAVE THE SHIPS TO MOVE THEM ALL...AND THE REFUGEES WON'T LEAVE THEIR SICK BEHIND.
IT IS A COLD DAY IN HELL WHEN I SEE EYE TO EYE WITH DEAR OLD DAD...
...BUT GETTING AS MANY PEOPLE OFF THAT PLANET AS POSSIBLE BEFORE HISTORY REPEATS ITSELF IS THE ONLY WISE THING THE COUNCIL HAS TRIED TO DO IN A LONG, LONG TIME.

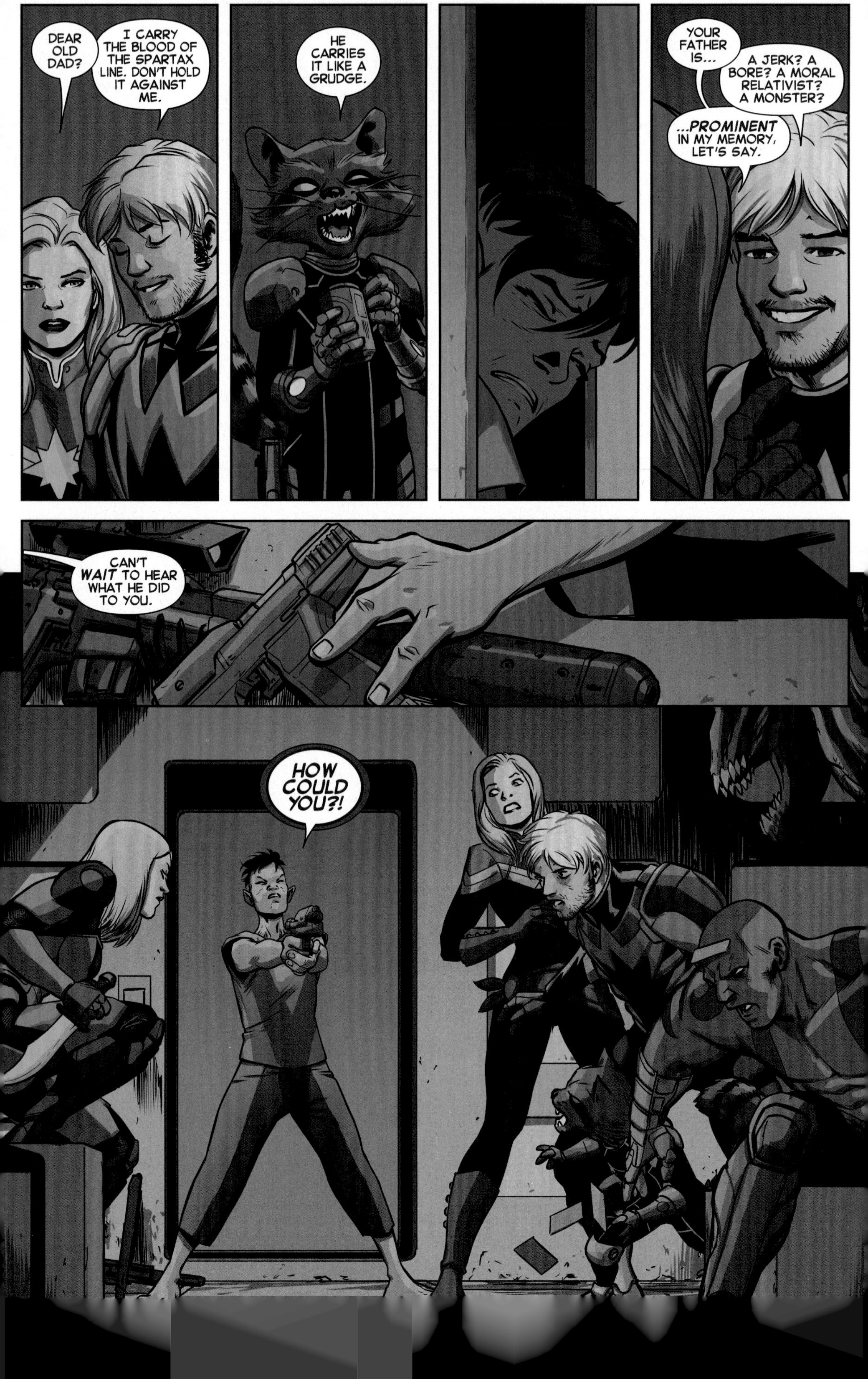
DEAR OLD DAD?
I CARRY THE BLOOD OF THE SPARTAX LINE. DON'T HOLD IT AGAINST ME.
HE CARRIES IT LIKE A GRUDGE.
YOUR FATHER IS...
A JERK? A BORE? A MORAL RELATIVIST? A MONSTER?
...PROMINENT IN MY MEMORY, LET'S SAY.
CAN'T WAIT TO HEAR WHAT HE DID TO YOU.
HOW COULD YOU?!

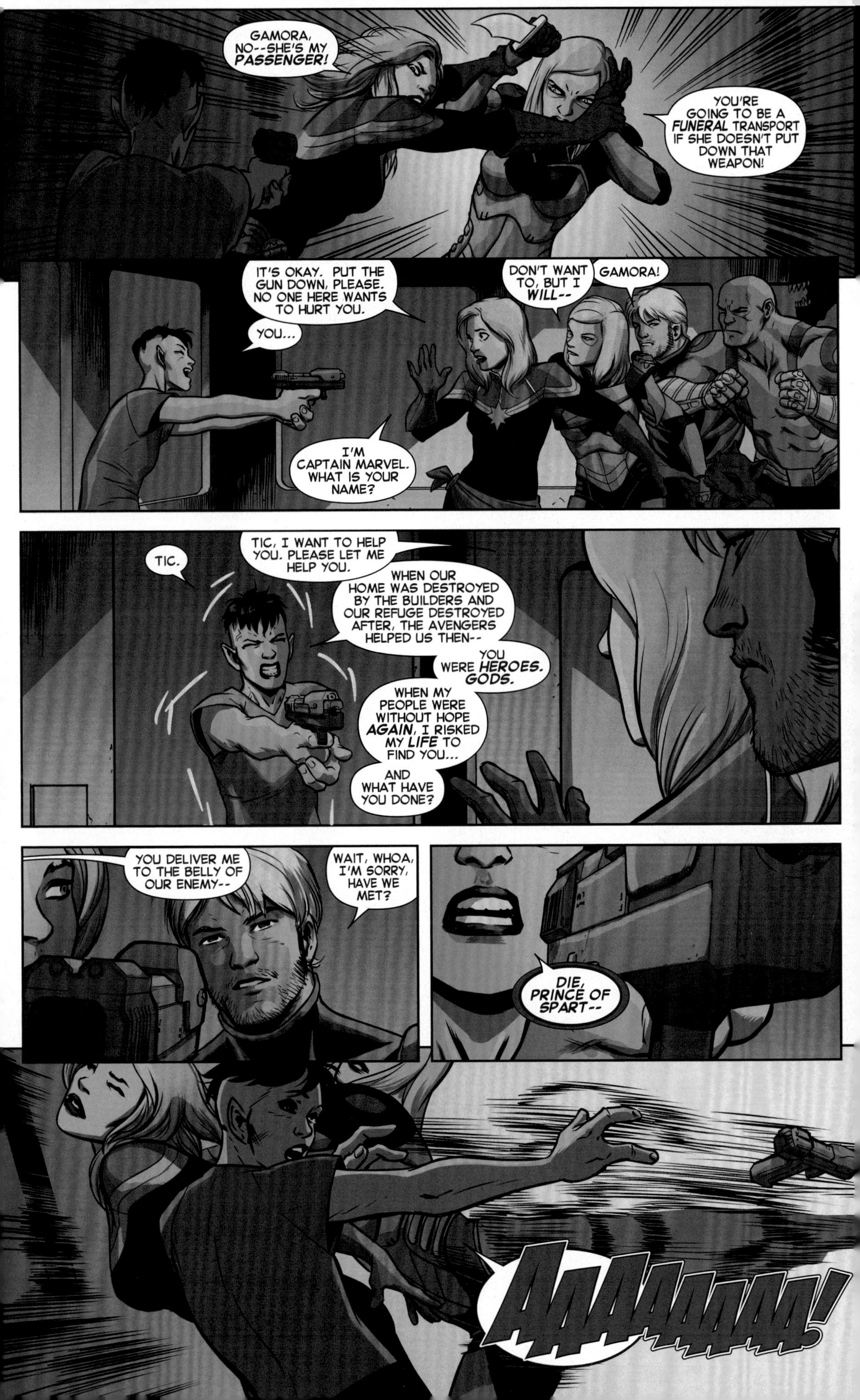
GAMORA, NO--SHE'S MY PASSENGER!
YOU'RE GOING TO BE A FUNERAL TRANSPORT IF SHE DOESN'T PUT DOWN THAT WEAPON!
IT'S OKAY. PUT THE GUN DOWN, PLEASE. NO ONE HERE WANTS TO HURT YOU.
YOU...
DON'T WANT TO, BUT I WILL--
GAMORA!
I'M CAPTAIN MARVEL. WHAT IS YOUR NAME?
TIC.
TIC, I WANT TO HELP YOU. PLEASE LET ME HELP YOU.
WHEN OUR HOME WAS DESTROYED BY THE BUILDERS AND OUR REFUGE DESTROYED AFTER, THE AVENGERS HELPED US THEN--
YOU WERE HEROES. GODS.
WHEN MY PEOPLE WERE WITHOUT HOPE AGAIN, I RISKED MY LIFE TO FIND YOU...
AND WHAT HAVE YOU DONE?
YOU DELIVER ME TO THE BELLY OF OUR ENEMY--
WAIT, WHOA, I'M SORRY, HAVE WE MET?
DIE, PRINCE OF SPART--
AAAAAAAA!

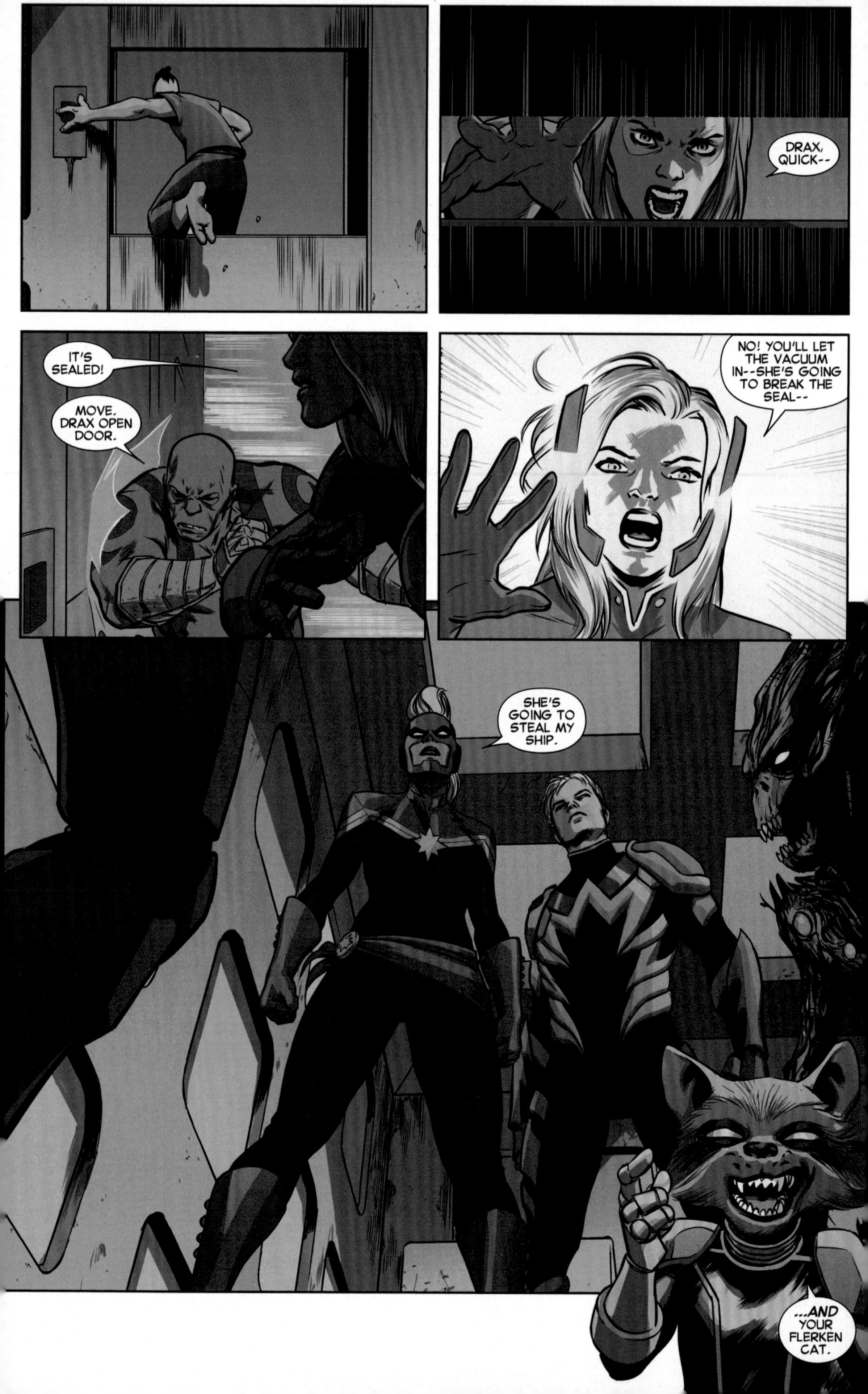
DRAX, QUICK--
IT'S SEALED!
MOVE. DRAX OPEN DOOR.
NO! YOU'LL LET THE VACUUM IN--SHE'S GOING TO BREAK THE SEAL--
SHE'S GOING TO STEAL MY SHIP.
...AND YOUR FLERKEN CAT.

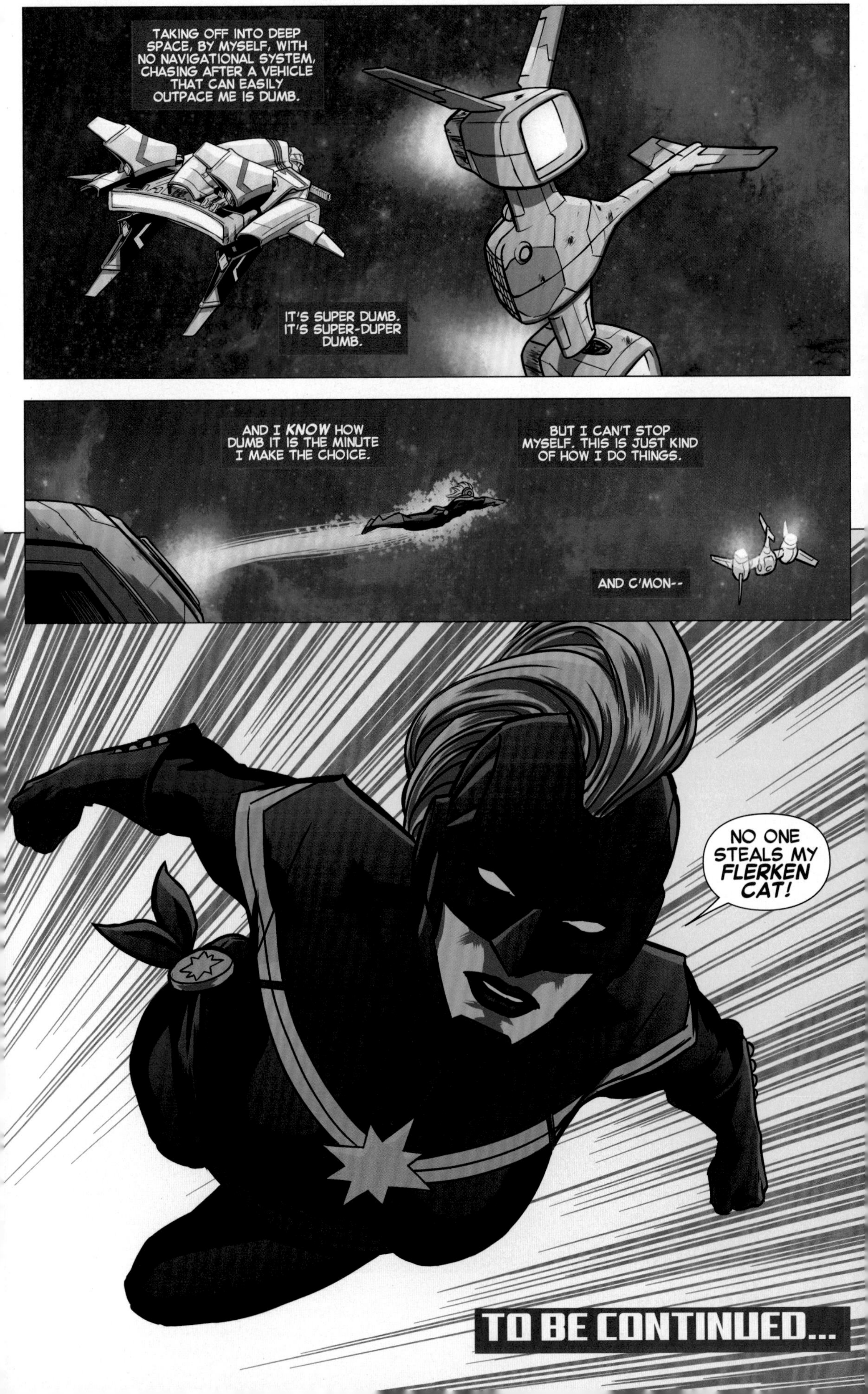
TAKING OFF INTO DEEP SPACE, BY MYSELF, WITH NO NAVIGATIONAL SYSTEM, CHASING AFTER A VEHICLE THAT CAN EASILY OUTPACE ME IS DUMB.
IT'S SUPER DUMB. IT'S SUPER-DUPER DUMB.
AND I KNOW HOW DUMB IT IS THE MINUTE I MAKE THE CHOICE.
BUT I CAN'T STOP MYSELF. THIS IS JUST KIND OF HOW I DO THINGS.
AND C'MON--
NO ONE STEALS MY FLERKEN CAT!
TO BE CONTINUED...

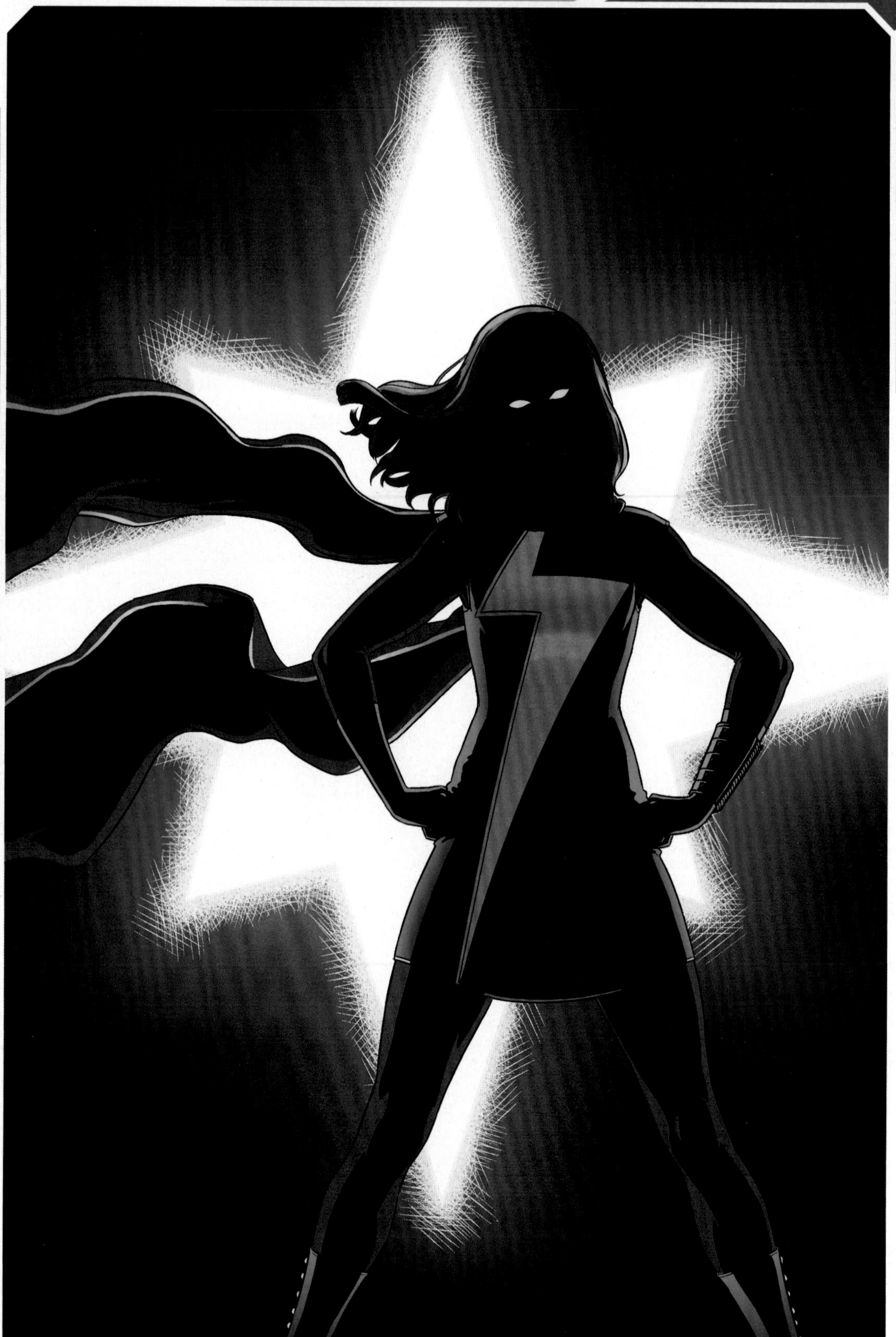

MS. MARVEL #2

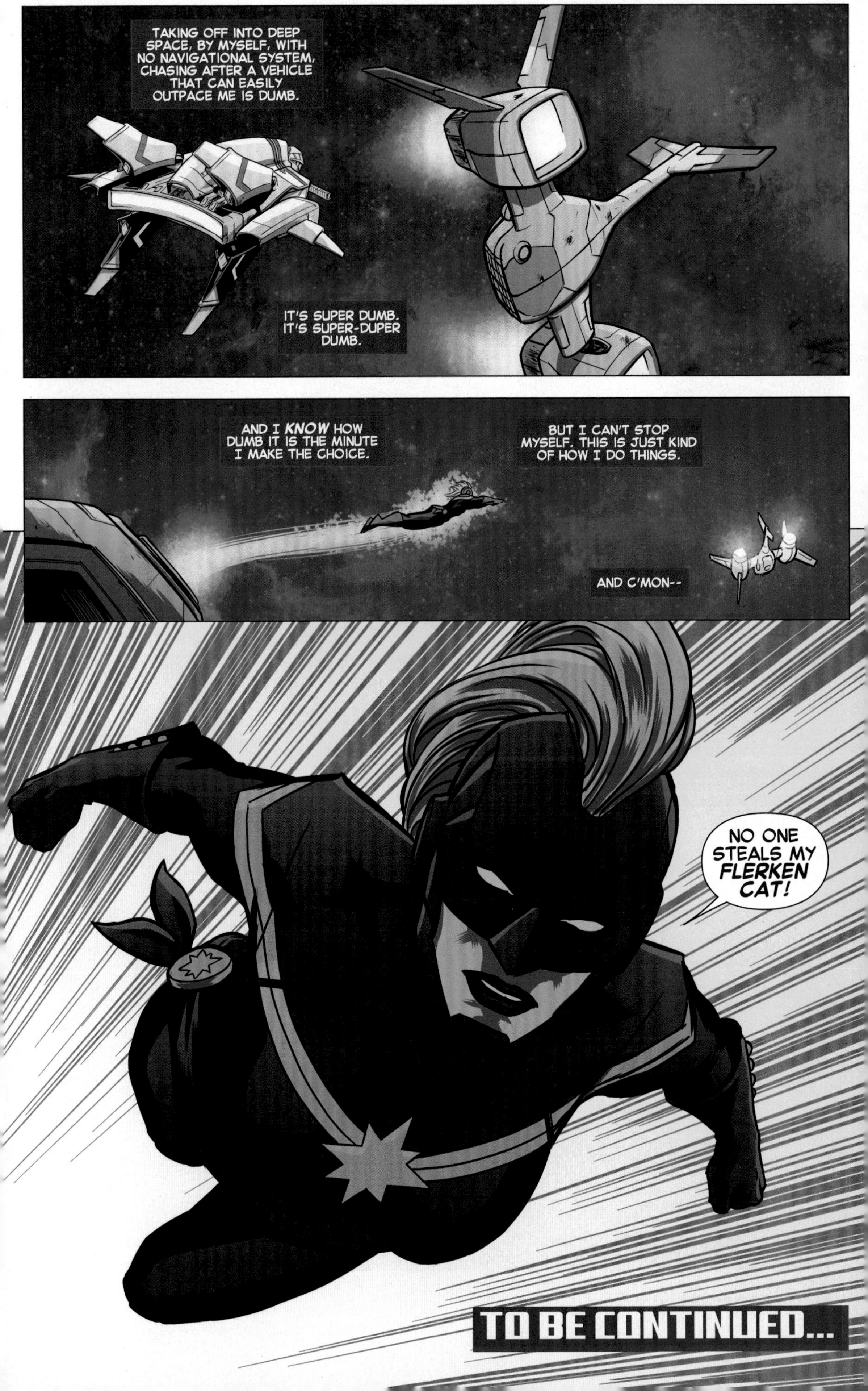
TAKING OFF INTO DEEP SPACE, BY MYSELF, WITH NO NAVIGATIONAL SYSTEM, CHASING AFTER A VEHICLE THAT CAN EASILY OUTPACE ME IS DUMB.
IT'S SUPER DUMB. IT'S SUPER-DUPER DUMB.
AND I KNOW HOW DUMB IT IS THE MINUTE I MAKE THE CHOICE.
BUT I CAN'T STOP MYSELF. THIS IS JUST KIND OF HOW I DO THINGS.
AND C'MON--
NO ONE STEALS MY FLERKEN CAT!
TO BE CONTINUED...

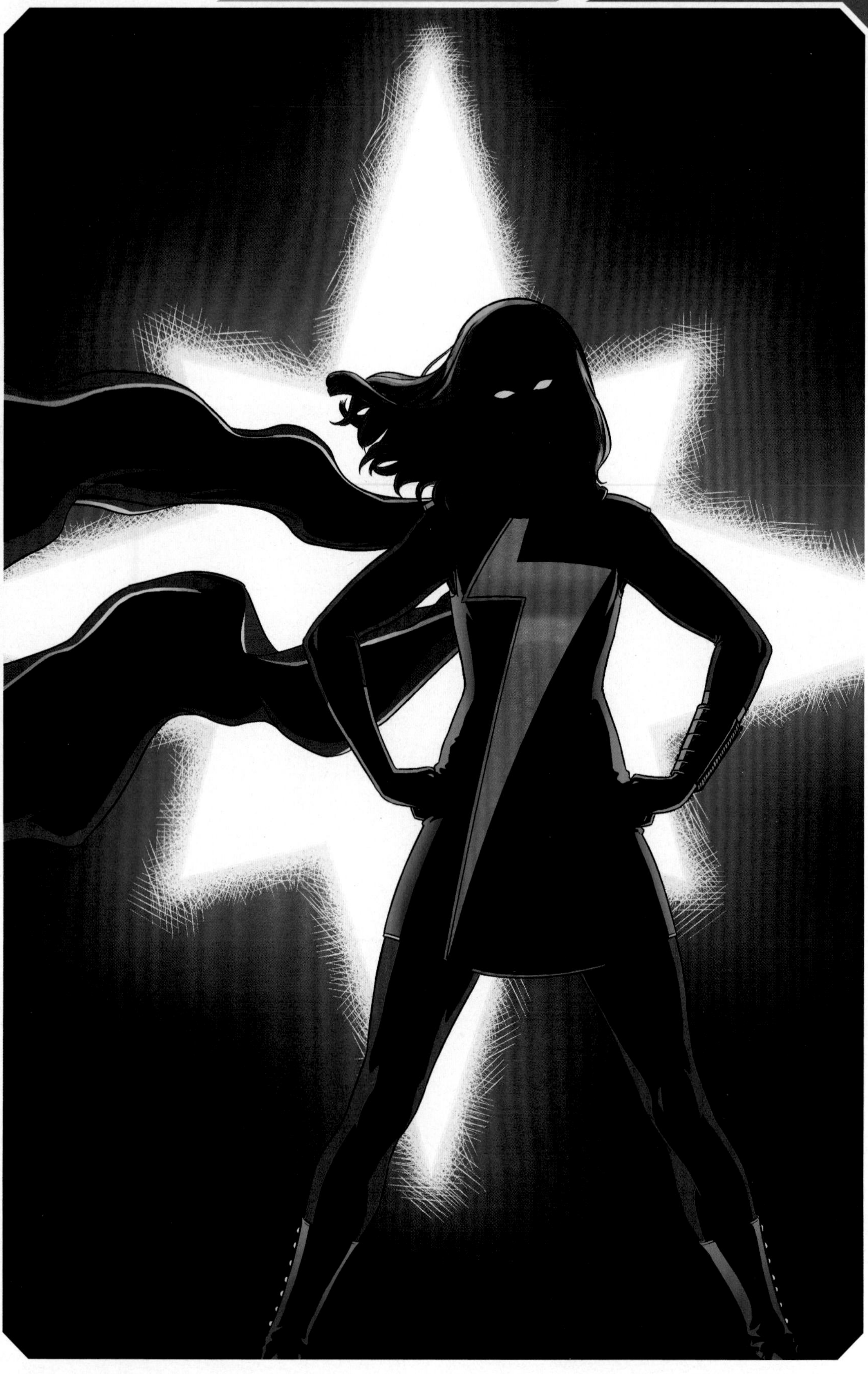

MS. MARVEL #2

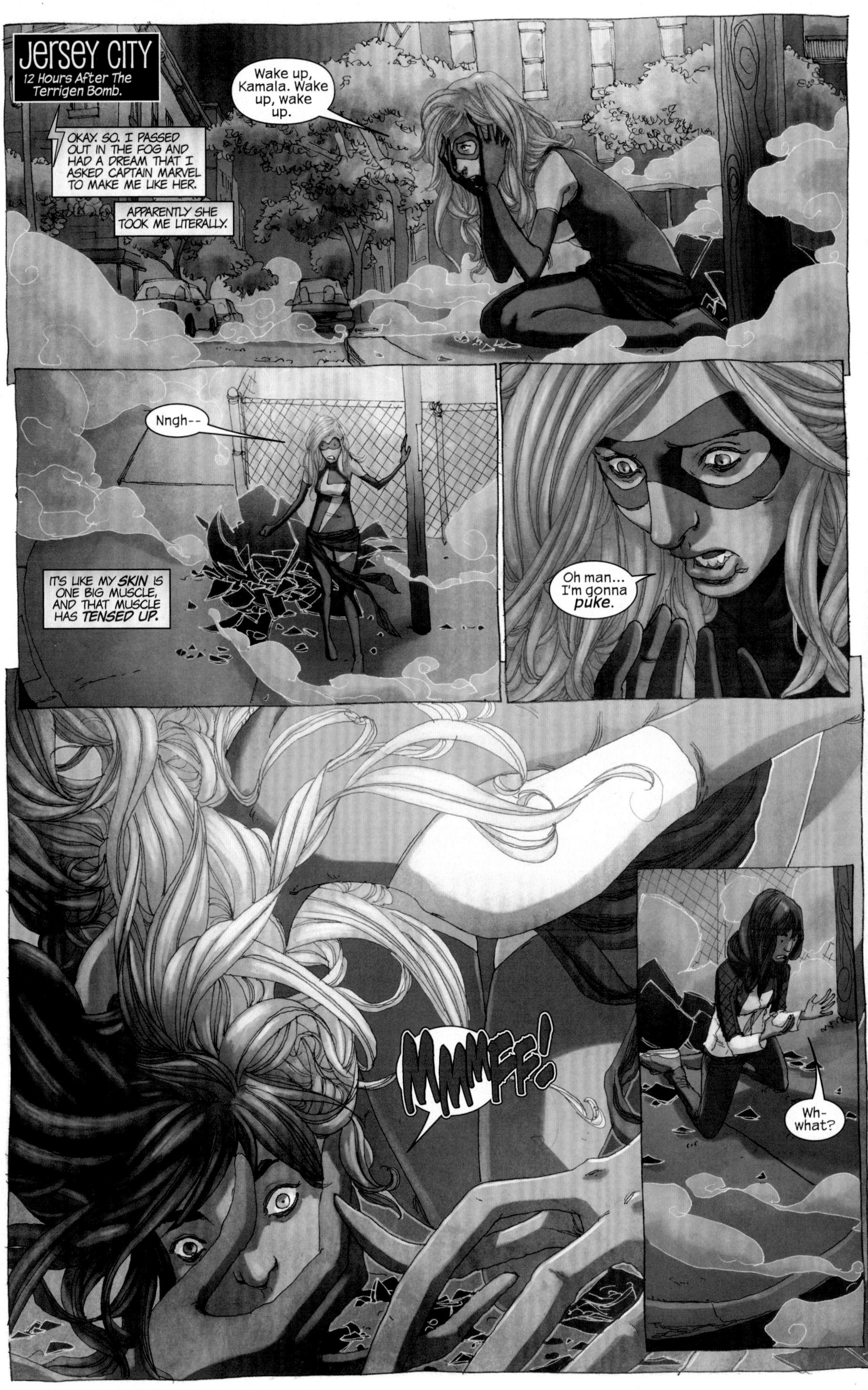

JERSEY CITY
12 Hours After The Terrigen Bomb.
Wake up, Kamala. Wake up, wake up.
OKAY. SO. I PASSED OUT IN THE FOG AND HAD A DREAM THAT I ASKED CAPTAIN MARVEL TO MAKE ME LIKE HER.
APPARENTLY SHE TOOK ME LITERALLY.
Nngh--
IT'S LIKE MY SKIN IS ONE BIG MUSCLE, AND THAT MUSCLE HAS TENSED UP.
Oh man... I'm gonna puke.
MMMFF!
Wh-what?

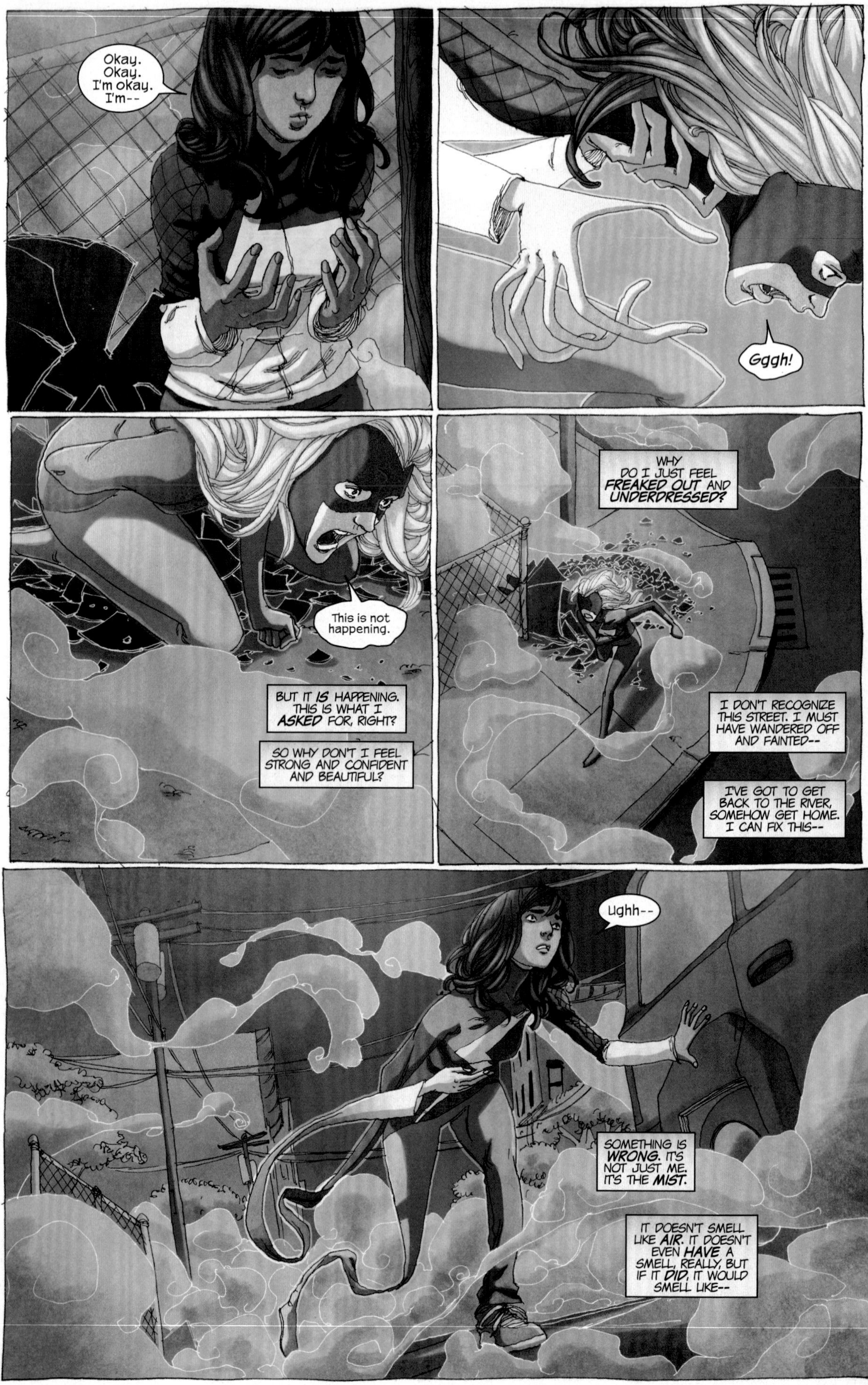
Okay. Okay. I'm okay. I'm--
Gggh!
This is not happening.
BUT IT IS HAPPENING. THIS IS WHAT I ASKED FOR, RIGHT?
SO WHY DON'T I FEEL STRONG AND CONFIDENT AND BEAUTIFUL?
WHY DO I JUST FEEL FREAKED OUT AND UNDERDRESSED?
I DON'T RECOGNIZE THIS STREET. I MUST HAVE WANDERED OFF AND FAINTED--
I'VE GOT TO GET BACK TO THE RIVER, SOMEHOW GET HOME. I CAN FIX THIS--
Ughh--
SOMETHING IS WRONG. IT'S NOT JUST ME. IT'S THE MIST.
IT DOESN'T SMELL LIKE AIR. IT DOESN'T EVEN HAVE A SMELL, REALLY, BUT IF IT DID, IT WOULD SMELL LIKE--

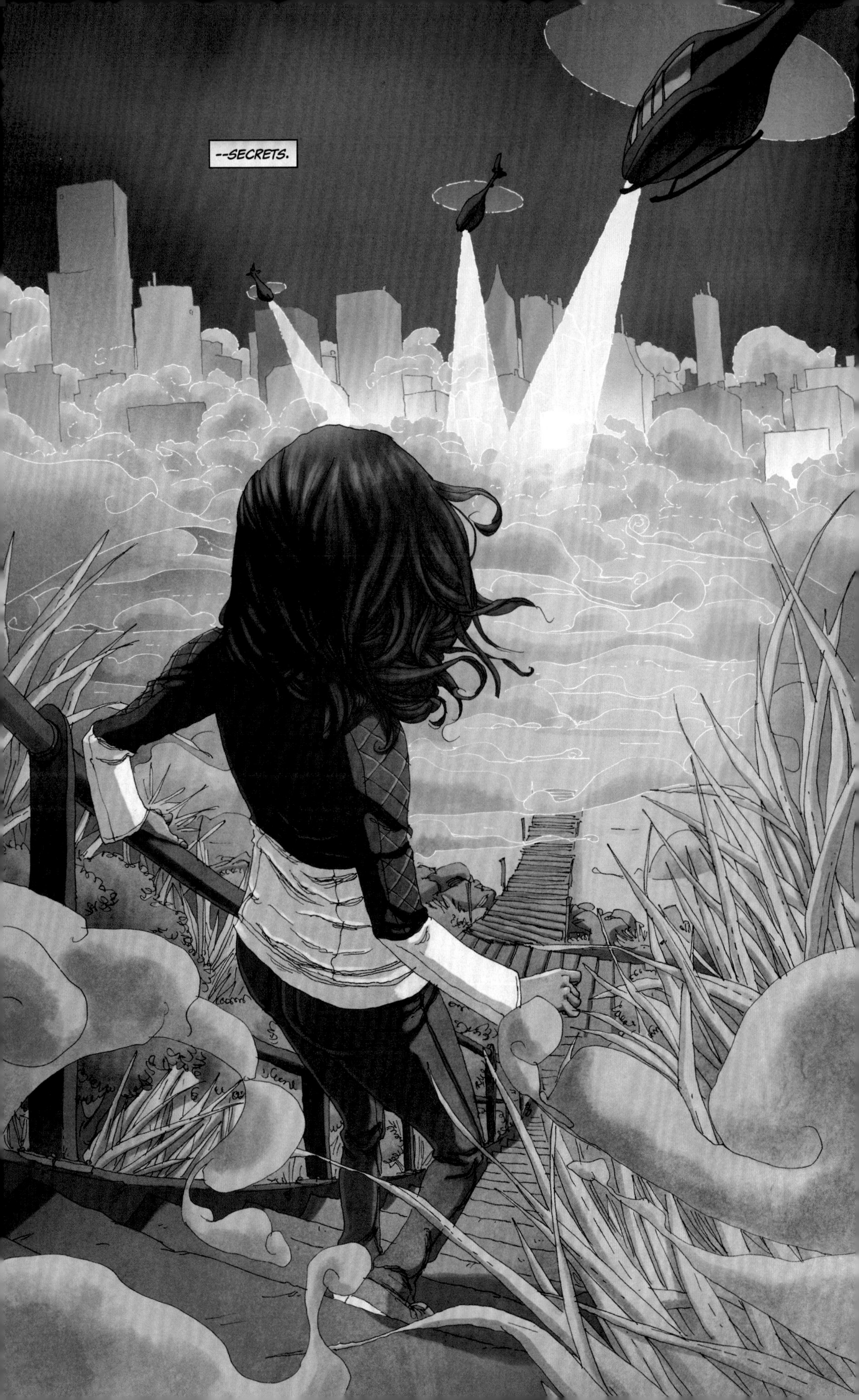
--SECRETS.

MARVEL COMICS
PROUDLY PRESENTS:

ALL MANKIND

PART TWO OF FIVE

MEET KAMALA KHAN.

SHE'S 16 YEARS OLD. INTO AVENGERS FAN FICTION.
GOOD AT SCHOOL. BAD AT FITTING IN.

SO WHEN A STRANGE MIST DESCENDS AND MORPHS KAMALA INTO A
SHAPE-SHIFTING SUPERHUMAN...
FITTING IN IS THE LEAST OF HER PROBLEMS.

G. WILLOW WILSON - WRITER   ADRIAN ALPHONA - ART

IAN HERRING - COLOR ART   VC'S JOE CARAMAGNA - LETTERING

JAMIE MCKELVIE &
MATT WILSON - COVER ART
JORGE MOLINA - VARIANT COVER

DEVIN LEWIS - ASSISTANT EDITOR
SANA AMANAT - EDITOR
STEPHEN WACKER - SENIOR EDITOR
AXEL ALONSO - EDITOR IN CHIEF
JOE QUESADA - CHIEF CREATIVE OFFICER
DAN BUCKLEY - PUBLISHER
ALAN FINE - EXECUTIVE PRODUCER

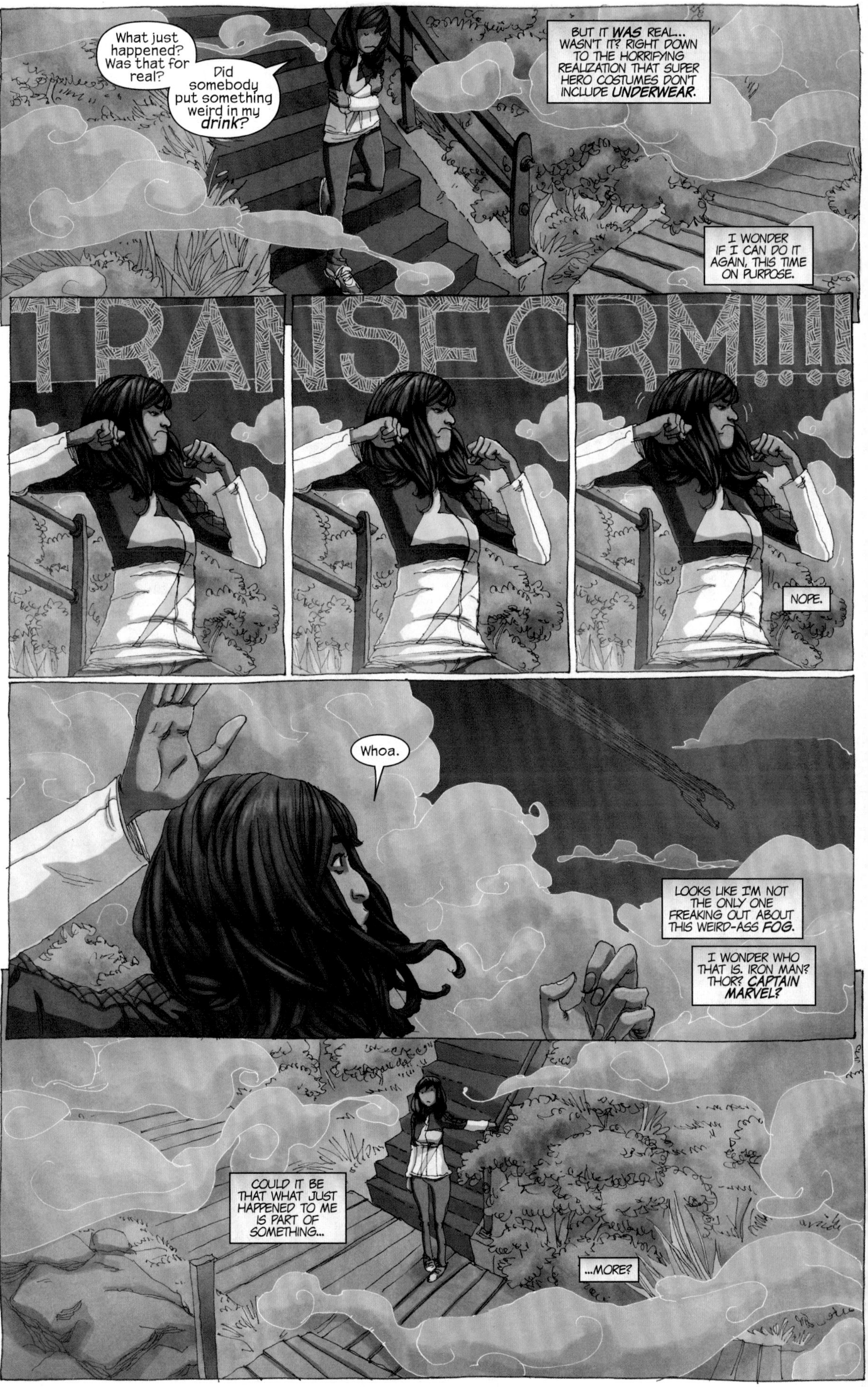
What just happened? Was that for real?
Did somebody put something weird in my drink?
BUT IT WAS REAL... WASN'T IT? RIGHT DOWN TO THE HORRIFYING REALIZATION THAT SUPER HERO COSTUMES DON'T INCLUDE UNDERWEAR.
I WONDER IF I CAN DO IT AGAIN, THIS TIME ON PURPOSE.
TRANSFORM!!!!
NOPE.
Whoa.
LOOKS LIKE I'M NOT THE ONLY ONE FREAKING OUT ABOUT THIS WEIRD-ASS FOG.
I WONDER WHO THAT IS. IRON MAN? THOR? CAPTAIN MARVEL?
COULD IT BE THAT WHAT JUST HAPPENED TO ME IS PART OF SOMETHING...
...MORE?

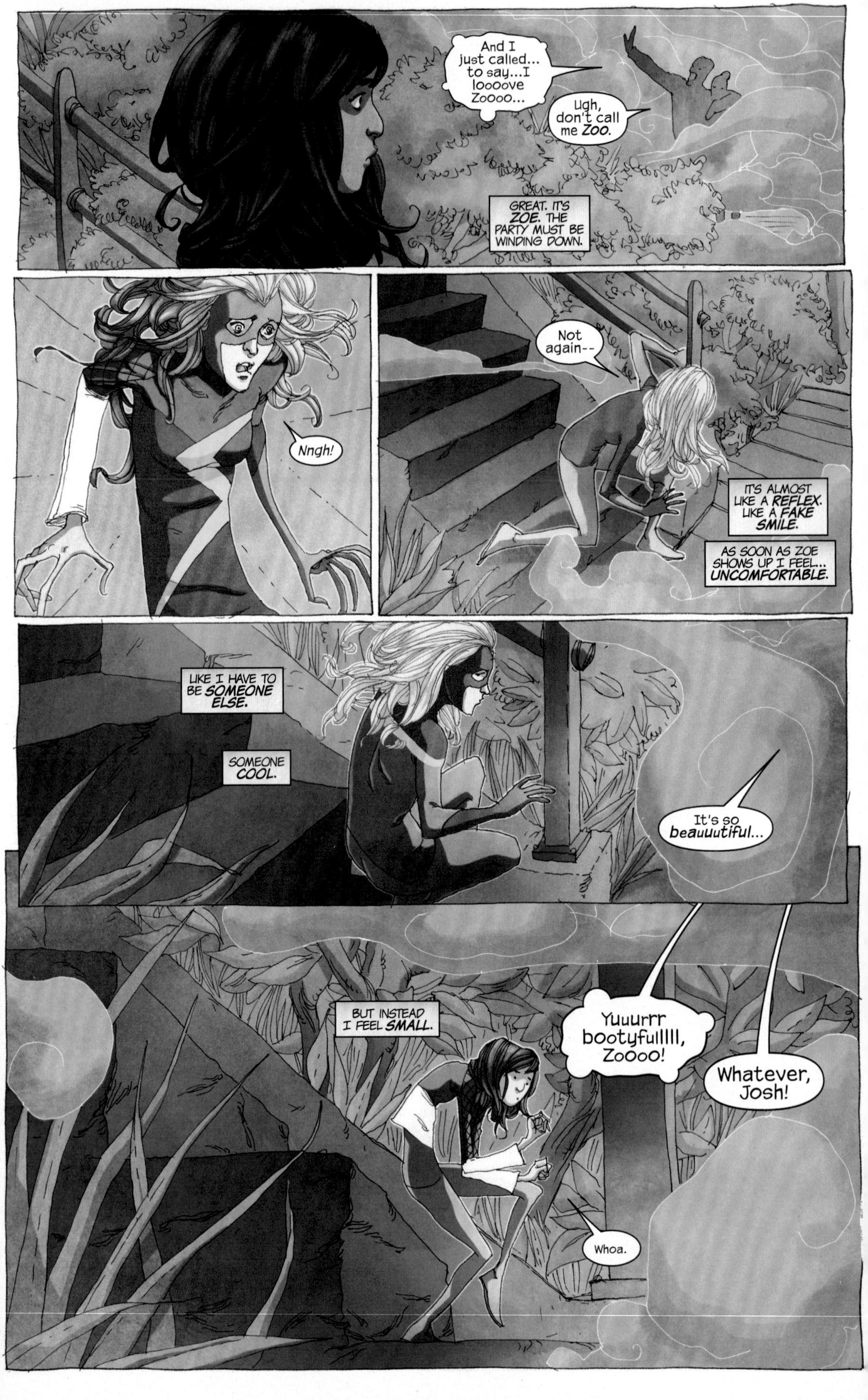
And I just called... to say...I loooove Zoooo...
Ugh, don't call me ZOO.
GREAT. IT'S ZOE. THE PARTY MUST BE WINDING DOWN.
Nngh!
Not again--
IT'S ALMOST LIKE A REFLEX. LIKE A FAKE SMILE.
AS SOON AS ZOE SHOWS UP I FEEL... UNCOMFORTABLE.
LIKE I HAVE TO BE SOMEONE ELSE.
SOMEONE COOL.
It's so beauuutiful...
BUT INSTEAD I FEEL SMALL.
Yuuurrr bootyfullllll, Zoooo!
Whatever, Josh!
Whoa.

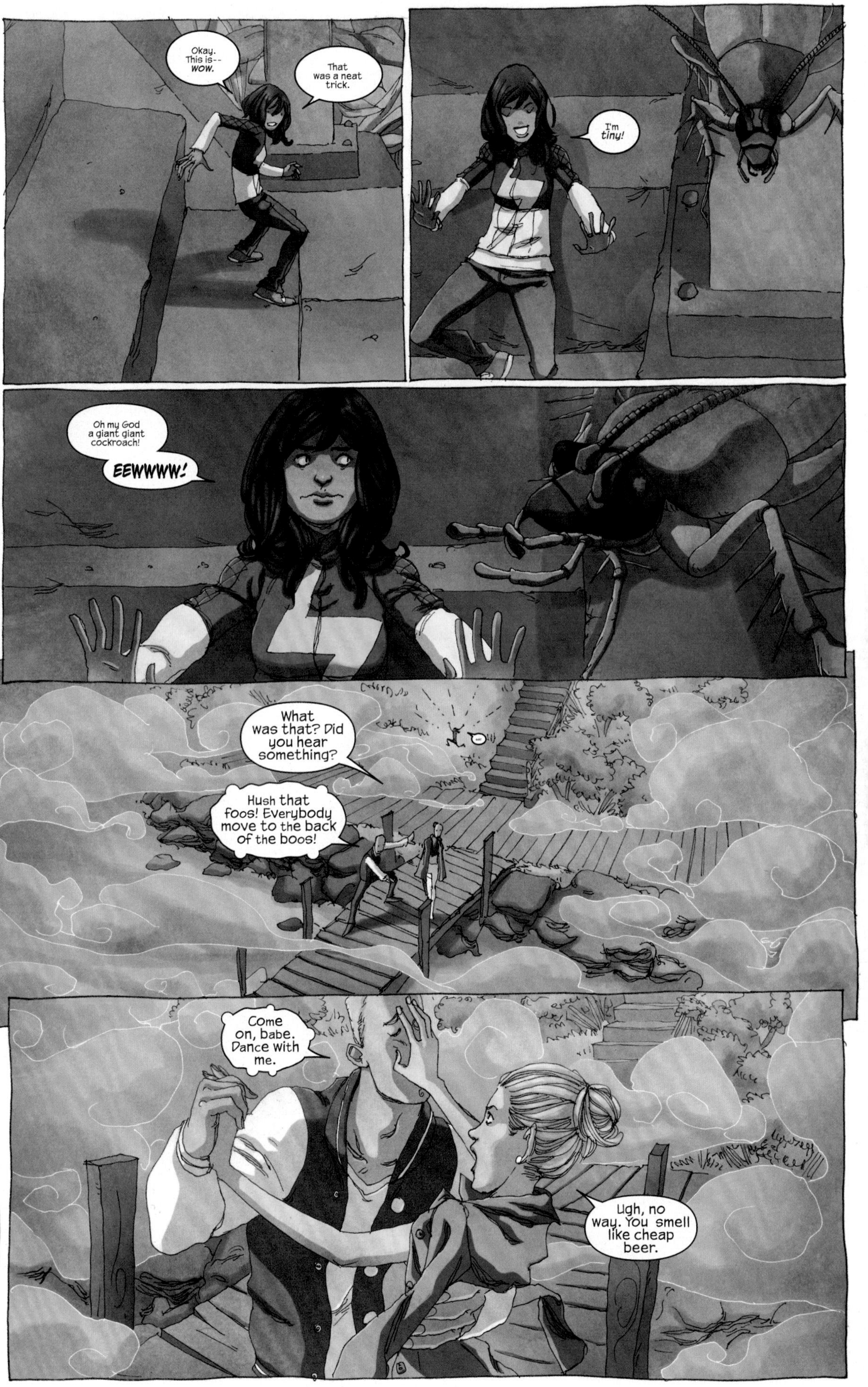
Okay. This is-- WOW.
That was a neat trick.
I'm tiny!
Oh my God a giant giant cockroach!
EEWWWW!
What was that? Did you hear something?
Hush that foos! Everybody move to the back of the boos!
Come on, babe. Dance with me.
Ugh, no way. You smell like cheap beer.

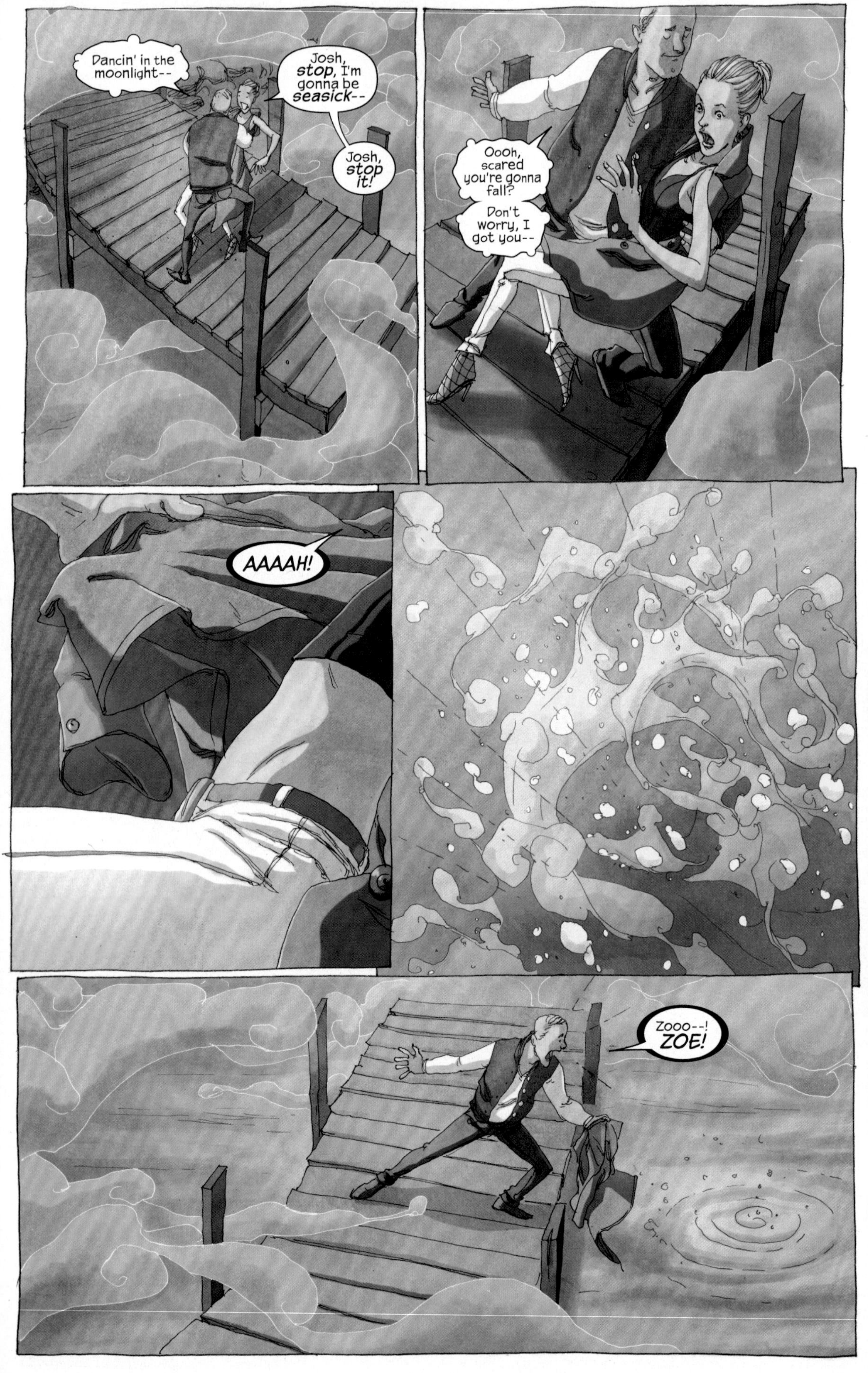
Dancin' in the moonlight--
Josh, stop, I'm gonna be seasick--
Josh, stop it!
Oooh, scared you're gonna fall?
Don't worry, I got you--
AAAAH!
Zooo--! ZOE!

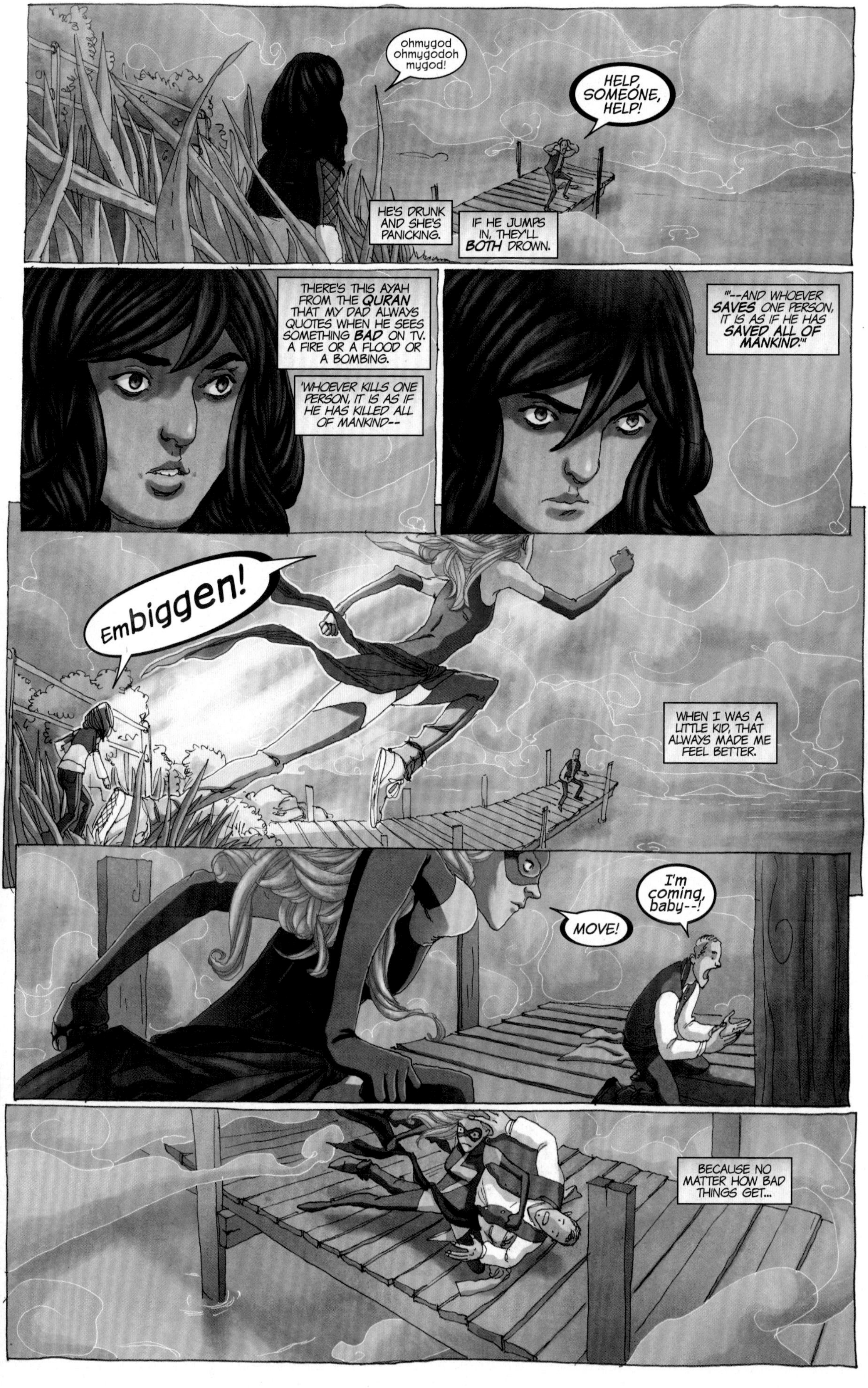
ohmygod ohmygodoh mygod!
HELP, SOMEONE, HELP!
HE'S DRUNK AND SHE'S PANICKING.
IF HE JUMPS IN, THEY'LL BOTH DROWN.
THERE'S THIS AYAH FROM THE QURAN THAT MY DAD ALWAYS QUOTES WHEN HE SEES SOMETHING BAD ON TV. A FIRE OR A FLOOD OR A BOMBING.
'WHOEVER KILLS ONE PERSON, IT IS AS IF HE HAS KILLED ALL OF MANKIND--
'--AND WHOEVER SAVES ONE PERSON, IT IS AS IF HE HAS SAVED ALL OF MANKIND.'
Embiggen!
WHEN I WAS A LITTLE KID, THAT ALWAYS MADE ME FEEL BETTER.
MOVE!
I'm coming, baby--!
BECAUSE NO MATTER HOW BAD THINGS GET...

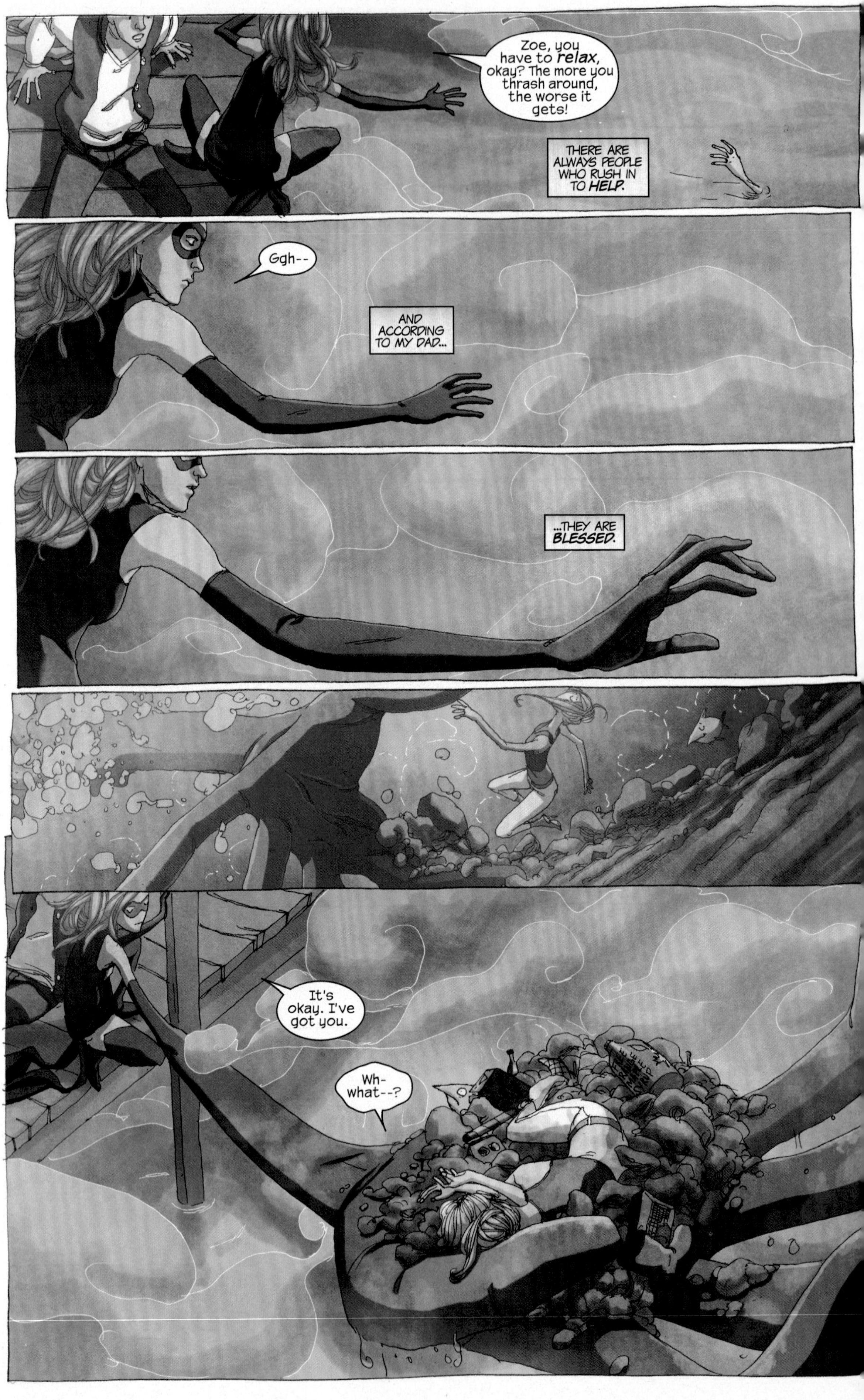

Zoe, you have to relax, okay? The more you thrash around, the worse it gets!
THERE ARE ALWAYS PEOPLE WHO RUSH IN TO HELP.
Ggh--
AND ACCORDING TO MY DAD...
...THEY ARE BLESSED.
It's okay. I've got you.
Wh-what--?

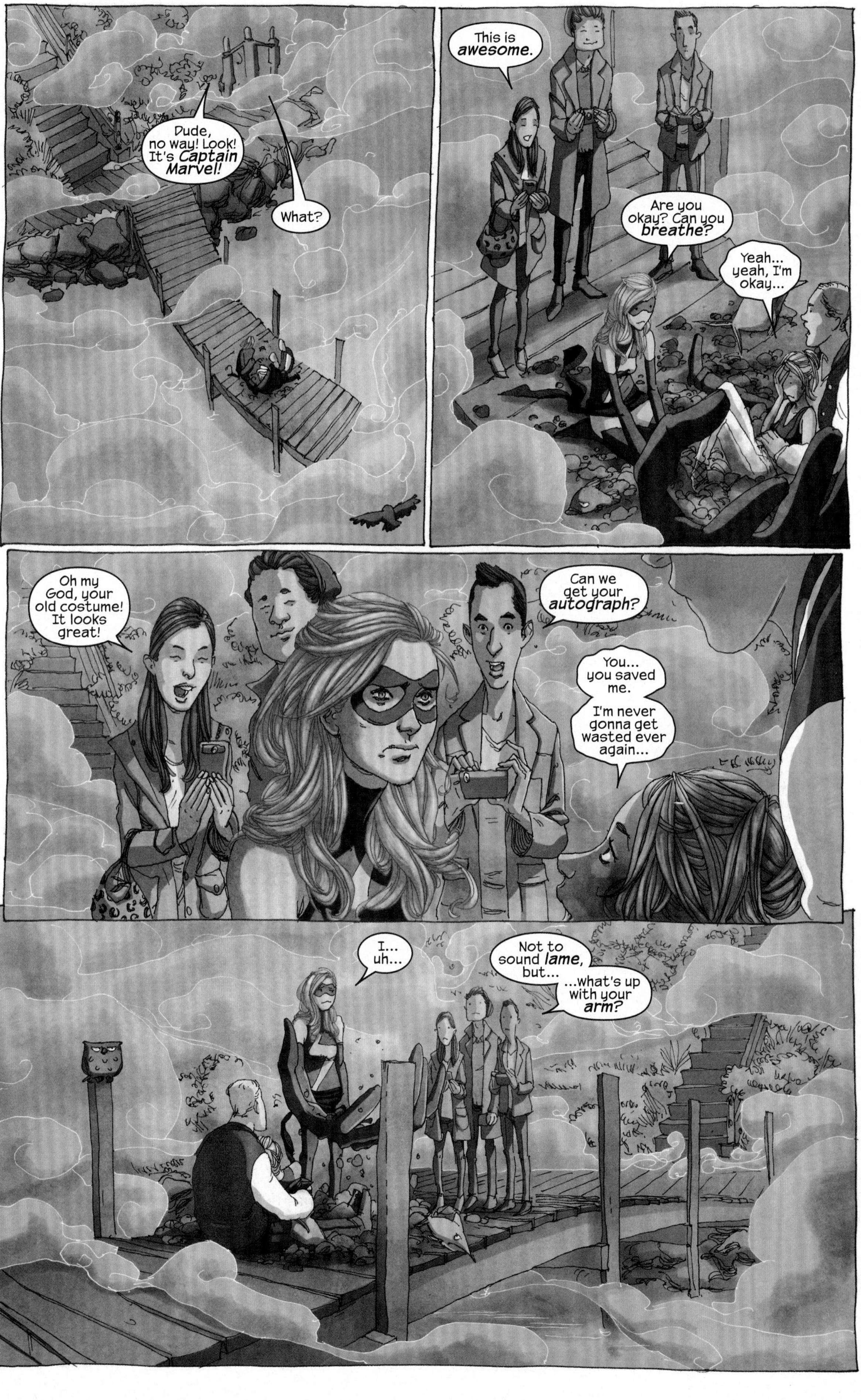

Dude, no way! Look! It's *Captain Marvel!*
What?
This is *awesome.*
Are you okay? Can you *breathe?*
Yeah... yeah, I'm okay...
Oh my God, your old costume! It looks great!
Can we get your *autograph?*
You... you saved me.
I'm never gonna get wasted ever again...
I... uh...
Not to sound *lame*, but...
...what's up with your *arm?*

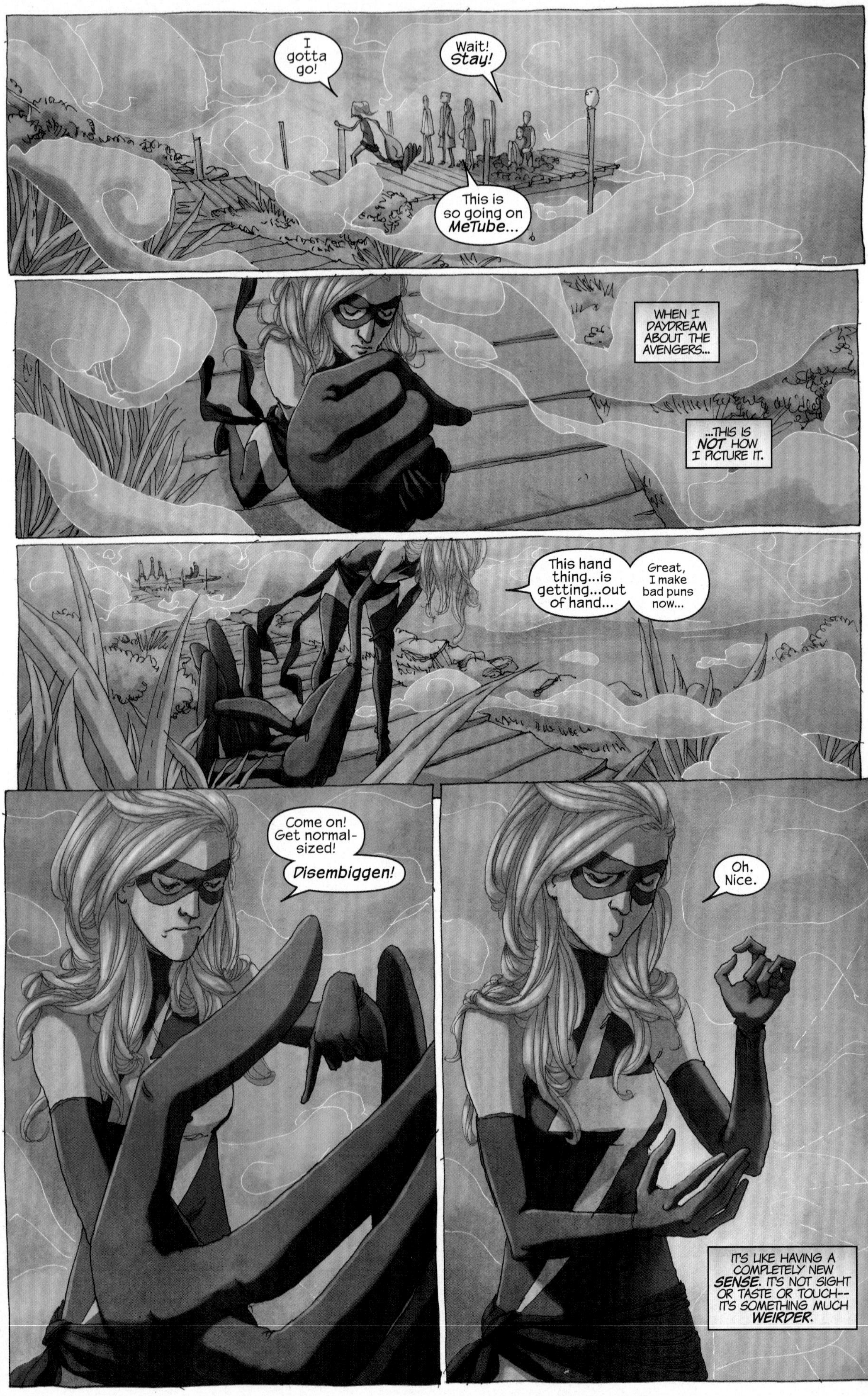
I gotta go!
Wait! Stay!
This is so going on MeTube...
WHEN I DAYDREAM ABOUT THE AVENGERS...
...THIS IS NOT HOW I PICTURE IT.
This hand thing...is getting...out of hand...
Great, I make bad puns now...
Come on! Get normal-sized!
Disembiggen!
Oh. Nice.
IT'S LIKE HAVING A COMPLETELY NEW SENSE. IT'S NOT SIGHT OR TASTE OR TOUCH-- IT'S SOMETHING MUCH WEIRDER.

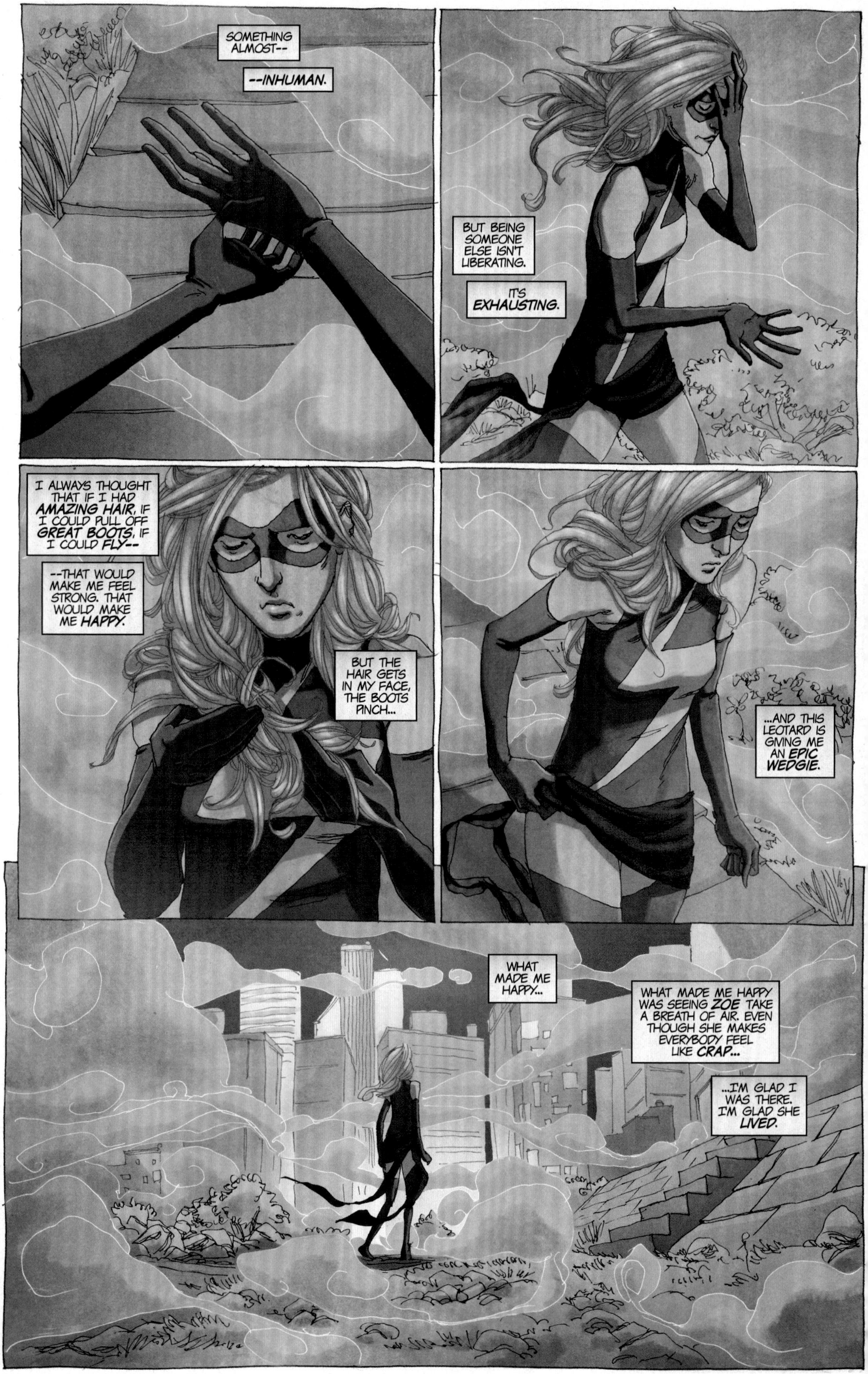
SOMETHING ALMOST--
--INHUMAN.
BUT BEING SOMEONE ELSE ISN'T LIBERATING.
IT'S EXHAUSTING.
I ALWAYS THOUGHT THAT IF I HAD AMAZING HAIR, IF I COULD PULL OFF GREAT BOOTS, IF I COULD FLY--
--THAT WOULD MAKE ME FEEL STRONG. THAT WOULD MAKE ME HAPPY.
BUT THE HAIR GETS IN MY FACE, THE BOOTS PINCH...
...AND THIS LEOTARD IS GIVING ME AN EPIC WEDGIE.
WHAT MADE ME HAPPY...
WHAT MADE ME HAPPY WAS SEEING ZOE TAKE A BREATH OF AIR. EVEN THOUGH SHE MAKES EVERYBODY FEEL LIKE CRAP...
...I'M GLAD I WAS THERE. I'M GLAD SHE LIVED.

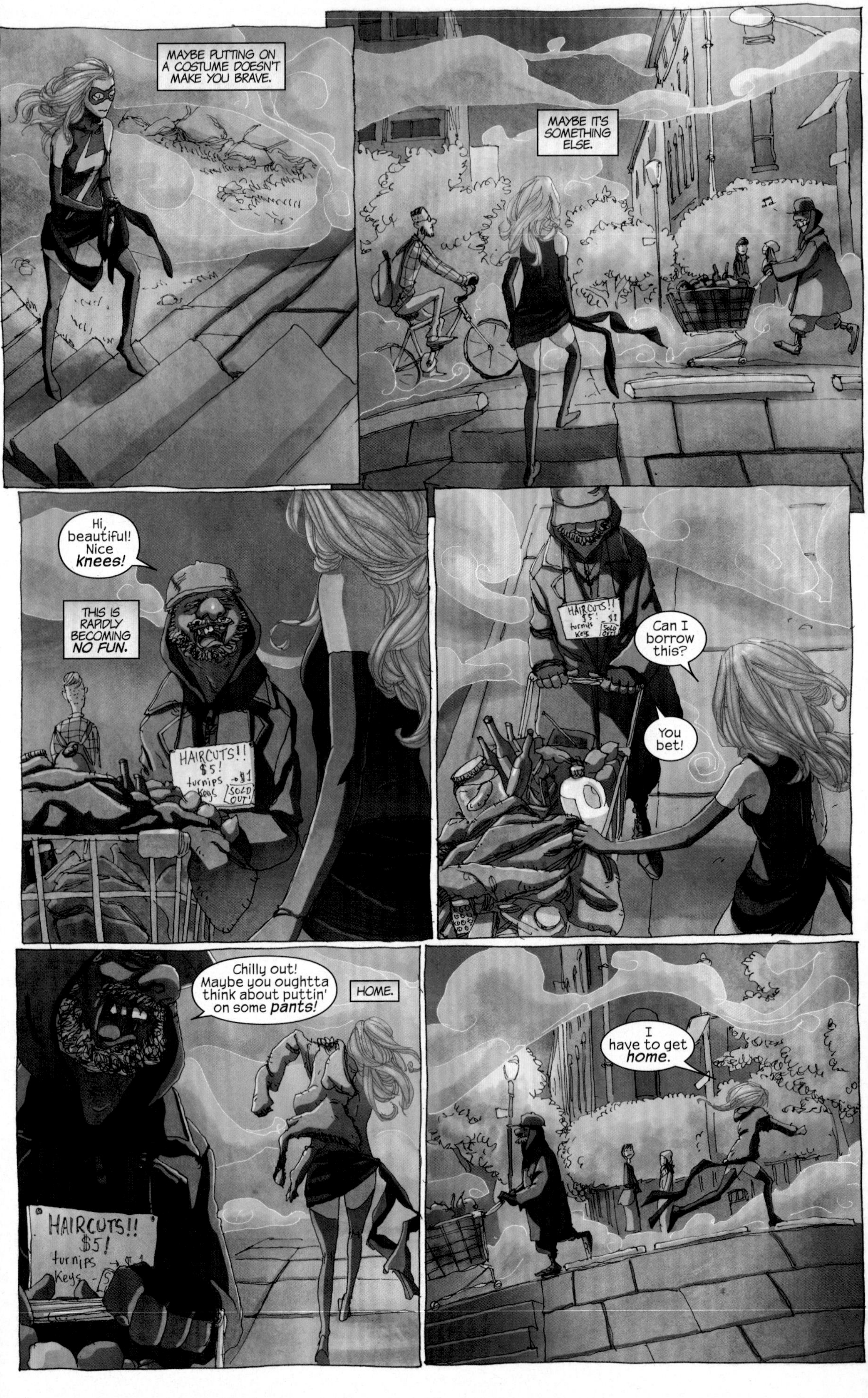
MAYBE PUTTING ON A COSTUME DOESN'T MAKE YOU BRAVE.
MAYBE IT'S SOMETHING ELSE.
Hi, beautiful! Nice *knees!*
THIS IS RAPIDLY BECOMING **NO FUN.**
HAIRCUTS!! $5! turnips →$1 Keys SOLD OUT!
HAIRCUTS!! $5! turnips $1 Keys SOLD OUT
Can I borrow this?
You bet!
Chilly out! Maybe you oughtta think about puttin' on some *pants!*
HOME.
HAIRCUTS!! $5! turnips → $1 Keys
I have to get *home.*

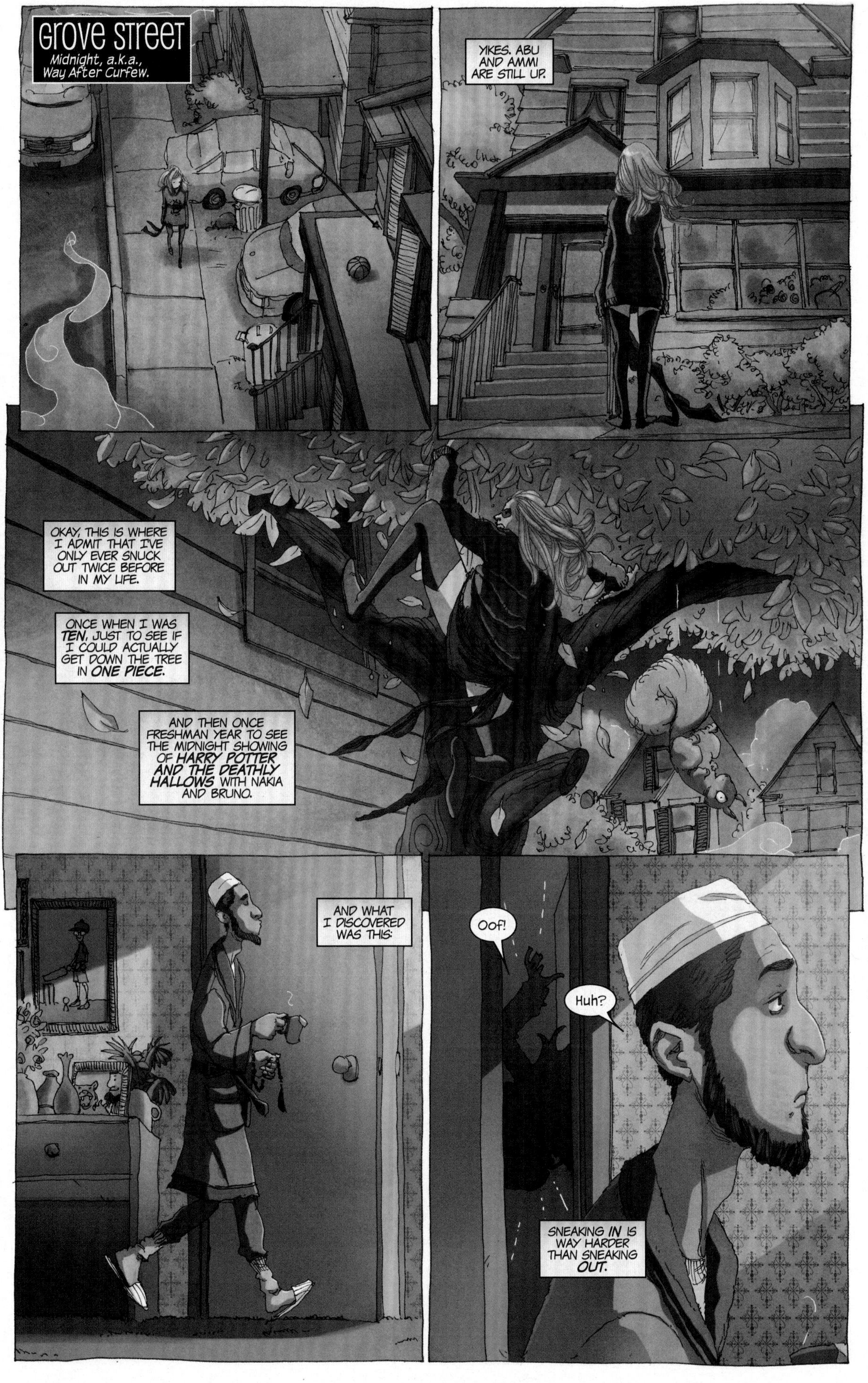
GROVE STREET
Midnight, a.k.a., Way After Curfew.
YIKES. ABU AND AMMI ARE STILL UP.
OKAY, THIS IS WHERE I ADMIT THAT I'VE ONLY EVER SNUCK OUT TWICE BEFORE IN MY LIFE.
ONCE WHEN I WAS TEN, JUST TO SEE IF I COULD ACTUALLY GET DOWN THE TREE IN ONE PIECE.
AND THEN ONCE FRESHMAN YEAR TO SEE THE MIDNIGHT SHOWING OF HARRY POTTER AND THE DEATHLY HALLOWS WITH NAKIA AND BRUNO.
AND WHAT I DISCOVERED WAS THIS:
Oof!
Huh?
SNEAKING IN IS WAY HARDER THAN SNEAKING OUT.

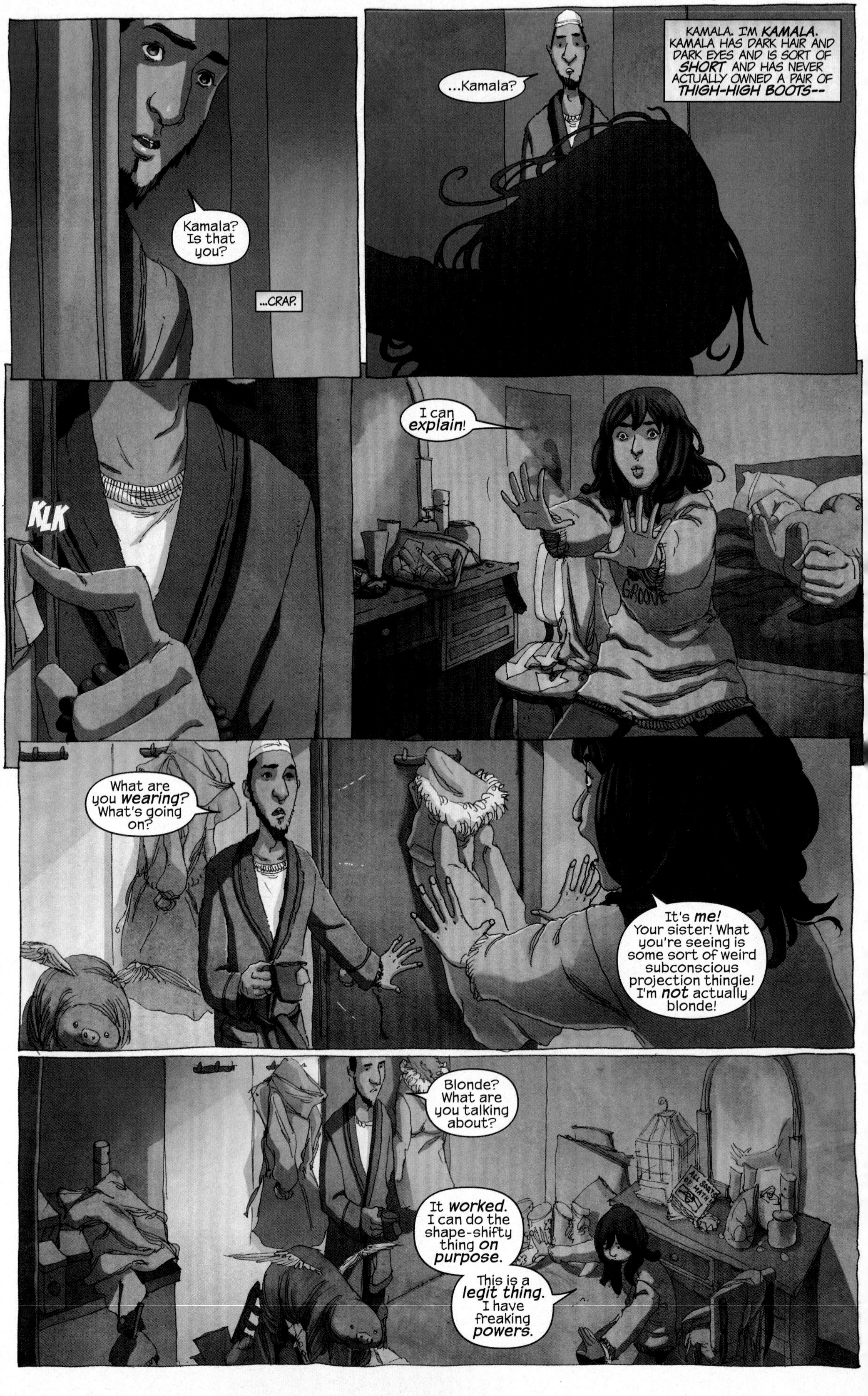
Kamala? Is that you?
...CRAP.
...Kamala?
KAMALA. I'M KAMALA. KAMALA HAS DARK HAIR AND DARK EYES AND IS SORT OF SHORT AND HAS NEVER ACTUALLY OWNED A PAIR OF THIGH-HIGH BOOTS--
KLK
I can explain!
GROOVE
What are you wearing? What's going on?
It's me! Your sister! What you're seeing is some sort of weird subconscious projection thingie! I'm not actually blonde!
Blonde? What are you talking about?
ALL SORTS OF MATH
It worked. I can do the shape-shifty thing on purpose.
This is a legit thing. I have freaking powers.

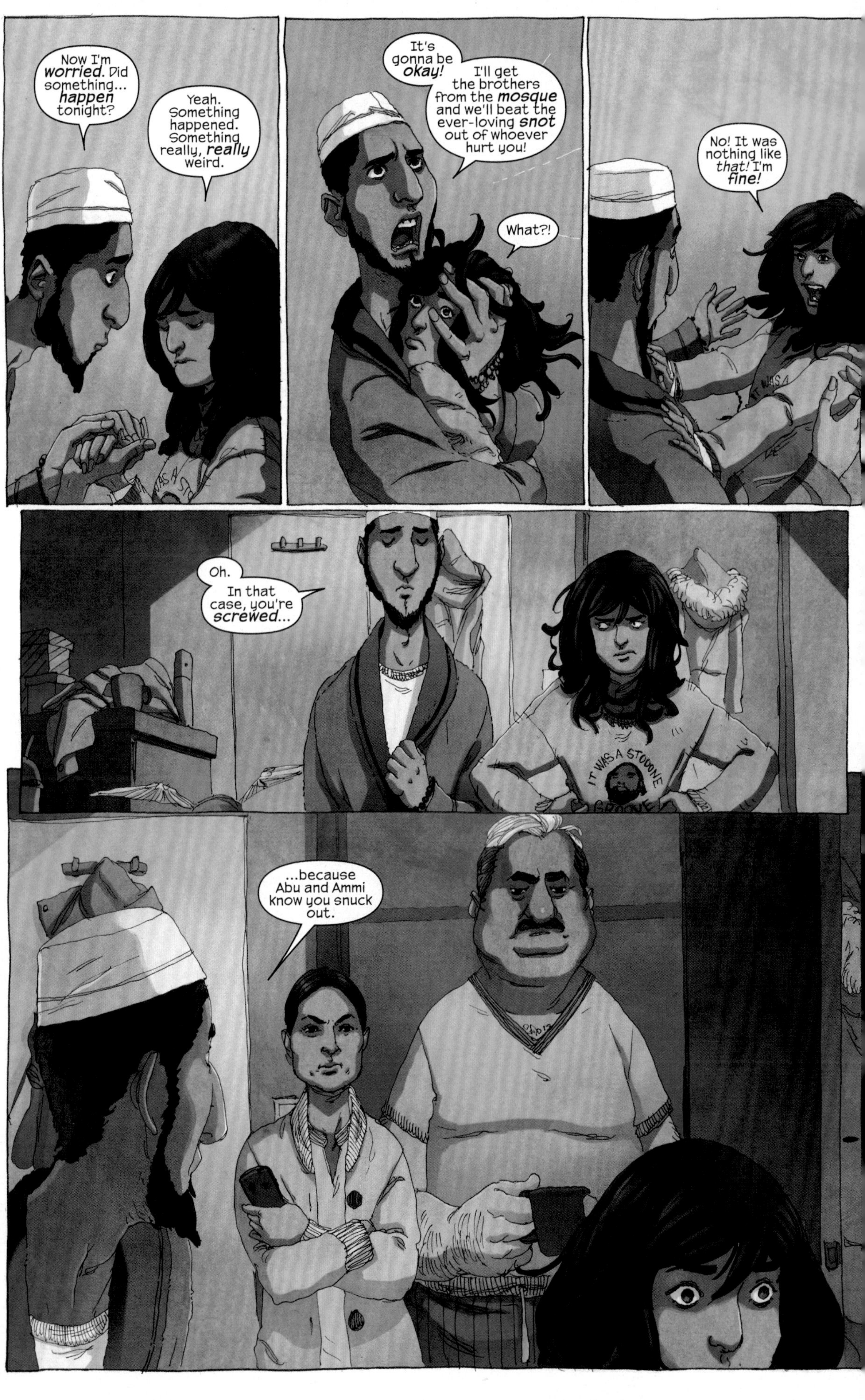
Now I'm worried. Did something... happen tonight?
Yeah. Something happened. Something really, really weird.
It's gonna be okay!
I'll get the brothers from the mosque and we'll beat the ever-loving snot out of whoever hurt you!
What?!
No! It was nothing like that! I'm fine!
Oh.
In that case, you're screwed...
IT WAS A STOOONE GROOVE
...because Abu and Ammi know you snuck out.

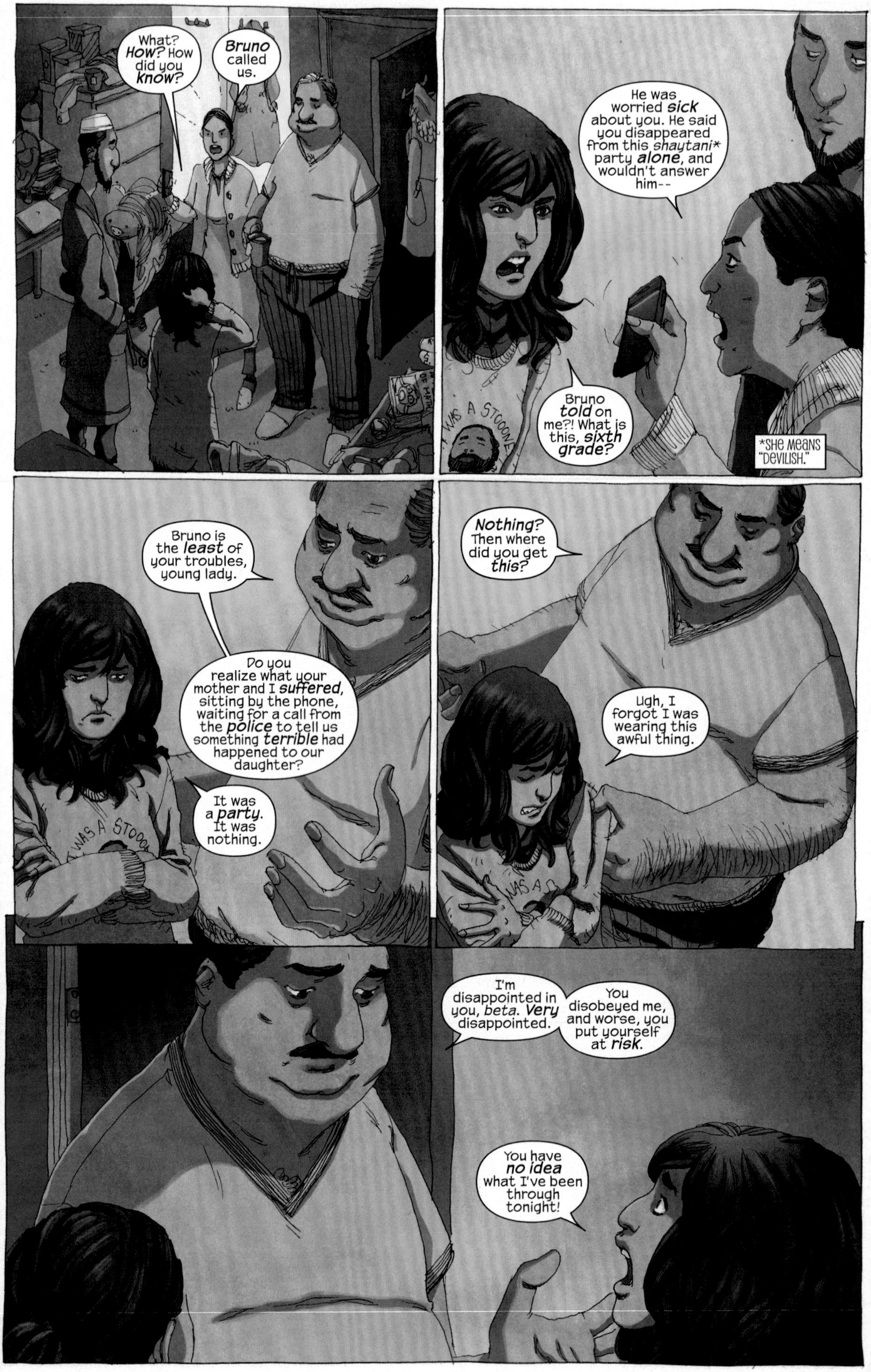
What? *How?* How did you *know?*
Bruno called us.
He was worried *sick* about you. He said you disappeared from this *shaytani** party *alone*, and wouldn't answer him--
Bruno *told* on me?! What is this, *sixth grade?*
*SHE MEANS "DEVILISH."
Bruno is the *least* of your troubles, young lady.
Do you realize what your mother and I *suffered*, sitting by the phone, waiting for a call from the *police* to tell us something *terrible* had happened to our daughter?
It was a *party*. It was nothing.
Nothing? Then where did you get *this?*
Ugh, I forgot I was wearing this awful thing.
I'm disappointed in you, *beta*. *Very* disappointed.
You disobeyed me, and worse, you put yourself at *risk*.
You have *no idea* what I've been through tonight!

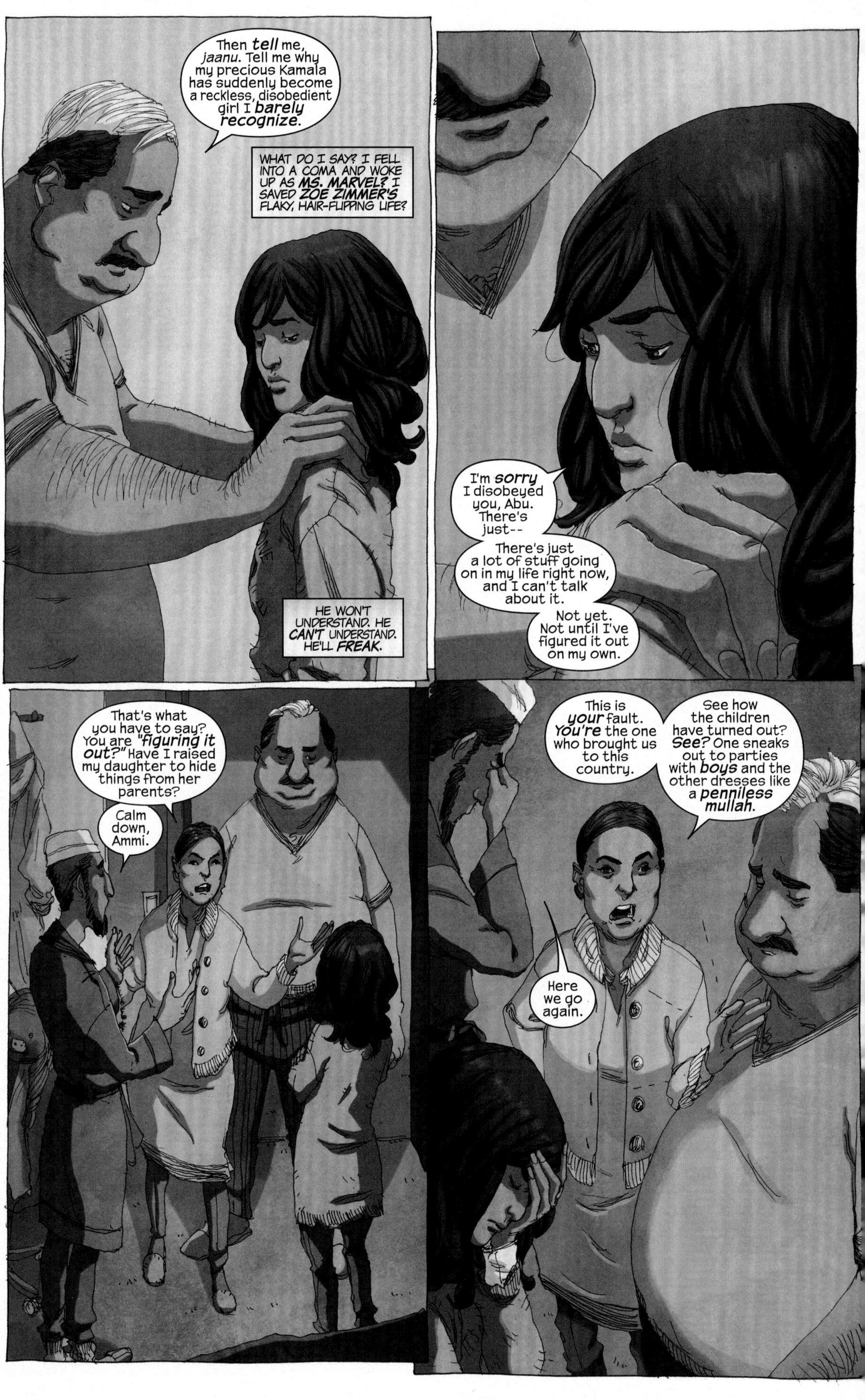
Then tell me, jaanu. Tell me why my precious Kamala has suddenly become a reckless, disobedient girl I barely recognize.
WHAT DO I SAY? I FELL INTO A COMA AND WOKE UP AS MS. MARVEL? I SAVED ZOE ZIMMER'S FLAKY, HAIR-FLIPPING LIFE?
HE WON'T UNDERSTAND. HE CAN'T UNDERSTAND. HE'LL FREAK.
I'm sorry I disobeyed you, Abu. There's just--
There's just a lot of stuff going on in my life right now, and I can't talk about it.
Not yet. Not until I've figured it out on my own.
That's what you have to say? You are "figuring it out?" Have I raised my daughter to hide things from her parents?
Calm down, Ammi.
This is your fault. You're the one who brought us to this country.
See how the children have turned out? See? One sneaks out to parties with boys and the other dresses like a penniless mullah.
Here we go again.

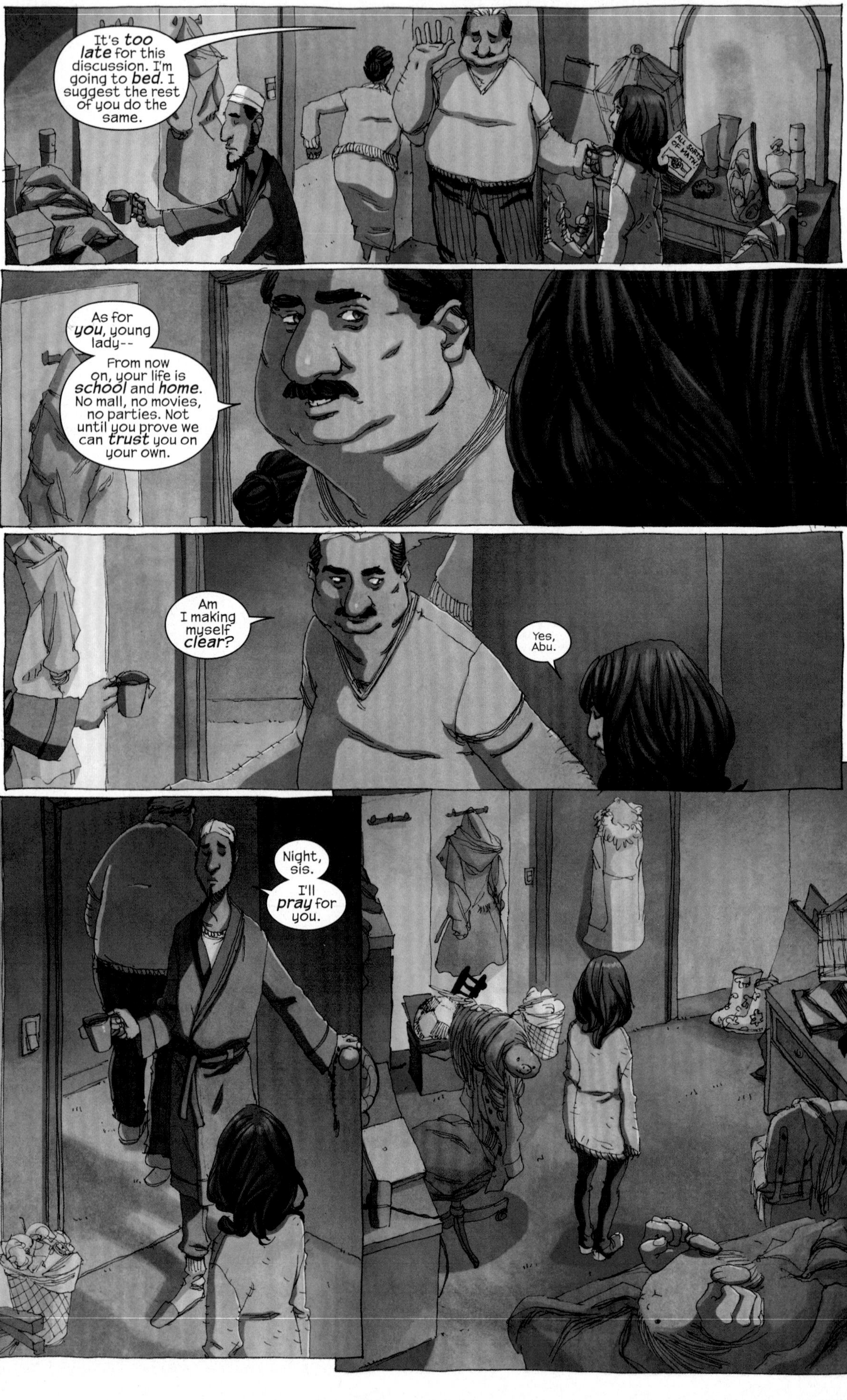
It's too late for this discussion. I'm going to bed. I suggest the rest of you do the same.
ALL SORTS OF MATH!
As for you, young lady--
From now on, your life is school and home. No mall, no movies, no parties. Not until you prove we can trust you on your own.
Am I making myself clear?
Yes, Abu.
Night, sis.
I'll pray for you.

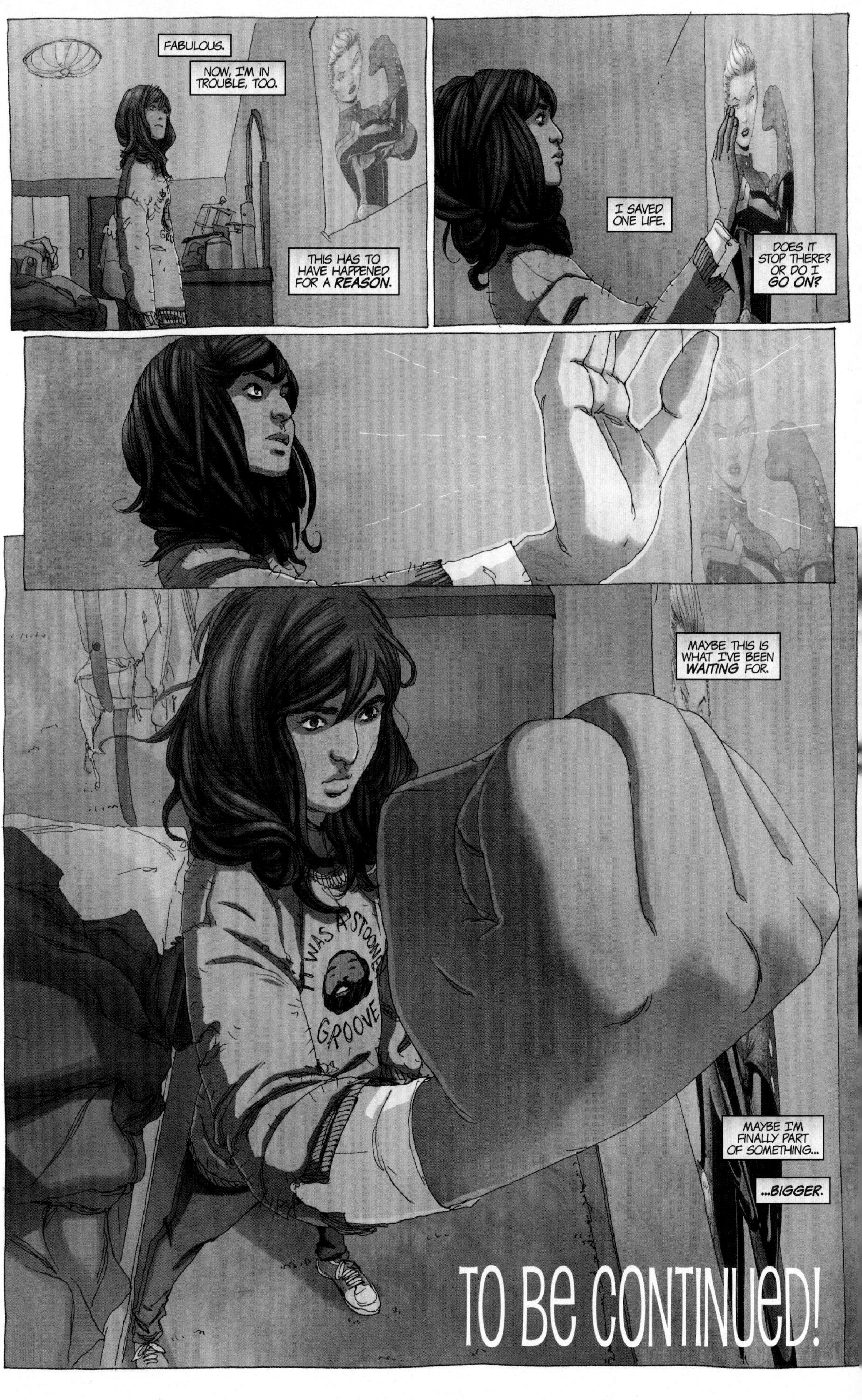
FABULOUS.
NOW, I'M IN TROUBLE, TOO.
THIS HAS TO HAVE HAPPENED FOR A **REASON**.
I SAVED ONE LIFE.
DOES IT STOP THERE? OR DO I **GO ON?**
MAYBE THIS IS WHAT I'VE BEEN **WAITING** FOR.
IT WAS A STOONER GROOVE
MAYBE I'M FINALLY PART OF SOMETHING...
...**BIGGER**.
TO BE CONTINUED!

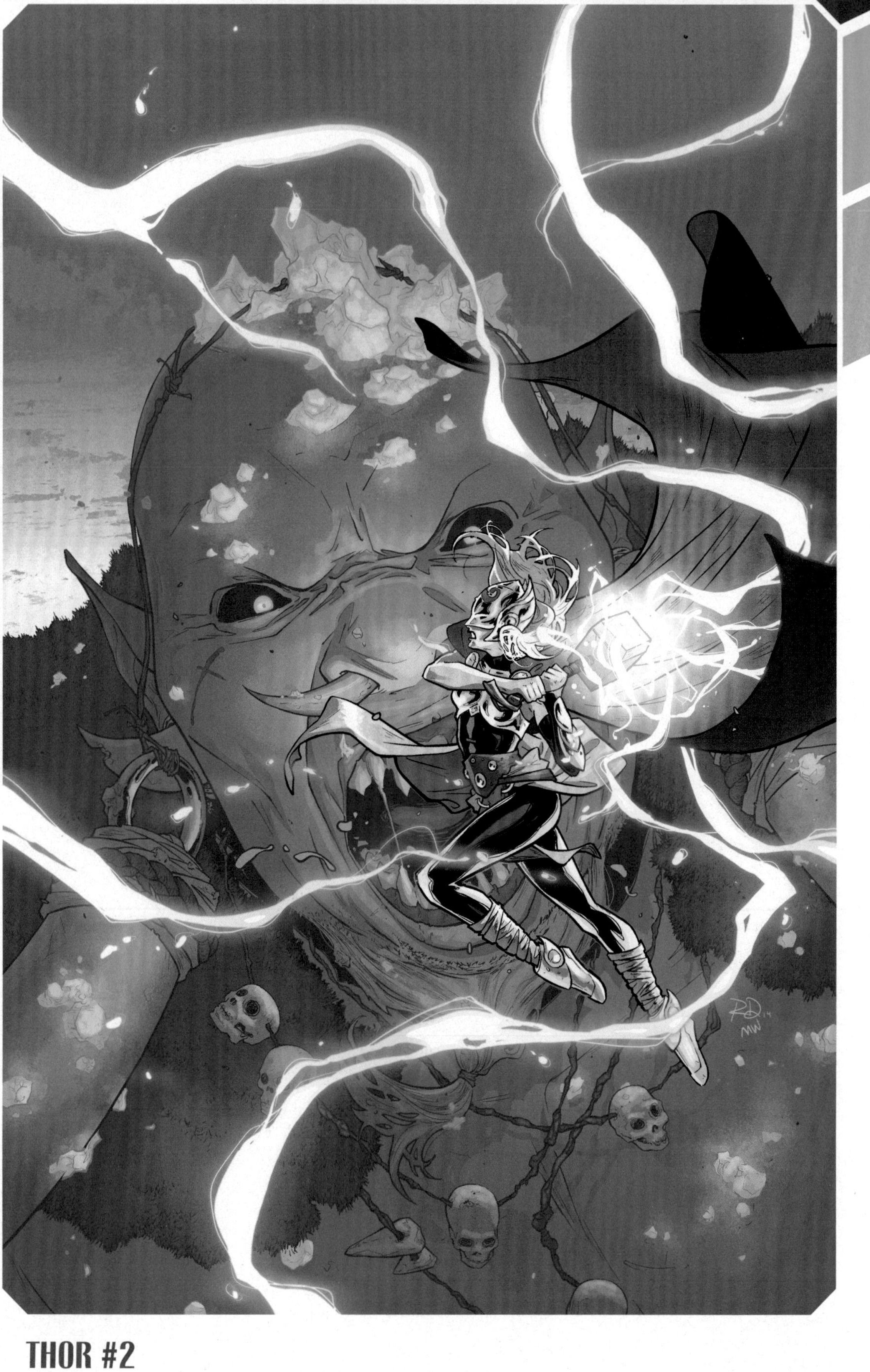

THOR #2

It's the dawning of a new age for Asgard.

After a self-imposed exile, Odin has returned to his former kingdom. But his wife Freyja, who had been ruling in his stead, has no intention of having things go back to the way they were. And their son Thor, the God of Thunder, finds himself no longer worthy of wielding Mjolnir, his enchanted hammer, which now rests on the surface of the moon.

Back on Earth, all of this is sure to be good news for the Roxxon Energy Company, which recently ran afoul of the God of Thunder. But Roxxon has other problems to deal with--one of their undersea mining stations was attacked by Frost Giants and the evil elf sorcerer Malekith. Thor attempted to stop them, but without his hammer he was quickly overpowered and had his arm chopped off. Things look bleak.

But back on the moon, a mysterious woman is able to lift Mjolnir and finds herself transformed into the all-new Goddess of Thunder!

THE GODDESS OF THUNDER

JASON AARON
WRITER

RUSSELL DAUTERMAN
ARTIST

MATTHEW WILSON
COLOR ARTIST

VC's JOE SABINO
LETTERER & PRODUCTION

RUSSELL DAUTERMAN & MATTHEW WILSON
COVER ARTISTS

ESAD RIBIC; CHRIS SAMNEE & MATTHEW WILSON; JAMES STOKOE
VARIANT COVER ARTISTS

JON MOISAN
ASSISTANT EDITOR

WIL MOSS
EDITOR

AXEL ALONSO
EDITOR IN CHIEF

JOE QUESADA
CHIEF CREATIVE OFFICER

DAN BUCKLEY
PUBLISHER

ALAN FINE
EXECUTIVE PRODUCER

THOR CREATED BY STAN LEE, LARRY LIEBER & JACK KIRBY

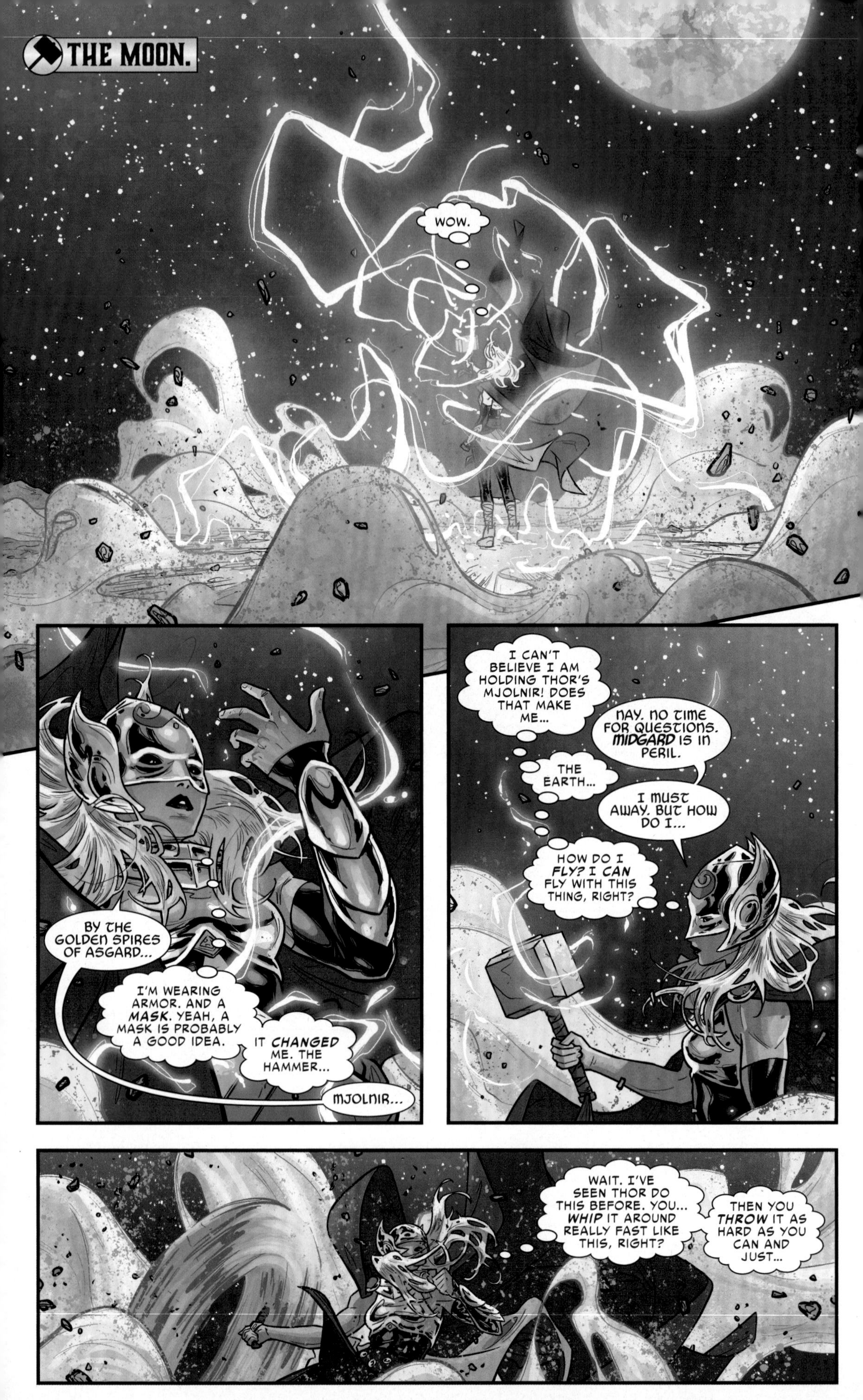
THE MOON.
WOW.
BY THE GOLDEN SPIRES OF ASGARD...
I'M WEARING ARMOR. AND A MASK. YEAH, A MASK IS PROBABLY A GOOD IDEA.
IT CHANGED ME. THE HAMMER...
MJOLNIR...
I CAN'T BELIEVE I AM HOLDING THOR'S MJOLNIR! DOES THAT MAKE ME...
NAY. NO TIME FOR QUESTIONS. MIDGARD IS IN PERIL.
THE EARTH...
I MUST AWAY. BUT HOW DO I...
HOW DO I FLY? I CAN FLY WITH THIS THING, RIGHT?
WAIT. I'VE SEEN THOR DO THIS BEFORE. YOU... WHIP IT AROUND REALLY FAST LIKE THIS, RIGHT?
THEN YOU THROW IT AS HARD AS YOU CAN AND JUST...

It's the dawning of a new age for Asgard.

After a self-imposed exile, Odin has returned to his former kingdom. But his wife Freyja, who had been ruling in his stead, has no intention of having things go back to the way they were. And their son Thor, the God of Thunder, finds himself no longer worthy of wielding Mjolnir, his enchanted hammer, which now rests on the surface of the moon.

Back on Earth, all of this is sure to be good news for the Roxxon Energy Company, which recently ran afoul of the God of Thunder. But Roxxon has other problems to deal with--one of their undersea mining stations was attacked by Frost Giants and the evil elf sorcerer Malekith. Thor attempted to stop them, but without his hammer he was quickly overpowered and had his arm chopped off. Things look bleak.

But back on the moon, a mysterious woman is able to lift Mjolnir and finds herself transformed into the all-new Goddess of Thunder!

THE GODDESS OF THUNDER

JASON AARON
WRITER

RUSSELL DAUTERMAN
ARTIST

MATTHEW WILSON
COLOR ARTIST

VC's JOE SABINO
LETTERER & PRODUCTION

RUSSELL DAUTERMAN & MATTHEW WILSON
COVER ARTISTS

ESAD RIBIC; CHRIS SAMNEE & MATTHEW WILSON; JAMES STOKOE
VARIANT COVER ARTISTS

JON MOISAN
ASSISTANT EDITOR

WIL MOSS
EDITOR

AXEL ALONSO
EDITOR IN CHIEF

JOE QUESADA
CHIEF CREATIVE OFFICER

DAN BUCKLEY
PUBLISHER

ALAN FINE
EXECUTIVE PRODUCER

THOR CREATED BY STAN LEE, LARRY LIEBER & JACK KIRBY

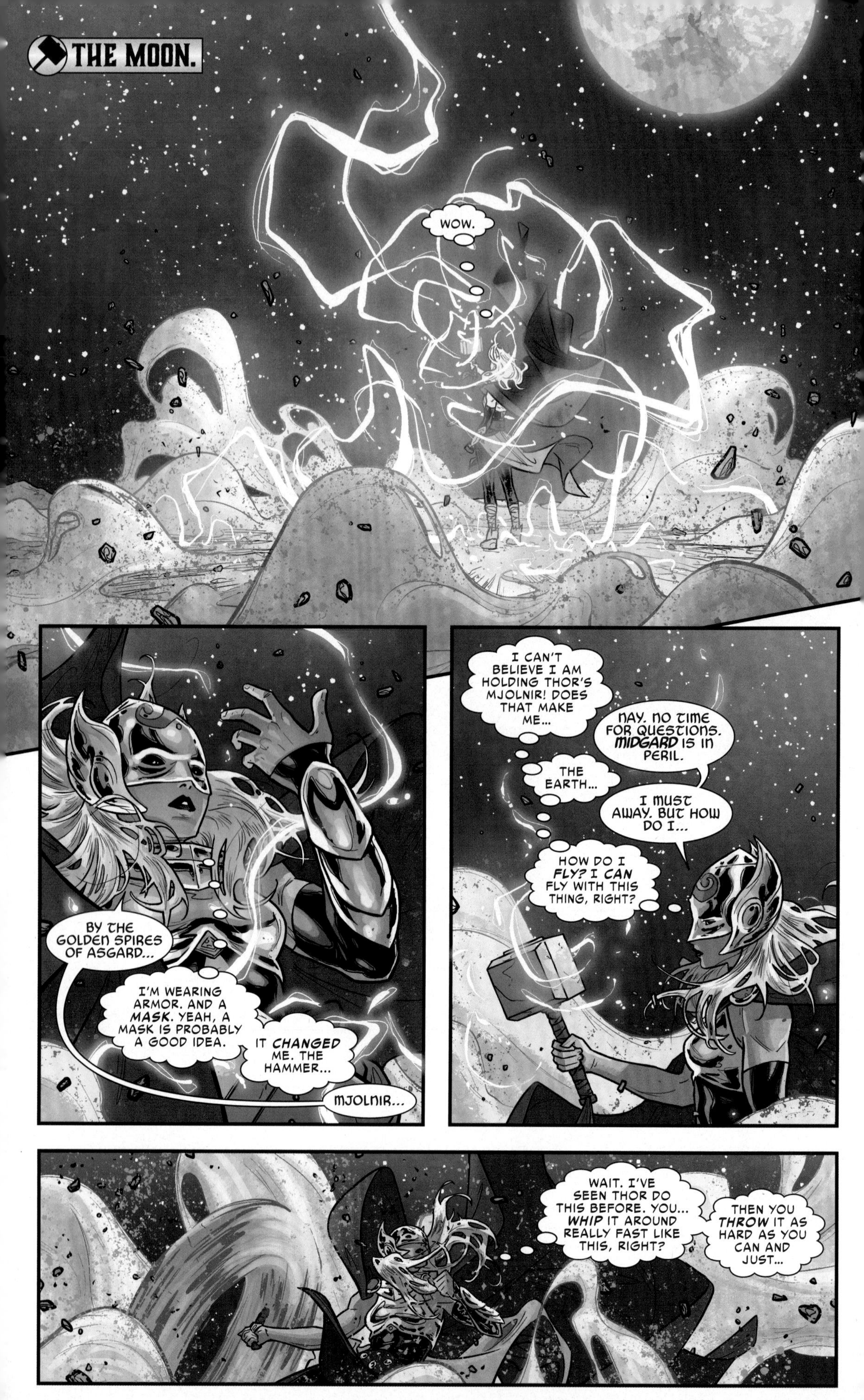
THE MOON.
WOW.
BY THE GOLDEN SPIRES OF ASGARD...
I'M WEARING ARMOR. AND A MASK. YEAH, A MASK IS PROBABLY A GOOD IDEA.
IT CHANGED ME. THE HAMMER...
MJOLNIR...
I CAN'T BELIEVE I AM HOLDING THOR'S MJOLNIR! DOES THAT MAKE ME...
NAY. NO TIME FOR QUESTIONS. MIDGARD IS IN PERIL.
THE EARTH...
I MUST AWAY. BUT HOW DO I...
HOW DO I FLY? I CAN FLY WITH THIS THING, RIGHT?
WAIT. I'VE SEEN THOR DO THIS BEFORE. YOU... WHIP IT AROUND REALLY FAST LIKE THIS, RIGHT?
THEN YOU THROW IT AS HARD AS YOU CAN AND JUST...

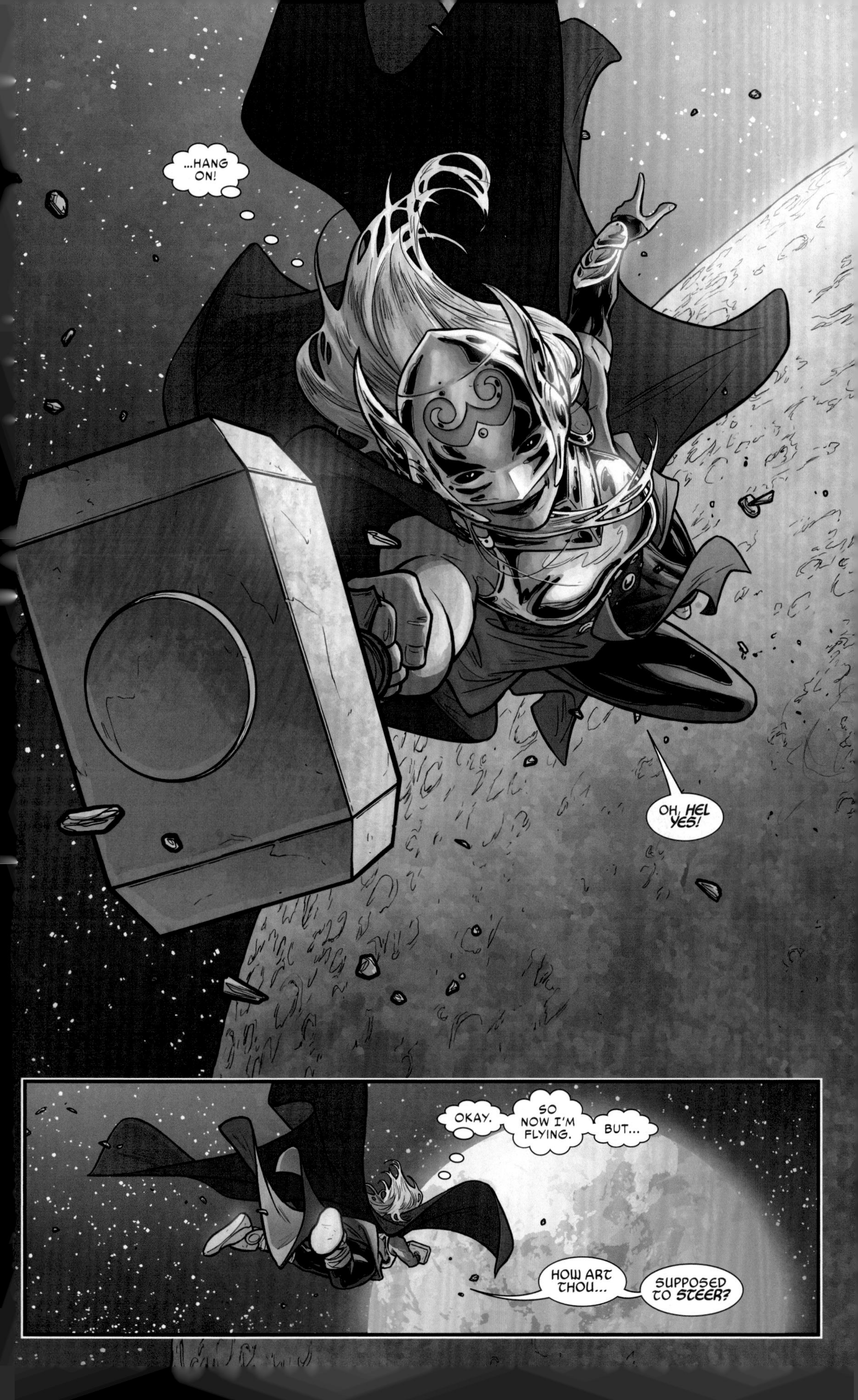

...HANG ON!
OH, HEL YES!
OKAY.
SO NOW I'M FLYING.
BUT...
HOW ART THOU...
SUPPOSED TO STEER?

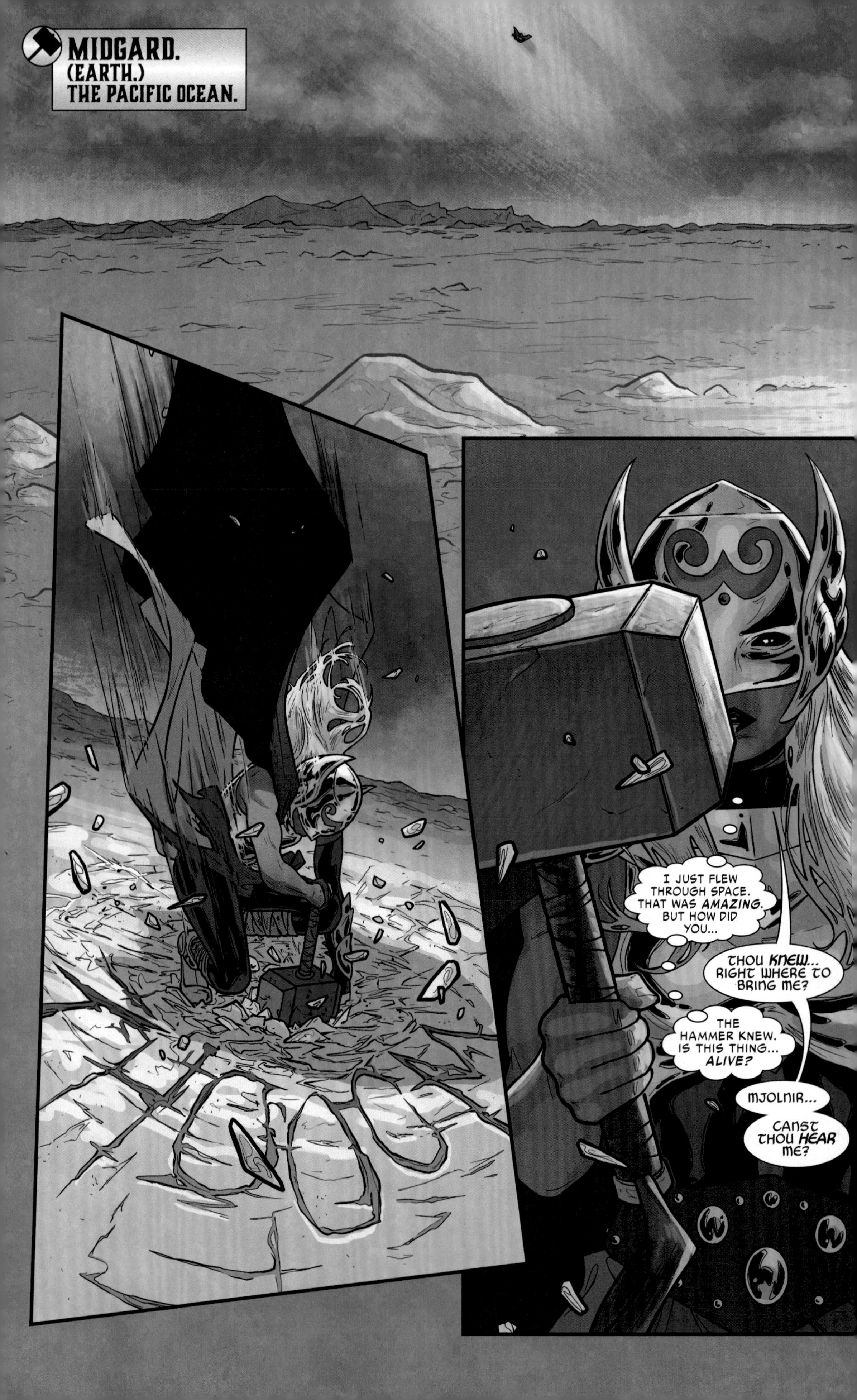
MIDGARD.
(EARTH.)
THE PACIFIC OCEAN.
I JUST FLEW THROUGH SPACE. THAT WAS AMAZING. BUT HOW DID YOU...
THOU KNEW... RIGHT WHERE TO BRING ME?
THE HAMMER KNEW. IS THIS THING... ALIVE?
MJOLNIR...
CANST THOU HEAR ME?

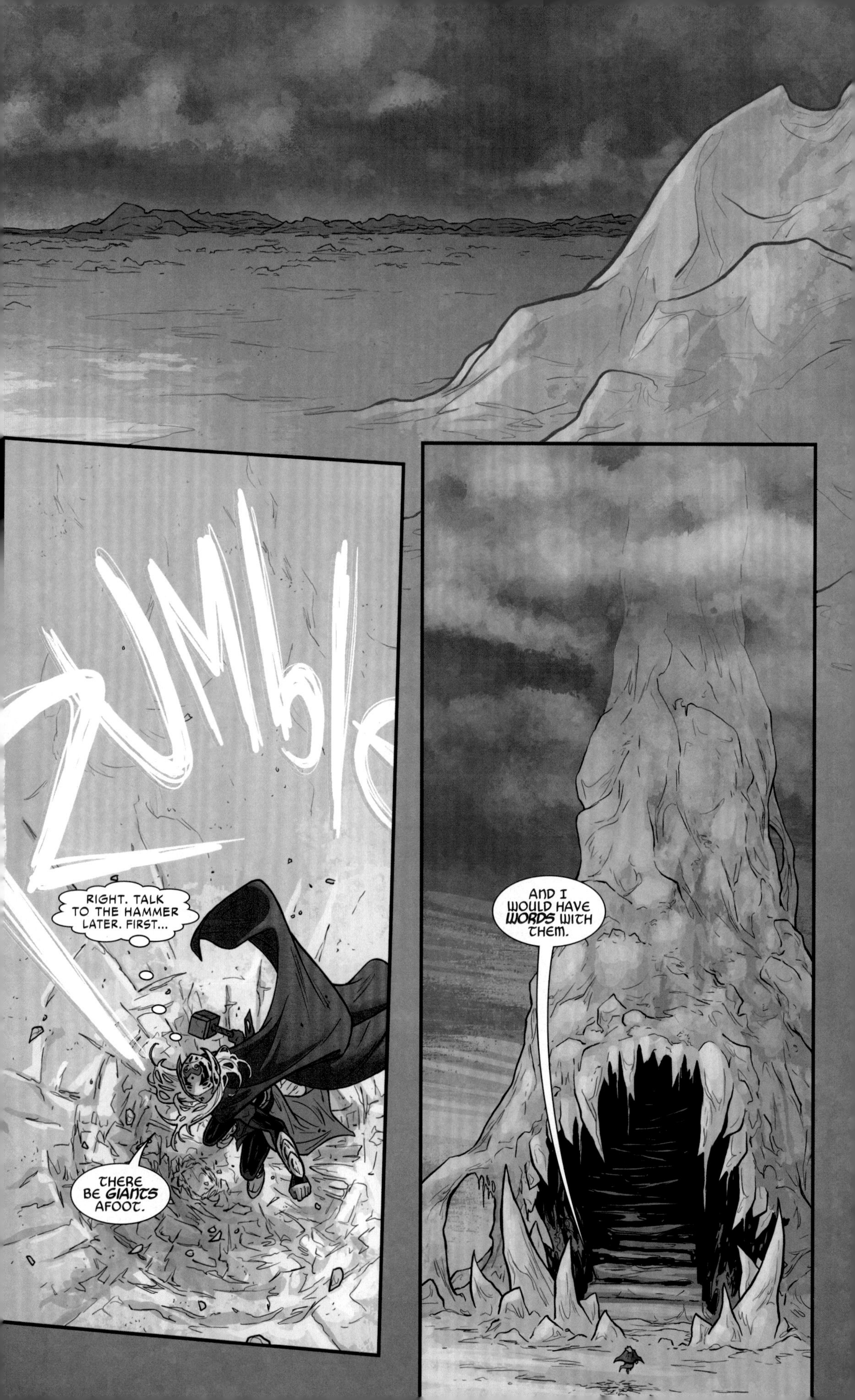
RUMBLE
RIGHT. TALK TO THE HAMMER LATER. FIRST...
THERE BE GIANTS AFOOT.
AND I WOULD HAVE WORDS WITH THEM.

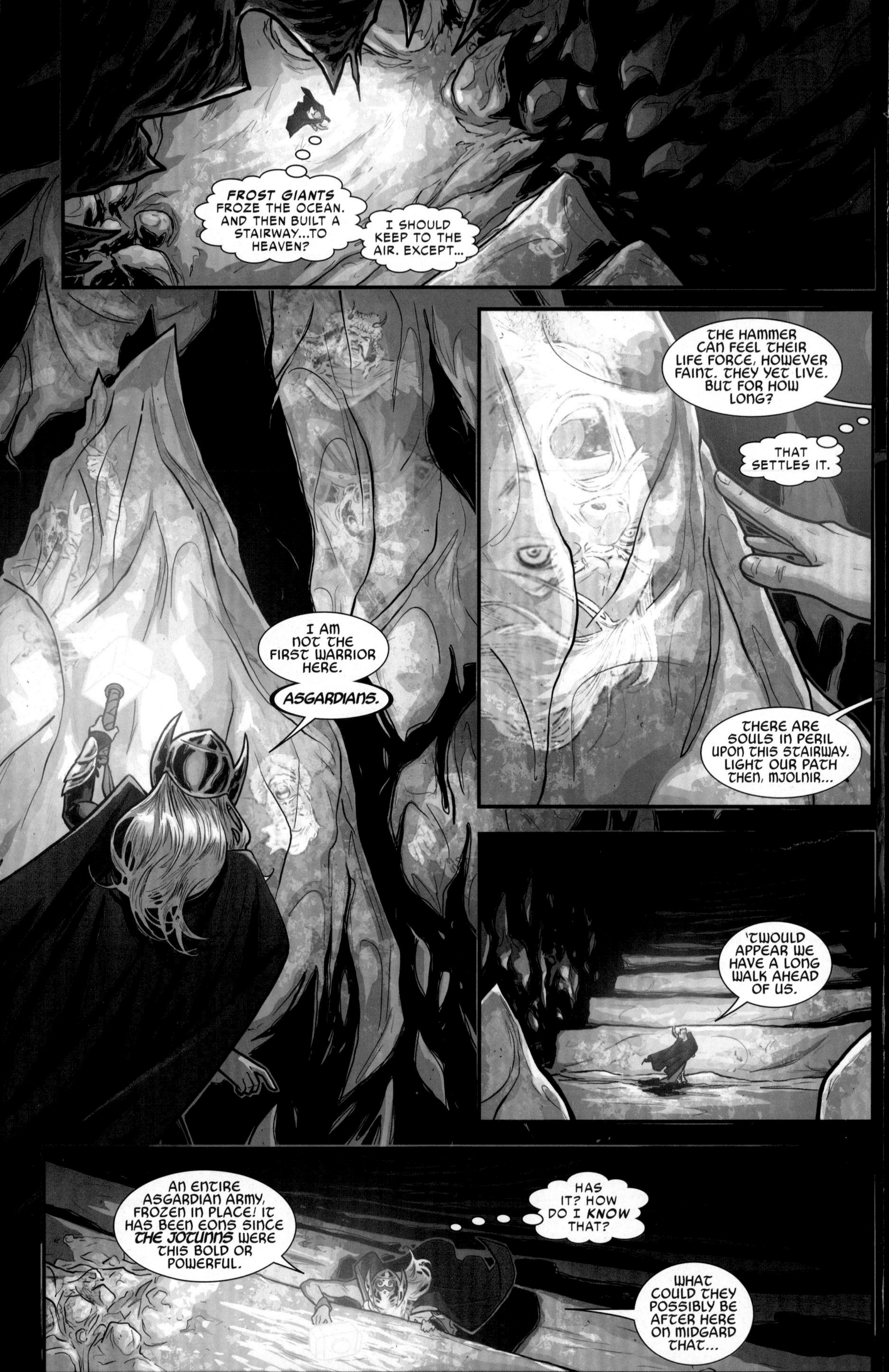
FROST GIANTS FROZE THE OCEAN. AND THEN BUILT A STAIRWAY...TO HEAVEN?
I SHOULD KEEP TO THE AIR. EXCEPT...
I AM NOT THE FIRST WARRIOR HERE.
ASGARDIANS.
THE HAMMER CAN FEEL THEIR LIFE FORCE, HOWEVER FAINT. THEY YET LIVE. BUT FOR HOW LONG?
THAT SETTLES IT.
THERE ARE SOULS IN PERIL UPON THIS STAIRWAY. LIGHT OUR PATH THEN, MJOLNIR...
'TWOULD APPEAR WE HAVE A LONG WALK AHEAD OF US.
AN ENTIRE ASGARDIAN ARMY, FROZEN IN PLACE! IT HAS BEEN EONS SINCE THE JOTUNNS WERE THIS BOLD OR POWERFUL.
HAS IT? HOW DO I KNOW THAT?
WHAT COULD THEY POSSIBLY BE AFTER HERE ON MIDGARD THAT...

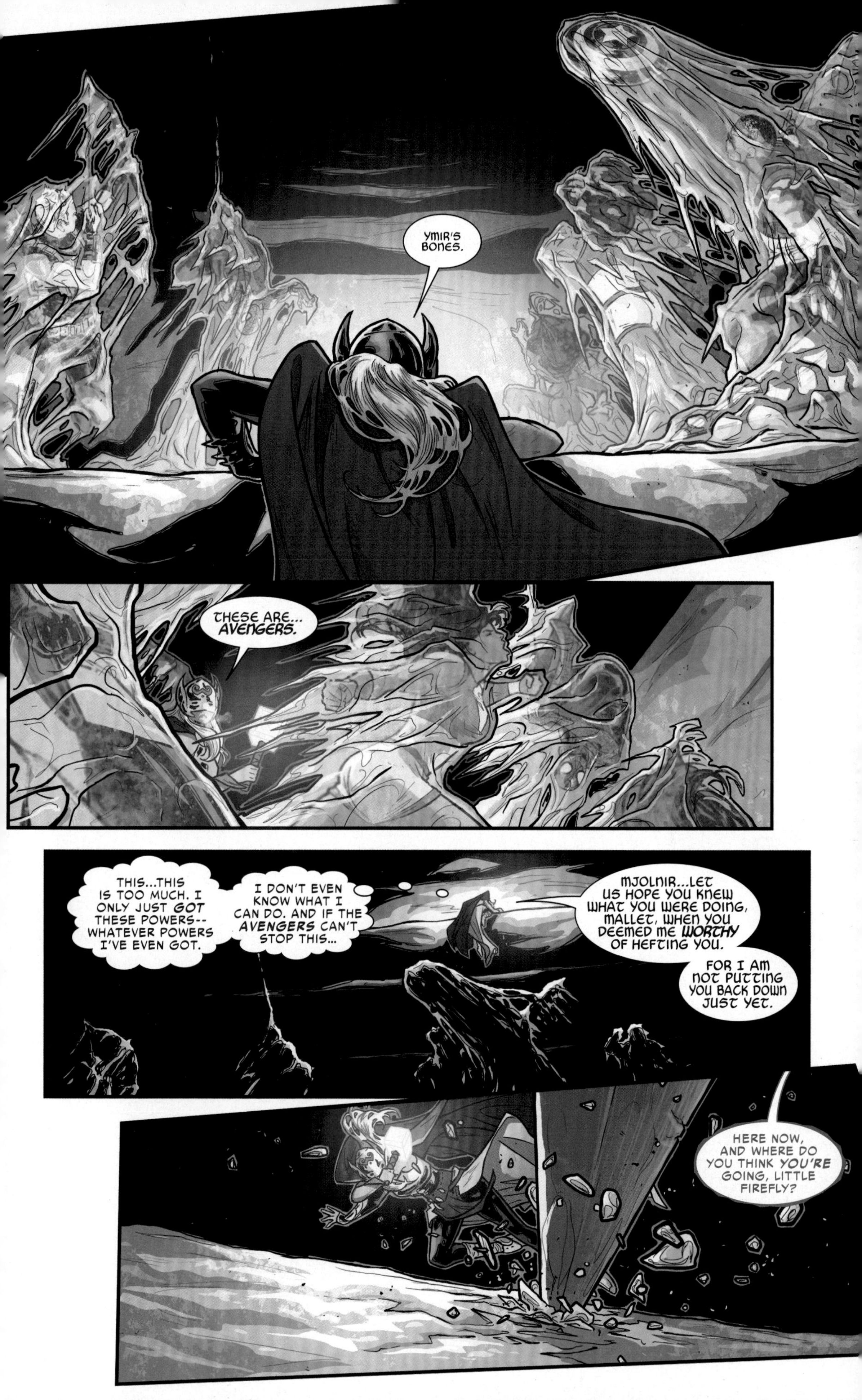
YMIR'S BONES.
THESE ARE... AVENGERS.
THIS...THIS IS TOO MUCH. I ONLY JUST GOT THESE POWERS-- WHATEVER POWERS I'VE EVEN GOT.
I DON'T EVEN KNOW WHAT I CAN DO. AND IF THE AVENGERS CAN'T STOP THIS...
MJOLNIR...LET US HOPE YOU KNEW WHAT YOU WERE DOING, MALLET, WHEN YOU DEEMED ME WORTHY OF HEFTING YOU.
FOR I AM NOT PUTTING YOU BACK DOWN JUST YET.
HERE NOW, AND WHERE DO YOU THINK YOU'RE GOING, LITTLE FIREFLY?

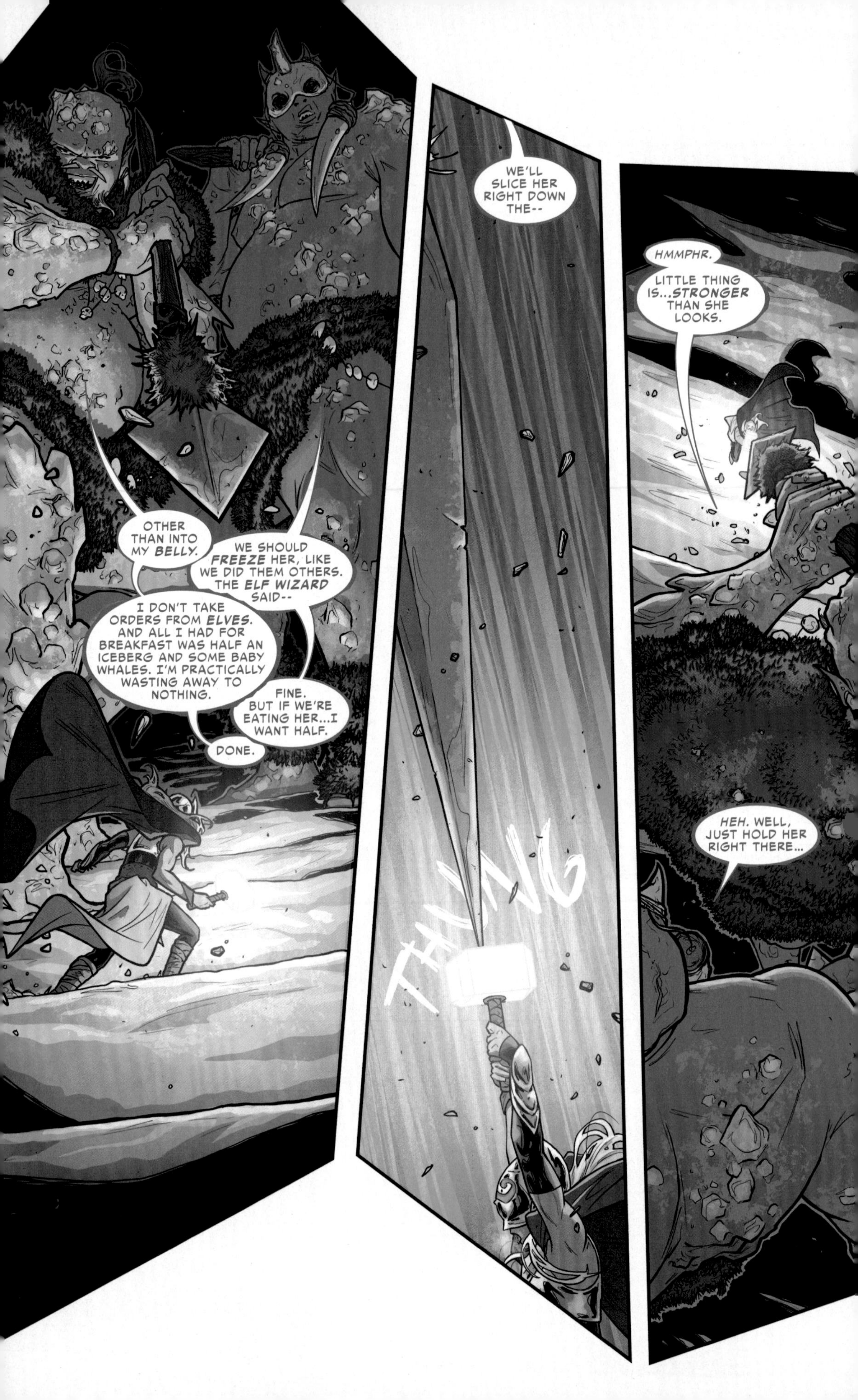

OTHER THAN INTO MY *BELLY*.
WE SHOULD *FREEZE* HER, LIKE WE DID THEM OTHERS. THE *ELF WIZARD* SAID--
I DON'T TAKE ORDERS FROM *ELVES*. AND ALL I HAD FOR BREAKFAST WAS HALF AN ICEBERG AND SOME BABY WHALES. I'M PRACTICALLY WASTING AWAY TO NOTHING.
FINE. BUT IF WE'RE EATING HER...I WANT HALF.
DONE.
WE'LL SLICE HER RIGHT DOWN THE--
THUNG
HMMPHR.
LITTLE THING IS...*STRONGER* THAN SHE LOOKS.
HEH. WELL, JUST HOLD HER RIGHT THERE...

I THINK THE *MUTTS* WANT A TASTE.

GGRRRRRRR

MJOLNIR... THIS TIME... LET ME STEER.

KRUNN

RRRROOOOORRR

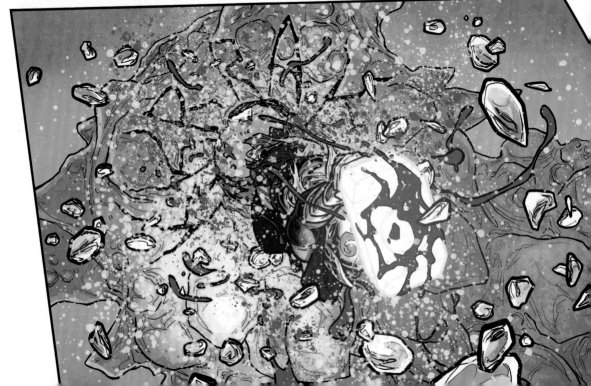

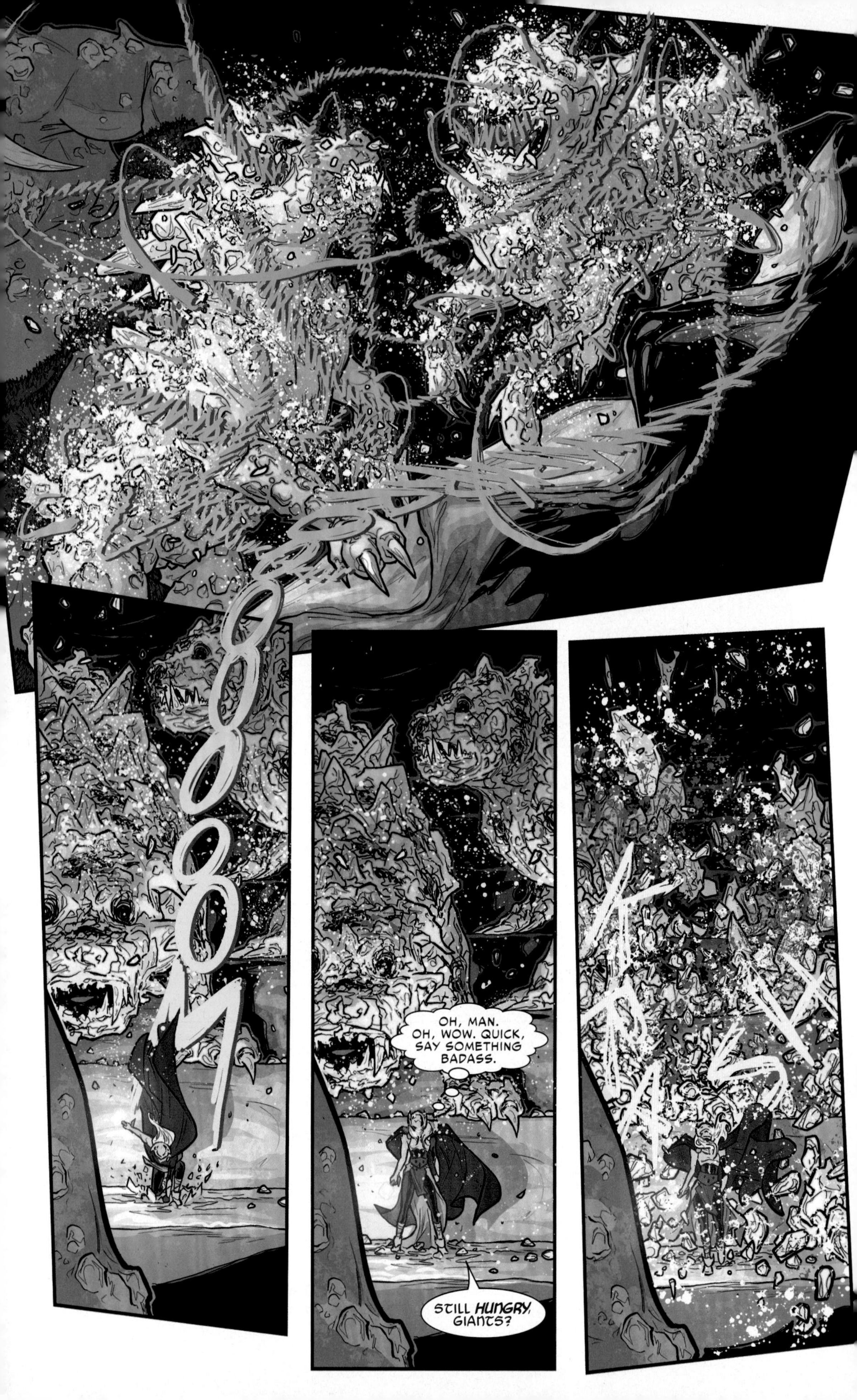
OH, MAN. OH, WOW. QUICK, SAY SOMETHING BADASS.
STILL HUNGRY, GIANTS?

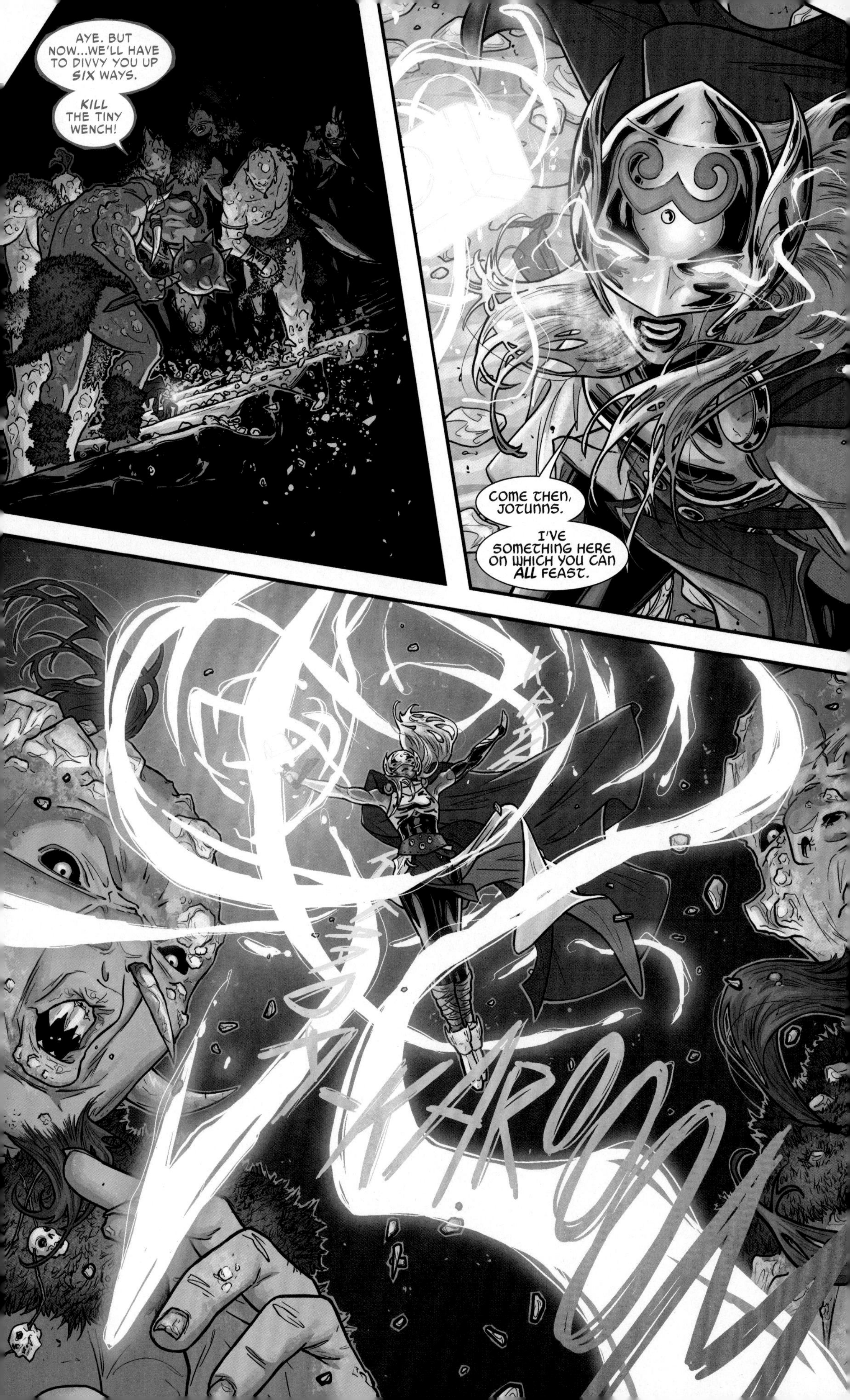
AYE. BUT NOW...WE'LL HAVE TO DIVVY YOU UP SIX WAYS.
KILL THE TINY WENCH!
COME THEN, JOTUNNS.
I'VE SOMETHING HERE ON WHICH YOU CAN ALL FEAST.

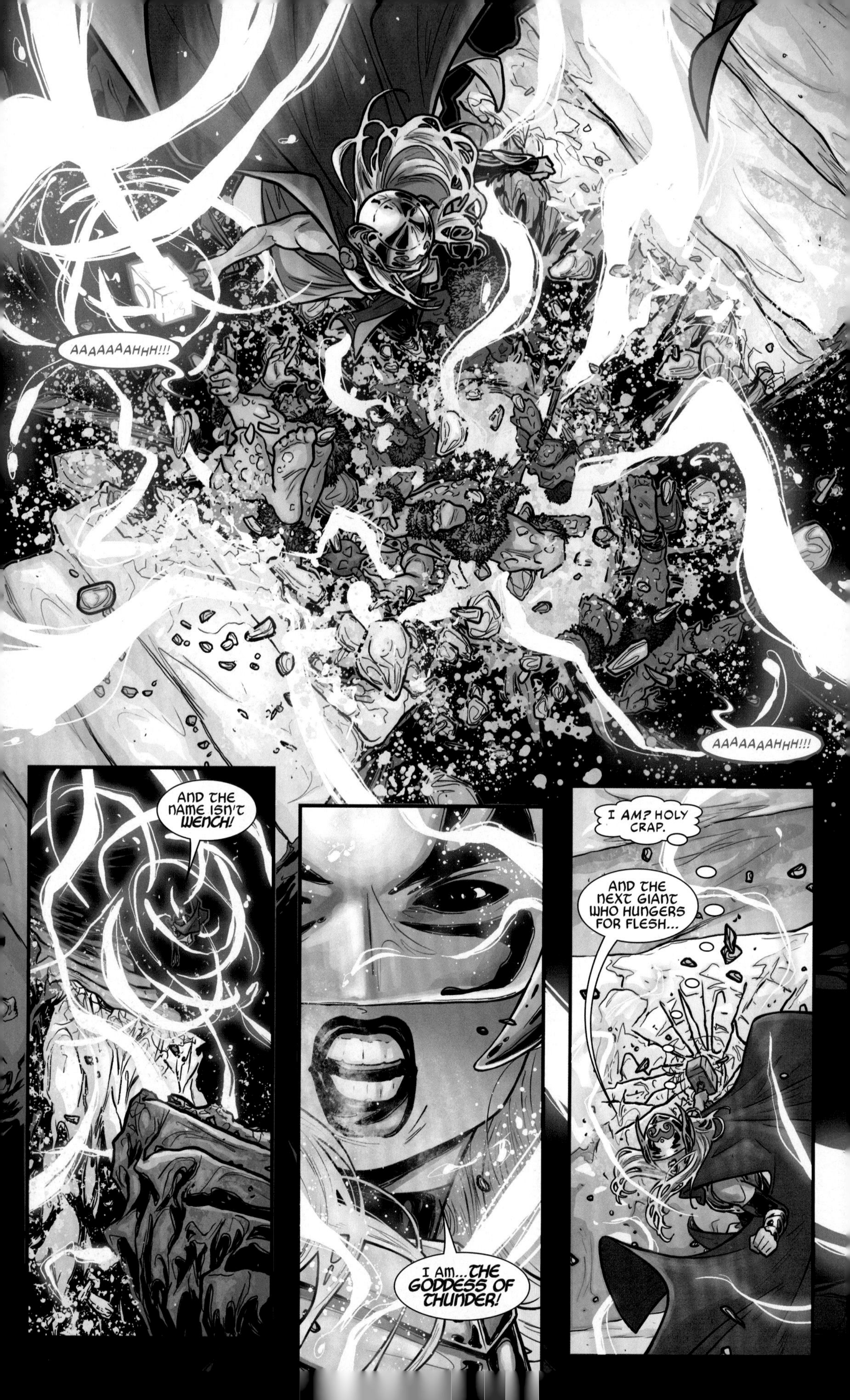
AAAAAAAHHH!!!
AAAAAAAHHH!!!
AND THE NAME ISN'T WENCH!
I AM...THE GODDESS OF THUNDER!
I AM? HOLY CRAP.
AND THE NEXT GIANT WHO HUNGERS FOR FLESH...

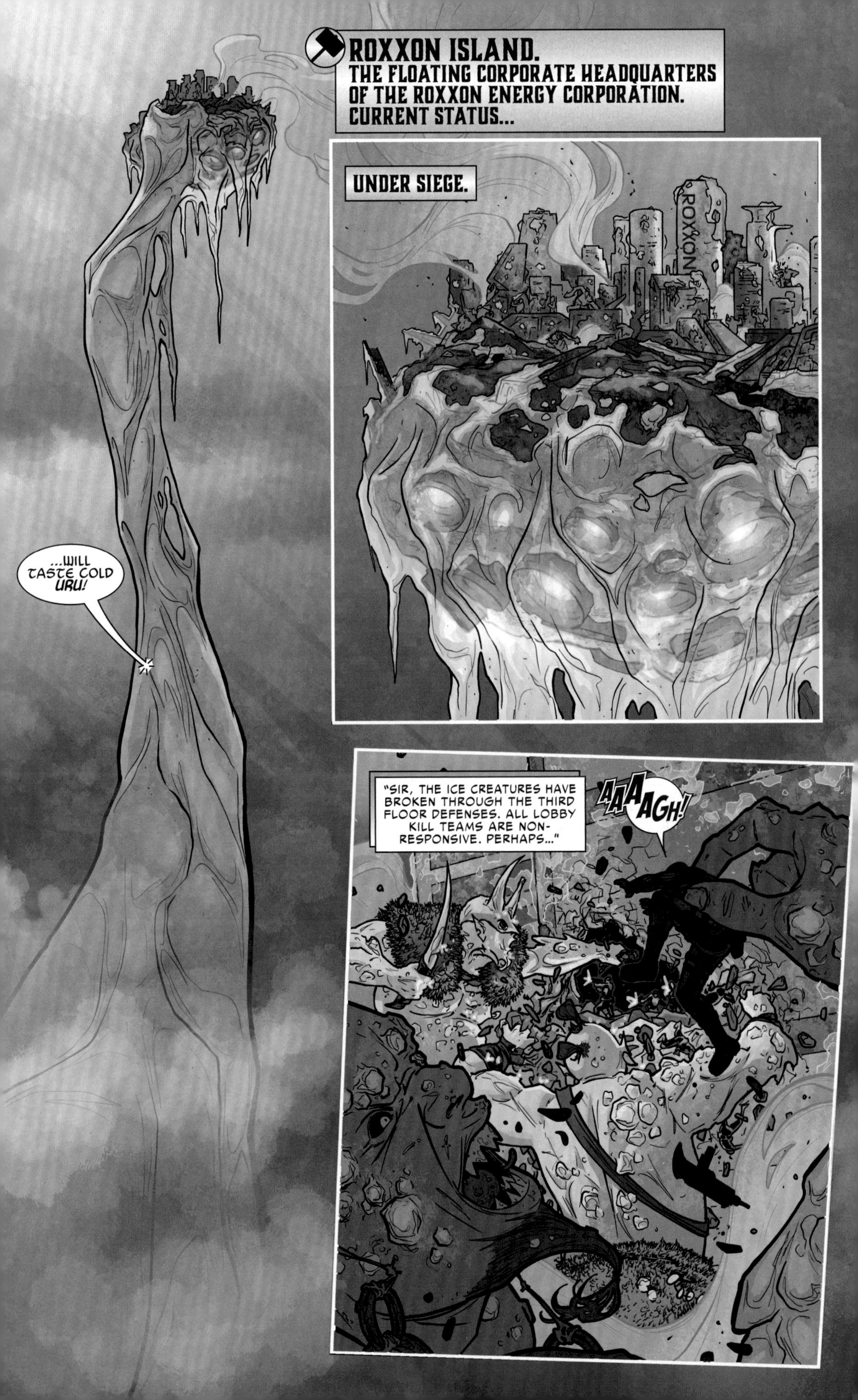
ROXXON ISLAND.
THE FLOATING CORPORATE HEADQUARTERS OF THE ROXXON ENERGY CORPORATION. CURRENT STATUS...
UNDER SIEGE.
ROXXON
...WILL TASTE COLD URU!
"SIR, THE ICE CREATURES HAVE BROKEN THROUGH THE THIRD FLOOR DEFENSES. ALL LOBBY KILL TEAMS ARE NON-RESPONSIVE. PERHAPS..."
AAAAGH!

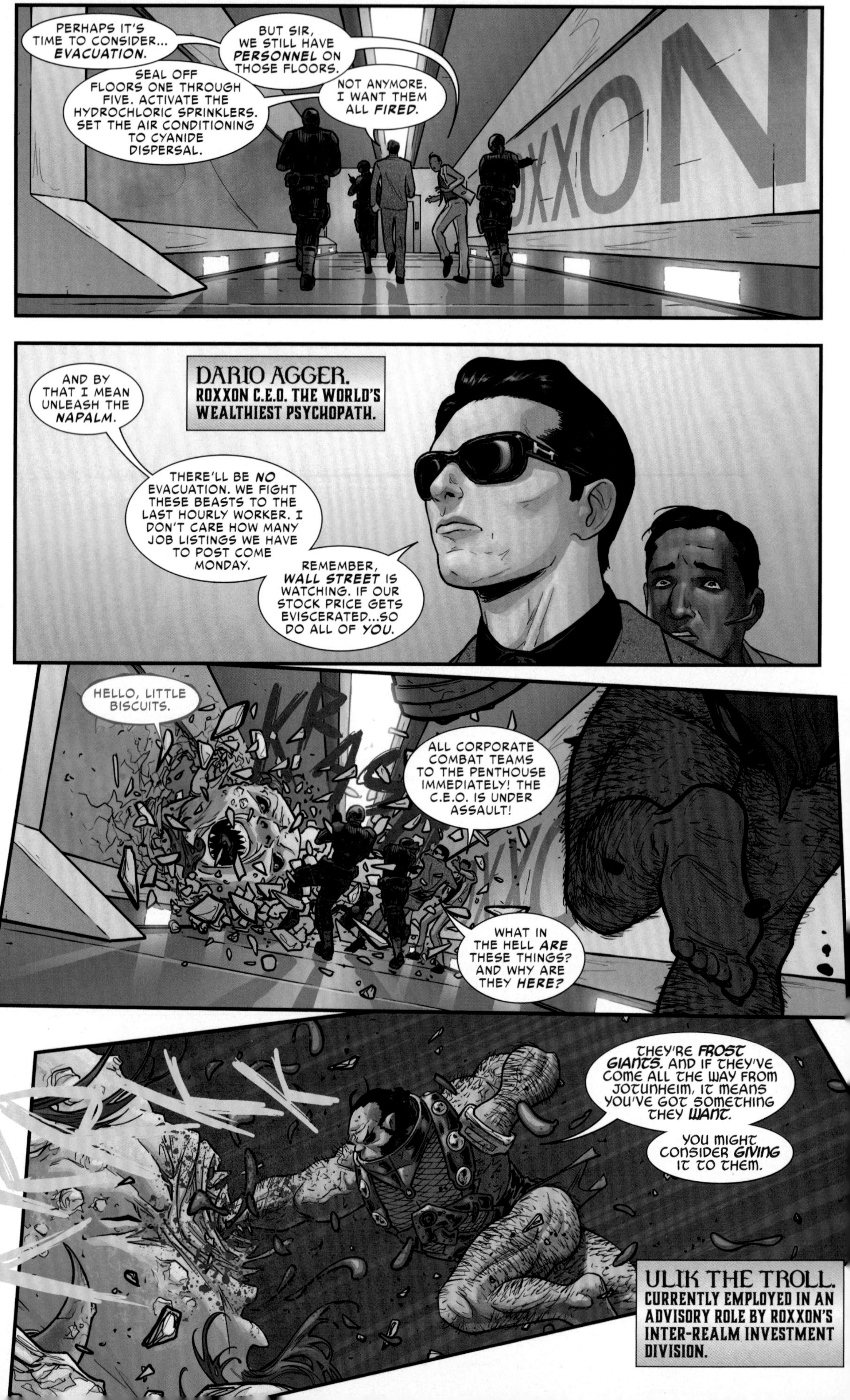
PERHAPS IT'S TIME TO CONSIDER... EVACUATION.
SEAL OFF FLOORS ONE THROUGH FIVE. ACTIVATE THE HYDROCHLORIC SPRINKLERS. SET THE AIR CONDITIONING TO CYANIDE DISPERSAL.
BUT SIR, WE STILL HAVE PERSONNEL ON THOSE FLOORS.
NOT ANYMORE. I WANT THEM ALL FIRED.
ROXXON
DARIO AGGER. ROXXON C.E.O. THE WORLD'S WEALTHIEST PSYCHOPATH.
AND BY THAT I MEAN UNLEASH THE NAPALM.
THERE'LL BE NO EVACUATION. WE FIGHT THESE BEASTS TO THE LAST HOURLY WORKER. I DON'T CARE HOW MANY JOB LISTINGS WE HAVE TO POST COME MONDAY.
REMEMBER, WALL STREET IS WATCHING. IF OUR STOCK PRICE GETS EVISCERATED...SO DO ALL OF YOU.
HELLO, LITTLE BISCUITS.
KRASH
ALL CORPORATE COMBAT TEAMS TO THE PENTHOUSE IMMEDIATELY! THE C.E.O. IS UNDER ASSAULT!
WHAT IN THE HELL ARE THESE THINGS? AND WHY ARE THEY HERE?
THEY'RE FROST GIANTS. AND IF THEY'VE COME ALL THE WAY FROM JOTUNHEIM, IT MEANS YOU'VE GOT SOMETHING THEY WANT.
YOU MIGHT CONSIDER GIVING IT TO THEM.
ULIK THE TROLL. CURRENTLY EMPLOYED IN AN ADVISORY ROLE BY ROXXON'S INTER-REALM INVESTMENT DIVISION.

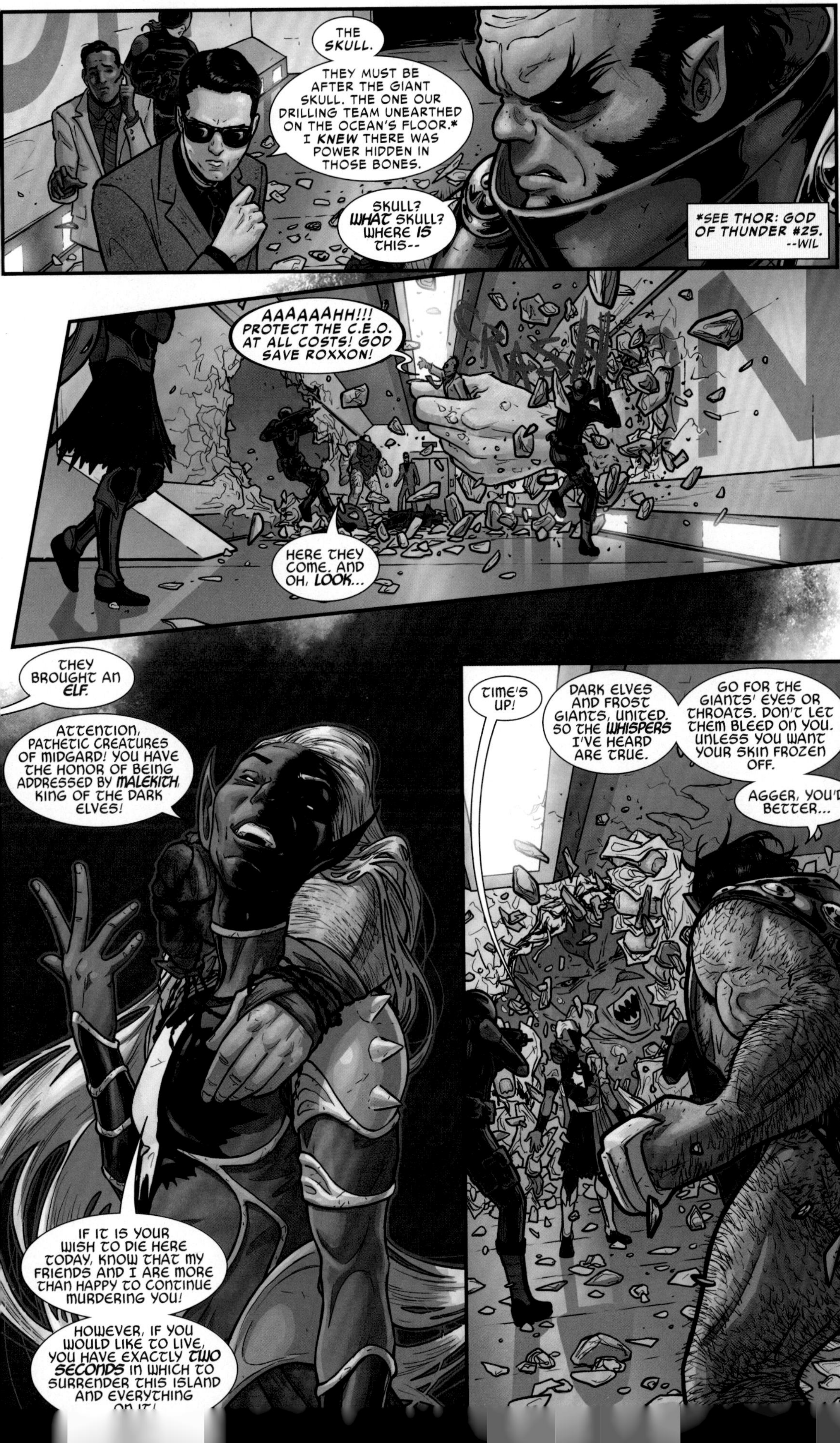

THE SKULL.
THEY MUST BE AFTER THE GIANT SKULL. THE ONE OUR DRILLING TEAM UNEARTHED ON THE OCEAN'S FLOOR.* I KNEW THERE WAS POWER HIDDEN IN THOSE BONES.
SKULL? WHAT SKULL? WHERE IS THIS--
*SEE THOR: GOD OF THUNDER #25. --WIL
AAAAAAHH!!! PROTECT THE C.E.O. AT ALL COSTS! GOD SAVE ROXXON!
CRASH
HERE THEY COME. AND OH, LOOK...
THEY BROUGHT AN ELF.
ATTENTION, PATHETIC CREATURES OF MIDGARD! YOU HAVE THE HONOR OF BEING ADDRESSED BY MALEKITH, KING OF THE DARK ELVES!
IF IT IS YOUR WISH TO DIE HERE TODAY, KNOW THAT MY FRIENDS AND I ARE MORE THAN HAPPY TO CONTINUE MURDERING YOU!
HOWEVER, IF YOU WOULD LIKE TO LIVE, YOU HAVE EXACTLY TWO SECONDS IN WHICH TO SURRENDER THIS ISLAND AND EVERYTHING ON IT!
TIME'S UP!
DARK ELVES AND FROST GIANTS, UNITED. SO THE WHISPERS I'VE HEARD ARE TRUE.
GO FOR THE GIANTS' EYES OR THROATS. DON'T LET THEM BLEED ON YOU. UNLESS YOU WANT YOUR SKIN FROZEN OFF.
AGGER, YOU'D BETTER...

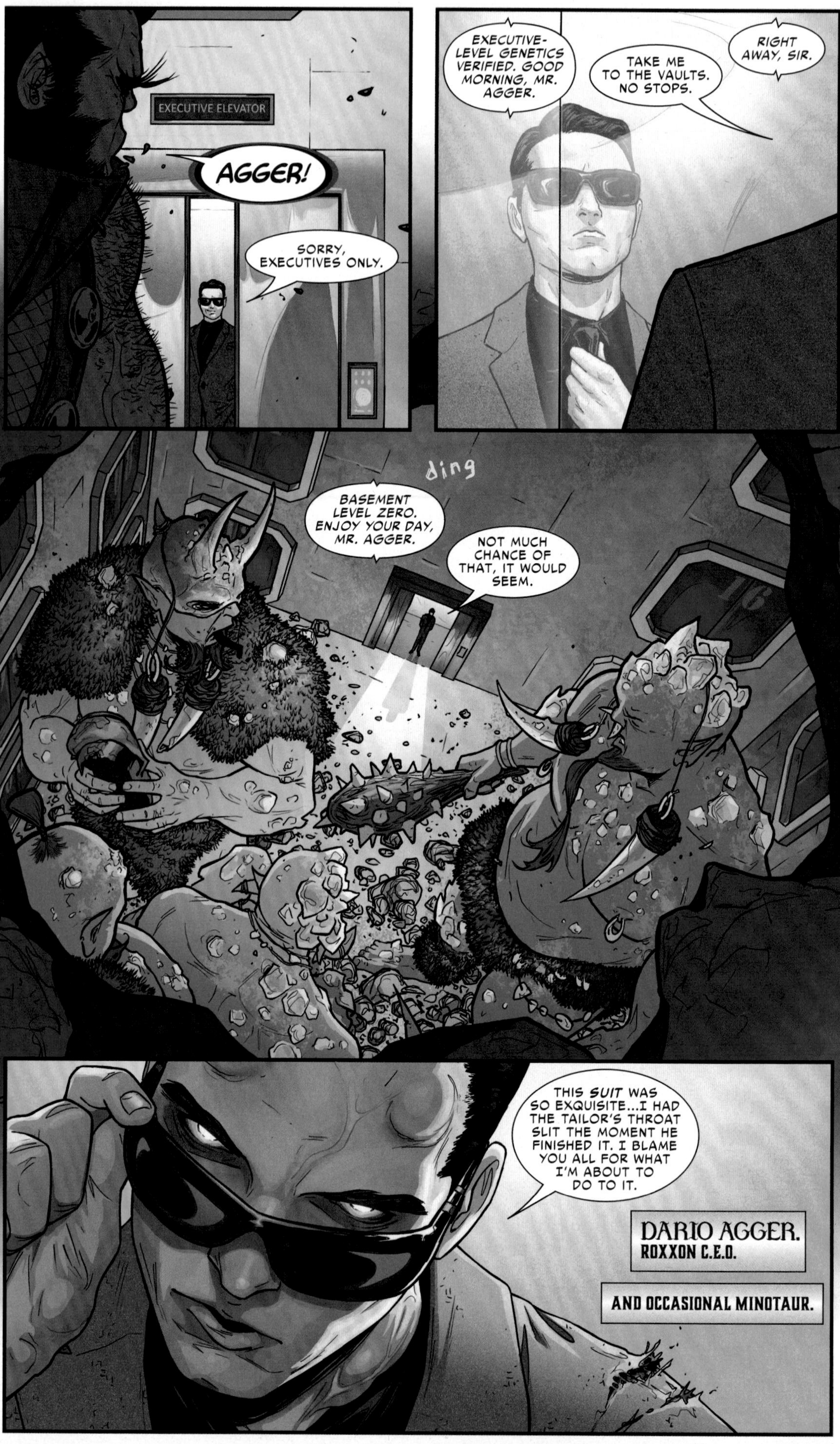
EXECUTIVE ELEVATOR
AGGER!
SORRY, EXECUTIVES ONLY.
EXECUTIVE-LEVEL GENETICS VERIFIED. GOOD MORNING, MR. AGGER.
TAKE ME TO THE VAULTS. NO STOPS.
RIGHT AWAY, SIR.
ding
BASEMENT LEVEL ZERO. ENJOY YOUR DAY, MR. AGGER.
NOT MUCH CHANCE OF THAT, IT WOULD SEEM.
THIS SUIT WAS SO EXQUISITE...I HAD THE TAILOR'S THROAT SLIT THE MOMENT HE FINISHED IT. I BLAME YOU ALL FOR WHAT I'M ABOUT TO DO TO IT.
DARIO AGGER.
ROXXON C.E.O.
AND OCCASIONAL MINOTAUR.

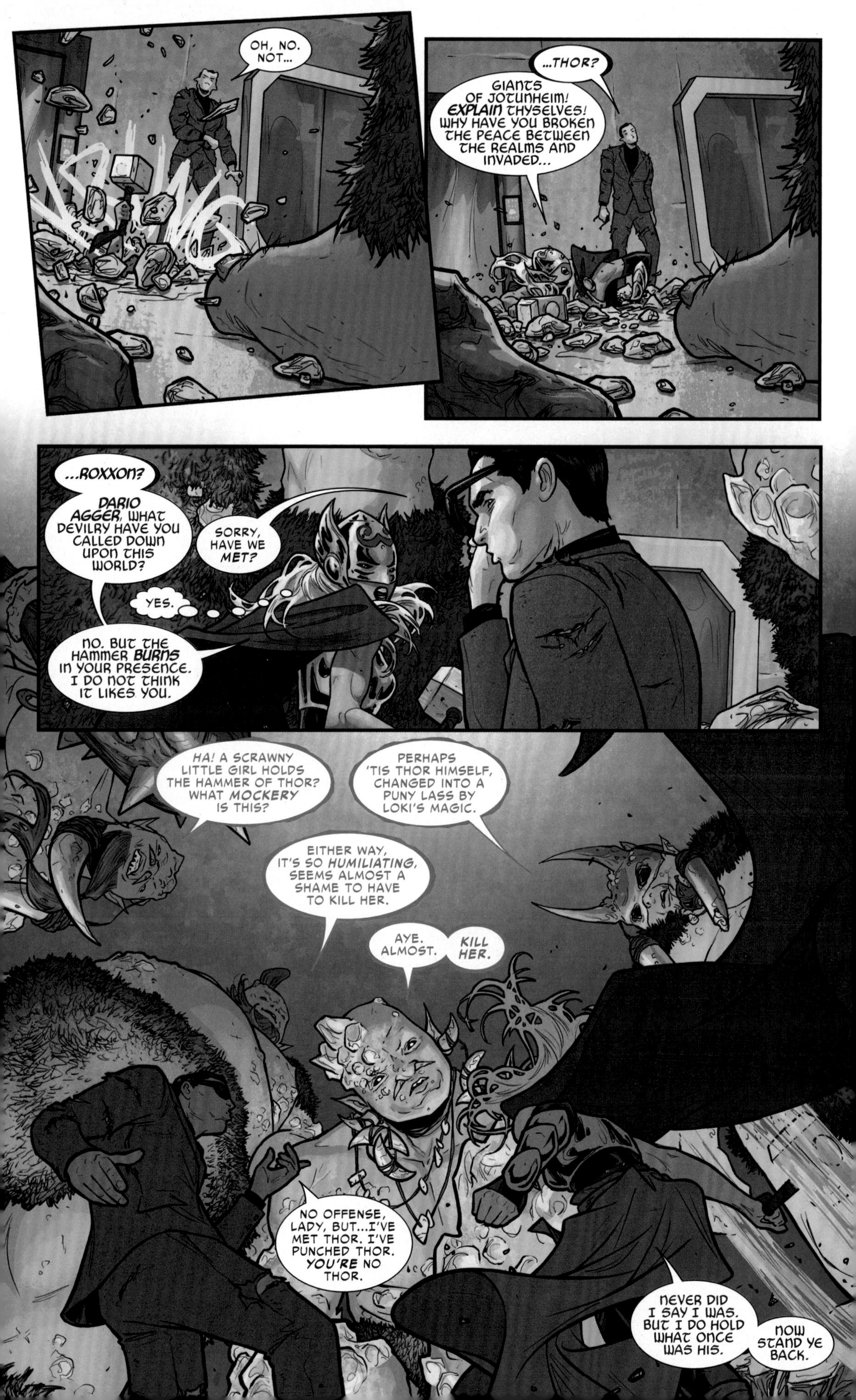
OH, NO. NOT...
...THOR?
GIANTS OF JOTUNHEIM! EXPLAIN THYSELVES! WHY HAVE YOU BROKEN THE PEACE BETWEEN THE REALMS AND INVADED...
...ROXXON?
DARIO AGGER, WHAT DEVILRY HAVE YOU CALLED DOWN UPON THIS WORLD?
SORRY, HAVE WE MET?
YES.
NO. BUT THE HAMMER BURNS IN YOUR PRESENCE. I DO NOT THINK IT LIKES YOU.
HA! A SCRAWNY LITTLE GIRL HOLDS THE HAMMER OF THOR? WHAT MOCKERY IS THIS?
PERHAPS 'TIS THOR HIMSELF, CHANGED INTO A PUNY LASS BY LOKI'S MAGIC.
EITHER WAY, IT'S SO HUMILIATING, SEEMS ALMOST A SHAME TO HAVE TO KILL HER.
AYE. ALMOST.
KILL HER.
NO OFFENSE, LADY, BUT...I'VE MET THOR. I'VE PUNCHED THOR. YOU'RE NO THOR.
NEVER DID I SAY I WAS. BUT I DO HOLD WHAT ONCE WAS HIS.
NOW STAND YE BACK.

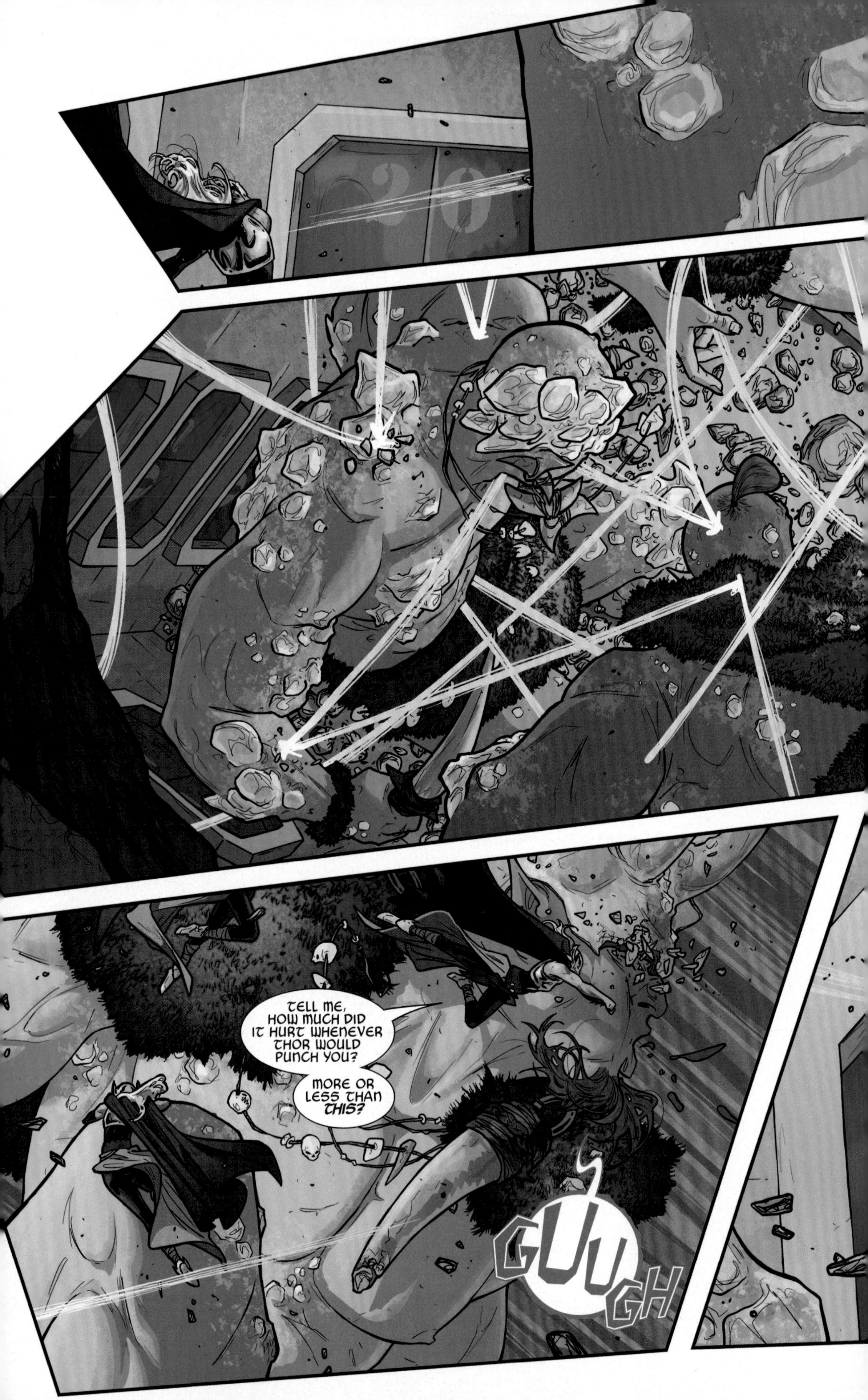
TELL ME, HOW MUCH DID IT HURT WHENEVER THOR WOULD PUNCH YOU?
MORE OR LESS THAN *THIS?*
GUUGH

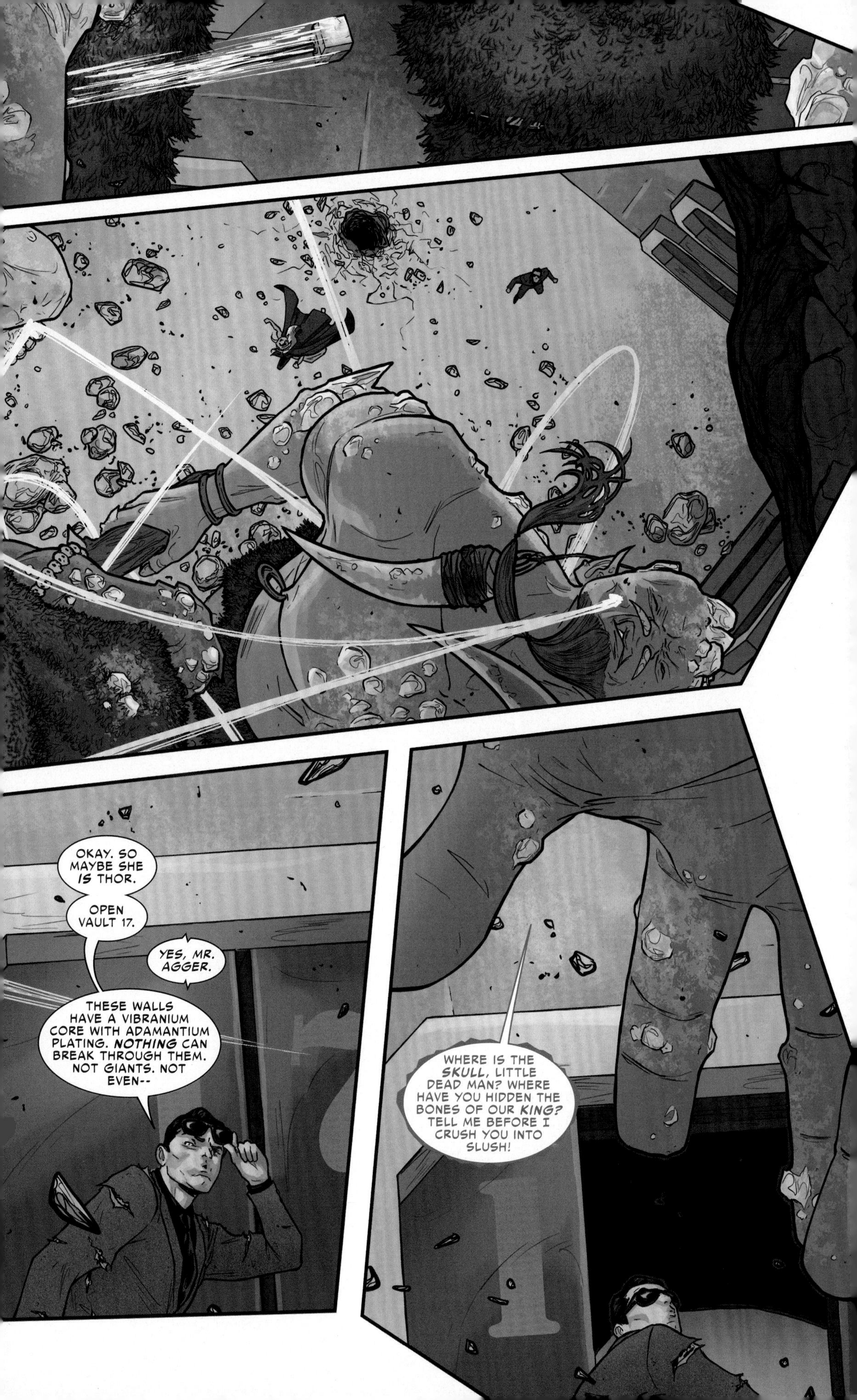
OKAY. SO MAYBE SHE *IS* THOR.
OPEN VAULT 17.
YES, MR. AGGER.
THESE WALLS HAVE A VIBRANIUM CORE WITH ADAMANTIUM PLATING. *NOTHING* CAN BREAK THROUGH THEM. NOT GIANTS. NOT EVEN--
WHERE IS THE *SKULL*, LITTLE DEAD MAN? WHERE HAVE YOU HIDDEN THE BONES OF OUR *KING?* TELL ME BEFORE I CRUSH YOU INTO SLUSH!

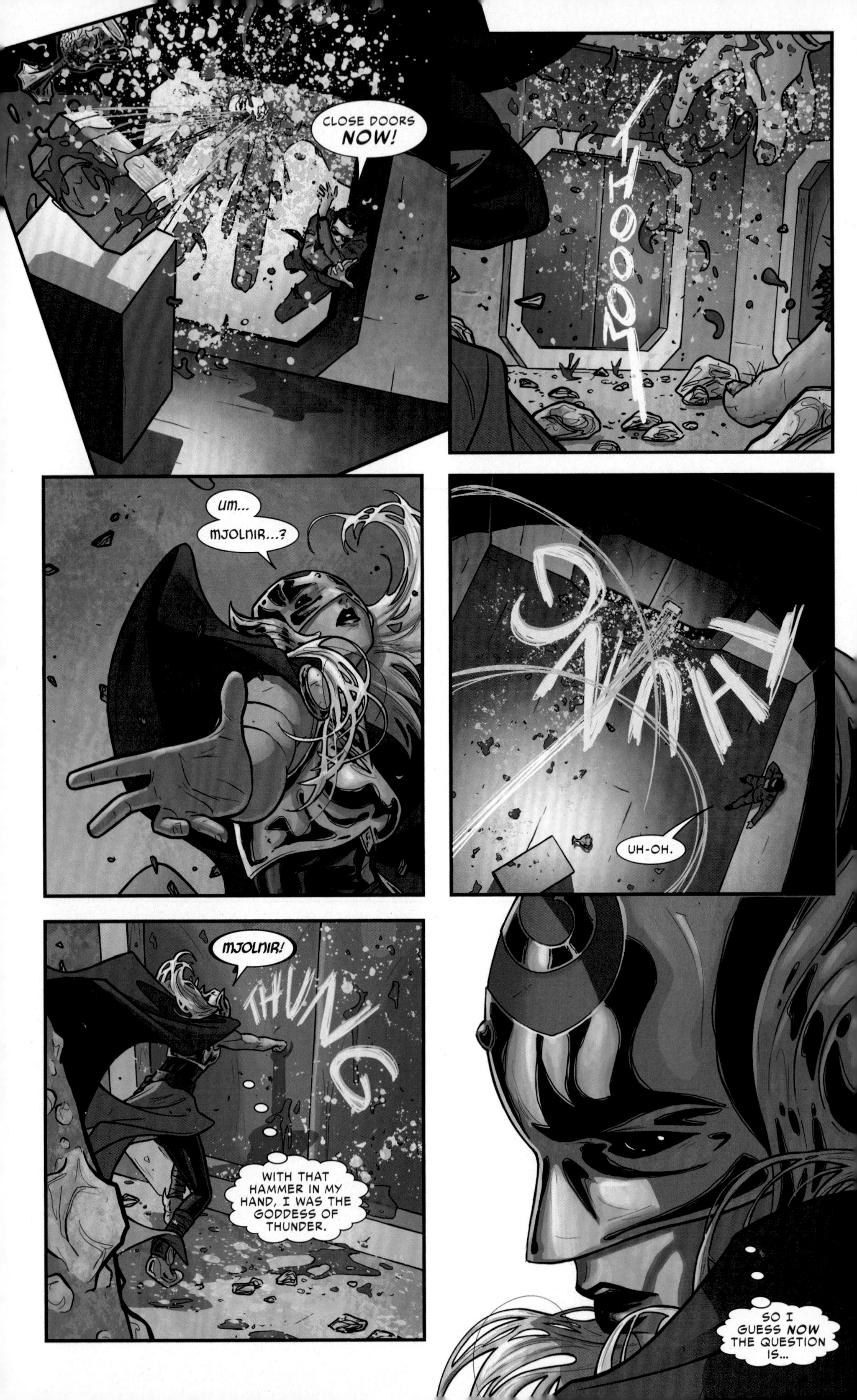
CLOSE DOORS NOW!
THOOOOM
UM... MJOLNIR...?
UH-OH.
MJOLNIR!
THUNG
WITH THAT HAMMER IN MY HAND, I WAS THE GODDESS OF THUNDER.
SO I GUESS NOW THE QUESTION IS...

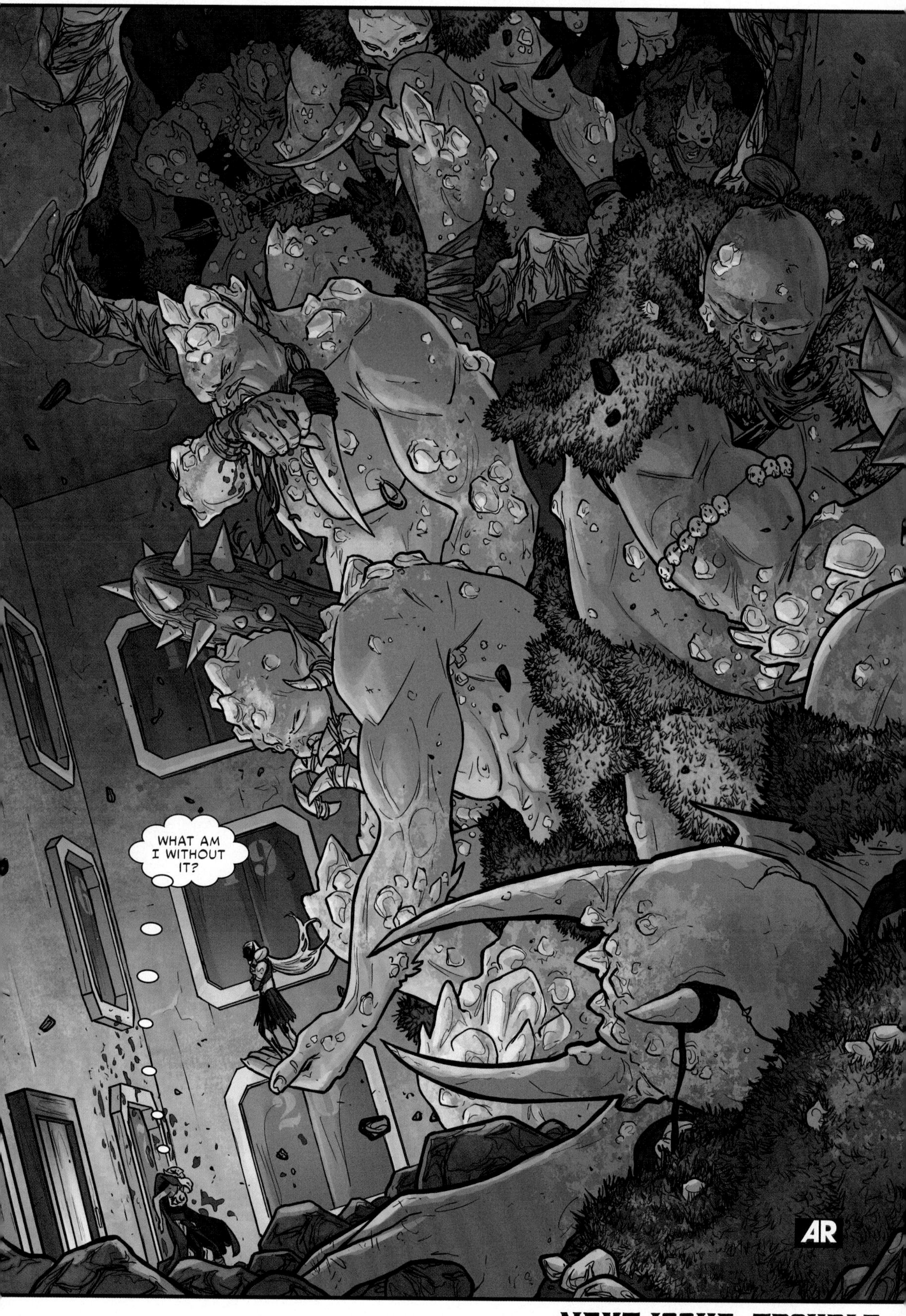
WHAT AM
I WITHOUT
IT?
AR

NEXT ISSUE: TROUBLE

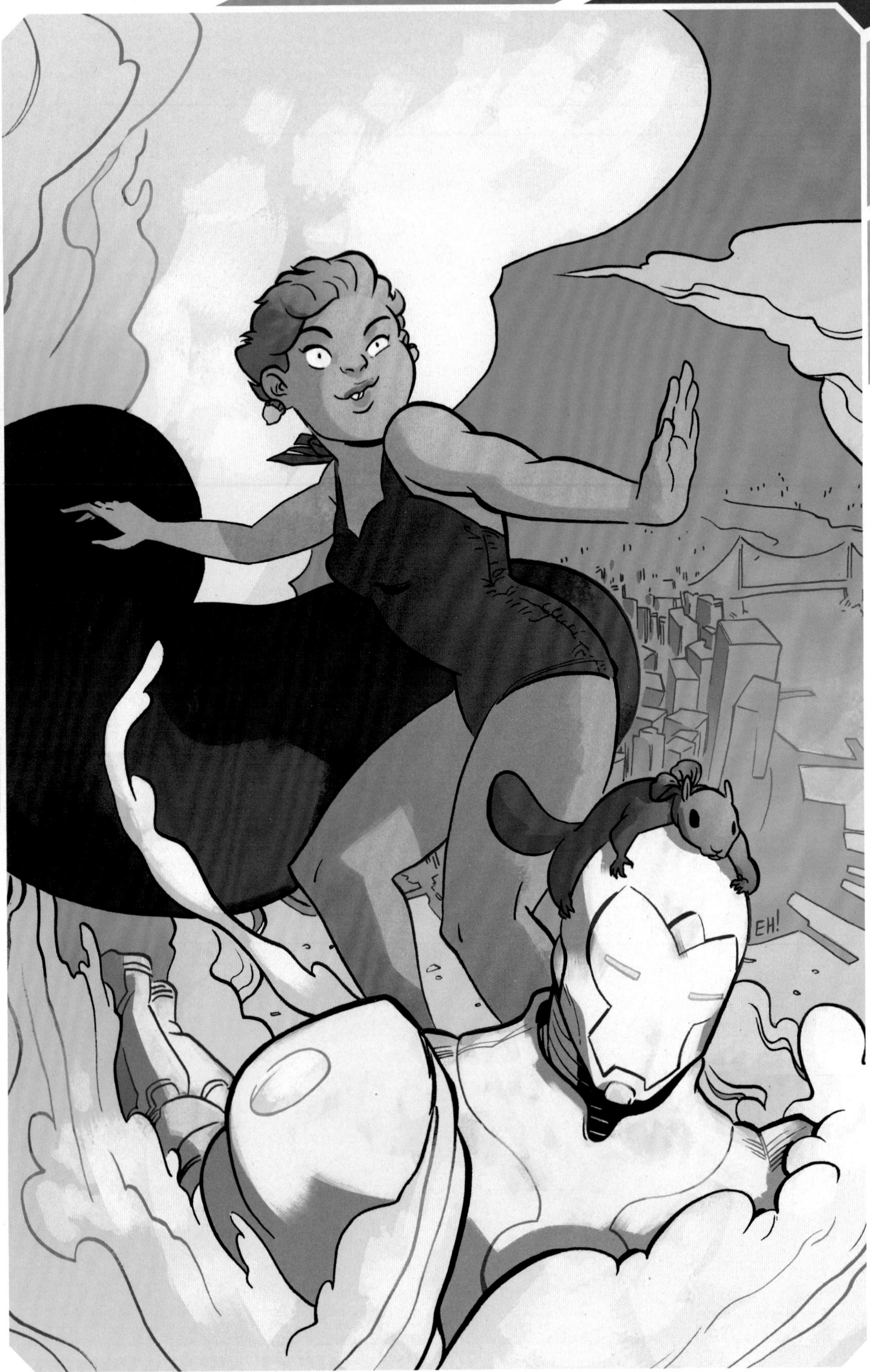
EH!

THE UNBEATABLE SQUIRREL GIRL #2